D0046779

BLUE LILY,
LILY BLUE

Also by Maggie Stiefvater

The Raven Boys
The Dream Thieves

The Scorpio Races

Shiver

Linger

Forever

Sinner

Lament: The Faerie Queen's Deception
Ballad: A Gathering of Faerie

BLUE LILY, LILY BLUE

BOOK III OF THE RAVEN CYCLE

MAGGIE STIEFVATER

SCHOLASTIC PRESS · NEW YORK

to Laura, one of the white knights

Copyright © 2014 by Maggie Stiefvater

All rights reserved. Published by Scholastic Press, an imprint of
Scholastic Inc., *Publishers since 1920.* SCHOLASTIC, SCHOLASTIC PRESS,
and associated logos are trademarks and/or registered trademarks
of Scholastic Inc.

No part of this publication may be reproduced, stored in a retrieval
system, or transmitted in any form or by any means, electronic,
mechanical, photocopying, recording, or otherwise, without written permission of the publisher. For information regarding
permission, write to Scholastic Inc., Attention: Permissions
Department, 557 Broadway, New York, NY 10012.

Library of Congress Cataloging-in-Publication Data available

ISBN 978-0-545-42496-7

10 9 8 7 6 5 4 3 2   15 16 17 18

Printed in the U.S.A.   23
First edition, November 2014

The text type was set in Centaur MT.

Book design by
Christopher Stengel

I'm looking for the face I had
Before the world was made.

— WILLIAM BUTLER YEATS,
"BEFORE THE WORLD
WAS MADE"

Let us be grateful to the mirror for revealing to
us our appearance only.

— SAMUEL BUTLER,
EREWHON

PROLOGUE

ABOVE

Persephone stood on the bare mountaintop, her ruffled ivory dress whipping around her legs, her masses of white-blond curls streaming behind her. She was gauzy, immaterial, something blown between these boulders and caught upon one of them. The wind was fierce up here with no trees to block it. The world below was gloriously autumnal.

Adam Parrish stood beside her with his hands shoved into the pockets of his grease-stained cargo pants. He looked tired, but his eyes were clear, better than when she'd seen him last. Because Persephone was only interested in important things, she hadn't considered her own age in a long time, but it struck her as she looked at him that he was quite *new*. That raw expression, that youthful hunch of his shoulders, the frantic sprawl of the energy inside him.

What a good day it is for this, she thought. It was cool and overcast, with no interference from the sun's force or the lunar schedule or nearby road construction.

"This is the corpse road," she said, aligning her body with the invisible path. As she did, she could feel something inside her begin to hum agreeably, a sensation very much like the satisfaction that came from aligning book spines on a shelf.

"The ley line," Adam clarified.

She nodded serenely. "Find it for yourself."

He stepped onto the line immediately, his face turning to gaze along its length as naturally as a flower looking into the sun. It had taken Persephone rather longer to master this skill, but then, unlike her youthful pupil, *she* had not made any bargains with supernatural forests. She was not much for bargains. Group projects, in general, were not her thing.

"What do you see?" she asked.

His eyes fluttered, his dusty lashes resting on his cheeks. Because she was Persephone, and because it was a good day for this, she could see what he was seeing. It was not anything related to the ley line. It was a confusion of shattered figurines on the floor of a lovely mansion. An official letter printed on county stationery. A friend convulsing at his feet.

"Outside of you," Persephone reminded him mildly. She herself saw so many events and possibilities along the corpse road that no single one stood out. She was a far better psychic when she had her two friends Calla and Maura with her: Calla to sort through her impressions and Maura to put them in context.

Adam seemed to have potential in this department, though he was too new to replace Maura — no, that was a ridiculous way to put it, Persephone told herself, you don't *replace* friends. She struggled to think of the proper word. Not *replace*.

Rescue. Yes, of course, that was what you did with your friends. Did Maura need rescuing?

If Maura had been there on the mountain, Persephone might have been able to say. But if Maura had been there on the mountain, Persephone wouldn't *need* to say.

She sighed deeply.

She sighed a lot.

"I see things." Adam's eyebrows formed either concentration or uncertainty. "More than one thing. It's like — like the animals at the Barns. I see things . . . sleeping."

"Dreaming," Persephone agreed.

As soon as he'd called her attention to the sleepers, they came to the forefront of her consciousness.

"Three," she added.

"Three what?"

"Three in particular," she murmured. "To be woken. Oh, no. No. Two. One should not be woken."

Persephone had never been very handy with the concept of right and wrong. But in this case, the third sleeper was definitely *wrong*.

For a few minutes, she and the boy — *Adam*, she reminded herself; it was so difficult to find birth-given names important — both stood there, feeling the ley line course beneath their feet. Persephone gently and unsuccessfully attempted to find the bright strand of Maura's existence in the tangled threads of energy.

Beside her, Adam was once again retreating inside himself, most interested, as always, in the thing that remained unknowable to him: his own mind.

"Outside," Persephone reminded him.

Adam didn't open his eyes. His words were so soft that the wind nearly destroyed them. "I don't mean to be rude, ma'am, but I don't know why this is worth learning."

Persephone wasn't sure how he thought such a reasonable question could be impolite. "When you were a baby, what made learning to talk worth it?"

"Who am I learning to communicate with?"

She was pleased that he immediately grasped the concept.

She replied, "Everything."

BETWEEN

Calla was overwhelmed by how much shit Maura had in her room at 300 Fox Way, and she told Blue this.

Blue didn't answer. She sorted through papers by the window, head tilted in consideration. From this angle, she looked exactly like her mother, compact and athletic and hard to tip over. She was weirdly lovely, even though she had unevenly clipped her dark hair all over her head and wore a shirt she'd attacked with a roto-tiller. Or perhaps *because* of these things. When had she gotten so pretty and so grown-up? Without getting any taller? This was probably what happened to girls when they lived on only yogurt.

Blue asked, "Have you seen these? They're really good."

Calla wasn't sure what Blue was looking at, but she believed her. Blue wasn't the sort of girl to hand out false compliments, even to her mother. Although she was kind, she wasn't *nice*. Good thing, too, because nice people made Calla irritable.

"Your mother is a woman of many talents," she growled. The mess was taking years from her life. Calla liked things you could rely on: filing systems, months with thirty-one days, purple lipstick. Maura liked chaos. "Such as aggravating me."

Calla picked up Maura's pillow. Sensations assaulted her. She *felt* all at once where the pillow had been procured, how Maura balled it up under her neck, the number of tears applied to the pillowcase, and the contents of five years of dreams.

The psychic hotline rang in the room next door. Calla's concentration fluttered away.

"Damn it," she said.

She was psychometric — just her touch could often reveal both an object's origin and the owner's feelings. But this pillow had been handled so often that it contained too many memories to sort through. If Maura had been there, Calla would have been able to easily isolate the useful ones.

But if Maura had been there, she wouldn't have needed to.

"Blue, get over here."

Blue theatrically clapped a hand on Calla's shoulder. Immediately, her natural amplifying talent sharpened Calla's ability. She saw Maura's hopefulness keeping her awake. Felt the impression of Mr. Gray's shadowed jaw on the pillowcase. Saw the contents of Maura's final dream: a mirrored lake and a distantly familiar man.

Calla sneered.

Artemus. Maura's long-gone ex-lover.

"Anything?" Blue asked.

"Nothing *useful*."

Blue snatched away her hand then, aware that Calla was able to pick up as many feelings from girls as from pillows. But Calla didn't need psychic powers to guess that Blue's sensible, pleasant expression was at odds with the fire that burned furiously inside. School was imminent, love was in the air, and Blue's mother had vanished on some mysterious personal quest more than a month before, leaving behind her newly acquired assassin beau. Blue was a hurricane lurking just offshore.

Ah, Maura! Calla's stomach twisted. *I told you not to go.*

"Touch that." Blue pointed to a large black scrying bowl. It sat askew on the rug, untouched since Maura had used it.

Calla didn't think much of scrying, or mirror magic, or anything that had to do with plumbing the mysterious ether of space and time in order to actually muck about on the other side of it. Technically, scrying was not dangerous; it was just meditating into a mirrored surface. But practically, it often involved freeing the soul from the body. And the soul was a fragile traveler.

The last time Calla, Persephone, and Maura had messed with mirror magic, they had accidentally made Maura's half sister, Neeve, disappear.

At least Calla had never liked Neeve.

But Blue was right. The scrying bowl probably held the most answers.

Calla said, "Fine. But don't touch me. I don't want you to make this any stronger than it already is."

Blue held her hands up as if proving she had no weapon.

Reluctantly, Calla touched the bowl's rim and darkness immediately billowed through her vision. She was sleeping, dreaming. Falling through endless black water. A mirrored version of her soared upward toward the stars. Metal bit into her cheek. Hair stuck to the corner of her mouth.

Where was Maura in all this?

An unfamiliar voice chanted in her head, strident and wry and sing-song:

"Queens and kings
Kings and queens

Blue lily, lily blue
Crowns and birds
Swords and things
Blue lily, lily blue"

Suddenly, she focused.

She was Calla again.

Now she saw what Maura had seen: three sleepers — light, dark, and in between. The knowledge that Artemus was underground. The certainty that no one was coming out of those caverns unless fetched. The realization that Blue and her friends were part of something huger, something vast and stretching and slowly waking —

"BLUE!" roared Calla, because she realized why her efforts had suddenly become so successful.

Sure enough, Blue was touching her shoulder, amplifying everything. "Hi."

"I *told* you not to touch me."

Blue didn't look sorry. "What did you see?"

Calla was still mired in that *other* awareness. She couldn't shake the idea that she was getting ready for a fight that, somehow, she'd already fought.

She couldn't remember if she'd won the last time.

BELOW

Maura Sargent had the nagging feeling that time had stopped working. Not that it had stopped functioning, exactly. Just that it had ceased to run forward in the manner she'd come to think of as "the usual way." Minutes stacking upon minutes to make hours and then days and weeks.

She was beginning to suspect that she might just be using the same minute over and over.

This might have troubled some people. Some people might not have noticed at all. But Maura was not *some people*. She had begun to dream the future when she was fourteen. She had spoken to her first spirit when she was sixteen. She had used remote viewing to see the other side of the world when she was nineteen. Time and space were bathtubs that Maura splashed in.

So she knew there were impossible things in the world, but she didn't believe that a cavern where time stood still was one of them. Had she been here for an hour? Two? A day? Four days? Twenty years? Her flashlight batteries hadn't died.

But if time's not moving forward here, they never will, will they?

She striped her flashlight from floor to ceiling as she crept through the tunnel. She didn't want to smash her head, but she didn't want to fall into a bottomless crevice, either. She'd already stepped into several deep puddles, and her scuffed boots were soaked and cold.

The worst part was the boredom. A poor childhood in West Virginia had left Maura with a strong sense of self-reliance, a high tolerance for discomfort, and a black sense of humor.

But this *monotony*.

It was impossible to tell a joke when you were alone.

The only indication Maura had that time might be moving *somewhere* was that sometimes she forgot who she was looking for down here.

Artemus is the goal, she reminded herself. Seventeen years before, she'd let Calla convince her that he'd merely run off. Maybe she had wanted to be convinced. Deep down, she'd known he was part of something bigger. She'd known that *she* was part of something bigger.

Probably.

So far, the only thing she had found in this tunnel was doubt. This was not the sort of place sun-loving Artemus would have ever chosen. She had half an idea that this was the kind of place someone like Artemus would die in. She was beginning to feel bad about the note she'd left behind. In its entirety, it read:

Glendower is underground. So am I.

At the time, she'd felt quite smug; the note was meant to enrage and inspire, depending on who read it. Of course, she had written it thinking she would be back by the next day.

She revised it now in her head:

Going into timeless caverns to search for ex-boyfriend. If it looks like I will miss Blue's graduation, send help.

P.S. Pie is not a meal.

She kept walking. It was inky black ahead and inky black behind. The sweep of her flashlight illuminated details: stubbled stalactites on the uneven ceiling. Water sheened on the walls.

But she was not lost, because there had only ever been one option: deeper and deeper.

She wasn't afraid yet. It took a lot to terrify someone who played in time and space like a bathtub.

Using a mud-slick stalagmite as a handhold, Maura hauled herself through a narrow opening. The scene on the opposite side was confusing. The ceiling was spiked; the floor was spiked; it was endless; it was impossible.

Then a tiny drip of water unspooled ripples through the image, momentarily ruining the illusion. It was an underground lake. The dark surface mirrored the golden stalactites on the ceiling, making it seem as if an equal number of stalagmites jabbed up from the lake floor.

The real bottom of the lake was hidden. The water could be two inches, two feet, depthless.

Ah. So here it was, finally. She had dreamt of this. She was still not quite afraid, but her heart skipped uneasily.

I could just go home. I know the way.

But if Mr. Gray had been willing to risk his life for what he wanted, surely she could be as brave. She wondered if he was alive. She was surprised by how much she desperately hoped that he was.

She revised the note in her head.

Going into timeless caverns to search for ex-boyfriend. If it looks like I will miss Blue's graduation, send help.

P.S. Pie is still not a meal.
P.P.S. Don't forget to take the car in for the oil change.
P.P.P.S. Look for me at the bottom of a mirrored lake.

A voice whispered in her ear. Someone from the future, or the past. Someone dead or alive or sleeping. It wasn't really a whisper, Maura realized. It was just hoarse. The voice of someone who had been calling for a long time without an answer.

Maura was a good listener.

"What did you say?" she asked.

It whispered again: *"Find me."*

It wasn't Artemus. It was someone else who'd gotten lost, or was in the process of getting lost, or was going to get lost. In these caverns, time wasn't a line; it was a mirrored lake.

P.P.P.P.S. Don't wake the third sleeper.

I

D o you think this is actually real?" Blue asked.

They sat between ascendant oaks under a stolen summer sky. Roots and rocks buckled up through the moist ground around them. The hazy air was nothing like the overcast fall chill they'd just left behind. They had longed for summer, and so Cabeswater had given them summer.

Richard Gansey III lay on his back, gazing up at the muzzy warm blue above the branches. Sprawled in his khakis and citrus-yellow V-neck sweater, he looked indolent, tossed, a sensuous heir to the forest around him. "What is real?"

Blue said, "Maybe we all come here and fall asleep and have the same dream."

She knew it was not true, but it was both comforting and thrilling to imagine they were so connected, that Cabeswater represented something they all thought of when they closed their eyes.

"I know when I'm awake and when I'm asleep," Ronan Lynch said. If everything around Gansey was soft-edged and organic, faded and homogenous, Ronan was sharp and dark and dissonant, standing out in stark relief from the woods.

Adam Parrish, curled over himself in a pair of battered, greasy coveralls, asked, "Do you?"

Ronan made an ugly sound of scorn or mirth. He was like Cabeswater: a maker of dreams. If he didn't know the difference between waking and sleeping, it was because the difference didn't matter to him.

"Maybe I dreamt *you*," he said.

"Thanks for the straight teeth, then," Adam replied.

Around them, Cabeswater hummed and muttered with life. Birds that didn't exist outside the forest flapped overhead. Somewhere close by, water ran over rocks. The trees were grand and old, furred with moss and lichen. Perhaps it was because she knew the forest was sentient, but Blue thought it *looked* wise. If she let her mind wander far enough, she could almost feel the sensation of the forest listening to her. It was hard to explain; it was sort of like the feeling of someone hovering a hand just over your skin, not quite touching.

Adam had said, "We have to earn Cabeswater's trust before we go into the cave."

Blue didn't understand what it meant for Adam to be so connected to the forest, to have promised to be its hands and eyes. She suspected that sometimes, Adam didn't, either. But under his advice, the group had returned again and again to the forest, walking between the trees, exploring carefully, taking nothing. Walking around the cave that might hold both Glendower — and Maura.

Mom.

The note she'd left more than a month before had not indicated when she intended to return. It hadn't indicated whether or not she intended to return *at all*. So it was impossible to tell if she was still gone because she was in trouble or because she didn't want to come home. Did other people's mothers vanish into holes in the ground during their midlife crises?

"I don't dream," Noah Czerny said. He was dead, so he probably didn't sleep, either. "So I think it must be real."

Real, but theirs, just theirs.

For a few more minutes, or hours, or days — what was time, here? — they lazed.

A little away from the group, Ronan's younger brother, Matthew, nattered away to their mother, Aurora, happy for this visit. The two of them were golden-haired and angelic, both of them looking like inventions of this place. Blue longed to hate Aurora because of her origin — literally dreamt up by her husband — and because she had the attention span and intellectual prowess of a puppy. But the truth was that she was endlessly kind and upbeat, as compulsively lovable as her youngest son.

She wouldn't abandon her daughter right before senior year.

The most infuriating part about Maura's disappearance was that Blue didn't know if she was supposed to be consumed by worry or anger. She vacillated wildly between the two, occasionally burning herself out and feeling nothing at all.

How could she do this to me now?

Blue lay her cheek against a boulder covered with warm moss, trying to keep her thoughts even and pleasant. The same ability that amplified clairvoyance also heightened Cabeswater's strange magic, and she didn't want to cause another earthquake or start a stampede.

Instead, she began a conversation with the trees.

She thought about birds singing — *thought* or *wished* or *longed* or *dreamt*. It was a thought turned on its side, a door left cracked in her mind. She was getting better at telling when she was doing it right.

A strange bird trilled high and off-key above her.

She thought-wished-longed-dreamt of leaves rustling.

Overhead, the trees shushed their leaves, forming vague, whispered words. *Avide audimus.*

She thought of a spring flower. A lily, blue, like her name.

A blue petal fell aimlessly into her hair. Another dropped onto the back of her hand, slipping down her wrist like a kiss.

Gansey's eyes opened as petals landed lightly on his cheeks. As his lips parted, ever-wondering, a petal landed directly on his mouth. Adam craned his head back to watch the floral, fragrant rain drift down around them, slow-motion butterflies of blue.

Blue's heart exploded with furious joy.

It's real, it's real, it's real —

Ronan looked at Blue, eyes narrowed. She didn't look away.

This was a game she sometimes played with Ronan Lynch: Who would look away first?

It was always a draw.

He had changed over the summer, and now Blue felt less unequal in the group. Not because she knew Ronan any better — but because she felt as if maybe Gansey and Adam now knew him less. He challenged them all to learn him again.

Gansey pushed himself up onto his elbows; petals tumbled from him as if he had been awoken from a long sleep. "Okay. I think it's time. Lynch?"

Rising, Ronan went to stand starkly beside his mother and brother; Matthew, who had been waving his arms like a performing bear, stilled. Aurora petted Ronan's hand, which Ronan permitted.

"Up," he said to Matthew. "Time to go."

Aurora smiled gently at her sons. She would stay here, in Cabeswater, doing whatever dreams did when no one was there to see them. It was unsurprising to Blue that she would fall into an instant sleep if she left the forest; it was impossible to imagine Aurora existing in the real world. More impossible still to imagine growing up with a mother like her.

My mother wouldn't just leave forever. Right?

Ronan put his hands on either side of Matthew's head, crushing the blond curls down, locking his brother's gaze on his.

"Go wait in the car," he said. "If we aren't back by nine, call Blue's house."

Matthew's expression was pleasant and unafraid. His eyes were the same color blue as Ronan's but infinitely more innocent. "How will I know the number?"

Ronan continued to clasp his brother's head. "Matthew. Focus. We talked about this. I want you to think. You tell me: How will you know the number?"

His younger brother laughed a little and patted his pocket. "Oh, right. It's programmed in your phone. I remember now."

"I'll stay with him," Noah offered at once.

"Chicken," said Ronan ungratefully.

"Lynch," said Gansey. "That's a good idea, Noah, if you're feeling up for it."

Noah, as a ghost, required outside energy to stay visible.

Both Blue and the ley line were powerful spiritual batteries; waiting in the car parked nearby should have been more than enough. But sometimes it wasn't the energy that failed Noah — it was his courage.

"He'll be a champ," Blue said, punching Noah's arm lightly.

"I'll be a champ," repeated Noah.

The forest waited, listening, rustling. The edge of the sky was grayer than the blue directly overhead, like Cabeswater's attention was so tightly focused on them that the real world was now able to intrude.

At the cave mouth, Gansey said, *"De fumo in flammam."*

"From the smoke into the fire," Adam translated for Blue.

The cave. The *cave.*

Everything in Cabeswater was magical, but the cave was unusual because it hadn't existed when they had first discovered the forest. Or maybe it *had* existed, but in a different place.

Gansey said, "Equipment check."

Blue dumped out the contents of her ragged backpack. A helmet (bicycle, used), knee pads (roller skating, used), and flashlight (miniature, used) rolled out, along with a pink switchblade. As she began to apply all of these things to her body, Gansey emptied his messenger bag beside her. His contained a helmet (caving, used), knee pads (caving, used), and a flashlight (Maglite, used), along with several lengths of new rope, a harness, and a selection of bolt anchors and metal carabiners.

Both Blue and Adam stared at the used equipment. It seemed impossible that Richard Campbell Gansey III would have thought to buy anything less than brand-new.

Unaware of their attention, Gansey effortlessly tied a carabiner to a rope by way of an accomplished knot.

Blue got it a moment before Adam did. The equipment was used because *Gansey* had used it.

It was hard to remember, sometimes, that he'd lived a life before they'd met him.

Gansey began to unwind a longer safety cable. "What we talked about. We're tied together, three tugs if you are alarmed *in the slightest*. Time check?"

Adam checked his battered watch. "My watch isn't working."

Ronan checked his expensive black one and shook his head.

Although this was not unexpected, Blue was still disconcerted, a kite cut free.

Gansey frowned as if he shared her thoughts. "Nor is my phone. Okay, Ronan."

As Ronan shouted some Latin into the air, Adam whispered the translation to Blue: "Is it safe for us to go in?"

And is my mother still in there?

The reply came in the form of hissing leaves and guttural scraping, wilder than the voices Blue had heard earlier. *"Greywaren semper est incorruptus."*

"Always safe," Gansey translated quickly, eager to prove that he wasn't entirely useless when it came to Latin. "The Greywaren is always safe."

The Greywaren was Ronan. Whatever they were to this forest, Ronan was more to it.

Adam mused, *"Incorruptus.* I never thought anyone would use *that* word to describe Lynch."

Ronan looked as pleased as a pit viper ever could.

What do you want from us? Blue wondered as they stepped inside. *How do you see us? Just four teens sneaking into an ancient forest.*

An oddly quiet earth-room lay just inside the cave entrance. The walls were dust and rock, roots and chalk, everything the color of Adam's hair and skin. Blue touched a reluctantly curled fern, the last foliage before the sunlight faded. Adam turned his head, listening, but there was only the muffled, ordinary sound of their footsteps.

Gansey turned on his headlamp. It barely penetrated the darkness of the narrowing tunnel.

One of the boys was shivering a little. Blue didn't know if it was Adam or Ronan, but she felt the cable trembling at her belt.

"I wish we'd brought Noah after all," Gansey said abruptly. "In we go. Ronan, don't forget to set the directional markers as we go. We're counting on you. Don't just stare at me. Nod like you understand. Good. You know what? Give them to Jane."

"What?" Ronan sounded betrayed.

Blue accepted the markers — round, plastic disks with arrows drawn on them. She hadn't realized how nervous she was until she had them in her hands; it felt good to have something concrete to do.

"I want you to whistle or hum or sing, Ronan, and keep track of time," Gansey said.

"You have got to be shitting me," Ronan replied. "Me."

Gansey peered down the tunnel. "I know you know a lot of

songs all the way through, and can do them the same speed and length every time. Because you had to memorize all of those tunes for the Irish music competitions."

Blue and Adam exchanged a delighted look. The only thing more pleasing than seeing Ronan singled out was seeing him singled out *and* forced to repeatedly sing an Irish jig.

"Piss up a rope," Ronan said.

Gansey, unoffended, waited.

Ronan shook his head, but then, with a wicked smile, he began to sing, "Squash one, squash two, s—"

"Not that one," both Adam and Gansey said.

"I'm not listening to that for three hours," Adam said.

Gansey pointed at Ronan until he began to breathily whistle a jaunty reel.

And they went in deeper.

Deeper.

The sun vanished. Roots gave way to stalactites. The air smelled damp and familiar. The walls shimmered like something living. From time to time, Blue and the others had to shuffle through pools and streams — the narrow, uneven path had been carved by water, and the water was still doing that work.

Every ten times around Ronan's reel, Blue deposited a marker. As the stack in her hand diminished, she wondered how far they would go, how they would know if they were even getting close. It seemed difficult to believe that a king might be hidden away down here. Harder still to imagine that her mother might be. This was not a place to *inhabit*.

She calmed her thoughts. No earthquakes. No stampedes.

She tried not to long or hope or think of or call for Maura. The last thing she wanted was for Cabeswater to produce a copy of her mother for her. She only wanted the real thing. The truth.

It became steeper. The blackness itself was fatiguing; Blue longed for the light, for space, for the sky. She felt buried alive.

Adam slipped and caught himself, hand outstretched.

"Hey!" Blue ordered. "Don't touch the walls."

Ronan broke off whistling to ask, "Cave germs?"

"It's bad for stalactite growth."

"Oh, *honestly* —"

"Ronan!" ordered Gansey from the front of the line, not turning, his canary sweater rendered light gray by the headlamps. "Get back to work."

Ronan had only just begun to whistle once more when Gansey disappeared.

"What?" said Adam.

Then he was snatched from his feet. He slammed the ground and skidded away on his side, fingers trailing.

Blue didn't have time to realize what this meant when she felt Ronan grab her from behind. Then the rope at her waist snagged tight, threatening to pull her off her feet as well. But he was well planted. His fingers were rooted into her arms so tightly they hurt.

Adam was still on the ground, but he'd stopped sliding.

"Gansey?" he called, the word doleful in the vast space beyond. "Are you okay down there?"

Because Gansey had not just *vanished* — he'd fallen into a hole.

Thank goodness we were tied together, Blue thought.

Ronan's arms were still locked around her; she felt them quivering. She didn't know if it was from muscle strain or worry. He had not even hesitated before grabbing her.

I can't let myself forget that.

"Gansey?" Adam repeated, and there was just an edge of something terrible behind it. He had spackled confidence too heavily over his anxiety for it to be invisible.

Three tugs. Blue felt them shiver through Adam to her.

Adam laid his face down on the mud in visible relief.

"What's going on?" Ronan asked. "Where is he?"

"He must be hanging," Adam replied, uncertainty letting his Henrietta accent snatch the last *g* from *hanging*. "The rope's cutting me in half it's pulling so hard. I can't get closer to help. It's slimy — his weight would just pull me in."

Freeing herself from Ronan's arms, Blue took an experimental step closer to where Gansey had disappeared. The rope between her and Adam slackened, but he slid no closer to the hole. Slowly, she said, "I think you can be a counterweight if you don't move, Adam. Ronan, stay up here — if anything happens and I start slipping, can you anchor yourself?"

Ronan's headlamp pointed at a muddy column. He nodded.

"Okay," she said. "I'm going to go over and take a look."

She crept slowly past Adam. His fingers were hooked uselessly into the sloppy ground by his cheek.

She nearly fell into the hole.

No wonder Gansey hadn't seen it. There was a rock ledge and then, just — nothing. She swept her headlamp back and forth and saw only inky black. The chasm was too wide to see the other side. Too deep to see the bottom.

The safety rope was visible, though, dark with mud, leading into the pit. Blue shone her flashlight into the black.

"Gansey?"

"I'm here." Gansey's voice was closer than she expected. Quieter than she expected, too. "I just — I believe I'm having a panic attack."

"*You're* having a panic attack? New rule: Everyone should give four tugs before suddenly disappearing. Have you broken anything?"

A long pause. "No."

Something about the tone of the single syllable conveyed, all at once, that he had not been kidding about his fear.

Blue wasn't sure that reassurance was her strong point, especially when she was the one who wanted it, but she tried. "It'll be okay. We're anchored up here. All you need to do is climb out. You're not going to fall."

"It's not that." His voice was a sliver. "There is something on my skin and it is reminding me of . . ."

He trailed off.

"Water," Blue suggested. "Or mud. It's everywhere. Say something again so I can point the flashlight at you."

There was nothing but the sound of his breathing, jagged and afraid. She swept the flashlight beam again.

"Or mosquitoes. Mosquitoes are everywhere," she said, voice bright.

No reply.

"There are over two dozen species of cave beetle," she added. "I read that before we came today."

Gansey whispered, "Hornets."

Her heart contracted.

In the wash of adrenaline, she talked herself down: Yes, hornets could kill Gansey with just a sting, but no, there were not hornets in this cave. And today was not the day that Gansey was going to die, because she had *seen* his spirit on the day he died, and that spirit had been wearing an Aglionby sweater spattered with rain. Not a pair of khakis and a cheery yellow V-neck.

Her flashlight beam finally found him. He hung limply in his harness, head tilted down, hands over his ears. Her flashlight beam traced his heaving shoulders. They were spattered with mud and grime, but there were no insects on them.

She could breathe again.

"Look at me," she ordered. "There are no hornets."

"I know," he muttered. "That's why I said I *think* I'm having a panic attack. I *know* there are no hornets."

What he wasn't saying, but what they both knew, was that Cabeswater was a careful listener.

Which meant he needed to stop thinking about hornets.

"Well, you're making me angry," Blue said. "Adam is lying on his face in the mud for you. Ronan's going home."

Gansey laughed tonelessly. "Keep talking, Jane."

"I don't *want* to. I want you to just grab that rope and pull yourself up here like I know you're perfectly capable of. What good does me *talking* do?"

He looked up at her then, his face streaked and unrecognizable. "It's just that there's something rustling down below me, and your voice drowns it out."

A nasty shiver went down Blue's spine.

Cabeswater was such a good listener.

"Ronan," she called quietly over her shoulder. "New plan: Adam and I are going to pull Gansey out very quickly."

"What! That is a fucking terrible idea," Ronan said. "Why is that the plan?"

Blue didn't want to shout it out loud.

Adam had been listening, though, and he said, quietly and clearly, *"Est aliquid in foramen.* I don't know. *Apis? Apibus? Forsitan."*

Latin hid nothing from Cabeswater; they only meant to spare Gansey.

"No," Ronan said. "No, there is not. That is not what is down there."

Gansey closed his eyes.

I saw him, Blue thought. *I saw his spirit when he died, and this was not what he was wearing. This is not how it happens. It's not now, it's later, it's later —*

Ronan kept going, his voice louder. "No. Do you hear me, Cabeswater? You promised to keep me safe. Who are we to you? Nothing? If you let him die, that is *not keeping me safe.* Do you understand? If they die, I die, too."

Now Blue could hear the humming sound from the pit, too.

Adam spoke up, voice half-muffled from the mud. "I made a deal with you, Cabeswater. I'm your hands and your eyes. What do you think I'll see if he dies?"

The rustling grew. It sounded *numerous.*

It is not hornets, Blue thought, wished, longed, dreamt. *Who are we to you, Cabeswater? Who am I to you?*

Out loud, she said, "We've been making the ley line stronger. We have been making *you* stronger. And we'll keep helping you, but you've got to help us —"

Blackness ate her flashlight beam, rising from the depths. The sound exploded. It was humming; it was wings. They filled the pit, hiding Gansey from view.

"*Gansey!*" Blue shouted, or maybe it was Adam, or maybe it was Ronan.

Then something flapped against her face, and another something. A body careened off the wall. Off the ceiling. The beams of their headlamps were cut into a thousand flickering pieces.

The sound of their wings. The *sound.*

Not hornets.

Bats?

No.

Ravens.

This was not where ravens lived, and this was not how ravens behaved. But they burst and burst from the pit below Gansey. It seemed as if the flock would never end. Blue had the disorienting sensation that it had always been this way, ravens coursing all around them, feathers brushing her cheeks, claws scraping over her helmet. Then, suddenly, the ravens began to shout, back and forth, back and forth. It grew more and more sing-song, and then it resolved into words.

Rex Corvus, parate Regis Corvi.

The Raven King, make way for the Raven King.

Feathers rained down as the birds careened toward the cave

mouth. Blue's heart burst with how *big* it was, this moment, and no other.

Then there was silence, or at least not enough sound to be heard over Blue's thudding heart. Feathers quivered in the mud beside Adam.

"Hold on," Gansey said. "I'm coming out."

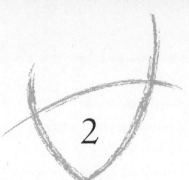

2

Adam Parrish was lonesome.

There is no good word for the opposite of *lonesome*. One might be tempted to suggest *togetherness* or *contentment*, but the fact that these two other words bear definitions unrelated to each other perfectly displays why *lonesome* cannot be properly mirrored. It does not mean *solitude*, nor *alone*, nor *lonely*, although *lonesome* can contain all of those words in itself.

Lonesome means a state of being apart. Of being other. Alone-some.

Adam was not always alone, but he was always lonesome. Even in a group, he was slowly perfecting the skill of holding himself separate. It was easier than one might expect; the others allowed him to do it. He knew he was different since aligning himself more tightly with the ley line this summer. He was himself, but more powerful. Himself, but less human.

If he were them, he would silently watch him draw away, too.

It was better this way. He had not fought with anyone for so long. He had not been angry for weeks.

Now, the day after their excursion into the cave of ravens, Adam drove his small, shitty car away from Henrietta, on his way to do Cabeswater's work. Through the soles of his shoes, he felt the ley line's slow pulse. If he didn't actively focus on it, his heartbeat unconsciously synced up with it. There was something comforting and anxious about the way it twined through him now; he could no longer tell if it was merely a powerful friend or if the power was now actually *him*.

Adam eyed the gas gauge warily. The car would make it back, he thought, if he didn't have to drive too far into the autumnal mountains. He wasn't yet sure what he was meant to do for Cabeswater. Its needs came to him in restless nights and twinging days, slowly becoming visible like something floating to the surface of a lake. The current feeling, a nagging sense of incompletion, wasn't really clear yet, but school was about to start, and he was hoping to get it taken care of before classes began. That morning, he'd lined his bathroom sink with tinfoil, filled it with water, and scryed for clarification. He'd only managed to glimpse a vague location.

The rest will come to me when I get closer. Probably.

Instead, though, as he drew nearer, his mind kept drifting back to Gansey's voice in the cave the day before. The tremulous note in it. The fear — a fear so profound that Gansey could not bring himself to climb out of the pit, though there was nothing physically preventing him.

He had not known that Richard Gansey III had it in him to be a coward.

Adam remembered crouching on the kitchen floor of his parents' double-wide, telling himself to take Gansey's oft-repeated advice to leave. *Just put what you need in the car, Adam.*

But he had stayed. Hung in the pit of his father's anger. A coward, too.

Adam felt like he needed to reconfigure every conversation he'd ever had with Gansey in light of this new knowledge.

As the entrance for Skyline Drive came into view, his thoughts switched abruptly to Cabeswater. Adam had not been to the park, but he knew from a lifetime in Henrietta that it was a national park that stretched along the Blue Ridge Mountains, following the ley line with an almost eerie precision. In front of him, three lanes fed into three squat brown booths. A short line of cars waited.

His gaze found the fee board. He hadn't realized he needed to pay to enter. Fifteen dollars.

Although he hadn't been able to pinpoint a precise location for Cabeswater's task, he was sure it was on the other side of these toll booths. There was no other way in.

But he also knew the contents of his pockets, and it was not fifteen dollars.

I can come back another day.

He was so tired of doing things another day, another way, a cheaper way, a day when Gansey could tidy the edges. This was supposed to be something he could do by himself, *his* power as the magician, tapped into the ley line.

But the ley line couldn't get him through a toll plaza.

If Gansey had been here, he would have breezily tossed the bills out of the Camaro. He wouldn't have even thought about it.

One day, Adam thought. *One day.*

As he sat in line, he plucked his wallet free, and then, when it failed to produce enough, he began digging for change under the seats. It was a moment that would have been both easier and worse if he'd been with Gansey, Ronan, and Blue. Because then IOUs would have had to be created, the *haves* assuring them it wasn't necessary to be paid back, the *have-nots* insisting that it was.

But since it was only Adam, lonesome Adam, he just silently looked at the meager sum he'd managed to scrape together.

$12.38.

He would not beg at the booth. He had very little of anything except for some damned dignity, and he couldn't bring himself to hand that through the driver's side window.

It would have to be another day.

He didn't get angry. There was no one to get angry at. He just allowed himself a brief moment of leaning his temple against the driver's side window, and then he pulled out of line and backed onto the shoulder to turn around.

As he did, his attention was drawn to the vehicles still in line. Two of the cars were exactly what Adam might imagine: a minivan with a young family in it, a sedan with a laughing college-aged couple in it. But the third car was not quite right. It was a rental car — he could see the bar code sticker stuck in the corner of the windshield. Perhaps that was not strange; a tourist might fly in and visit the park. But on the dashboard was a device Adam was very familiar with: an electromagnetic frequency reader. Another device sat next to it, although he wasn't sure what that one was. A geophone, maybe.

The sort of tools Gansey and the others had used for hunting for the ley line. The sort they'd used to find Cabeswater.

Then he blinked, and the dashboard of the car was empty. Had always been empty. It was just a rental car with a bored family in it. A month ago, Adam wouldn't have understood why he was seeing things that weren't real. But now he knew Cabeswater better, and he understood that what he had just seen *was* real — just real in a different place, or a different time.

Someone else had come to Henrietta looking for the ley line.

3

M apey neat downer," Blue said, "to see how far it goes."
"How far *what* goes?" Gansey demanded. He replayed her words, but they remained nonsense. "Lynch, turn that *down*."

It had been several days since their trip into the cave of ravens and now they were on the way to the airport to pick up Dr. Roger Malory, international ley line expert and aged mentor of Gansey's. Ronan lounged in the passenger seat. Adam keeled against a window in the back, his mouth parted in the unaware sleep of the exhausted. Blue sat behind Gansey, clutching his headrest in an effort to be heard.

"This *car*," she despaired.

Gansey knew his reliable and enormous Suburban would have been a more logical choice for the trip, but he wanted the old Camaro to be the first thing the professor saw, not the expensive new SUV. The Camaro was shorthand for the person he had become, and he wanted, more than anything, for Malory to feel that person had been worth the trip. The professor did not fly, but he had flown three thousand miles for him. Gansey couldn't fathom how to repay such a kindness, especially considering the circumstances under which he had left England.

"I said maybe we should just rappel down into that pit you helpfully found." Blue's voice warred with the engine and Ronan's still-abusive electronica. It seemed impossible that Adam could sleep through it.

"I just don't — *Ronan.* My ears are bleeding!"

Ronan turned down the music.

Gansey started again. "I just can't imagine why Glendower's men would have gone to the trouble of lowering him into that hole. I just can't, Jane."

Even thinking about the pit made long-ago venom hum and burn in his throat; effortlessly, he conjured the image of warning-striped insects prowling the thin skin between his fingers. He had nearly forgotten how horrifying and compelling it was to relive the moment.

Eyes on the road, Gansey.

"Maybe it's a recent hole," she suggested. "The collapsed roof of a lower cavern."

"If that's true, we'd have to get *across* it, not *in* it. Ronan and I would have to climb the walls like spiders. Unless you and Adam have rock climbing experience I don't know about."

Outside the car, Washington, D.C., slunk closer; the deep-blue sky got smaller. The widening interstate grew guardrails, streetlights, BMWs, airport taxis. In the rearview mirror, Gansey saw a corner of Blue's face. Her wide-awake gaze snagged on something outside, fast, and she craned to look out the window, like this was another country.

It kind of was. He was, as ever, a reluctantly returning expatriate. He felt a pang, a longing to run, and it surprised him. It had been a long time.

Blue said, "Ronan could dream a bridge for us."

Ronan made a noise of glorious disdain.

"Don't just snort at me! Tell me why not. You're a magical creature. Why can't you do magic?"

With acidic precision, Ronan replied, "For starters, I'd have to sleep right there by the pit, since I have to be touching something to pull it out of a dream. And I'd have to know what was on the other side to even know what kind of bridge to make. And then, even if I pulled all that off, if I took something that big out of my dream, it would drain the ley line, possibly making Cabeswater disappear again, this time with us in it, sending us all to some never-never land of time-space fuckery that we might never escape from. I figured after the events of this summer, all this was self-evident, which was why I summed it up before like so —"

Ronan repeated the noise of glorious disdain.

"Thanks for the super helpful alternative suggestions, Ronan Lynch. Your contribution at the end of the world will be tallied accordingly," Blue said. She turned her attention back to Gansey, persisting, "So, then, what? It has to be important, or Cabeswater wouldn't have shown it to us."

That, Gansey thought, *assumes Cabeswater's priorities are the same as ours.* Out loud, he said, "We find another way in. One that brings us in on the other side of that hole. Since it's not a normal cave — it's all tied in with the ley line — Malory can help us."

He couldn't believe Malory was really here. He'd spent nearly a year with the professor, the longest he had stayed anywhere, and it had started to feel like there would never be a time when he wasn't searching. Now he was looking in a narrowing grave, and somewhere in that vast darkness was Glendower and the end.

Gansey felt off-kilter; time played in jittery fast-forward.

In the rearview mirror, he caught Blue's eyes by accident.

Strangely enough, he saw his own thoughts reflected in her face: excitement and consternation. Casually, out of view of Ronan, making sure Adam was still sleeping, Gansey dangled his hand between the driver's seat and the door. Palm up, fingers stretched back to Blue.

This was not allowed.

He knew it was not allowed, by rules he himself had set. He would not permit himself to play favorites between Adam and Ronan; he and Blue couldn't play favorites in this way, either. She would not see the gesture, anyway. She would ignore it if she did. His heart hummed.

Blue touched his fingertips.

Just this —

He pinched her fingers lightly, just for a moment, and then he withdrew his hand and put it back on the wheel. His chest felt warm.

This was not allowed.

Ronan had not seen; Adam was still sleeping. The only casualty was his pulse.

"Your exit, dick!" Ronan snapped. Or *Dick*. It could have been either, really.

Gansey steered in a hurry. Adam blinked awake. Ronan swore. Gansey's heart restarted.

Eyes on the road, Gansey.

At the airport, the professor was not waiting at the outdoor passenger pick-up area as arranged, nor did he pick up his phone. They finally found him sitting by the baggage carousel, near a group of chattering people, a tower of luggage, and an irritable-looking service dog. He looked precisely as Gansey remembered him. There was something of a turtle in his visage, and he had not only one chin, but another waiting in line behind it. His nose and his ears appeared to be fashioned whimsically from rubber. The round bags beneath his eyes perfectly mirrored his round brow lines. His expression was befuddled.

"Mr. Malory!" Gansey said gladly.

"Oh, God," Ronan said under his breath. "He's so *old*."

Adam punched Ronan, saving Gansey the trouble.

"Gansey," Malory said, clasping hands with him. "What a relief."

"I'm terribly sorry to keep you waiting — I called!"

"My blasted phone. The battery on these things is rubbish. It is like a conspiracy to sell us something. Blood pressure medication, possibly. Are airplanes always like that? So full of *people*?"

"I'm afraid so," Gansey said. Out of the corner of his eye, he noticed that Adam was regarding Malory in a not entirely *Adam* sort of way, his head cocked, pensive concentration in his eyes. Disconcerted, Gansey hurried on. "Let me introduce you. These are my friends: Ronan, Adam Parrish, and Jane."

Adam's expression focused. Became Adam-like. He blinked over to Gansey.

"Blue," Blue corrected.

"Oh, yes, you are blue," Malory agreed. "How perceptive you are. What was the name? Jane? This is the lady I spoke to on the phone all those months ago, right? How small she is. Are you done growing?"

"*What!*" Blue said.

Gansey felt it was time to remove Malory from the terminal. "Which of these is your bag?"

"All of them," Malory said tragically.

Ronan was trying his best to meaningfully catch Gansey's eye, but Gansey wouldn't let him. The teens collected the bags. The service dog got up.

Blue, friend to all canines, said, "Whoa there, fellow. You stay here."

"Oh, no," Malory protested. "The Dog is mine."

They eyed the Dog. It wore a smart blue vest that advertised its usefulness without providing further details.

"Okay," Gansey said.

He avoided another meaningful look from Ronan. On the curb outside, they all stopped for Malory to remove the Dog's vest and then they watched the Dog relieve itself on the sign for the rental car shuttle.

Ronan asked, "What's the Dog for?"

Malory's turtle mouth got very small. "He is a service animal."

"What nature of service does he provide?"

"Excuse *you*," Malory replied.

Gansey avoided a third meaningful look from both Adam and Malory.

They reached the car, which had gotten no larger since they entered the terminal. Gansey disliked confronting the consequences of his folly so directly.

Ladies and gentlemen, my trick for you today will be to take this 1973 Camaro —

Removing the spare tire from the trunk, Gansey abandoned it beside a streetlight. The price of Malory's visit.

— and fit five people, a dog, and a hell of a lot of luggage inside.

After performing this magic trick, he sank into the driver's seat. The Dog was panting anxiously. Gansey knew how it felt.

"May I pet her? Him?" Blue asked.

"Yes," Malory replied. "But he won't enjoy it. He's very highly strung."

Gansey allowed Blue to exchange a meaningful glance with him in the rearview mirror as they got back onto the interstate.

"The food on the plane was appalling; it is amazing the staff has not perished of bleeding ulcers," said Malory. He slapped Gansey's arm so suddenly that both Gansey and the Dog jumped in surprise. "Do you know anything about the drapery that was lost to the English in Mawddwy?"

"Drapery? Oh. *Oh.* It had women with red hands on it? I thought they'd decided it was a flag," Gansey said.

"Yes, yes, that's the very one. You *are* good!"

Gansey thought he was no better than one would expect after seven years of fairly single-minded study, but he appreciated the sentiment. He raised his voice so as to include the backseat in the conversation. "It's actually very interesting. The English pursued some of Glendower's men, and though they got away, the English got ahold of this ancient drapery. Flag, whatever. The red hands are interesting because red hands are associated with the *Mab Darogan,* a mythic title. It was given to people like King Arthur and Llewellyn the Great and of course Owain Lawgoch —"

"Of course," echoed Ronan sarcastically. "Of course Owain Lawgoch."

"Don't be such a shitbag," Adam murmured.

"This lane ends," Blue said.

"So it does," Gansey said, merging. "Anyway, the *Mab Darogan* was a kind of Welsh 'Son of Destiny.'"

Malory broke in, "Blame the poets. It's easier to stir people to rebellion if they think they're on the side of a demigod or some chosen one. Never trust a poet. They —"

Gansey interrupted, "The flag was destroyed, right? Oh, sorry, I didn't mean to cut you off."

"It's quite all right," Malory said, and sounded as if it was more than all right. This — plucking threads from the tight weave of history — was their common ground. Gansey was relieved to realize their relationship was still intact, just built upon a very different foundation than his relationship with the people currently in the backseat. As a Honda blew past them, its occupants giving Gansey the finger, the professor continued, "It was indeed thought destroyed. Repurposed, really. Skidmore wrote that it was made into nightgowns for Henry the Fourth, though I couldn't find *his* sources."

"Nightgowns!" repeated Blue. "Why *nightgowns*?"

Gansey said, "For maximum ignominy."

"No one knows what *ignominy* means, Gansey," Adam muttered.

"Disgrace," supplied Malory. "Destruction of dignity. Much like airplane travel. But the drapery was, in fact, just rediscovered this past week."

Gansey swerved. "You're joking!"

"It's in terrible shape — textiles don't preserve nicely, as you well know. And it took them forever to suss out what it was. Now, now, get off at this exit, Gansey, so I can show you this. By curious accident, the drapery was found under a barn in Kirtling. Flooding cut a deep path through the topsoil, which revealed the edge of an older foundation. Meters and meters of dirt were dislodged."

Adam asked, "All that water didn't destroy the flag?"

The professor swiveled. "Exactly the question! By a trick of physics, the water didn't fill the foundation but instead managed to cut a separate course slightly uphill! And in answer to your unasked question, yes! The barn was located on a ley line."

"That was the very question I was about to ask," Ronan said.

"Ronan," Blue said, "don't be such a shitbag."

Gansey caught a corner of Adam's laugh in the rearview mirror as he pulled into a parking spot at a bedraggled gas station. Malory had produced an old digital camera from some place on his person and was now clicking back through the photos on it. "They're now blaming the flooding on a flash thunderstorm or some such. But people who were *there* say it was because the walls of the barn were weeping."

"Weeping!" exclaimed Blue. It was impossible to tell if she was horrified or delighted.

"What do you believe?" Gansey asked.

In response, Malory simply handed him the camera. Gansey looked at the display.

"Oh," he said.

The photo showed a badly degraded textile painted with three women, each in simple robes from a time well before Glendower. They stood in identical poses, hands lifted on either side of their heads, palms bloody red, heralding the *Mab Darogan*.

They each wore Blue Sargent's face.

Impossible.

But no. Nothing was impossible these days. He zoomed the photo larger for a better look. Blue's wide eyes looked back at him. Stylized, yes, but still, the resemblance was uncanny: her dubious eyebrows, her curious mouth. He pressed a knuckle to his lips as hornets hissed in his ears.

He was suddenly overwhelmed, as he had not been in a long time, with the memory of the voice in his head as his life was saved. *You will live because of Glendower. Someone else on the ley line is dying when they should not, and so you will live when you should not.* He was filled with the need to see Glendower himself, to touch his hand, to kneel before him, to thank him, to be him.

Hands reached from the back; he didn't know whose they were. He let them take the camera.

Blue murmured something he didn't catch. Adam whispered, "She looks like you."

"Which one?"

"All of them."

"Fuck me," Ronan said, voicing all of their thoughts.

"The photo is so close," Gansey said finally. "The quality is excellent."

"Well, of course," Malory answered. "Don't you understand? That is the barn outside my holiday cottage. I was the one who saw the tears. My team found the drapery."

Gansey struggled to piece this together. "How did you know to look there?"

"That, Gansey, is the thing. I wasn't looking for anything. I was on a well-deserved holiday. After the summer I had, battling that wretched Simmons neighbor about his beastly sewage issue,

I was in desperate need of some time away. I assure you, my presence in Kirtling was a coincidence."

"Coincidence," echoed Adam, dubious.

What was this thing, this huge thing? Gansey was alive with anticipation and fear. The enormity of it felt like the black pit in the cave — he could see neither the bottom nor the other side.

"I must say, Gansey," Malory said brightly. "I am so excited to meet your ley line."

4

Blue couldn't sleep that night. She couldn't stop waiting for the sound of the front door. Some ingrained, foolish part of her couldn't believe that her mother would not come home before school began tomorrow. Her mother always had an answer for everything, even if it was wrong, and Blue had taken for granted that she would be unchanging as everything else turned sideways.

Blue missed her.

She went to the hall and listened. Outside, Orla was conducting a midnight chakra clearing with a few ardent clients. Downstairs, Calla angrily watched television alone. On her floor, she heard nothing, nothing — and then a series of short, purposeful sighs from Persephone's room at the end of the hall.

When she knocked, Persephone said in her tiny voice, "You might as well."

Inside, the lamplight reached only to a shoddy little desk and the end of Persephone's high, elderly twin bed. Persephone sat cross-legged in the Victorian desk chair, her enormous nimbus of curly hair lit golden by the single bulb. She worked away at an old sweater.

As Blue climbed onto the worn mattress, several bobbins of thread raced down to nestle against her bare feet. She tugged her oversized shirt down over her knees and watched Persephone for a few minutes. She seemed to be adding length to the sleeves by sewing on mismatching cuffs. Every so often, she sighed as if she were annoyed with herself or the sweater.

"Is that yours?" Blue asked.

"Is what mine?" Persephone followed her eyes to the sweater. "Oh. Oh, no. I mean, it was. Once. But you see I'm changing it."

"For someone with giant long arms?"

Persephone held out the garment to verify if this was the case. "Yes."

Blue slowly lined up the thread by color on the bed beside her. "Do you think Mom went looking for Butternut?"

"Your father. Artemus," Persephone corrected. Or clarified. *Butternut* was not really Blue's father's name — it was a pet name Maura had apparently given him in Ye Olde Days. "I think that's oversimplifying it. But yes, that is one of the reasons why she went."

"I thought she had the hots for Mr. Gray."

Persephone considered. "The problem with your mother, Blue, is she likes to touch things. We told her that Artemus was in the past. He made his choices long before you, I said. But no, she had to keep touching it! How can you expect something to heal if you keep *poking*?"

"Sooooo she's . . . gone . . . to . . . get . . . him?"

"Oh, no!" Persephone said with a little laugh. "I don't think that would — no. As you said, she has the hots for Mr. Gray. Do young people really say that anymore?"

"I just said it. I'm young."

"Ish."

"Are you asking me or not? Either you accept my authority on this point or we move on."

"We move on. But it is up to her, you know, if she wants to go looking for him. She never gets to be all on her own, and this is her chance to have some time to herself."

Maura did not strike Blue as a *time to herself* person, but maybe that had been the problem. "So you're saying we shouldn't keep looking for her."

"How should I know?"

"You're a psychic! You charge people to tell their future! Look into the future!"

Persephone gazed at Blue with her all-black eyes until she felt a little bad about her outburst, and then Persephone added, "Maura went into Cabeswater. That's not the future. Besides, if she had wanted help, she would have asked. Probably."

"If I had paid you," Blue said dangerously, "I would be asking for my money back right now."

"Fortunate that you didn't pay me, then. Does this look even to you?" Persephone held up the sweater. The two sleeves were nothing alike.

With a rather blasted *pshaw!* Blue leapt off the bed and stormed out of the room. She heard Persephone call, "Sleep is brain food!" as she headed down the hall.

Blue was not comforted. She did not feel in any way as if she had just had a meaningful exchange with a human.

Instead of going to her bedroom, she crept into the dim Phone/Sewing/Cat Room and sat beside the psychic hotline, folding her bare legs beneath her. The window, ajar, let in the chilly air. The streetlight through the leaves cast familiar, living shadows over the bins of sewing materials. Snatching a pillow from the chair, Blue rested it on top of her goose-bumped legs before picking up the handset. She listened to make sure there was a dial tone and not psychic activity on the other end.

Then she called Gansey.

It rang twice, three times, and then: "Hello?"

He sounded boyish and ordinary. Blue asked, "Did I wake you up?"

She heard Gansey fumble for and scrape up his wireframes.

"No," he lied, "I was awake."

"I called you by accident anyway. I meant to call Congress, but your number is one off."

"Oh?"

"Yeah, because yours has 6-6-5 in it." She paused. "Get it?"

"Oh, you."

"6-6-5. One number different. *Get it?*"

"Yeah, I got it." He was quiet for a minute then, though she heard him breathing. "I didn't know you could call hell, actually."

"You can call in," Blue said. "The thing is that you can't call *out*."

"I imagine you could send letters, though."

"Never with enough postage."

"No, faxes," Gansey corrected himself. "Pretend I didn't say letters. *Faxes* is funnier."

Blue laughed into the pillow. "Okay, that was all."

"All what?"

"All I had to say."

47

"I've learned a lot. I'm glad you misdialed."

"Well. Easy mistake to make," she said. "Might do it again."

A very, very long pause. She opened her mouth to fill it, then changed her mind and didn't. She was shivering again, even though she wasn't cold with the pillow on her legs.

"Shouldn't," Gansey said finally. "But I hope you do."

5

The following morning, Gansey and Malory went out to investigate the ley line. Adam agreed to join them, which surprised Gansey. It wasn't that the two of them had been fighting. It was that they'd been . . . *not* fighting. Not talking. Not anything. Gansey had kept going on the same road he always had, and Adam had taken a fork onto a second road.

But for the moment, at least, they were headed in the same direction. Goal: Find another entrance to the raven cave. Method: Retrace steps from previous ley line searches. Resources: Roger Malory.

It was a good time of year to show off the town. Henrietta and her environs were a paint box of colors. Green hayfields, golden cornfields, yellow sycamores, orange oaks, periwinkle mountains, cerulean cloudless sky. The freshly paved road was black and snaking and inviting. The air was crisp and breathable and insistent on action.

The three of them moved quickly until Malory's attention was caught and held at their fourth stop of the morning, Massanutten Mountain. It was not the most mystical of locales. Neighborhoods bubbled from its sides and a ski resort crowned it. Gansey found it coarse, tourist and student fodder, but if he'd said it out loud, Adam would've torn out his throat in a minute for being elitist.

The three of them stood just off the road, avoiding the stares of slowing drivers. Malory was all turtled over behind his tripod, lecturing either Adam or himself. "The procedure of ley hunting is quite different in the States! In England, a true ley must have at least one aligned element — church, barrow, standing stone — every two miles, or it is considered coincidental. But of course here in the Colonies" — both boys smiled good-naturedly — "everything is much farther apart. Moreover, you never had the Romans to build you things in wonderfully straight lines. Pity. One misses them."

"I *do* miss the Romans," Gansey said, just to see Adam smirk, which he did.

Malory sighted his transit through a gap in the trees, toward the gaping valley down below. "And although your line is now awake and profound — positively *profound* — with energy, the secondary line we're looking for today is n— curses!" He had tripped over the Dog.

The Dog looked at Malory. His expression said, *Curses!*

"Hand me that pencil." Malory took the pencil from Adam and marked something on the map. "Go sit in the car!"

"Excuse me?" Adam asked, polite and shocked.

"Not you! The Dog!"

The Dog sulkily retreated. Another car slowed down to stare. Malory muttered to himself. Adam absently tapped a finger against his own wrist, a gesture somehow disconcerting and otherworldly. Insects buzzed around them; wings brushed Gansey's cheek.

A bee, maybe; I could be dead in a minute here, maybe, by the side of this road, before Malory can get his cell phone out of the car, before Adam realizes what's going on.

He didn't swat the insect. It buzzed away, but his heart still beat fast.

"Talk me through what you're doing," Gansey said. Then he corrected: "*Us.* Talk us."

Malory adopted his professor voice. "Your cave is tied to the ley line, and it has no fixed location. Therefore, if we're looking for a cave to join up with it, there's no sense searching for ordinary cave entrances. Only an entrance on a ley will do. And as your cave mapping suggests that you were traveling perpendicular to the ley instead of along it, I believe the cave network in its entirety exists on multiple lines. So we seek a crossroads! Tell me, what is this?"

He indicated something on one of the maps that a younger Gansey had heavily notated. Older Gansey lifted Malory's finger to look beneath it. "Spruce Knob. Highest peak in West Virginia. Forty-five hundred feet or something like that?"

"Highest peak in Virginia?" echoed Malory.

"West," said Gansey and Adam at the same time.

"*West* Virginia," Gansey repeated, studiously avoiding eye contact with another slowing driver. "Sixty miles west of here. Seventy, perhaps?"

Malory dragged his square fingertip a few inches along one of the many short highlighter paths. "And what's this?"

"Coopers Mountain."

Malory tapped it. "What's this note? Giant's Grave?"

"It's another name for the mountain."

The professor raised his hairy eyebrows. "Interesting name for the new world."

Gansey recalled how excited he had been to learn Coopers Mountain's old name. It had felt like a stunning bit of detective work to stumble across it in an old court document, and then it had been even more thrilling to discover that the mountain was appropriately odd: situated all by itself in the middle of sloping fields, two miles away from the main ridge.

"Why is it interesting?" Adam asked.

Gansey explained, "Kings were often giants in British mythology. A lot of British locations associated with kings have the word *giant* in them, or are giant-*sized*. There's a mountain in Wales, what is it . . . Idris? Dr. Malory, help me."

Malory smacked his lips. "Cadair Idris."

"Right. It translates to *the chair of Idris*, who was a king, and a giant, and so the chair in the mountain is giant-sized, too. I got permission to hike on Giant's Grave — there was some rumor of Native American graves on there, but I couldn't find them. No cave, either."

Malory continued tracing the highlighter line. "And this?"

"Mole Hill. Used to be a volcano. It's out in the middle of a flat field. No cave there, either, but lots of geology students."

Malory tapped on the last location on the line. "And this is us, yes? Mass-a-nut-ten. My, this line of yours. I've waited a life-time to see something like it. Remarkable! Tell me, there must be others prowling around poking at it as well?"

"Yes," Adam replied immediately.

Gansey looked at him. The *yes* had left no place for doubt; a *yes* not of paranoia, but observation.

In a lower voice, for Gansey, not Malory, Adam said, "Because of Mr. Gray."

Of course. Mr. Gray had come looking for a magical parcel, and when he'd failed to deliver it to his employer Colin Greenmantle, Greenmantle had flooded the town with people looking for Mr. Gray. It would be foolish to assume they'd all left.

Gansey preferred to be foolish.

"Unsurprising!" Malory concluded. He clapped a hand on Gansey's shoulder. "Lucky for both of you that this young man has a better ear than most; he'll hear that king long before anyone else has thought to even listen. Now, let us flee this coarse place before it rubs off. Here! To Spruce Knob. By way of these other two lumps."

Out of old habit, Gansey gathered up the transit and GPS and laser rod as Malory climbed into the Suburban to wait. Adam went into the woods a bit farther to pee, an action that always made Gansey wish that he was not too inhibited to do the same.

When he returned, Adam said suddenly, "I'm glad we're not fighting. It was stupid for it to go on so long."

"Yes," Gansey replied, trying not to sound relieved, exhausted, pleased. He was afraid to say too much; he'd destroy this moment, which already felt imaginary.

Adam continued, "That thing with Blue. I should've known it would be weird trying to date her once she was one of . . . you know, with us all. Whatever."

Gansey thought of his fingers on Blue's and how foolish such a gesture had been. This equilibrium was so hard-won.

He preferred being foolish, but he couldn't keep on that way.

Both boys looked out through the bare spot in the trees toward the valley. Thunder rumbled somewhere, though there was not a cloud in the sky. It didn't feel like it came from the sky, anyway. It felt like it came from below them, down in the ley line.

Adam's expression was ferocious and pleased; Gansey was at once proud to know him and uncertain he did at all.

"I can't believe we're doing this," Gansey said.

Adam replied, "I can."

6

This was not Blue's real life.

As she leaned against the wall outside the guidance counselor's office, she wondered when she would start to think of school as an important thing again. After an extraordinary summer full of chasing kings and disappearing mothers, it was hard to really, truly picture herself going to class every day. What would any of this matter in two years? Nobody here would remember her, or vice versa. She would only remember that this was the fall her mother vanished. This was the year of Glendower.

She peered across the linoleum-basted hall to the clock. In an hour she could walk back home to her real life.

You are coming back tomorrow, Blue told herself. *And the next day.*

But it felt like more of a dream than Cabeswater.

She touched her palm with the fingers of her other hand and thought about that flag Malory had found, painted with three women with red hands and her face. She thought about how the boys were off exploring without her.

She became aware of Noah's presence. At first she just sort of knew that he was there, and when she considered how it was that she happened to know, she realized she could see him slouching beside her in his rumpled Aglionby uniform.

"Here?" Blue demanded, though really she was pleased. "Here, and not in the raven cave of death?"

Noah shrugged, apologetic and smudgy. His proximity chilled Blue as he pulled energy from her to stay visible. He blinked at two girls who walked by pushing a cart. They didn't seem to notice him, but it was difficult to tell if it was because he was invisible to them or just because he was Noah.

"I think I miss this part," he said. "The beginning. This *is* the beginning, right?"

"First day," Blue replied.

"Oh, *yeah*." Noah leaned back and inhaled. "Oh, wait, no, it's the other one. I forgot. I actually hate this part."

Blue did not hate it, because that would require acknowledging that it was really happening.

"What are you doing?" Noah asked.

She handed him a brochure, even though she felt self-conscious sharing it, as if she were giving him a list for Santa Claus. "Talking to the counselor about that."

Noah read the words as if they were in a foreign language. "Ex-per-ie-ence di-verse fo-rest types in the A-ma-zon. The Sch-ooool for E-col-o-gy fea-tures a stud-y a-broad — oh, you can't *go somewhere*."

She was very aware that he was probably right. "Thanks for the vote of confidence."

"People are going to see you talking to nobody and think you're weird." This amused him.

It neither amused nor worried Blue. She'd gone through eighteen years as the town psychic's daughter, and now, in her senior year, she had already held every single possible conversation about that fact. She had been shunned and embraced and bullied and cajoled. She was going to hell, she had the straight line to spiritual nirvana. Her mother was a hack, her mother was a witch. Blue dressed like a hobo, Blue dressed like a fashion mogul. She was untouchably hilarious, she was a friendless bitch. It had faded into monotonous background noise. The disheartening and lonesome upshot was that Blue Sargent was the strangest thing in the halls of Mountain View High School.

Well, with the exception of Noah.

"Do you see other dead people?" Blue asked him.

Meaning: *Do you see my mother?*

Noah shuddered.

A voice came from the cracked office door. "Blue? Sweetie, you can come in now."

Noah slid into the office ahead of her. Even though he looked solid and living in the strong sunlight through the office window, the counselor looked right through him. His invisibility seemed downright miraculous as he sat down on the floor in front of the metal desk to pleasantly eavesdrop.

Blue shot him a withering look.

There were two sorts of people: The ones who could see Noah, and the ones who couldn't. Blue generally only got along with the former.

The counselor — Ms. Shiftlet — was new to the school, but not to Henrietta. Blue recognized her from the post office. She was one of those impeccably dressed older women who liked things done right the first time. She sat perfectly straight in a chair designed for slouching, out of place behind a cheap shared desk cluttered with mismatching personal knickknacks.

Ms. Shiftlet efficiently checked the computer. "I see someone just had a birthday."

"It was your *birthday*?" Noah demanded.

Blue struggled to address the counselor instead of Noah. "What — oh — yes."

It had been two weeks ago. Ordinarily, Maura made sludgy brownies, but she hadn't been there. Persephone had tried her best to re-create their undercooked glory, but the brownies had accidentally turned out pretty and precise with powdered sugar dusted in lace patterns on top. Calla had seemed worried Blue would be angry, which bemused Blue. Why would Blue be angry at *them*? It was Maura she wanted to slap. Or hug.

"I can't believe you didn't tell us," muttered Noah. "We could have gone for gelato."

Noah couldn't eat, but he liked the gelato parlor in town for reasons that escaped Blue.

Ms. Shiftlet inclined her head to Blue without disrupting her perfect posture. "I see here you talked to Mr. Torres before he left. He has a note here about an incident in —"

"That's all taken care of and done with," Blue interrupted, avoiding Noah's eyes. She slid the brochure across the desk. "Pretend like it never happened. All I'd like to know is if there is any way to get here from what I'm doing now."

Ms. Shiftlet was visibly eager to get off the topic of anything that could be considered an *incident*. She consulted the brochure. "Well, this looks like a barrel of monkeys, pun intended! Do you have an interest in wildlife? Let me pull up some information on this school."

Noah leaned over. "You should see her shoes. Pointy."

Blue ignored him. "I'd *like* to do something with river systems, or forest —"

"Oh, this school is *very* competitive." Ms. Shiftlet was too efficient to let Blue finish her sentence. "Here, let me show you the average scores of the students who get accepted."

"Rude," Noah commented.

Ms. Shiftlet turned the monitor so that Blue could see a somewhat demoralizing graph. "You see how few students get accepted. That means financial aid would also be very competitive. You'd be applying for aid?"

She said it like a statement instead of a question, but she wasn't wrong. This was Mountain View High. No one was paying outright for a private school. Most of Blue's peers considered community college or state schools, if they considered college at all.

"I don't know if Mr. Torres went over the types of schools you need." Ms. Shiftlet sounded as if she suspected he hadn't, and that she judged him for it. "What you need is three different types. *Reach* schools, *match* schools, and *safety* schools. This one is a wonderful example of a reach school. But now it's time to add some others to your list. Some schools that you can be sure you can get into and afford. That's just good sense."

Ms. Shiftlet wrote *reach*, *match*, and *safety* on an index card. Underlining *safety*, she slid it across the desk. Blue wasn't sure if she was supposed to keep it.

"Have you filled out your application fee waiver form?"

"Four of them. I read online I could get up to four waived?"

This show of efficiency visibly pleased Ms. Shiftlet. "So maybe you already know this is your *reach* school! Now it's time to make a sensible backup plan."

Blue was so tired of compromises. She was tired of *sensible*.

Noah scratched his fingernails on the desk leg. The sound — which was admittedly uncomfortable — made Ms. Shiftlet frown.

He said, "I'd be way more sunshiney if I was a counselor."

"If I *did* get in," Blue said, "could I get loans and aid to cover it all?"

"Let me get you some paperwork," Ms. Shiftlet said. "FAFSA will pay for a *percentage* depending on your *need*. The amount varies."

Blue couldn't expect any help from the lean budget at 300 Fox Way. She thought about the bank account she'd slowly been filling. "How much will be left over? Could you guess?"

Ms. Shiftlet sighed. *Guessing* clearly fell outside her realm of interests. She flipped the monitor around again to reveal the school's tuition rate. "If you were staying in the dorm, you'd probably be obligated for ten thousand dollars a year. Your parents could take out a loan, of course. I have paperwork for that, too, if you would like it."

Blue leaned back as her heart vacated her chest cavity. Of course it was impossible. It had been impossible before she arrived and would continue being impossible forever. It was just that spending time with Gansey and the others had made her think that the impossible might be more possible than she'd thought before.

Maura was always telling her, *Look at all the potential you hold inside yourself!*

Potential for other people, though. Not for Blue.

It wasn't worth shedding tears over something she had known for so long. It was just that *this*, on top of everything *else* —

She swallowed. *I will not cry in front of this woman.*

Suddenly, Noah scrambled out from under the desk. He leapt to his feet. There was something wrong about the action, something about it that meant it was too fast or too vertical or too violent for a living boy to perform. And he kept going up, even after he'd already stood. As he stretched to the ceiling, the card that said *reach*, *match*, and *safety* hurtled into the air.

"Oh?" said Ms. Shiftlet. Her voice wasn't even surprised, yet.

The warmth sucked from Blue's skin. The water in Ms. Shiftlet's glass creaked.

The business card holder upended. Cards splayed across the desk. A computer speaker fell onto its face. An array of paper swirled up. Someone's family photo shot upward.

Blue jumped up. She didn't have any immediate plan but to stop Noah, but as she flung her hands out, she realized that Noah wasn't there.

There was just a tossed explosion of tissues and business envelopes and business cards, a frenetic tornado losing propulsion.

The material collapsed back to the desk.

Blue and Ms. Shiftlet stared at each other. The paper rustled as it settled completely. The knocked-over computer speaker buzzed; one of its cables had been knocked ajar.

The temperature was slowly rising in the room again.

"What just happened?" Ms. Shiftlet asked.

Blue's pulse galloped.

Truthfully, she replied, "I have no idea."

7

Blue arrived at Monmouth Manufacturing before anyone else. She knocked to be sure, and then let herself in. Immediately, she was enveloped with the comfortable scent of the room: the faded library-smell of old books, the cool odor of mint, the must-and-rust scent of century-old brick and ancient pipes, the note of funk from the heap of dirty laundry against the wall.

"Noah?" Her voice was small in the huge expanse. She dropped her backpack on the desk chair. "Are you here? It's okay, I'm not upset. You can use my energy if you need."

There was no answer. The space was turning gray and blue as one of the strange flash thunderstorms roiled over the mountains, filling the floor-to-ceiling windows of the warehouse with clouds. The sharp afternoon shadows behind the stacks of books mutated and diffused. The room felt heavy, sleepy.

Blue peered into the dark gathering at the far-above peak of the roof. "Noah? I just want to talk about what happened."

She put her head in the door of Noah's room. Malory's things occupied it currently, and it smelled mannish and evergreen. One of his bags was open and Blue could see that it was entirely filled with books. This struck her as impractical and Gansey-like and made her feel a bit more benevolent toward the professor.

Noah was not there.

She checked the bathroom, which was also sort of the laundry room and kitchen. The doors hung open on a small stacked washer-dryer unit; socks draped over the sink's edge, either drying or flung. A small fridge lurked dangerously close to the toilet. A length of rubber tubing strangled a showerhead above a grimy drain; the shower curtain was strung from the ceiling with fishing line. Blue was disturbed by the number of chip bags that were reachable from the toilet. A dark red tie on the floor pointed a jagged line toward the exit.

Some foreign impulse urged Blue to pick up any of the mess, any single component, to improve upon the disaster.

She did not.

She backed out.

Ronan's room was forbidden, but she looked inside anyway. His raven's cage sat with its door ajar, impeccably and incongruously clean. His room was filled not so much with filth, but clutter: shovels and swords leaned in the corners, speakers and printers piled by the wall. And bizarre objects in between: an old suitcase with vines trailing out of it, a potted tree that seemed to be humming to itself, a single cowboy boot in the middle of the floor. A mask hung high on the wall, eyes wide, mouth gaping. It was blackened, as if by fire, and the edges were badly bitten, as if by a saw. Something that looked suspiciously like a tire track ran over one of its eyes. The mask made Blue think of words like *survivor* and *destroyer*.

She didn't like it.

A crash behind Blue made her leap — but it was only the apartment door opening. Guilt had amplified the sound.

Blue darted out of Ronan's room. Gansey and Malory trailed in slowly, deep in conversation. The Dog sulked behind them, excluded by virtue of not speaking English.

"Of course Iolo Goch would make sense as a companion," Gansey was saying, sloughing off his jacket. "Him or Gruffudd Llwyd, I suppose. But — no, it's impossible. He died in Wales."

"But are we sure?" Malory asked. "Do we know where he was buried? That he *was* buried?"

"Or if he was just made into nightgowns, you mean?" Gansey caught sight of Blue then, and he rewarded her with his best smile — not his polished one, but the more foolish number that meant he was excited. "Hallo, Jane. Tell me what Iolo Goch means to you."

Blue pulled her thoughts from Ronan's mask and Noah and school. "A chest cold?"

"Glendower's closest poet," Gansey corrected. "Also, very funny."

"Did you find anything?" she asked.

"Absolutely nothing," he replied, but he sounded cheerful about it.

Malory lowered his mass onto the leather couch. The Dog lay on top of him. It didn't seem as if it would be very comfortable; the Dog draped over the professor like a slip cloth over a chair. But Malory merely closed his eyes and stroked him in an uncharacteristic show of affection. "Gansey, I perish for a cup of tea. Can such a thing be had in this place? I cannot possibly hope to survive this jet lag without a cup of tea."

"I got tea just for you," Gansey said. "I'll make some."

"Please not with loo water," Malory called after him, not opening his eyes. The Dog kept lying on him.

For an overwhelming moment, Blue was afraid she was going to be unable to prevent herself from asking what the Dog was for. Instead, she followed Gansey back to the kitchen-bathroom-laundry.

He rummaged through the cluttered shelves. "We were just talking about the mechanics of bringing Glendower over here. The books say he traveled with mages — are they the ones who put him to sleep? Did he *want* it? Was he sleeping before he left, or did he fall asleep here?"

It suddenly seemed like a lonesome thing to be buried a sea away from your home, like being shot off into space. "Iolo Goch was one of the mages?"

"No, just a poet. You heard Malory in the car. They were very poetlitical — poet — political." Gansey laughed at his own stumble. "*Poets* were *political*. I know that's not really a tongue twister. I've been listening to Malory all day. P-p-political. Poets. Iolo composed these really flattering poems about Glendower's past prowess and his house and lands. His family. And such. Oh, what am I even looking for here?"

He paused to locate a tiny microwave. He examined the interior of a mug before filling it. Pulling a mint leaf from his pocket to suck on, he spoke around it as the water heated. "Really, if Glendower were Robin Hood, Iolo Goch would have been . . . that other guy."

"Maid Marian," Blue said. "Little John."

Gansey pointed at her. "Like Batman and Robin. But he died in Wales. Are we to believe he returned to Wales after leaving Glendower here? No. I reject it."

Blue loved this ponderous, scholarly Gansey, too involved with facts to consider how he appeared on the outside. She asked, "Glendower had a wife, right?"

"Died in the Tower of London."

"Siblings?"

"Beheaded."

"Children?"

"A million of them, but most imprisoned and dead, or just plain dead. He lost his entire family in the uprising."

"Poet it is, then!"

Gansey asked, "Have you ever heard that rumor that if you boil water in the microwave it will explode when you touch it?"

"Has to be pure," she replied. "Distilled water. Regular water won't explode because of the minerals. You shouldn't believe everything you read on the Internet."

A roaring sound interrupted them, sudden and complete. Blue started, but Gansey just cast his eyes upward. "It's rain on the roof. Must be dumping."

He turned, mug in hand, and suddenly they were an inch apart. She could smell the mint in his mouth. She saw his throat move as he swallowed.

She was furious at her body for betraying her, for wanting him differently than any of the other boys, for refusing to listen to her insistence that they were just friends.

"How was your first day of school, Jane?" he asked, voice different than before.

Mom's gone. Noah exploded. I'm not going to college. I don't want to go home where everything is strange, and I don't want to go back to school where everything is normal.

"Oh, you know, public school," she said, not meeting his eyes. She concentrated instead on Gansey's neck, which was right at eye level, and on how his collar didn't lay quite flat against his skin all the way around because of his Adam's apple. "We just watched cartoons all day."

She'd meant it to be wry, but she didn't think it quite worked.

"We'll find her," he said, and her chest twinged again.

"I don't know if she wants to be found."

"Fair enough. Jane, if —" He stopped and swirled the tea. "I hope Malory doesn't want any milk. I completely forgot."

She wished she could still evoke that Blue who despised him. She wished she knew if Adam would feel terrible about this. She wished she knew if fighting this feeling would make Gansey's foretold end destroy her any less.

She shut the microwave. Gansey left the room.

Back on the sofa, Malory viewed the tea as a man would view a death sentence.

"What else?" Gansey asked kindly.

Malory shoved the Dog off him. "I'd like a new hip. And better weather. Ah — however. This is your home and I know that I'm an outsider, so far be it from me to chastise or generally overstep. That being said, were you aware there was someone under . . . ?"

He indicated the storm-dark area beneath the pool table. If Blue squinted, she could make out a form in the black.

"Noah," Gansey said. "Come out at once."

"No," Noah replied.

"Well! I see you two know each other and all is well," Malory said, in the voice of someone who sensed trouble coming and hadn't brought an umbrella. "I will be in my room nursing my jet lag."

After he had retreated, Blue said with exasperation, "Noah! I called and called for you."

Noah remained where he was, arms hugged around his body. He looked markedly less alive than he had earlier; there was something smudgy about his eyes, something uncertain about his edges. It was kind of hard to look at the place where Noah stopped and the shadow below him began. Something unpleasant happened in Blue's throat when she tried to make out what was off about his face.

"I'm tired of it," Noah said.

"Tired of what?" Gansey asked, voice kind.

"Decaying."

He had been crying. That was what was wrong with his face, Blue realized. Nothing supernatural.

"Oh, Noah," she said, crouching down.

"What can I do?" Gansey asked. "We. What can we do?"

Noah shrugged in a watery way.

Blue was suddenly desperately afraid that Noah might want to actually die. This seemed like something most ghosts wanted — to be laid to rest. It was a dreadful notion, a forever good-bye. Her selfishness warred mightily with every bit of ethics she had ever learned from the women of her family.

Blast. She had to.

She asked, "Do you want us to find a way to, um, to properly, to lay . . ."

Before she'd even finished, Noah started shaking his head. He hugged his legs closer. "No. Nonono."

"You don't have to be ashamed," Blue said, because it sounded like what her mother would have said. She was certain her mother would have added something comforting about the afterlife, but she was unable, this time, to sound comforting when she herself wanted to be comforted. Lamely, she finished, "You don't have to be afraid."

"You don't know!" Noah said, vaguely hysterical. "You don't know!"

She stretched out a hand. "Okay, hey —"

Noah repeated, "You don't know!"

"We can talk this out," Gansey said, as if a decaying soul was something that could be solved through conversation.

"You don't know! You don't know!"

Noah was standing. It was impossible, because there was not room beneath the pool table for him to stand. But he was somehow escaping on either side, surrounding Gansey and Blue. The maps fluttered frantically against the green surface. A flock of dust wads tumbled from beneath the table and raced down the streets of Gansey's miniature model of Henrietta. The desk lamp flickered.

The temperature dropped.

Blue saw Gansey's eyes widen behind a cloud of his own breath.

"Noah," Blue warned. Her head felt swimmy as Noah robbed her of energy. She caught a whiff, strangely, of the old-carpet smell of the guidance counselor's office, and then the living, green scent of Cabeswater. "This isn't you!"

The swirl of wind was still rising, flapping papers and knocking over stacks of books. The Dog was barking from behind the closed door of Noah's old room. Goose bumps rippled on Blue's skin, and her limbs felt heavy.

"Noah, *stop*," Gansey said.

But he didn't. The door to the apartment rattled.

Blue said, "Noah, I'm asking you now."

He wasn't attending, or there wasn't enough of the true Noah to attend.

Standing up on her wobbly legs, Blue began to use all of the protective visualizations she'd been taught by her mother. She imagined herself inside an unbreakable glass ball; she could see out, but no one could touch her. She imagined white light piercing the stormy clouds, the roof, the darkness of Noah, finding Blue, armoring her.

Then she pulled the plug on the battery that was Blue Sargent.

The room went still. The papers settled. The light flickered once more and then strengthened. She heard a little gasp of a sob, and then absolute quiet.

Gansey looked shocked.

Noah sat in the middle of the floor, papers all around him, a mint plant spilling dirt by his hand. He was all hunched over and shadowless, his form slight and streaky, barely visible at all. He was crying again.

In a very small voice, he told Blue, "You said I could use your energy."

She knelt in front of him. She wanted to hug him, but he wasn't really there. Without her energy, he was a paper-thin boy, he was a skull, he was air in the shape of Noah. "Not like that."

He whispered, "I'm sorry."

"Me too."

He covered his face, and then he was gone.

Gansey said, "That was impressive, Jane."

8

That night, Blue leaned against the spreading beech tree in her backyard, her eyes cast up to the stars and her fingers touching the chilly, smooth bark of one of the roots. The kitchen light through the sliding door seemed far away.

That was impressive, Jane.

Although Blue was perfectly aware of the positive effects of her ability, she had never really considered the opposite. And yet Noah would have destroyed Monmouth Manufacturing if she hadn't cut herself off from him.

The stars winked through the beech leaves. She'd read that new stars tended to form in pairs. Binary stars, orbiting in close proximity, only becoming single stars when their partner was smashed off them by another pair of wildly spinning new stars. If she pretended hard enough, she could see the multitude of pairs clinging to each other in the destructive and creative gravity of their constellations.

Impressive.

Maybe she was a little impressed. Not by pulling the plug on a dead boy — that seemed sad, nothing to brag about. But because she'd learned something about herself today, and she'd thought there was nothing left there to discover.

The stars moved slowly above her, an array of possibilities, and for the first time in a long time, she felt them mirrored in her heart.

Calla opened the sliding door. "Blue?"

"What?"

"If you're done gallivanting for the day, I could use your body," Calla said. "I have a reading."

Blue raised her eyebrows. Maura only asked for her help during important readings, and Calla never asked, period. Curiosity rather than obedience pulled Blue to her feet. "This late? Now?"

"I'm asking now, aren't I?"

Once inside, Calla fussed over the reading room and called for Persephone so many times that Orla screamed back that some people were trying to conduct phone calls and Jimi shouted, "Is it something I can help with?"

All of the fuss made Blue strangely nervous. At 300 Fox Way, readings happened so often that they ordinarily felt both perfunctory and unmagical. But this felt like chaos. This felt like anything could happen.

The doorbell rang.

"PERSEPHONE, I TOLD YOU," Calla roared. "Blue, get that. I'll be in the reading room. Bring him in there."

When Blue opened the front door, she discovered an Aglionby student standing in the glow of the porch light. Moths fluttered around his head. He wore salmon-colored pants and white Top-Siders and boasted flawless skin and tousled hair.

Then her eyes adjusted and she realized that he was too old to be a raven boy. Quite a bit too old; it was hard to imagine how she would have thought it before even for a moment.

Blue scowled at his shoes and then at his face. Although everything about him had been cultivated to impress, she found him less impressive than she might have a few months before. "Hola."

"Howdy," he replied, with a cheery smile full of unsurprisingly straight teeth. "I'm here for a probing of my future. I expect the timing is still good?"

"You expect right, sailor. Come in."

In the reading room, Calla had been joined by Persephone. They sat on one side of the table like a jury. The man stood across from them, idly drumming his fingers on a chair back.

"Sit," intoned Calla.

"Any old chair," Persephone added mildly.

"Not any old chair," Calla said. She pointed. "That one."

He sat opposite, his bright eyes all over the room as he did, his body dynamic. He looked like a person who *got things done*. Blue couldn't decide if he was handsome or if his demeanor was fooling her into believing him so.

He asked, "Well, how does this work? Do I pay you up front or do you decide how much it is after you see how complicated my future is?"

"Any old time," Persephone said.

"No," Calla said. "Now. Fifty."

He parted with the bills without malice. "Could I get a receipt? Business expense. That is a fantastic portrait of Steve Martin over there, by the way. Behold how its eyes follow you around the room."

"Blue, would you get the receipt?" Persephone asked.

Blue, lingering by the door, went for a business card to write the amount on. When she returned, Persephone was saying to Calla, "Oh, we will have to use just yours. I don't have mine."

"Don't have yours!" Calla replied incredulously. "What happened to them?"

"Coca-Cola shirt has them."

With a mighty snort, Calla retrieved her tarot cards and instructed the man on how to shuffle them. She finished, "Then you pass them back to me, facedown, and I'll draw them."

He began.

"As you shuffle them, you should be thinking about what you'd like to know," Persephone added in her small voice. "That will focus the reading quite a bit."

"Good, good," he replied, shuffling the cards more aggressively. He glanced up at Blue. Then, without warning, he flipped the deck so that the cards were faceup. He fanned them out, eyes darting over the selection.

This was *not* how Calla had instructed him.

Something in Blue's nerves tingled a warning.

"So, if the question is 'How can I make *this* happen?' " — he plucked a card free and set it on the table — "that's a good start, right?"

There was dead silence.

The card was the three of swords. It depicted a bloody heart stabbed with the aforementioned three swords. Gore dripped down the blades. Maura called it "the heartbreak card."

Blue needed no psychic perception to feel the threat oozing from it.

The psychics stared at the man. With a cool curl in her stomach, Blue realized that they hadn't seen this coming.

Calla growled, "What's your game?"

He kept smiling his cheery, congenial smile. "Here's the question: Is there another one of you? One that looks more like that one?" He pointed at Blue, whose stomach turned over unpleasantly once more.

Mom.

"Go to hell," Calla burst out.

He nodded. "That's what I thought. You expecting her anytime soon? I'd love to have a chat with her in particular."

"Hell," Persephone said. "I actually agree in this case. Insofar as going there is concerned."

What does this man want with Mom?

Blue frantically memorized everything about him so that she could describe him later.

The man stood, sweeping up the three of swords. "You know what? I'm keeping this. Thanks for the info."

As he turned to go, Calla started after him, but Persephone put a single finger on Calla's arm, stopping her.

"No," Persephone said softly. The front door closed. "That one's not to be touched."

9

Adam was reading and re-reading his first-quarter schedule when Ronan hurled himself into the desk beside him.

They were the only two in the navy-carpeted classroom; Adam had arrived very early to Borden House. It seemed wrong that the first day of school should carry the same emotional weight as the anxious afternoon in the cave of ravens, but there was no denying that the gleeful and anticipatory jitter in his veins now was as pronounced as those breathless minutes when birds sang around them.

One more year, and he had done it.

The first day was the easiest, of course. Before it had really all begun: the homework and the sports, the school-wide dinners and the college counseling, the exams and the extra credit. Before Adam's night job and studying until three A.M. conspired to destroy him.

He read his schedule again. It bristled with classes and extracurriculars. It looked impossible. Aglionby was a hard school: harder for Adam, though, because he had to be the best.

Last year, Barrington Whelk had stood at the front of this room and taught them Latin. Now he was dead. Adam knew that he had seen Whelk die, but he couldn't seem to remember what the event had actually looked like — though he could, if he tried hard enough, imagine what it *should* have looked like.

Adam closed his eyes for a moment. In the quiet of the empty classroom, he could hear the rustling of leaves against yet more leaves.

"I can't take it," Ronan said.

Adam opened his eyes. "Take what?"

Take sitting, apparently. Ronan went to the whiteboard and began to write. He had furious handwriting.

"Malory. He's always complaining about his hips or his eyes or the government or — oh, and that *dog*. It's not like he's blind or crippled or anything."

"Why couldn't he have something normal like a raven?"

Ronan ignored this. "And he got up three times in the night to piss. I think he has a tumor."

Adam said, "You don't sleep anyway."

"Not *anymore*." Ronan's dry-erase marker squeaked in protest as he jabbed down Latin words. Although Ronan wasn't smiling and Adam didn't know some of the vocabulary, Adam was certain it was a dirty joke. For a moment, he watched Ronan and tried to imagine that he was a teacher instead of a Ronan. It was impossible. Adam couldn't decide if it was how he'd shoved up his sleeves or the apocalyptic way he had tied his tie.

"He knows everything," Ronan said in a casual way.

Adam didn't immediately reply, though he knew what Ronan meant, because he also found the professor's omniscience uncomfortable. When he thought harder about the source of the unpleasantness — the idea of Malory spending a year with fifteen-year-old Gansey — he had to admit that it was not paranoia, but jealousy.

"He's older than I expected," Adam said.

"Oh, God, the oldest," Ronan replied at once, as if he had been waiting for Adam to mention it. "He never chews with his mouth shut."

A floorboard popped. Immediately, Ronan put down his marker. One couldn't open the front door of Borden House without making the floor creak two rooms over. So both boys knew what the noise meant: School was under way.

"Well," Ronan said, sounding nasty and unhappy, "here we go, cowboy."

Returning to his desk, he threw his feet up on it. This was forbidden, of course. He crossed his arms, tilted his chin back, closed his eyes. Instant insolence. This was the version of himself he prepared for Aglionby, for his older brother, Declan, and sometimes, for Gansey.

Ronan was always saying that he never lied, but he wore a liar's face.

In the students came. It was such a familiar sound — desk legs scraping the floor, jackets swooshing over chair backs, notebooks slapping worktops — that Adam could've closed his eyes and still seen the scene with perfect clarity. They were chattering and hateful and oblivious. *Where have you been on break, man? Cape, always, where else? So boring. Vail. Mom broke her ankle. Oh, you know, we did Europe, hobo style. Granddad said I needed to get some muscles because I was looking gay these days. No, he didn't really say that. Speaking of which, here's Parrish.*

Someone cuffed the back of Adam's head. He blinked up. One way, then the other. His assailant had come up on Adam's deaf side.

"Oh," Adam said. It was Tad Carruthers, whose worst fault was that Adam didn't like him and Tad couldn't tell.

"Oh," mimicked Tad benevolently, as if Adam's standoffishness charmed him. Adam wanted desperately and masochistically for Tad to ask him where he had summered. Instead, Tad turned to where Ronan was still reclined with his eyes closed. He lifted a hand to cuff Ronan's head but lost his nerve an inch into the swing. Instead, he just drummed on Ronan's desk and moved off.

Adam could feel the pulse of the ley line in the veins of his hands.

The students kept coming in. Adam kept watching. He was good at this part, the observing of others. It was himself that he couldn't seem to study or understand. How he despised them, how he wanted to be them. How pointless to summer in Maine, how much he wanted to do it. How affected he found their speech, how he coveted their lazy monotones. He couldn't tell how all of these things could be equally true.

Gansey appeared in the doorway. He was speaking to a teacher in the hall, thumb poised on his lower lip, eyebrows furrowed handsomely, uniform worn with confident ease. He stepped into the classroom, shoulders square, and for just a second, it was like he was a stranger again — once more that lofty, unknowable Virginia princeling.

It hit Adam like a real thing. Like somehow he had stopped being friends with Gansey and forgotten until this moment. Like Gansey would take a seat on the other side of Ronan instead of the one by Adam. Like the last year had not happened and once more it would be just Adam against all the rest of these overfed predators.

Then Gansey sat down in the seat in front of Adam with a sigh. He turned around. "Jesus Christ, I haven't slept a second."

He remembered his manners and extended his fist. As Adam bumped knuckles with him, he felt an extraordinary rush of relief, of fondness. "Ronan, feet down."

Ronan put his feet down.

Gansey turned back to Adam. "Ronan told you all about the Pig, then."

"Ronan told me nothing."

"I told you about the pissing," Ronan said.

Adam ignored him. "What about the car?"

Gansey glanced around at Borden House as if he expected to see that it had changed over the summer. Of course it had not: navy carpet over everything, baseboard heating on too early in the year, bookshelves crowded with elegantly tattered books in Latin and Greek and French. It was your favorite aunt who smelled when you hugged her. "Last night we went out for bread and jam and more tea in the Pig, and the power steering went out. Then the radio, the lights. Jesus. Ronan was singing that awful murder squash song the whole damn time and he only made it through half a verse before I had absolutely nothing. Had to wrestle it out of the road."

"Alternator again," Adam observed.

"Right, yes, yes," Gansey said. "I opened up the hood and saw the alternator belt just hanging there ragged. We had to go get another one, and it was just an absolute *zoo* to find one in stock for some reason, like there was a run on this precise size. Of course, putting on the new belt by the side of the road was the fast part."

He said it in the most offhanded way, like it was nothing to have thrown on a new belt, but once upon a not-very-long time ago, Richard Gansey III had only one automotive skill: calling a tow truck.

Adam said, "You were smart to figure it out."

"Oh, I don't know," Gansey replied, but it was clear he was proud. Adam felt like he had helped a bird hatch from an egg.

Thank God we're not fighting thank God we're not fighting thank God we're not fighting how can I keep it from happening again—

Ronan said, "Keep it up, and you just might be a mechanic after you graduate. They'll put *that* in the alumni magazine."

"Ha and —" Gansey swiveled in his seat to watch as the new Latin teacher made his way to the front.

Every student watched him.

In his glove box, Adam kept a cutout advertisement for inspiration. The photo featured a sleek gray car made by happy Germans. A young man leaned against the vehicle in a long coat of black virgin wool, collar turned up against the wind. He was confident and snub-nosed, like a powerful child, with lots of dark hair and white teeth. His arms were crossed over his chest like a prizefighter.

That was what their new Latin teacher looked like.

Adam was badly impressed.

The new teacher swept his dark coat off as he observed Ronan's handiwork on the whiteboard. Then he turned his gaze on the seated students with the same confidence as the man in the car advertisement.

"Well, look at you," he said. His eyes lingered on Gansey, on Adam, on Ronan. "America's youth. I can't decide if you are the best or the worst thing I've seen this week. Whose work is this?"

Everyone knew, but no one copped to it.

He clasped his hands behind his back and took a closer look. "Vocabulary's impressive." He tapped a knuckle against a few of the words. He was kinetic. "But what's going on with the grammar in here? And here? You'd want a subjunctive here in this fear clause. 'I fear that they *may* believe this'— there should be a vocative here. *I* know what's being said here because I already know the joke, but a native speaker would've just stared at you. This is not usable Latin."

Adam didn't have to turn his head to *feel* Ronan simmering.

Their new Latin teacher turned, swift and compact and keen, and again Adam felt that rush of both intimidation and awe. "Good thing, too, or I'd be out of a job. Well, you little runts. Gentlemen. I'm your Latin teacher for the year. I'm not really a fan of languages for the sake of languages. I'm only interested in how we can use them. And I'm not really a Latin teacher. I'm a historian. That means I'm really only interested in Latin as a mechanism to — to — rifle through dead men's papers. Any questions?"

The students eyed him. This was the first period of the first day of school and nothing could make Latin class less full of Latin. This man's fervent energy sank uselessly into moss-covered stones.

Adam put up his hand.

The man pointed at him.

"*Miserere nobis,*" Adam said. "*Timeo nos horrendi esse.* Sir."

Have mercy on us — I'm afraid we are terrible.

The man's smile widened at *sir.* But he had to know that students were to address teachers as *sir* or *madam* to show respect.

"*Nihil timeo,*" he replied. "*Solvitur ambulando.*"

The nuances of his first statement — *I fear nothing!* — escaped most of the class, and the second statement — an idiom embracing the merit of practice, blew by the rest.

Ronan smiled lazily. Without raising his hand, he said, "Heh. *Noli prohicere maccaritas ad porcos.*"

Don't throw pearls before swine.

He did not add *sir*.

"Are you pigs, then?" the man asked. "Or are you men?"

Adam wasn't eager to watch either Ronan or their new Latin teacher run out to the end of their respective ropes. He asked quickly, *"Quod nomen est tibi,* sir?"

"My name" — the man swept out a big swath of Ronan's bad grammar with the edge of an eraser and used the space to replace it with efficient letters of his own — "is Colin Greenmantle."

10

ere we are, living among the provincials!" Colin Greenmantle leaned out the window. Down below, a herd of cows looked up at him. "Piper, come look at these cows. This one asshole is looking right at me. 'Colin,' says this cow, 'you are really living among the provincials now.'"

Piper said, "I'm in the bath."

Her voice was coming from the kitchen, though. His wife (although he didn't like to use that word, *wife*, because it made him think that he was now over thirty, which he was, but still, he didn't need to be reminded, and anyway, he still had his boyish good looks; in fact, the cashier at the grocery store had flirted with him just last night, and even though it could have been the fact that he was overawingly overdressed for a cheese-cracker run, he thought it was probably his aquamarine eyes because she had been virtually swimming in them) was taking the move to Henrietta better than he had expected. So far, the only act of rebellion Piper had performed had been to wreck the rental car by driving it aggressively through a shopping center sign to demonstrate just how unsuited she was for living in a place where she couldn't walk to shops. It was possible she hadn't done it on purpose, but there was very little Piper did by accident.

"They are basically monsters," Greenmantle said, although now he was thinking less of the cows and more of his new pupils.

"Accepting handouts all day long, but they'd eat you in a second, if they had the right teeth for it."

They'd only just moved into their "historic" rental on a cattle farm. Greenmantle, who had made plenty of history, doubted the farmhouse's *historic* claim, but it was charming enough. He liked the idea of farming; in the most basic linguistic sense, he was now a farmer.

"They'll be here for your blood on Friday," Piper called.

The cows lowed curiously. Greenmantle experimentally flipped them off; their expressions didn't change. "They're here now."

"Not the cows. I'm getting more life insurance for you and they need your blood. Friday. Be here."

He ducked back inside and creaked down to the kitchen. Piper stood at the counter in a pink bra and underwear, chopping a mango. Her blond hair was a curtain around her head. She didn't look up.

"I'm teaching Friday," he said. "Think of the *children*. How much life insurance do we need?"

"I have certain standards of living I want to maintain if something terrible happens to you in the middle of the night." She stabbed at him with the knife as he stole a piece of mango. He avoided a wound only because of his speed, not her lack of intention. "Just come right back after class. Don't fritter around like you've been doing."

"I'm not frittering," Greenmantle said. "I am being quite purposeful."

"Yes, I know, getting revenge, having testicles, whatnot."

"You can help, if you want. You're so much better with directions and things."

She couldn't quite hide that the appeal to her ego pleased her. "I can't until Sunday. I have eyebrows on Wednesday. Bikini line on Thursday. Don't come home on Saturday. Fritter on Saturday. I'm having people come sage the house."

Greenmantle swiped another piece of mango; the knife came a little closer this time. "What does that mean?"

"I saw a flier. It's getting rid of the bad energy in a place. This house is full of it."

"That's just you."

She tossed the knife into the sink, where it would remain until it died. Piper was not much for housework. She had a very narrow skill set. She drifted toward the bedroom, on her way to have a bath or take a nap or start a war. "Don't get us killed."

"No one's going to kill us," Greenmantle said with certainty. "The Gray Man knows the rules. And the others . . ." He rinsed the knife and put it back in the knife block.

"The others what?"

He hadn't realized she was still in the room. "Oh, I was just thinking about how I saw one of Niall Lynch's sons today."

"Was he a bastard, too?" Piper asked. Niall Lynch had been responsible for seven moderately unpleasant and four extremely unpleasant months in their collective lives.

"Probably. God, but he looked just like that fucker. I can't wait to fail him. I wonder if he knows who I am. I wonder if I should tell him."

"You are such a sadist," she said carelessly.

He knocked his knuckles on the counter. "I'm going to go see which jaw those cows have teeth on."

"Bottom. I saw it on Animal Planet."

"I'm going anyway."

As he tried to remember which door led to the mudroom, he heard her say something to him, but he didn't catch it. He'd already dialed the number of a Belgian contact who was supposed to be looking into a fifteenth-century belt buckle that gave the wearer bad dreams. It was taking this guy forever to run it down. Too bad he couldn't put the Gray Man on it; he'd been the best. Right up until he'd betrayed Greenmantle, of course.

He wondered how long it would take the Gray Man to come to him.

11

When Gansey and Ronan arrived at 300 Fox Way after school, Calla was being attacked in the living room by a man dressed entirely in gray. Blue, Persephone, and the furniture lurked against the walls. The man stood in perfect fighting form, legs a little wider than his shoulders, one foot forward. He had a solid grip on one of her hands. In Calla's other hand she held a Manhattan, which she was trying not to spill.

The Gray Man was smiling thinly. He had extraordinary teeth.

The boys had entered without knocking, familiarly, and now Gansey eased his messenger bag to the old buckled floorboards and stood in the doorway to the living room. He wasn't sure if the situation required intervention. The Gray Man was a (possibly retired) hit man. Nothing to be trifled with.

But still, if Calla wanted help, surely she would've put her drink down. Surely Blue would not be merely eating yogurt.

"Show me again," Calla said. "I didn't see it, I don't think."

"I'll do it a little harder," Mr. Gray replied, "but I don't want to actually break your arm."

"You were nowhere close," she assured him. "Put your back into it."

She sipped her Manhattan. He clasped her hand and wrist again, his skin pale against hers, and swiftly turned her entire arm. Her shoulder tipped downward sharply; she snatched at her drink and cackled. "That one I felt."

"Now do it to me," Mr. Gray said. "I'll hold your drink."

Putting his hands in his pockets, Gansey leaned against the doorjamb, watching. He knew instinctively that the dreadful news he carried was the sort of burden that would only get heavier once shared. He allowed himself a moment before the storm, letting the atmosphere of the house do its usual work on him. Unlike Monmouth Manufacturing, 300 Fox Way was cramped with extraneous people and whimsical objects. It hummed with conversation, music, telephones, old appliances. It was impossible to forget that all of these women were plugged into the past and tapped into the future, connected to everything in the world and to one another.

Gansey didn't so much visit as get absorbed.

He loved it. He wanted to be a part of this world, even though he understood there were endless reasons why he could never be. Blue was the natural result of a home like this: confident, strange, credulous, curious. And here *he* was: neurotic, rarified, the product of something else entirely.

"What else?" Calla asked.

"I can show you how to unhinge my jaw, if you like," Mr. Gray said kindly.

"Oh, yes, that — well, there is Richard Gansey the Third," Calla said, catching sight of him. "And the snake. Where is Coca-Cola?"

"Work," Gansey said. "He couldn't get off."

Persephone waved vaguely from behind a tall, light pink drink. Blue didn't wave. She had seen Gansey's expression.

"Does the name Colin Greenmantle mean anything to you?" Gansey asked Mr. Gray, though he already knew the answer.

Handing Calla her drink, the Gray Man wiped his palms on his slacks. The excellent teeth had vanished. "Colin Greenmantle was my employer."

"He's our new Latin teacher."

"Oh, dear," said Persephone. "Would you like a drink?"

Gansey realized she was talking to him. "Oh, no, thank you."

"I need another one," she said. "I'm making one for you, too, Mr. Gray."

The Gray Man crossed to the window. His car, an unsubtle white Mitsubishi with an enormous spoiler, was parked outside, and both he and Ronan studied it pensively. After a very long moment, the Gray Man said, "He's the man who asked me to kill Ronan's father."

Gansey knew that he could not be hurt by the casualness of the statement — Mr. Gray was a hit man, Niall Lynch had been his mark, he had not known Ronan then, and ethically Mr. Gray's profession was probably no worse than a professional mercenary — but it did not change that Ronan's father was dead. He reminded himself that the Gray Man had merely been the uncaring weapon. Greenmantle was the hand that wielded it.

Ronan, silent to this point, said, "I'm going to kill him."

Gansey had a sudden, terrible vision of it: Ronan's hands painted with blood, his eyes blank and unknowable, a corpse at his feet. It was a savage and unshakeable image, made worse because Gansey had seen enough of the pieces separately to know accurately how they'd appear added together.

The Gray Man turned swiftly.

"You will *not*," he said, with as much force as Gansey had ever heard from him. "Do you hear me? You cannot."

"Oh, can't I?" Ronan asked. His voice was low and dangerous; infinitely more threatening than if he'd snarled his response.

"Colin Greenmantle is untouchable," the Gray Man said. He spread his fingers wide, hand hanging in the air. "He is a spider clinging in a web. Every leg touches a thread, and if anything happens to the spider, hell rains down."

Ronan said, "I already lived through hell."

"You have no idea what hell is," the Gray Man said, but not unkindly. "Do you think you're the first son to want revenge? Do you think your father was the first he had killed? And yet Greenmantle is alive and untouched. Because we all know how it works. Before coming down here from Boston, he would have attached sixteen little threads to people like me, to computer programs, to bank accounts. The spider dies, the web twitches, suddenly your accounts are wiped clean, your younger brother becomes an amputee, your older brother dies behind the wheel of a car in D.C., Mrs. Gansey's campaign immolates over faked scandalous photos, Adam's scholarship vanishes, Blue loses an eye —"

"Stop," Gansey said. He thought he might throw up. "Jesus, please stop."

"I just want Ronan to understand that he cannot do anything stupid," the Gray Man said. "To kill Greenmantle is to end your lives as you know it. And what good will revenge do you?"

"Says the killer," Ronan said. Now his snarl was back, which meant he was hurting.

"Says the killer, yes, but I'm good at it," Mr. Gray replied. "Even if he was not a spider in a dazzling web, would you be willing to go to prison for the satisfaction of killing him?"

Without a word, Ronan departed through the front door, slamming it. Gansey didn't follow. He was torn between the impulse to mitigate Ronan's pain and the one to let him stay hurt but cautious. Violence was a disease Gansey didn't think he could catch. But all around him, his friends were slowly infected.

Persephone brought the Gray Man a drink; she had another one of her own. They knocked them back in unison.

"Want this?" Blue asked Gansey. She tipped the yogurt container to him so he could see that all that was left was the fruit in the bottom. He didn't nod, but she brought it to him anyway, giving him her spoon. It had a grounding effect — the shocking slime of the blueberries, the sugar hitting his stomach, empty from school, the knowledge that her mouth had been the last thing to touch the spoon.

Blue watched him take the first bite and then turned quickly to Mr. Gray. "He's the one who came for a reading last night, wasn't he?"

"Yes," Mr. Gray said. "As I thought. And now he is teaching Latin to the boys."

"Why?" Gansey asked. "Why us?"

"Not you," Mr. Gray replied. "Me. Clearly, he didn't believe my story of fleeing with the Greywaren. He came to this house looking for Maura, because he thinks she is important to me. He has infiltrated the school because he has found out that you and I are acquainted. He wants me to know he knows I am still here and he wants me to know how much he knows about my life here."

"What do we do?" Gansey asked. He was beginning to feel like this day had been a mistake; this was not the real first day of school; he should have stayed in bed until tomorrow and tried again.

"He's not your problem; he's mine," Mr. Gray said tersely.

"He's in my school, every day. Ronan has to look *at his face every day*. How is that not my problem?"

Mr. Gray said, "Because it's not you that he wants. I will address it. Your problem is to let me address it."

Gansey sank to a crouch. He believed in Mr. Gray's intention, but not the statement. If he had learned anything in the last year, it was that everything in this town was tangled up.

Calla took Mr. Gray's wrist and slowly pretended to break his arm. Shaking his head a little, he traded with her, taking her palm in one hand and her wrist in the other. He turned it with slow precision. A few times, so she could see how he was doing it. There was something satisfying about watching him competently demonstrate this act of pretend violence, something controlled and beautiful, like a dance. Everything about his clean, muscled appearance and clean, intentional process said, *I've got it under control.* Where *it* stood for *everything.*

How badly Gansey wanted to let Greenmantle be the Gray Man's problem. But again he saw that narrowing black tunnel and the pit, and at the bottom, a grave.

Calla cursed and held her shoulder.

"Sorry," Mr. Gray said. To Gansey, "I'll find out what he wants."

"Don't get killed," Blue said immediately.

"I don't intend to."

Persephone finally spoke up in her tiny voice. "I think it's good you've nearly found that king."

Gansey realized she was speaking to him. "Have I?"

"Surely," Calla said. "It's taken you long enough."

12

That night, not long after he returned from work, Adam heard a knock at his church apartment door. When he answered it, he was first surprised that the person on the other side was real, and then he was surprised that the person was Gansey and not Ronan.

"Oh," he said. "It's late."

"I know." Gansey was in his overcoat and his wireframes; he had clearly tried to sleep and failed. "I'm sorry. Have you done your calculus yet? I can't get number four."

He did not say the word *Greenmantle.* There was nothing more to say until they heard more from Mr. Gray.

"I have, but you can look at it." Adam let Gansey in, sweeping the letter — *the letter* — behind the little shelf by the door as he did. Unlike Ronan, Gansey appeared out of place inside the apartment. The hipped ceiling cramped him more; the cracks in the plaster were etched more starkly; the utilitarian plastic bins containing Adam's things seemed even more bereft of aesthetic charm. Gansey belonged with old things, but this place was not just old, but cheap.

The letter was hidden, yes? It was. Adam could feel the outline of it glowing from behind the shelf. Gansey would pity him and hire a lawyer and Adam would feel like dirt and then they would fight —

We will not fight.

Gansey tossed off his overcoat — beneath it, he was in a T-shirt and pajama pants, which was possibly the most metaphorical outfit Adam could imagine for his friend, unless he could manage to wear another overcoat beneath the T-shirt, and another set of pajamas beneath that second overcoat, so on and so on, an endless matryoshka of Ganseys — and cast himself onto the end of the bed.

"Mom called," Gansey said. "Do I want to meet the governor the weekend after next because it would be great if I did and did I want to bring my friends? No, Mother, I would in fact not like that. Helen will be there! Yes, Mother, I assumed so but hardly consider it a plus, as I am worried she will kidnap Adam. Fine, fine, you don't have to, I know you're busy but oh dot dot dot *et cetera et cetera*. Oh, I forgot, I brought payment for my intrusion."

He dragged his coat closer by the arm and retrieved two candy bars from the pocket. He chucked one onto Adam's lap and peeled the other for himself.

Adam badly wanted to eat it, but he put it aside to eat during his break at work tomorrow evening. "It'll keep me up." He liked the notion that Gansey's elegant older sister found him handsome. The impossibility of her rendered it merely a pleasant ego stroke. "Are you going?"

"I don't know. If I do, will you come?"

Adam felt an instinctive pang of nerves. Muscle memory, from the last time he had traveled to a Gansey political event. "Better invite Blue, too. She reamed me out for not getting invited to the last one."

Gansey blinked up, eyes startled behind his glasses. "Because *I* didn't invite her?"

"No, me. But she'll want to go. Trust me. She was something fearful."

"I believe you. Oh, Jesus, I just imagined her meeting the governor. I have a slideshow of her questions playing in my head."

Adam grinned. "He deserves all of them."

Gansey ran a pencil down his homework, checking it against Adam's, although Adam could see that he had done number four quite adequately before he arrived. Adam eyed the candy bar and rubbed the backs of his hands. Every winter they chapped hideously despite his best efforts, and they had already begun to dry. He realized the tapping had ceased, and when he looked up, he saw that Gansey was frowning into space.

"Everyone says, *Just find Glendower*," Gansey said suddenly, "but all around me the cave walls are crumbling."

It was not the cave walls that crumbled. Now that Adam had heard Gansey's anxiety in the cave, he was acutely attuned to its reappearance now. He looked away to give Gansey a chance to compose himself and then he asked, "What does Malory say to do next?"

"He seems enthused about Giant's Grave for no reason I can fathom." Gansey had indeed taken the moment Adam granted him to carefully school his tone; anxiety transubstantiated to wry deprecation in an oft-practiced ritual. "He's talking about visual cues and energy readings and how they all point there. How he adores our ley line, he says. He's all starry-eyed over it."

"You were once," Adam reminded him. They both had been. How ungrateful they'd become, how greedy for better wonders.

Gansey tapped his pencil in wordless agreement.

In the quiet, Adam heard whispers from the direction of the bathroom. From experience, he knew they came from the water that dripped from the tap and that the language was gibberish to him. Ronan might have been able to identify a word or two; he had his puzzle box that translated whatever the old language was. But Adam still listened, waiting to hear if the voices would ascend or ebb, waiting to hear if the ley line was surging or if Cabeswater was trying to communicate.

He realized Gansey was looking at him, brow furrowed. Adam wasn't sure what his expression had been or how long he had been focused on something Gansey couldn't hear. From Gansey's face, a while.

"Is Malory trapped in Monmouth all day?" Adam quickly asked.

Gansey's face cleared. "I've given him the Suburban to drive around in. God help us; he drives like he walks. Oh, but I can tell he doesn't like Monmouth."

"Treason," said Adam, because he knew it would please Gansey, and he saw that it did. "Where's Ronan at?"

"To the Barns, he said."

"You believe him?"

"Probably. He took Chainsaw," Gansey said. "I don't think he'll mess with Greenmantle — Mr. Gray was very persuasive. And what else would he get into? Kavinsky's dead, so — Jesus Christ, listen to me. Jesus Christ."

The cave walls crumbled yet more; the ritual before had been imperfect. Gansey sat back against the wall and closed his eyes. Adam watched him swallow.

Again he heard Gansey's voice in the cave.

"It's okay," Adam said. He did not care that Joseph Kavinsky was dead, but he liked that Gansey did. "I know what you meant."

"No, it's not. It's disgusting of me." Gansey didn't open his eyes. "Everything has gotten so ugly. It wasn't supposed to be this way."

Everything had *begun* ugly for Adam, but he knew what Gansey meant. His noble and oblivious and optimistic friend was slowly opening his eyes and seeing the world for what it was, and it was filthy, and violent, and profane, and unfair. Adam had always thought that was what he wanted — for Gansey to *know*. But now he wasn't sure. Gansey wasn't like anyone else, and suddenly Adam wasn't sure that he really wanted him to be.

"Here," Adam said, standing, fetching their history text. "Do the reading. Out loud. I'll take notes."

An hour passed this way, Gansey reading out loud in his lovely old voice, and Adam jotting in his overambitious hand, and when Gansey reached the end of the assignment, he closed the text carefully and set it on the upside-down plastic bin Adam used as a bedside table.

Gansey stood and put on his coat.

"I think," he said, "that if — when — we find Glendower, I will ask him for Noah's life. Do you think that would work?"

It was such a non sequitur from the previous conversation topic that Adam didn't immediately answer. He merely looked at Gansey. Something was different about him; he'd changed while Adam's back had been turned. The crease between his eyebrows?

The way he ducked his chin? The tighter set to his mouth, perhaps, as responsibility tugged the corners down.

Adam couldn't remember how they had managed to fight so continuously over the summer. Gansey, his best friend, his stupid and kind and marvelous best friend.

He replied, "No. But I think it is worth asking."

Gansey nodded, once. Twice. "Sorry for keeping you up late. See you tomorrow?"

"First thing."

After Gansey had gone, Adam fetched the hidden letter. In it was his father's rescheduled court date. A remote part of Adam marveled that the mere sight of the words *Robert Parrish* could twist his stomach in a muddy, homesick way.

Eyes forward, Adam. Soon it would be behind him. Soon this school year, too, would be behind him. Soon they would find Glendower, soon they would all be kings. Soon, soon.

13

The next day after school, Blue sat at the table with a spoon in one hand and *Lysistrata*, the play she'd chosen to analyze for English, in the other. (*It's not easy, you know, for women to get away. One's busy pottering about her husband; poking the servant awake; putting her child asleep or washing the brat or feeding it.*) Gray drizzle pressed against the windows of the cluttered kitchen.

Blue was not thinking about *Lysistrata*. She was thinking about Gansey and the Gray Man, Maura and the cave of ravens.

Suddenly, a shadow the exact size and shape of her cousin Orla fell across the table.

"I get that Maura is away, but that is no reason to go around being a social tard," Orla said by way of hello. "Also, when was the last time you ate a food that wasn't yogurt?"

Sometimes Blue couldn't take Orla. This was one of those times. She didn't look up. "Don't be offensive."

"Charity told me that T.J. asked you out today and you just stared at him."

"What?"

"T.J. asked you out. You just stared at him. Ringing bells?" Orla had long since graduated from Mountain View High, but she was still friends or ex-girlfriends with her entire class, and the collective power of all of those younger siblings served to provide Orla with a view, somewhat incomplete, of Blue's current high school life.

Blue looked up (and up, and up) at her tall cousin. "At lunch, T.J. came over to my table and drew a penis on the unicorn on my binder. Is that the incident Charity is referring to?"

"Don't Richard Gansey the Third at me," Orla replied.

"Because if that's what she meant, then yes, I just stared at him. I didn't realize it was a conversation because *penis*."

Orla flared her nostrils magnificently. "Here's some advice: Sometimes people are just trying to be friendly. You can't expect everyone to be profound all the time. There's just chatting."

"I *chat*," Blue retorted. The T.J. incident hadn't offended her, although she'd preferred her unicorn non-gendered. It had just made her feel wearily older than everyone in the school. "Do you mind? I'm trying to get this done before Gansey gets here." (*O Zeus, what throbbing suffering!*)

"You can be just friends with people, you know," Orla said. "I think it's crazy how you're in love with all those raven boys."

Orla wasn't wrong, of course. But what she didn't realize about Blue and her boys was that they were *all* in love with one another. She was no less obsessed with them than they were with her, or one another, analyzing every conversation and gesture, drawing out every joke into a longer and longer running gag, spending each moment either with one another or thinking about when next they would be with one another. Blue was perfectly aware that it was possible to have a friendship that wasn't all-encompassing, that wasn't blinding, deafening, maddening, quickening. It was just that now that she'd had this kind, she didn't want the other.

Orla snapped her fingers in between Blue and her book. "Blue. This is what I was just talking about."

Blue folded her finger in the pages to keep her place. "I didn't ask for any advice."

"No, but you should," Orla said. "What do you think's going to happen in a year? All of your boys are going to go off to fancy schools, and where will you be? Here in Henrietta with the people you didn't *chat* with."

Blue opened her mouth and closed it, and Orla's eyes flashed with victory. She knew she'd dug down to marrow.

Outside, the familiar grumble of an old Camaro sounded, and Blue leapt up. She dumped her spoon in the sink. "My ride's here."

"*Temporary* ride."

Blue exploded, hurling her yogurt container into the recycling bin. "What is it, Orla? Jealousy? Or what? You just don't want me to like them as well as I do because . . . you're trying to save me from being hurt? You know what else is temporary? *Life.*"

"Oh, please, don't you think you're taking this a bit —"

"So maybe I should have spread my love out through some other mothers, too!" Blue snatched up her jacket and stormed down the hall toward the door. "If I didn't love *her* as much, then it wouldn't feel so bad when she was gone! I could have some fallback parents, each containing a *tiny* piece of my affection so that when one goes away, I barely notice! Or maybe I should just not love anyone or anything! That makes it the easiest, really, because then I'll never get let down! I will build a tower for my heart!"

"Oh, calm your ass down," Orla said, clomping after Blue in her platform clogs. "That wasn't what I meant."

"You know what I think, Orla? I think you're a big, fat *bully* —" Blue barreled right into Gansey, who had stepped inside the front hall. For a moment she smelled mint, felt the solidness of his chest, and then she wheeled back.

Gansey untangled his watch from Blue's crochet jacket. "Hi. Oh, Orla."

"Oh, *Orla*," echoed Orla, not pleasantly. It was not at him, but he didn't know that; he flinched.

From upstairs, Calla roared, "SHUT UP!"

"You'll remember this conversation later and say sorry to me," Orla told Blue. "You forget who you are." She whirled with as much grace as she could manage on her long legs and massive shoes.

Gansey was too gracious to inquire after the source of the argument.

"Get me out of here," Blue said.

Outside, it was a miserable day, soggy and cool, late fall come too early. Malory was already installed in the Pig's front seat; Blue was at once regretful and glad that he was along. He would keep her from doing something stupid.

Now she sat beside the Dog, looking out the backseat window as they passed Mole Hill on the way to Coopers Mountain, feeling her bad mood leach into the gray. This was a very different part of the world than Henrietta. Rural, but less wild. More cows, fewer woods. And very poor. The houses that lined the highway were smaller than single-wide trailers.

"I'm not hopeful about this," Gansey was saying to Malory. He plucked at his left shoulder; rain was coming in through his window, though it was rolled up. Water also dripped onto the dash beneath the rearview mirror. Malory shook water off the map in his hands. "I crawled all over this mountain a year ago and saw no cave. If there is one, it's someone else's secret."

Blue leaned forward; so did the Dog. She said, "There's this super clever way that folks in the country find out someone else's secrets. We *ask* them."

Gansey met her eyes, and then the Dog's, in the rearview mirror. "Adam keeps his secrets pretty close."

"Oh, not *Adam's* sort of country people."

Blue had discovered that there were two distinct stereotypes for the rural population of her part of Virginia: the neighbors who loaned one another cups of sugar and knew everything about everyone, and the rednecks who stood on their porches with shotguns and shouted racist things when they got drunk. Because she grew up so thoroughly entrenched in the first group, she hadn't believed in the second group until well into her teens. School had taught her that the two kinds were almost never born into the same litter.

"Look," she said. "When we get there, I'll show you the houses to stop at."

Coopers Mountain turned out to be more of a mountainette than a proper mountain, impressive mostly because of its sudden appearance in the middle of sparsely populated fields. A small neighborhood lay on one side. Widely flung farmhouses dotted the rest of the surrounding area. Blue directed Gansey past the former and toward the latter.

"People in neighborhoods only know about people in neighborhoods," she said. "No caves in neighborhoods. Here, here, this one's good! You better wait in the car with your fancy face."

Gansey was too aware of his face's fanciness to protest. He minced the Camaro down a long gravel drive that ended at a white farmhouse. A shaggy dog of no breed or all breeds burst out to bark at her as she climbed out into the rain.

"Hey, you," Blue greeted it, and the dog retreated immediately under the porch. At the door, an older woman holding a magazine answered her knock. She looked friendly. In Blue's experience, everyone who lived in remote tired farmhouses generally looked friendly, until they didn't.

"What can I do for you?"

Blue slathered on her accent as slow and local as possible. "I'm not selling anything, I promise. My name's Blue Sargent and I live in Henrietta and I'm doing a geology project. I heard there was a cave round here. Could you possibly point me in the right way?"

Then she smiled as if the woman *had* already helped her. If there was one thing Blue had learned while being a waitress and dog walker and Maura Sargent's daughter, it was that people generally became the kind of person you expected them to be.

The woman considered. "Well, that does sound familiar, but I don't reckon I . . . Have you asked Wayne? Bauer? He's good with this area."

"Which one's he, now?"

The woman pointed kitty-corner across the highway.

Blue gave her a thumbs-up. The woman wished her luck.

It turned out Wayne Bauer wasn't home, but his wife was, and she didn't know anything about a cave, but had they asked Jimmy down the road, because he was always digging ditches and you knew you found all kinds of things in ditches. And Jimmy didn't know, but he thought Gloria Mitchell had said something about it last year. They discovered that Gloria wasn't home, but her elderly sister was, and she asked, "What, you mean Jesse Dittley's cave?"

"You don't have to look so smug," Gansey said to Blue as she buckled her seat belt.

"Sure I do," Blue replied.

The Dittley farm was directly at the base of Coopers Mountain. The swaybacked wood-frame house was surrounded by partial cars and entire sofas, all overgrown. The abandoned tires and broken window air conditioners inspired the same feeling in Blue as the cluttered kitchen-bathroom-laundry in Monmouth had: the urge to tidy and impart order.

As she climbed out, she turned the name *Jesse Dittley* over and over in her mind. Something about it poked the back of her mind, but she couldn't think what. Old family friend? Sex offender from a newspaper story? Character from a picture book?

Just in case he was the middle one, she made certain that she had her pink switchblade knife in her pocket. She didn't really think she would have to stab anyone, but she liked being prepared.

She stood on the slanted porch with fourteen empty milk jugs and ten cats and knocked. It took a long time for the door to open, and when it did, a puff of cigarette smoke came out with it.

"WHAT THE HELL ARE YOU?"

She peered up at the man. He peered down at her. He must have been close to seven feet tall and was wearing the largest white wife-beater that she'd ever seen (and she'd seen a lot). His face was mild, if surprised; the booming, Blue decided, was from chest capacity and not from malice. He stared at her shirt, which she had made from ribbons and soda can tabs, and then at her face.

"Excited to meet you, is what I am." She peered past him into the house. She saw more recliners than she'd ever seen in her life (and she'd seen a lot). Nothing hinted where she might have heard his name before. "Are you Jesse Dittley?"

"I AM JESSE DITTLEY. DID YOU NEVER EAT YOUR GREENS?"

It was true that Blue was just shy of five feet and it was also true that she hadn't eaten her greens, but she'd done the research and she didn't think the two were related. She said, "I lost the genetic roll of the dice."

"DAMN STRAIGHT."

"I'm here because folks are saying you have a cave."

He considered this. He scratched his chest. Finally, he looked to where the Camaro sat sodden in the pitted driveway. "WHO'S THAT?"

"My friends," Blue replied, "who are also interested in the cave. If it exists."

"OH, IT EXISTS." He let out a hurricane-sized sigh. "MIGHT AS WELL TELL THEM TO COME IN OUT OF THE RAIN."

The Camaro *was* theoretically already out of the rain — well, perhaps not Gansey's left shoulder — but Blue didn't argue the point. She gestured for the others to join her.

Inside the farmhouse was much like the outside. Machines half-dissected, dead plants in dry pots, dusty bedspreads balled in corners, cats peering from inside sinks. It was gray and colorless and dark in the rain. There was something sort of *sideways* about it, like the hallways were a little too narrow, or a little slanted, or just slightly wrong in some way.

Jesse Dittley. The familiarity of it was driving her crazy.

In the living room, Malory sat on a brown recliner without blinking an eye. Gansey remained standing. He looked a bit faint.

Blue sat on an ottoman without a chair. Jesse Dittley stood next to a card table covered with empty glasses. He didn't offer them a drink.

"WHAT DO YOU WANT TO KNOW ABOUT THE CAVE?" Before they could answer, he added gloomily, "IT'S CURSED."

"My," said Malory.

"I don't so much mind about curses," Gansey said, his old-money Virginia accent sounding elegant and affected beside Jesse's. "Is it near here?"

"RIGHT OVER THERE," Jesse reported.

"Oh! Do you know how long it is?" Gansey asked, at the same time that Blue asked, in a friendly way, "What sort of curse?"

"MY DADDY DIED IN IT. AND MY DADDY'S DADDY. AND MY DADDY'S DADDY'S DADDY." Jesse concluded, possibly erroneously, "IT PROBABLY HAS NO END. YOU ONE OF THEM AGLIONBY BOYS, THEN?"

"Yes," Gansey replied precisely.

"DOES THAT DOG WANT WATER?"

They all looked at the Dog. The Dog looked a bit faint.

"Oh, if it's not too much trouble," Malory said.

Jesse went to get water. Gansey exchanged a look with Blue. "This has turned unexpectedly ominous."

"Do you think there's a curse?" she asked.

"Of course there is," Malory replied. "It is on a ley line. Apparitions and lightning storms, black beasts and time slipping."

"To us, just the ley line. To everyone else, a curse," Gansey finished wonderingly. "Of course."

Jesse returned with a chipped glass mixing bowl full of water. The Dog drank ravenously. The Camaro had an exhaust leak, which had a dehydrating effect upon its occupants.

"WHAT IS IT YOU WANT WITH THE CAVE? I RECKON THERE ARE PLENTY OF CAVES WITHOUT CURSES HERE."

Gansey replied, "We're exploring another cave system and we've reached a section that's blocked. We're trying to find another way into it, and we think your cave might do it."

How neatly the truth worked.

Jesse took them out the back door, through another screen porch, and into the mist.

Outside, he was even bigger than Blue had thought he was. Or possibly, now it was easier to compare his size with the house and find the house wanting. As he led them across a vast cow pasture, he didn't duck his head against the rain. This lack of concern struck Blue as noble, though she couldn't quite convince her own head to follow his lead as rain dripped off her earlobes.

"This weather reminds me of this dreadful climb I went on with this fellow Pelham," Malory muttered, producing an umbrella from his person and sharing it with Blue. "Fourteen kilometers each way, and all for a standing stone that looked like a dog in certain lights. The man went on and on about football and his girlfriend — a terrible time was had by all."

With great, sloped strides, Jesse led them to a barbed-wire fence. On the other side, a ruined stone structure of indeterminate age grew out of the rocky hillside. It was roofless and about twenty feet square. Although it was only a single crumbled story, something about it gave the impression of height, as if it had once been taller. Blue struggled to imagine what its original purpose might have been. Something about the tiny aspect of the windows seemed wrong for a residence. If it had not been Virginia, if it had been someplace *older*, she would have thought it looked like the ruin of a stone tower.

"THIS IS IT."

Blue and Gansey exchanged a look. Gansey's look said, *We did tell him "cave," right?* Blue's said, *We definitely did.*

Jesse used a stick to push down the top string of the barbed wire so they could step over — all except the Dog, who remained pissily behind. Then, feet slipping on damp leaves, they climbed up the hill. On the backside of the building, a considerably newer door had been set into the old door frame. A padlock held it closed. Jesse produced a key, which he handed to Blue.

"Me?" she asked.

"I'M NOT GOING INSIDE."

"Gallant," Blue observed. She wasn't exactly nervous; it was just that she hadn't set out that morning with the intention of broaching a curse.

"ONLY KILLS DITTLEYS," Jesse reassured her. "UNLESS YOU HAVE DITTLEY BLOOD IN YOU?"

Blue said, "I don't reckon so."

She fit the key into the lock and let the door fall open.

Inside were saplings, crumbled stones, and then, amid the debris, a hole. It was nothing like the inviting cavern open-ing Cabeswater had provided for them. It was smaller, blacker, more uneven, steeper from the outset. It looked like a place for secrets.

"Look at that cave, Gansey," Malory said. "I wonder who said there was a cave here."

"Leave the smugness to Jane," Gansey told him.

"Don't come in here," Blue warned him, picking her way through the rubble. "In case there are nests or something."

"IT LOOKS BAD WHEN YOU LOOK IN," Jesse said as she peered in the hole. It was utter black inside, blacker because there was no sun. "BUT IT'S NOT STEEP. JUST CURSED."

"How do you know it's not steep?" she asked.

"BEEN IN IT BEFORE FOR MY DADDY'S BONES. CURSE DOESN'T TAKE YOU UNTIL IT'S READY."

It was difficult to argue with this brand of logic.

"Do you think we could go in?" Gansey asked. "Not now, but coming back with proper equipment?"

Jesse peered at him and then at Malory and finally at Blue. "I LIKE THE LOOKS OF YOU, SO —"

He shook his head.

"NO."

"Beg your pardon, did you say no?" Gansey asked.

"COULDN'T IN ALL GOOD CONSCIENCE. GO ON NOW, COME OUT OF THERE. LET'S LOCK IT BACK UP."

He accepted the key from Blue's shocked fingers.

"Oh, but we'd be very careful," she told him.

Jesse locked the door again as if she hadn't spoken.

"We could pay for your expenses?" Gansey suggested carefully, and Blue kicked his leg hard enough to leave a muddy scuff on his pants. "Jesus, Jane!"

"DON'T TAKE THE LORD'S NAME IN VAIN," Jesse said. "YOU KIDS HAVE A GOOD TIME EXPLORING SOMEWHERE ELSE NOW."

"Oh, but —"

"SHORT WAY IS ACROSS THE FIELD. HAVE A GOOD ONE."

They had been dismissed. Impossibly, they'd been dismissed.

"Just as well," Malory said as they headed back across the damp field, shoulders hunched miserably. "Caves are terrible places to die."

"What now?" Blue asked.

"We're supposed to hurry, apparently. Hurry, hurry," Gansey said. "So we find a way to persuade him, I guess. Or we trespass."

After he got into the car, she realized he was wearing his Aglionby uniform, shoulders spattered with rain, just as his spirit had been when she saw it on the ley line. He could have died in that field and she would have been warned. But she hadn't even thought about it until afterward.

It was so impossible to live life backward.

14

This one says 'grass-fed organic cheddar from New Zealand,' " said Greenmantle, shutting the door behind him. The empty hall immediately fell dark without the evening light from outside. Holding his parcel close to his face in order to see the label, and speaking loudly to be heard through the house, he continued, " 'A mild cheddar cheese made from grass-fed, farm-fresh organic milk. Ingredients: cow's milk, salt, starter cultures' — so, like, Dave Brubeck, Warhol, things like that — 'coagulating enzyme,' oh, that is mainstream media."

He dropped his coat on the chair by the front door, and then, after a moment's consideration, his pants as well. Piper's lust was like a single bear trap in the wilderness. It was nearly impossible to find if you were looking for it, but it was something you wanted to be prepared for if you stepped into it by accident.

"I hope that silence means you are getting the crackers out." Greenmantle stepped into the kitchen. Cracker-fetching was not, in fact, the cause of Piper's silence. She stood in the dining area with a pissy look on her face and pink yoga pants on her legs and a gun pointed to her head.

Greenmantle's former employee, the Gray Man, was the holder of said gun. Both he and Piper were silhouetted against the window that looked into the cow pasture. The Gray Man looked good, healthy, tan, as if Henrietta and mutiny suited him. Piper looked angry, not at the Gray Man, but at Greenmantle.

It had taken the Gray Man longer to appear than Greenmantle had expected.

Well, at least he was here now.

"I guess I'll just get the crackers myself, then," Greenmantle said, dropping the block of cheese on the center island. "Sorry I'm not dressed for company."

"Don't move," the Gray Man said, cocking his chin toward the gun in his hand. It was black and shocking-looking, although Greenmantle had no idea what kind it was. The silvery ones looked less dangerous to him, although he supposed that was a fallacy that could get him into trouble. "Do not move."

"Oh, *stop*," Greenmantle said with exasperation, turning to get the cutting board from the counter. "You're not going to shoot Piper."

"Are you certain?"

"Yeah, I think so." Greenmantle fetched the crackers and a plate and a knife from the knife block and assembled them in a reasonable way. Squinting one eye closed, he held up a piece of cheese. "Do you think this is the right size? Should I slice it thinner? These are the crackers we have to go with it."

"That piece is the size of an entire udder," Piper said.

"I'm sorry, this knife isn't very sharp. Mr. Gray. Seriously. The gun? Don't you think it's a bit theatrical?"

The Gray Man didn't lower the weapon. It continued looking dangerous, as did the Gray Man. He was very good at looking scary, but his job description was to be the most intimidating thing in the room at any given time.

Mr. Gray asked, "Why are you here?"

Ah, and the dance began.

"Why *I'm* here?" Greenmantle said. "I'm more bewildered about why *you're* here, since you specifically told me you had stolen my things and run away to West Palm Springs."

What a day that had been, with Laumonier being Laumonier and those damn Peruvian textiles getting stopped in customs before he ever even got to see them and then the Gray Man shitting the bed.

"I told you the truth first. And that wasn't good enough."

Greenmantle butchered a piece of cheese. "Oh right, the . . . 'truth.' Which one was that again? Of course. The *truth* was the one where you told me that the artifact that had been rumored to be in this area for over a decade and had in fact been traced pretty conclusively back to that loser Niall Lynch *didn't even exist*. I rejected that truth, as I recall. I'm trying to remember why I'd do such a thing. Do you remember, treasure, why I decided that was a lie?"

Piper clucked her tongue. "Because you're not a total idiot?"

Greenmantle shook the knife in the direction of his wife. Spouse. Partner. Lover. "Yes, it was that one. I remember now."

The Gray Man said, "I told you it wasn't an artifact, and I stand by that. It's a phenomenon, not a thing."

"Don't bullshit me, Mr. Gray," Greenmantle said pleasantly. He put a cheese cracker in his mouth and spoke around it. "How do you think I knew what it was called? Niall Lynch told me. Fucking braggart. He thought he was invincible. Can I pour you some wine? I've got this abusive red I brought with me. It's a thing of beauty."

The Gray Man gave him a cool look. His hit man look. Greenmantle had always liked the idea of being a mysterious hit man, but that career goal invariably paled in comparison with his enjoyment of going out on the town and having people admire his reputation and driving his Audi with its custom plate (GRNMNTL) and going on cheese holidays in countries that put little hats over their vowels like so: ê.

"What do you want from me?" Mr. Gray asked.

Greenmantle replied, "If we had a time machine, I'd say you could zip back and do what I asked the first time, but I guess *that* ship has sailed off into the sea of clusterfuck. Do you want to open the wine? I always cork it. No? All right, then. I guess you understand that you're going to have to be an example."

He crossed the kitchen and placed a cheese cracker on Piper's tongue. He offered one to the Gray Man, who neither accepted it nor lowered the gun. He continued, "I mean, what would the others think if I let you get away with this? Would not be good. So, although I've enjoyed our time together, I guess that means you're probably going to have to be destroyed."

"Then shoot me," the Gray Man said without fear.

He really was a work of art, the Gray Man. A hit man action figure. All his nobility did was prove what Greenmantle already knew: There were things in this town the Gray Man considered more important than his own life.

"Oh, Mr. Gray. Dean. You know better. No one remembers a corpse. I know you are aware of how this works." Greenmantle cut another piece of cheese. "First I'm going to hang out here, just *observing*. Taking in the view. Figuring out the best breakfast places, seeing the tourist sights, watching you sleep, figuring out everything that's important to you, finding that woman you fell in love with, planning the best way to make destroying all of the above publicly excruciating for you. Et cetera and so forth."

"Give me another one, but not so much cheese," Piper said.

He did so.

The Gray Man said, "If you are going to dismantle my life anyway, there's no motivation for me to not just kill you and Piper right now."

"Talk dirty to me," Greenmantle said. "Like old times. There's actually another option, Mr. Gray. You can give me the Greywaren, just like I asked, and then we'll film a short video of you cutting off your own trigger finger, and then we'll call it a day."

He held up his hands like Lady Justice, weighing the cheese in one hand with the knife in the other. "Either/or."

"And if there's no Greywaren?"

Greenmantle said, "Then there's always the public destruction of everything you love. Options: the American Dream."

The Gray Man seemed to be considering. Usually everyone else looked frightened by this point of this conversation, but it was possible the Gray Man didn't have emotions.

"I'll need to think about it."

"Sure you do," Greenmantle said. "Shall I give you a week? No, nine days. Nine's very three plus three plus three. I'll just keep looking around while you decide. Thanks for dropping by."

The Gray Man backed away from Piper, gun still pointed at her, and then disappeared through a door behind her. The room was silent.

"Isn't that a closet?" Greenmantle asked.

"It's the door to the garage, you piece of shit," Piper said with characteristic affection. "Now I've missed yoga, and what am I going to tell them? Oh, I had a gun pointed to my head. Also, I told you to throw out those boxers months ago. The band's all stretched out."

"That was me," he said. "I stretched it. Get it?"

Piper's voice remained as the rest of her left. "I'm tired of your hobbies. This is the worst vacation I've ever been on."

15

Adam was alone in the shop.

In the still-rainy evening, it grew prematurely dark inside, the corners of the garage consumed by a gloom that the fluorescents overhead couldn't reach. He had spent countless hours working there, though, so his hands knew where to find things even when his eyes did not.

Now he was stretched over the engine of an old Pontiac, the grimy radio on the shop shelves keeping him company. Boyd had set him on the task of changing a head gasket and closing up shop. Dinner, he said, was for old men like him. The long monotony of head gaskets was for young men like Adam.

It wasn't difficult work, which was worse, in a way, because his unoccupied mind whirred. Even as he mentally went over the details of the major events of 1920s United States history for a quiz, he had plenty of leftover brainpower to consider how his back ached from leaning over the engine, the grease he could feel in his ear, the frustration of this rusted head stud, the proximity of his court date, and the presence of others here on the ley line.

He wondered if Gansey and the others had really gone out in the rain to explore Coopers Mountain. Part of him hoped that they hadn't, though he tried his best to kill the baser emotions regarding his friends — if he let them run wild, he would be jealous of Ronan, jealous of Blue, jealous of Gansey with either of the other two. Any combination that didn't involve Adam would provoke a degree of discomfort, if he let it.

He wouldn't let it.

Don't fight with Gansey. Don't fight with Blue. Don't fight with Gansey. Don't fight with Blue.

There was no point telling himself not to fight with Ronan. They would fight again, because Ronan was still breathing.

Outside the shop, the wind blew, spattering rain against the small, streaky windows of the garage doors. Dry leaves rustled up against the walls and skittered away. It was that time of year when it could be hot or cold from day to day; it was neither summer nor fall. An in-between, liminal time. A border.

As he shifted to better reach the engine block, he felt a cool breeze around his ankles, playing just inside the cuff of his slacks. His hands ached; they were even more chapped. When he was a kid, he used to lick the back of them, not realizing at first that it made them even more chapped in the long run. It had been a hard habit to break. Even now, as they stung, he resisted the impulse to relieve the discomfort for just a second.

Outside, the wind blew again, more leaves rattling the windows. Inside, something shifted and clicked. Something settling in the garbage can, maybe.

Adam rubbed his arm against his cheek, realizing only as he did it that his arm had a smear of grease on it. There was no point wiping off his face, though, until he was done for the night.

There was another click from inside the shop. He paused in his work, wrench hovered above the engine, top of his skull touching the open hood overhead. Something seemed different, but he couldn't figure out what it was.

The radio was no longer playing.

Adam warily eyed the old radio. He could just see it, two bays away, on the other side of the Pontiac and a pickup truck and a little Toyota. The power light was off; possibly it had finally died.

But still, Adam asked the empty garage, "Noah?"

It was unlike Noah to be intentionally scary, but Noah had been less *Noah* than usual lately. Less Noah and more dead.

Something popped.

It took Adam a second to realize that it was the portable work light he had hanging from the edge of the hood. It had gone dark.

"Noah? Is that you?"

Adam suddenly had the terrible and looming *feeling* that something was behind him, watching him behind his back. Something close enough to blow a chill around his ankles again. Something big enough to block out some of the light from the incandescent bulb by the side door.

It was not Noah.

Outside, thunder suddenly crashed. Adam broke. He scrambled out from beneath the hood, spinning, pressed back against the car.

There was nothing there but concrete block, calendars, tools on walls, posters. But one of the wrenches on the tool wall was swinging. The other side of the garage was dim in a way that Adam couldn't remember it being.

Go away, go away —

Something touched the back of his neck.

He closed his eyes.

All at once, Adam understood. This was Cabeswater, trying to make itself understood. Persephone had been working with him to improve their communication: Normally, he asked it each morning what it needed, while he flipped tarot cards or scryed into his bathroom sink. But he hadn't asked since school began.

So now it forced him to listen.

Cabeswater, Persephone had said once, quiet and stern, *is not the boss of you.*

Something clattered on the table by the opposite wall.

Adam said, "Wait!"

He dove for his messenger bag as the room darkened further. His fingers found his notebooks, textbooks, envelopes, pens, the forgotten candy bar. Something else fell over, closer by. For an airless minute he thought he had left the tarot cards back in the apartment.

It won't hurt me. This will be scary, but it won't hurt me —

But fear hurt, too.

Just because it tantrums, Persephone had added, *doesn't make it more right than you.*

The cards. Crouching by his bag, Adam snatched out the velvet bag and tumbled the deck into his hands. Persephone had been teaching him all kinds of meditation methods, but there would be no meditating now. Shivering, he shuffled the deck as oil in the pan beneath the Pontiac began to tip, a furious ocean.

He slapped down three cards on the concrete floor. *Death, the Empress, the Devil.*

Think, Adam, think, get inside it —

The closest fluorescent buzzed harshly, suddenly over-bright, then just as suddenly out.

Adam's subconscious fled through Cabeswater's consciousness, both of them tangled up in this strange bargain he'd made.

Death, the Empress, the Devil. Three sleepers, yes, yes, he knew that, but they only needed one, and anyway, what did Cabeswater care about who was sleeping on the ley line, what did it *need* from Adam?

His mind focused on a branched thought, traveled along a limb, to a trunk, down to roots, into the ground. In that darkness and dirt and rock, he saw the ley line. Finally, he saw the connection and where it broke and understood what Cabeswater was asking him to repair. Relief washed over him.

"I get it," he said out loud, falling back, catching himself on the cold concrete. "I'll do it this week."

The shop immediately returned to normal. The radio had resumed playing; Adam hadn't heard the moment it had started up again. Although Cabeswater's means of communication could be terrifying — apparitions, black dogs, howling winds, faces in mirrors — the point was never to intimidate. He knew that. But it was hard to remember it as the walls shifted and water beaded on the inside of windows and imaginary women sobbed in his ear.

It always stopped as soon as Adam understood. It only ever wanted him to understand.

He heaved a big breath next to his tarot cards. Time to get back to work.

But.

He heard something. There should not have been anything, not anymore.

But something was scraping on the shop door. It was a dry, thin noise, like paper tearing. A claw. A nail.

But he'd *understood.* He'd promised to do the work.

He wanted to tell himself that it was only a leaf or a branch. Something ordinary.

But Henrietta was no longer someplace ordinary. *He* was no longer someone ordinary.

"I said I understood," Adam said. "I *get* it. This week. Does it need to be sooner?"

There was no response from within the garage, but outside, something light and uneasy moved past one of the windows, high off the ground. There was just enough light to see its scales.

Scales.

Adam's pulse sped, his heart beating so hard that it hurt.

Surely Cabeswater believed him; he had never let it down before. There were not rules, but there was trust.

A noise came just outside the door: *tck-tck-tck-tck.*

The garage door hurtled open. It sounded like a freight train as it roared along its tracks on the ceiling.

In the grim evening, in the deep-blue-black rain of it, a pale monster reared. It was needle claws and savage beaks, ragged wings and greasy scales. It was so against everything that was real that it was hard to even see it truly.

Terror owned Adam. The old terror, the one that was just as much confusion and betrayal as fear itself.

He had done everything right. Why was this still happening if he'd done everything right?

The horror of an animal took a scratching, slithering step toward Adam.

"Shoo, you ugly bastard," said Ronan Lynch.

He stepped out of the rain and into the shop; he had been hidden in the dark in his jacket and his dark jeans. Chainsaw clung to his shoulder. Ronan lifted a hand to the white beast as if casting off a ship. The creature drew its head back, side-by-side beaks parting.

"Go on," Ronan said, unafraid.

It took flight.

Because it was not just any monster; it was Ronan Lynch's monster. A night horror brought to vicious life. It floated up into the dark, strangely graceful once its face was out of sight.

"Damn, Ronan, damn," Adam gasped, ducking his head. "Oh, God. You scared the shit out of me."

Ronan smirked. He didn't understand that Adam's heart was actually going to explode. Adam wrapped his arms over the back of his neck, curling into a ball on the concrete, waiting to feel like he wasn't going to die.

He heard the garage door rattle closed again. The temperature rose immediately as the wind was locked out.

A boot shoved Adam's knee.

"Get up."

"You asshole," Adam muttered, still not lifting his head.

"Get up. It wasn't going to hurt you. I don't know why you're pissing yourself."

Adam uncurled. He was slowly getting enough function back to be more annoyed than afraid. He pushed to his feet. "There's more going on in the world than just you, Lynch."

Ronan turned his head sideways to read the cards. "What's this?"

"Cabeswater."

"What the fuck is wrong with your face?"

Adam didn't reply to this. "Why was it with you?"

"I was at the Barns. It followed the car." Ronan prowled around the Pontiac, peering at the process inside with a disinterested lack of comprehension. Chainsaw flapped down to crouch on the engine block, head ducked.

"Don't," Ronan warned. "That's toxic."

Adam wanted to ask what it was that Ronan had been doing at the Barns all of these days and evenings, but he didn't press. The Barns was Ronan's family business, and family was private.

"I saw your shitbox in the lot on the way back," Ronan said. "And I figured, anything to avoid Malory for a few more minutes."

"Touching."

"What do you think of the idea of researching Greenmantle's spiderweb? Possible? Not possible?"

"Anything's possible."

"Do it, then, for me," Ronan said.

Adam laughed in disbelief. "Do it for you! Some of us have homework, you know."

"Homework! What's the point?"

"Passing grades? Graduation?"

Ronan swore in a way that indicated further disinterest.

"Are you just trying to make me angry?" Adam asked.

Ronan picked up a socket from the worktable on the other side of the Pontiac. He studied it in a way that suggested he contemplated its merit as a weapon. "Aglionby is kind of pointless for people like us."

"What is 'people like us'?"

"I'm not going to use it," Ronan said, "to get some job with a tie —" He made a hanging motion above his neck, head tilted. "And you could find a way to make the ley line work for you since you've already bargained with it."

Adam retorted, "What's it you see me doing right now? Where is it we even are?"

"Insultingly close to that Toyota is where *I* am."

"I'm at work. Two hours from now, I'm going to my next job for another four hours. If you're trying to convince me that I don't need Aglionby after I have *killed* myself over it for a year, you're wasting your breath. Be a loser if you want to, but don't make me part of it to make yourself feel better."

Ronan's expression was cool over the top of the Pontiac. "Well," he said, "fuck you, Parrish."

Adam just looked at him witheringly. "Do your homework."

"Whatever. I'm getting out of here."

By the time Adam had leaned to get a rag to get the grease out of his ear, the other boy had gone. It was as if he had taken all of the noise of the garage with him; the wind had died down, so the leaves no longer rattled, and the radio's tuning had shifted so that the station was ever so slightly fuzzy. It felt safer, but also lonelier.

Later, Adam walked out through the cool, damp night to his small, shitty car. As he sank into the driver's seat, he found something already sitting on the seat.

He retrieved the object and held it up under the feeble interior cab light. It was a small white plastic container. Adam twisted off the lid. Inside was a colorless lotion that smelled of mist and moss. Replacing the lid with a frown, he turned the container over, looking for more identifying features. On the bottom, Ronan's handwriting labeled it merely: *manibus.*

For your hands.

16

I mean this in the kindest possible way," Malory said, reclined in Gansey's desk chair, "but you cannot make tea for love or money."

The night outside the wall of windows was black and damp; the lights of Henrietta seemed to move as the dark trees blew back and forth before them. Gansey sat on the floor beside his model of town, working slowly at it. He hadn't had time to add anything new; instead he'd snatched minutes here and there to repair the damage incurred that summer. It was distinctly less satisfying to restore something to what it had been than to grow it.

"I'm not sure what I'm doing wrong," Gansey admitted. "It seems like a straightforward process."

"If I wasn't terrified to spend time in that bathroom you call a kitchen, I would advise you," Malory said. "But I'm afraid that one day I will enter that room and never come out."

Gansey fixed a tiny cardboard staircase with a tube of glue and looked up to find the Dog watching him with narrow eyes. The Dog wasn't wrong; he'd placed the stairs a little crookedly. Gansey straightened them.

"Better?" he asked.

"Don't mind him," Malory replied. "He's highly strung. I'm bemused, Gansey, by the lack of thought you've put into the action of sending Glendower to sleep for six hundred years."

"I've put thought into it," Gansey said. "Well. *Conjecture.* I have no way of proving or disproving theories. And even though it's interesting, it's ultimately irrelevant."

"I disagree, from the point of view of a scholar, as should you."

"Oh, should I?"

"By your own assumption, Glendower traveled here via ley line. A perfectly straight line across the sea, not an easy thing to accomplish. Quite a lot of fuss to undergo to hide a prince. Why not hide him on a Welsh line?"

"The English would not have rested until they found him," Gansey said. "Wales is too small for a secret like that."

"Is it? You and I walked Wales. Tell me there are not places in those mountains that would have hid him."

Gansey could not.

"So why sail three thousand miles on a one-way trip to a new world where no one can make a decent cup of tea?" Malory trundled to the pool table maps. As Gansey joined him, he trailed a finger across an overflowing sea, from Wales to tiny Henrietta. "Why would one undertake the nearly impossible task of sailing a perfectly straight line across this sea?"

Gansey said nothing. This map was unmarked, but he could not unsee all of the places he had been on it. Outside, wind gusted abruptly, plastering damp, dead leaves against the windowpanes.

"The ley lines, the corpse roads, the death roads, *Doodwegen* if you believe the Dutch, but who does, this is how we used to carry our dead," Malory said. "Coffin-bearers traveled along the funeral roads in order to keep the souls intact. To take a crooked path was to unseat the soul and create a haunting, or worse. So when they traveled in a straight line with Glendower, it was because he was to be handled like the dead."

"So he was already sleeping when they left," Gansey said, although now *sleeping* seemed like too light a word for it. He had a flash of memory, though it was not a true memory; it was a vision he'd had in Cabeswater. Glendower supine in his coffin, arms folded over his chest, sword by one hand, cup by the other. Gansey, hand hovering over the helmet, afraid and ecstatic to finally look into the face of his king after six hundred years. "They were keeping his soul with his body."

"Precisely. And now that I am here, now that I have seen your line — I believe they sailed all this way because they were looking for this place." Malory tapped on the map.

"Virginia?"

"Cabeswater."

The word hung in the room.

"If not Cabeswater itself, then a place like it," Malory continued. "They may have merely followed energy readings until they could find a place with enough force to maintain a soul in stasis for hundreds of years. Or at least for longer than his attendants thought they themselves would live."

Gansey considered all of this. "The psychics have said there are three sleepers. Not just Glendower, but two others. I suppose what you're saying would explain why there might be others here, too. Not necessarily because no one has tried to put anyone else to sleep elsewhere, but because it has failed anywhere but here."

This inspired a shivery, unpleasant thought, of imagining you were being sent to sleep and instead being sent off to a trusting, accidental death.

The two of them gazed at the map for several minutes. Then Malory said, "I'm off to bed. Are we exploring tomorrow, or may I drive to that other Virginia again for some more cartography?"

"Other —? West. West Virginia. I think we should be able to come with you after class."

"Excellent."

Malory left his substandard cup of tea on the pool table and retired with the Dog.

Gansey stood unmoving in the warehouse after the door had shut. He stood so long that he felt disoriented; he could have been standing a minute, he could have been standing an hour. It could be now, it could be a year ago. He was as much a part of this room as his telescope and his stacks of books. Unchanging. Unable to change.

He could not decide if he was tired, or tired of waiting.

He wondered where Ronan had gone.

He did not call Blue.

"Look, I found this."

Gansey jumped at the precise same moment that he recognized Noah's voice. The dead boy sat cross-legged on the end of Gansey's mattress in the middle of the room. Gansey was relieved to see that Noah looked more firmly himself than when he'd seen him last. In his hands, he held a lump of dark gray clay that he had formed into a small, negative-image snowman.

"Frosty the clayman," Noah said, amusing himself. "I took it from Ronan's room. Look, it melts."

Gansey regarded it more closely as he settled himself cross-legged, mirror image from Noah. "Did he get it from a dream?"

"Gas station, I think. The clay's got metal flakes in it or something," Noah said. "See, it's standing on that magnet. It slurps down and eats the magnet after a while."

They watched. They watched a lot. It moved so slowly that it took Gansey a full minute to even believe that eventually, the metallicized putty probably would engulf the magnet.

"Is this supposed to be a toy?" Gansey asked.

"Ages six and up."

"This is the worst toy I have ever seen."

Noah grinned. He said, "Piss up a rope."

They both laughed uproariously at Ronan's words coming out of Noah's mouth.

The bottom of the clay figure had managed to hide the magnet without Gansey noticing any movement.

"What's that *slowly* phrase?" Noah asked. "Slowly, slowly . . ."

". . . catchy monkey," Gansey finished. "Noah, don't go. I'm going to ask you a question, and I don't want you to go like you always do."

The dead boy lifted his head to meet Gansey's eyes. Though he was not transparent or incorrect looking in any way, he was unintentionally unsettling in this light. Something about his unblinking eyes.

That could have been me. That should have been me.

"Did you hear him? When you . . . when you died?" Gansey regretted asking it already, but he pressed on. "Did you hear a voice as well?"

Noah's fingers touched his smudgy cheek, though he didn't seem to notice. He shook his head.

If both Gansey and Noah had been dying on the ley line at the same time, why had Gansey been chosen to live and Noah been chosen to die? By all rights, Noah's death was the more wrongful one: He had been murdered for no reason. Gansey had been stung by a death that had been dogging his steps for more than a decade.

"I think . . . Cabeswater wanted to be awake," Noah said. "It knew I wouldn't do what needed to be done, and you would."

"It couldn't know that."

Noah shook his head again. "It's easy to know a lot of things when time goes around instead of straight."

"But —" said Gansey, but he didn't know what he had meant to protest. Really it was just the fact of Noah's slow death, and there didn't seem to be anyone he could direct that protest toward. He touched one of his ears; he could feel ghosts of those hornets crawling over it. "When we find Glendower, I'm asking him to fix you. As the favor."

He didn't like saying it out loud; not because he didn't mean it, but because they weren't clear on how the favor worked, or if it worked at all, and he didn't like to make false promises.

Noah prodded his clayman. It was not much of a man anymore; it was only because Gansey had seen it before that he could still see the suggestion of the figure in the featureless lump. "I know. It's . . . it's nice of you."

"But . . . ?"

"Don't be afraid," Noah said unexpectedly. Reaching out, he pulled Gansey's hand away from his ear. Gansey hadn't even realized that he was still touching it softly. Leaning forward, Noah blew his cool, corpse breath over Gansey's ear. "Nothing there. You're just tired."

Gansey shivered a little.

Because it was Noah and no one else, Gansey could admit, "I don't know what I'll do if I find him, Noah. I don't know what I'll be if I'm not looking for him. I don't know the first thing about how to be that person again."

Noah put the clay in Gansey's hands. "That's exactly how I feel about the idea of being alive again."

17

"Tell my future," Blue said that night, throwing herself down in front of Calla, who had blanketed the reading room table with receipts. The entirety of 300 Fox Way was howlingly loud; Orla had yet another group over, as did Orla's mother, Jimi. Plus, Trinity — Jimi's sister or cousin or friend — had brought over about one thousand little cousins or something to make soap. The reading room was the quietest place. "Tell me if I'm an orphan in it."

"Go away," Calla said, punching buttons on a calculator. She and Maura had generally worked the house finances together, Calla operating the calculator like an adult, and Maura sitting cross-legged in the middle of the table nearby. But now there was no Maura. "I'm busy."

"I think you don't actually know," Blue said. "I think that's what it is. You and Persephone are pretending to be all wise about it and 'oh she needs to find her own way in the world' blah blah, but really, you're just saying that because you have no idea whatsoever."

"This is paperwork," Calla said. "And you are a pest. Go away."

Blue picked up a handful of receipts and threw them in Calla's face.

Calla looked at her through the fluttering sheets, unmoving.

They settled on the table.

Blue and Calla stared at each other.

"I'm so sorry," Blue said, shrinking. "I really am."

She started to pick up one of the receipts, and Calla grabbed her wrist.

"Don't," she said.

Blue's shoulders slumped more.

Calla said, "Look. This isn't easy for any of us. You're right. We could never see into Cabeswater, and it's harder to see everything else now, when there's just two of us. Harder to agree when there's no tiebreaker, especially when it's *about* the tiebreaker . . ." Her face changed. "I'll tell you this: There are three sleepers."

"You've told me that. Everyone's told me that."

"Well, I think your job is to wake up one of them, and I think it's Maura's job to *not* wake up another one."

"That's only two jobs and three sleepers."

"Persephone and I disagree slightly on the existence of a third job or not."

Blue asked, "What kind of job are we talking about here anyway? Like, a job where we pull a salary and at the end we get our faces put up on the wall of a magical forest with Most Valuable Employee of the Epoch?"

"A job like, at the end of it, everything settles into balance and we all live happily the damn ever after."

"Well, that sounds great, except a, what about that sleeper in the middle and b, you can't actually complete a negative job ever, i.e., when does Mom know she's successfully *not* woken someone, and three, does this still involve Gansey dying? Because f, that is not my idea of a happy ending."

"I regret this conversation," Calla said, and began stacking receipts.

"Also g, I don't want to do school anymore."

"Well, you're not quitting, so I'm sorry for your loss."

"I didn't say I was quitting. I just have a very low level of job satisfaction right now. Morale is low. The troops don't want to go to community college."

Calla punched another button on the calculator. Her mouth was making a very unimpressed shape. "The troops shouldn't whine to someone who worked her ass off to be able to go to community college, then."

"Is this going to be one of those 'I hiked uphill both ways to school' thing? Because if so —"

"This is a you-should-go-contemplate-your-entitlement-Blue-Sargent-thing."

Blue, shamed, huffed and stood up. "Whatever. Where is the list from the church watch?"

"That won't make Gansey less dead."

"Calla."

"It's in the box over the fridge, I think."

Blue stormed from the room, deeply unsatisfied, and dragged a chair through hordes of soap-making children to the fridge. Sure enough, she found the church watch notebooks in the box on top. Taking the entire collection, she pushed back through the industrious children and then out the sliding door into the dark backyard.

It was instantly quieter. The yard was empty except for some mums waiting to be planted, the massive beech tree with its great yellow canopy, and the Gray Man.

He sat so quietly in one of the lawn chairs that Blue didn't notice him until she turned to sit in the other.

"Oh! Sorry. Are you having a moment? I can go back inside."

His expression was pensive. He tipped his mostly full beer toward the other chair. "No, I'm the intruder. I should be asking you if you want this space to yourself."

She flapped a diffident hand toward him as she sat. The night smelled foxy and damp, all rain and failed leaf fires. For a moment they sat in quiet as Blue shuffled through the papers and the Gray Man nursed his beer in a contemplative way. The breeze was cool, and the Gray Man doffed his jacket without any particular ceremony and handed it to Blue.

As she draped it over her shoulders, he asked, "So what do you have there? Sonnets, I hope."

Blue drummed her fingers on the pages, thinking how to sum it up. "Every May, we hold a vigil and we see the spirits of people who are going to die within a year. We ask their names, and if they're clients, we let the living people know we saw their spirits so they can get their things in order. This is the list of names."

"Are you all right?"

"Oh, yeah, I just have, this, eyelid in my eye or something," Blue said, wiping her right eye. "What's that face for?"

"The ethical and spiritual ramifications dazzle."

"Don't they?" Blue held the most recent list up over her head so the kitchen light illuminated her handwriting. "Oh, well."

"What?"

She had just found what she was looking for: *JESSIE DITTLEY.*

Spelled wrong, but there nonetheless.

Blue sat back. "Gansey and I met someone and I thought I remembered his name."

"And he's there."

"Yeah. The thing is that I don't know if he'll die because we're in his life, or die because we're not, or if he'll die either way."

The Gray Man rested his neck on the back of his chair and gazed up at the low clouds reflecting light from Henrietta. "Fate versus mere prognostication? I suppose you know more about how the psychic business works."

Blue shrank further into his jacket as the breeze ruffled the beech leaves. "I only know what they've told me."

"And what have they told you?"

She liked the way he asked. It was less that he needed the information and more that he was enjoying her company. It seemed strange that she felt the least lonesome and uneasy sitting here with him, instead of with Calla or Persephone.

She felt more eyelids prickling in her eye.

"Mom says it's like a memory," Blue said. "Instead of looking backward, you're looking forward. Remembering the future. Because time isn't like this —" She drew a line. "It's like this —" She drew a circle. "So I guess, if you think about it that way, it's not that we can't change the future. It's that if you see the future, it already reflects the changes you might have made based upon seeing the future. I don't know. I don't know! Because Mom is always telling people that her readings are a promise, not a guarantee. So you can break a promise."

"Some guarantees, too," the Gray Man observed, voice wry. Then, suddenly, "Is Maura on the list?"

Blue shook her head. "She was born in West Virginia. The church watch only seems to show us people who were born in the area."

Or, in the case of Richard Gansey III: reborn.

Mr. Gray asked, "May I see it?"

She handed it over and watched the slowly moving leaves overhead as he made his way through the names. How she loved this beech tree. So often as a little girl she'd come out to rest her hands against its cool, smooth bark, or sat herself down in its twisted, exposed roots. She had written a letter to it, once, she remembered, and put it in a pencil case that she'd wedged in the roots. They had long since grown around the box, hiding it completely. Now she wished she could read the letter again, as she remembered only its existence and not its content.

Mr. Gray had gone still. Voice careful, he said, "Gansey?"

The very last name on the last of the pages.

She just chewed on her lower lip.

"Does he know?"

She shook her head, just a little.

"Do you know how long?"

She shook her head again.

His eyes were heavy on her, and then he just sighed and nodded, the solidarity of being the one left behind, the one not on the list.

Finally, he said, "A lot of promises get broken, Blue."

He sipped his beer. She folded the piece of paper to hide *JESSIE DITTLEY* and then reveal it again. In the dark, she asked, "Do you love my mother?"

He gazed up through the darker lace of the leaves. Then he nodded.

"Me too."

He somberly flexed his index finger. With a frown, he said, "I didn't mean to put your family in danger."

"I know you didn't. I don't think anyone thinks that."

"I have a decision to make," he said. "Or a plan. I suppose I will make it by Sunday."

"What's magical about Sunday?"

"It's a date that used to be very important to me," the Gray Man said. "And it seems fitting to make it the day I start to be the person your mother thinks I could be."

"I hope the person my mother thought you could be is a person who finds mothers," Blue replied.

He stood up and stretched. *"Helm sceal cenum, ond a þæs heanan hyge hord unginnost."*

"Does that mean 'I'm going to be a hero'?"

He smiled and said, "'A coward's heart is no prize, but the man of valor deserves his shining helmet.'"

"So, what I said," she replied.

"Basically."

18

Gansey was not sleeping.

Because Blue had no cell phone, there was no way for him to break the rules and call her. Instead, he had begun to instead lie in his bed each night, eyes closed, hand resting on his phone, waiting to see if she was going to call him from the Phone/Sewing/Cat Room at her house.

Stop it, he told himself. *Stop wanting it —*

His phone buzzed.

He put it to his ear.

"You're still not Congress, I see."

He was wide-awake.

Glancing toward Ronan's closed bedroom door, Gansey got his wireframes and his journal and climbed out of bed. He shut himself in the kitchen-bathroom-laundry and sat down in front of the refrigerator.

"Gansey?"

"I'm here," he said in a low voice. "What do you know about the blue-winged teal?"

A pause. "Is this what you discuss in Congress when the doors are closed?"

"Yes."

"Is it a duck?"

"Ding! Point to Fox Way. The bank holiday crowd goes wild! Did you know they become flightless for a month during the summer when they molt all of their flight feathers at once?"

Blue asked, "Isn't that all ducks?"

"Is it?"

"This is the problem with Congress."

"Don't be funny with me, Sargent," Gansey said. "Jane. Did you know that the blue-winged teal has to eat one hundred grams of protein to replace the sixty grams of body and tail feathers shed at this time?"

"I didn't."

"That's about thirty-one thousand invertebrates they have to eat."

"Are you reading off notes?"

"No." Gansey closed his journal.

"Well, this was very educational."

"Always is."

"Okay, then."

There was another pause, and Gansey realized she'd hung up. He leaned back against the fridge, eyes closed, guilty, comforted, wild, contained. In twenty-four hours, he'd be waiting for this again.

You know better you know better you know better

"What the hell, man?" Ronan said.

Gansey's eyes flew open just as Ronan hit the lights. He stood in the doorway, headphones looped around his neck, Chainsaw hulking like a tender thug on his shoulder. Ronan's eyes found the phone by Gansey's leg, but he didn't ask, and Gansey didn't say anything. Ronan would hear a lie in a second, and the truth wasn't an option. Jealousy had ruined Ronan for the first several months of Adam's introduction into their group; this would hurt him more than that.

"I couldn't sleep," Gansey said truthfully. Then, after a pause, "You're not going to try to kill Greenmantle, are you?"

Ronan's chin lifted. His smile was sharp and humorless. "No. I've thought of a better option."

"Do I want to know what it is? Is it acceptance of the pointlessness of revenge?"

The smile widened and sharpened yet more. "It's not your problem, Gansey."

He was so much more dangerous when he wasn't angry.

And he was right: Gansey didn't want to know.

Ronan pulled the fridge door open, shoving Gansey several inches across the floor. He retrieved a soda and handed Chainsaw a cold hot dog. Then he eyed Gansey again.

"Hey, I heard this great song," he said. Gansey tried to tune out the sound of a raven horking down a hot dog. "Want a listen?"

Gansey and Ronan rarely agreed on music, but Gansey shrugged an agreement.

Removing his headphones from his neck, Ronan placed them on Gansey's ears — they smelled a little dusty and birdy from proximity to Chainsaw.

Sound came through the headphones: "Squash one, squash tw —"

Gansey tore them off as Ronan dissolved into manic laughter, which Chainsaw echoed, flapping her wings, both of them terrible and amused.

"You bastard," Gansey said savagely. "You *bastard*. You betrayed my trust."

"That is the best song invented," Ronan told him, through breathless laughs. He got himself back together. "Come on, bird, let's give the man some privacy with his food." As he departed, he turned off the lights, returning Gansey to the dark. Gansey heard him whistling the remainder of the murder squash song on his way to his room.

Gansey pushed himself to his feet, collecting his phone and his journal, and then he went back to bed. The guilt and the worry had already worn off by the time his head hit the pillow, and all that was left was the happiness.

19

Gansey had forgotten how much time school occupied. Perhaps it was because he now had more to do outside of school, or perhaps it was because, now, he could not stop thinking about school even when he was not in it.

Greenmantle.

"Dick! Gansey! Gansey boy! *Richard Campbell Gansey the Third.*"

The Gansey in question strode down the colonnade with Ronan and Adam after school, headed toward the office. Though he was dimly aware of the shouting, his mind was too noisy for the words to register. Part of it was donated to Greenmantle, part to Maura's disappearance, part to Malory's exploration of the perpendicular ley line, part to the cave of ravens, part to the knowledge that in seven hours, Blue might call him. And a final, anxious part — an ever-growing part — was occupied with the color of the fall sky, the leaves on the ground, the sense that time was passing without being replaced, that it was running out and spooling to the end.

It was a uniform-free day in honor of the school's win at a regional quiz bowl, and the lack of uniforms somehow made Gansey's anxiety worse. His classmates sprawled across the historic campus in down vests and plaid pants and brand-name pullovers. It reminded him that he was existing *now* and no other

time. The other students had marked themselves as unmistak-
able inhabitants of this century, this decade, this year, this season,
this income bracket. Human clocks. It wasn't until they all
returned to the identical navy V-neck sweaters that Aglionby
slipped out of time and all times started to feel like they were in
fact the same time.

Sometimes Gansey felt as if he had spent the last seven years
of his life chasing places that made him feel like this.

Greenmantle.

Every morning this week had begun with Greenmantle
standing at the front of their Latin class, eternally smiling.
Ronan stopped coming to first period. There was no way he
would graduate if he failed Latin, but could Gansey blame him?

The walls crumbled.

Adam had asked why Gansey needed to go to the office.
Gansey had lied. He was done fighting with Adam Parrish.

"Ganseeeeeeey!"

The night before, Mr. Gray had told Ronan, "Dream me a
Greywaren to give Greenmantle."

And Ronan had replied, "You want me to give that bastard
the keys to Cabeswater? Is that what you're asking?"

So they were at an impasse. "Gansey boy! *DICK.*"

Ronan whirled and walked backward to face the shouter.
He spread his arms wide. "Not now, Cheng. The king's a little busy."

"I wasn't talking to you, Lynch. I need someone with a soul."

The light that glinted off Ronan's snarl caught Gansey's
eye, bringing him back to the present. He checked his stride

and his watch before doubling back to Henry, who sat at a card table situated between columns. His hair looked like pitch-black fire.

The two boys exchanged a comradely handshake over the table. They had some things in common: Before quitting last spring, Gansey had once been the captain of the crew team, and Henry had once signed up for the crew team at breakfast before scratching out his name by dinnertime. Gansey had been to Ecuador; Henry had once done a modeling photo shoot with a racehorse named Ecuador in Love. Gansey had once been killed by hornets; Henry's family business was on the cutting edge of designing robotic drone bees.

The two boys were friendly, but not friends. Henry ran with the Vancouver crowd, and Gansey ran with dead Welsh kings.

"What can I do for you, Mr. Cheng?" Gansey asked pleasantly.

Henry threw a hand at him. "Do you see, Ronan? That is the way you talk to a man. I'm. Glad. You. Asked, Gansey. Look, I need your help. Sign this."

Gansey observed *this*. The wording was rather official but it seemed to be a petition to establish a student-chosen student council. "You want me to vote for the right to vote?"

"You've grasped the salient point of my position much faster than the rest of our peers. I see why you're always in the newsletter." Henry offered him a pen, and when Gansey didn't immediately take it, a Sharpie, and then a pencil.

Instead of accepting a writing tool, Gansey tried to decide if signing the petition promised any of his time.

Rex Corvus, parate Regis Corvi.

"Gansey, come on," Henry said. "They'll listen to you. Your vote counts double because you're a Caucasian with great hair. You're Aglionby's golden boy. The only way you could score more points is if your mom gets that seat."

Ronan smirked at Adam. Gansey rubbed a thumb over his lower lip, unpleasantly aware that Henry hadn't said anything untrue. He would never know how much of his place here was fairly earned and how much had been bequeathed with his gilded pedigree. It used to bother him, a little.

Now it bothered him a lot.

"I'll sign, but I want to be exempt from nominations." Gansey accepted a pen. "My plate's full."

Henry rubbed his hands together. "Sure thing, old man. Parrish?"

Adam merely shook his head. He did it in a remote, cool way that didn't invite Henry to ask again.

Henry said, "Lynch?"

Ronan flicked his gaze from Adam to Henry. "I thought you said I didn't have a soul."

He didn't look at all Aglionby just then, with his shaved head and black biker jacket and expensive jeans. He looked altogether very grown-up. It was, Gansey thought, as if time had carried Ronan a little more swiftly than the rest of them this summer.

Who are these two? Gansey wondered. *What are we doing?*

"It turns out politics have already eroded my principles," Henry said.

Ronan selected a large-caliber marker and leaned deep over

the petition. He wrote *ANARCHY* in enormous letters and then tossed the instrument of war at Henry's chest.

"Hey!" Henry cried as the marker bounced off him. "You *thug*."

"Democracy's a farce," Ronan said, and Adam smirked, a private, small thing that was inherently exclusionary. An expression, in fact, that he could've very well learned from Ronan.

Gansey spared Henry a pitying glance. "Sorry, he didn't get enough exercise today. Or there's something wrong with his diet. I'll take him away now."

"When I get elected president," Henry told Ronan, "I'm making your face illegal."

Ronan's smile was thin and dark. "Litigation's a farce."

As they headed back down the shadowed colonnade, Gansey asked, "Do you ever consider the possibility that you might be growing up to be an asshole?"

Ronan kicked a piece of gravel. It skittered across the bricks in front of them before skipping off into the grassy courtyard. "Rumor has it that his father gave him a Fisker for his birthday and he's too afraid to drive it. I want to see it if he has it. Rumor has it he biked here."

"From Vancouver?" Adam asked.

Gansey frowned as a pair of impossibly young ninth graders ran across the courtyard — had he ever been that small? He knocked on the headmaster's door. *Am I doing this?* He was. "Are you waiting out here for me?"

"No," said Ronan. "Parrish and I are going for a drive."

"We are?" Adam asked.

"Good," Gansey said. He was relieved that they would be doing something, not thinking about the headmaster, not wondering if Gansey was, after all, behaving like a Gansey. "I'll see you later."

And before they could say anything else, he let himself in and shut the door.

20

Ronan took Adam to the Barns.

Ever since the disastrous Fourth of July party, Ronan had taken to disappearing to his family home, returning late without an explanation. Adam would have never pried — secrets were secrets — but he couldn't deny that he'd been curious.

Now it seemed he would find out.

He had always found the Barns disconcerting. The Lynch family property might not have carried the patina of lush wealth that the Gansey house did, but it more than made up for it with a sense of claustrophobic history. These barn-studded fields were an island, untouched by the rest of the valley, seeded by Niall Lynch's imagination and grazed by his dreams.

It was another world.

Ronan navigated the narrow driveway. The gravel cut through an embankment and a tangle of twisted trees. Cherry-red leaves of poison ivy and blood-spikes of raspberry vines flashed between the trunks. Everything else was green here: canopy dense enough to block out the afternoon sun, grass rippling up the banks, moss clinging damply.

And then they were through the forest and in the vast, protected fields. Here it was more saturated still: pastures green and gold; barns red and white; dense, messy autumn roses hanging on crowded bushes; purple, drowsy mountains half-hidden behind the tree line. Yellow apples, bright as butter, peeked from trees on one side of the drive. Some sort of blue flower, improbable, dreamt, ran amok through the grass on the other side. Everything was wild and raw.

But that was the Lynches.

Ronan made a big showy sideways slide at the end of the drive — Adam silently reached up to hold the strap on the ceiling — and the BMW scuffed sloppily into the gravel parking area in front of the white farmhouse.

"One day, you're going to blow out a sidewall," Adam said as he got out of the car.

"Sure," Ronan agreed. Climbing out of the car, he peered up into the branches of the plum trees beside the parking area. As always, Adam was reminded of how Ronan *belonged* in this place. Something about the familiar way he stood as he searched for ripe fruit implied that he had done it many times before. It made it easy to understand that Ronan had grown up here and would grow old here. Easy to see how to exile him was to excise his soul.

Adam allowed himself a wistful moment to imagine an Adam Parrish grown from these fields instead of the dusty park outside Henrietta — an Adam Parrish who was allowed to want this home for himself. But it was as impossible as trying to imagine Ronan as an Aglionby teacher.

He couldn't figure how Ronan had learned to be fierce in this protected place.

Ronan found two black-purple plums that he liked. He tossed one to Adam and then jerked his chin to indicate Adam should follow.

For some reason, Adam had gotten it in his mind that all of the times Ronan had vanished to the Barns, he had been preparing the house for himself and Matthew. It was so convincing an idea that he was surprised when Ronan led him around the farmhouse to one of the many barns that were built on the property.

It was a grand, long barn that was probably supposed to hold horses or cattle but instead contained junk. A closer inspection revealed that it was in fact dream junk, subtly dated by dust and fading.

Ronan moved through the dim expanse with ease, picking up a clock, a lantern, a bolt of strange cloth that somehow hurt Adam to look at. Ronan found a sort of ghostly light on a strap; he slung it over his shoulder to bring with him. He had already scarfed his plum.

Adam lingered in the doorway, watching through the dust motes, making the plum last. "This is what you've been working on?"

"No, this is Dad's." Ronan picked up a little stringed instrument. He turned it so Adam could see that its strings were pure gold. "Look at this."

Adam joined him. Although he had homework to do and Cabeswater to tend, it was difficult to feel hurried. The air in the barn was drowsy and timeless, and there was nothing disagreeable about rifling through the wonders and follies. Some of the things in the barn were machines that still ran by means mysterious. But others were things that Niall Lynch must have dreamt into life, because now they slept. They found sleeping birds among the clutter, and a sleeping cat, and an old-fashioned stuffed bear that must have been alive, too, because its chest rose and fell. With their creator dead, all of them were beyond waking — unless, like Ronan's mother, they were returned to Cabeswater.

As they moved through the old barn, Adam felt Ronan's eyes glance off him and away, his disinterest practiced but incomplete. Adam wondered if anyone else noticed. Part of him wished they did and immediately felt bad, because it was vanity, really: *See, Adam Parrish is wantable, worthy of a crush, not just by anyone, someone like Ronan, who could want Gansey or anyone else and chose Adam for his hungry eyes.*

Maybe he was wrong. He could be wrong.

I am unknowable, Ronan Lynch.

"You want to see what I've been working on?" Ronan asked. All casual.

"Sure," Adam replied. All casual.

Pausing only to sling the ghost light over a fence post for later retrieval, Ronan led Adam across the damp fields to a barn they had visited before. Adam knew what he would find before Ronan pulled open the big, rusted door, and sure enough, inside was a vast herd of cattle of all colors. Like all the other living things in these barns, they slept. Waited.

Inside, the light was dull and brown, filtered through dirt-covered skylights in the far-above roof. It smelled warm, alive, familiar, like fur and crap and humidity. Who dreamt a herd of cattle? No wonder Cabeswater had been unable to appear until Ronan's father died. Even Ronan's and Kavinsky's careless dreaming had drained the ley line of enough energy to make the forest disappear. That had been trinkets, drugs, cars.

Not fields full of living creatures. Not an invented valley.

This was why Greenmantle could not have even a forged Greywaren. Ferocious Cabeswater was also strangely fragile.

Ronan had come to a door inside the barn; behind it was a tattered office. Everywhere was dust thick enough to be dirt. Vet records and feed receipts yellowed on the desktop. A garbage can held ancient Coke cans. Unframed prints were tacked to the walls — a flier for some Irish folk band playing in New York; a vintage print of some children running on a faraway, older pier in a faraway, older country. It was so different from what Adam's father had pinned to his workspace walls that again Adam considered Ronan's admiration of him. Someone like him treating someone like Adam as someone worthy —

Ronan swore as he tripped. He found the light switch, and a benevolent fluorescent came on overhead. It was full of dead flies.

In the slightly improved light, Adam saw dustless trails leading from the desk to an office chair by the wall. A blanket — not dusty — nested on the chair, and it was not difficult to imagine the shape of a young man sleeping in it. There was something unexpectedly lonely about the image.

Ronan dragged a metal tack box out from the wall and flipped up the lid with a terrific crash. "I've been trying to wake my father's dreams."

"What?"

"They aren't dead. They're sleeping. If I dragged them all to Cabeswater, they'd get up and walk away. So I began to think, what if I brought Cabeswater to them?"

Adam wasn't sure what he'd expected as a reveal, but it wasn't this. "To the cows."

"Some of us have family, Parrish."

Aurora was trapped in Cabeswater. Of course Ronan would want her to be able to come and go. Shamed, Adam replied, "Sorry. Got it."

"It's not just that. It's Matthew —" Ronan broke off, very completely, and Adam understood. This was another secret, one Ronan wasn't ready to tell.

After a moment of rummaging in the box, Ronan turned around, a clear glass ball in his hand. The air inside it shimmered mistily. It was pretty, something you'd hang in a garden or in an old lady's kitchen. It struck Adam as *safe*. Not very Ronan-like.

Ronan held it up to the light. The air inside rolled from one side to the other. Maybe not air at all. Maybe a liquid. Adam could see it reflected in his blue eyes. Ronan said, "This was my first attempt."

"You dreamed it."

"Of course."

"Mm. And Cabeswater?"

Ronan sounded offended. "I asked."

He asked. So easy. As if it was a simple thing for him to communicate with this entity that could only make itself known to Adam through grand and violent gestures.

"In the dream, it had some of Cabeswater inside it," Ronan continued, and intoned, "If it works in the dream, it works in real life."

"Does it work? Give me the short version."

"Asshole. No. It doesn't. It does, in fact, jack shit." Ronan dug back through the tack box, lifting out various other failed attempts, all of them puzzling. A shimmering ribbon, a tuft of grass still growing from a lump of dirt, a forked branch. He let Adam hold some of them; they all felt strange. Too heavy, like gravity weighted them more than it should. And they smelled vaguely familiar, like Ronan, or like Cabeswater.

If Adam thought about it — or rather, if he *didn't* think about it — he could feel the pulse of the ley line in each.

"I had a bag of sand, too," Ronan said, "but I spilled it."

Hours of dreaming. He had driven an hour each day to park his car and curl in this chair and sleep alone.

"Why here? Why do you come here to do it?"

Voice toneless, Ronan said, "Sometimes I dream of wasps."

Adam imagined it then: Ronan waking in Monmouth Manufacturing, a dream object clutched in his hands, wasps crawling in his bedsheets, Gansey unaware in the other room.

No, he could not dream wildly in Monmouth.

Lonesome.

"Aren't you afraid you'll get hurt out here by yourself?" Adam asked.

Ronan scoffed. Him, fear for his own life. But there was something in his eyes, still. He studied his hands and admitted, "I've dreamt him a box of EpiPens. I dream cures for stings all the time. I carry one. I put them in the Pig. I have them all over Monmouth."

Adam felt a ferocious and cruel hope. "Do they work?"

"I don't know. And there's no way to find out before it actually happens. There won't be a rematch." Ronan took two objects from the tack box and stood. "Here. Field trip time. Let's go to the lab."

With one arm he braced a bright blue polar fleece blanket against his body. On the other he draped a slab of moss like a waiter's towel.

"Do you want me to carry one?" Adam asked.

"Fuck, no."

Adam got the door for him.

In the main room of the barn, Ronan took his time walking among the cows, pausing to look into their faces or cocking his head to observe their markings. Finally, he stopped by a chocolate-brown cow with a jagged stripe down her friendly face. He shoved her motionless side with the toe of his boot and explained, "It works better if they seem more . . . I don't know. Particular. If it looks like something I might have dreamt myself."

It looked like a cow to Adam. "So what is it about this one?"

"Looks fucking friendly. Bovine the boy wizard." He set the blue blanket on the floor. Carefully. Then he ordered, "Feel its pulse. Don't just stare at it. Pulse. On its face. There. There, Parrish, God. There."

Adam gingerly trailed his fingers across the cow's short facial hair until he felt the animal's slow pulse.

Ronan hefted the blanket of moss across the cow's withers. "And now?"

Adam wasn't sure what he was supposed to see. He felt nothing, nothing, nothing — ah, but there it was. The cow's pulse had accelerated fractionally. Again, he imagined Ronan here on his own, so hopeful for a change that he would have noted such a subtle difference. It was far more dedication than he had thought Ronan Lynch capable of.

Lonesome.

He asked, "Is this the closest you've gotten?"

Ronan scoffed. "Did you think I would bother showing you just this? There's one more. Do you need to piss first?"

"Ha."

"No, seriously."

"I'm good."

Ronan turned to the other object he'd brought out. It was not the blue blanket, as Adam had expected, but rather something wrapped inside the blanket. Whatever was inside couldn't be larger than a shoe box or a large book. It didn't seem very heavy.

And if Adam's eyes didn't deceive him, Ronan Lynch was afraid of it.

Ronan took a deep breath. "Okay, Parrish."

He unwrapped it.

Adam looked.

Then he looked away.

Then he looked back.

It was a book, he thought. And then he didn't know why he thought it was a book; it was a bird. No, a planet. A mirror.

It was none of those things. It was a word. It was a cupped word in Ronan's hand that wanted to be said out loud, but he didn't want to, but actually he did —

Then Adam looked away again, because he couldn't keep his eyes on it anymore. He could feel himself going mad trying to name it.

"What is it?" he asked.

Ronan eyed it, but sideways, with his chin tilted away from it. He looked younger than he usually did, his face softened by uncertainty and caution. Sometimes Gansey would tell stories of the Ronan he had known before Niall had died; now, looking at this fallible Ronan, Adam thought he might be able to believe them.

Ronan said, "A piece of Cabeswater. A piece of a dream. It's what I asked for. And this is . . . this is what I think it should look like, probably."

Adam felt the truth of it. This awful and impossible and lovely object was what a dream was when it had nothing to inhabit. Who was this person who could dream a dream into a concrete shape? No wonder Aglionby bored Ronan.

Adam looked at it. He looked away.

He asked, "Does it work?"

Ronan's expression sharpened. He held the dream *thing* beside the cow's face. Light, or something like light, reflected off it onto Ronan's chin and cheeks, rendering him stark and handsome and terrifying and someone else. Then he blew on it. His breath passed through the word, the mirror, the unwritten line.

Adam heard a whisper in his ear. Something moved and stirred inside him. Ronan's eyelashes fluttered darkly.

What are we doing —

The cow shifted.

Not a lot. But her head tilted; one ear flicked. Like she was sleepily jostling a fly from it. A muscle shivered near her spine.

Ronan's eyes were open; fires burned in them. He breathed again, and again the cow twitched her ear. Tensed her lips.

But she did not wake, and she did not rise.

He retreated, hiding the dream from Adam's maddened sight.

"I'm missing something still," Ronan said. "Tell me what I'm missing."

"Maybe you just can't wake someone else's dream."

Ronan shook his head. He didn't care if it was impossible. He was going to do it anyway.

Adam gave in. "Power. It takes a lot of power. Most of what I'm doing when I repair the ley line is making better connections so the energy can run more efficiently. Maybe you could find a way to direct a stub of the line out here."

"Already thought of it. Not interested. I don't want to make a bigger cage. I want to open the door."

They regarded each other. Adam fair and cautious, Ronan dark and incendiary. This was Ronan at his most truthful.

Adam asked, "Why? Tell me the real reason."

"Matthew —" Ronan began again, and stopped again.

Adam waited.

Ronan said, "Matthew's mine. He's one of mine."

Adam didn't understand.

"I *dreamt* him, Adam!" Ronan was angry — every one of his emotions that wasn't happiness was anger. "That means that when — if something happens to me, he becomes just like them. Just like Mom."

Every memory Adam possessed of Ronan and his younger brother reframed itself. Ronan's tireless devotion. Matthew's similarity to Aurora, a dream creature herself. Declan's eternal position as an outsider, neither a dreamer nor a dream.

Only half of Ronan's surviving family was real.

"Declan told me," Ronan said. "A few Sundays ago." Declan had left for college in D.C., but he still made the four-hour drive each Sunday to attend church with his brothers, a gesture so extravagant that even Ronan seemed forced to admit that it was kindness.

"*You* didn't know?"

"I was three. What did I know?" Ronan turned away, lashes low over his eyes, expression hidden, burdened by being born, not made.

Lonesome.

Adam sighed and sat down beside the cow, leaning against her warm body, letting her slow breaths lift him. After a moment, Ronan slipped down beside him and the two of them looked out over the sleepers. Adam felt Ronan glance at him and away. Their shoulders were close. Overhead, rain began to tap on the roof again, another sudden storm. Possibly their fault. Possibly not.

"Greenmantle," Ronan said abruptly. "His web. I want to wrap it around his neck."

"Mr. Gray's right, though. You can't kill him."

"I don't want to kill him. I want to do to him what he's threatening to do to Mr. Gray. To show him how I could make his life hell. If I can dream *that*" — Ronan jerked his chin toward the blanket that held his dream object — "surely I can dream something to blackmail him with."

Adam considered this. How difficult would it be to frame someone if you could create any kind of evidence you needed? Could it be done in such a way that Greenmantle couldn't undo it and come after them twice as dangerous?

"You're smarter than I am," Ronan said. "Figure it out."

Adam made a noise of disbelief. "Didn't you just ask me to research Greenmantle in all my spare time?"

"Yeah, and now I'm telling you why I asked you."

"Why me?"

Ronan laughed suddenly. That sound, as crooked and joyful and terrible as the dream in his hand, should have woken these cattle if nothing else did.

"I hear if you want magic done," he said, "you ask a magician."

21

It was quite late when Blue called that night, long after Malory had returned in the Suburban, long after Ronan had returned in the BMW.

No one else was awake.

"Gansey?" Blue asked.

Something anxious in him stilled.

"Tell me a story," she said. "About the ley line."

He went at once to the kitchen-bathroom-laundry, moving as quietly as he could, thinking of something to tell her. As he sat on the floor, he said in a low voice, "When I was in Poland, I met this guy who had sung his way across Europe. He said as long as he was singing he could always find his way back to 'the road.'"

Blue's voice was quiet, too, on the other end of the phone. "I assume you mean a corpse road, not an interstate."

"Mystical interstate." Gansey scrubbed a hand through his hair, remembering. "I hiked with him for about twenty miles. I had a GPS. He had the song. He was right, too. I could turn him around a million times and lead him astray two million times and he could always head back to the ley line. Like he was mag-netized. So long as he was singing."

"Was it always the same song? Was it *the murder squash song*?"

"Oh, God." The floorboards felt cool on the bottoms of his bare feet. For some reason, the feeling was sensuous and distracting, a reminder of Blue's skin. Gansey closed his eyes. "This was a simpler time, before that had been unleashed on the world. I cannot believe how obsessed Ronan and Noah are with that song. Ronan was talking about getting the T-shirt. Can you imagine him in it?"

Blue snickered. "What happened to the Polish guy?"

"I assume he's singing his way across Russia now. He was going left to right. West-to-east, I mean."

"What was Poland like?"

"Prettier than you're thinking. So pretty."

She paused. "I'd like to go, one day."

He didn't give himself time to doubt the wisdom of saying it out loud before he replied, "I know how to get there, if you want company."

After a long pause, Blue said, in a different voice, "I'm going to go sing myself to sleep. See you tomorrow. If you want company."

The phone went quiet. It was never enough, but it was something. Gansey opened his eyes.

Noah sat against the doorjamb of the kitchen-bathroom-laundry. When Gansey thought about it, he thought that possibly he had been sitting there for a long time.

There was nothing inherently guilty about the moment except that Gansey burned with guilt and thrill and desire and the nebulous feeling of being truly known. It was on the inside of him, and the inside was all Noah ever really paid attention to.

The other boy wore a knowing expression.

"Don't tell the others," Gansey said.

"I'm dead," Noah replied. "Not stupid."

22

I'm very angry at you," Piper said, voice very close. Greenmantle was lying on top of the replacement rental, his arms crossed over his chest and his knees close together, thinking about early medieval burial positions.

"I know," Greenmantle replied, opening his eyes. The sky overhead was jeeringly blue. "What about now?"

"The blood draw people were here today and you weren't. I *told* you to be here."

"I was here." He had spent the first hour after coming home lying on his face. A small percentage of medieval bodies were buried such; historians thought they were the graves of suicides or witches, though really, historians were such Guesser McGuessers, him the biggest of them all.

"You didn't answer when I called!"

"It doesn't change the fact that I was here."

"Was I supposed to come look for you on the car? Why are you even out here?"

"I'm having a creative block," Greenmantle said.

"About what?"

He rolled over to face her. She stood beside the car, wearing a dress that looked like it would take a wearying number of steps to remove. She was also holding a small animal with a jeweled collar. It had no hair apart from a long, silky tuft that grew from its head, the precise same shade of blond that Piper sported.

"What is that?" Greenmantle asked. He deeply suspected it was the physical manifestation of his bad mood.

"Otho."

He sat up. The rental car sighed noisily. "Is it a cat? A rodent? What species, pray?"

"Otho is a Chinese crested."

"Chinese crested what?"

"Don't be a dick."

Because Greenmantle had humans to pant and follow him around with mindless fidelity, he had never felt the urge to get a dog, but when he was younger, he had sometimes imagined acquiring a canine with a fringey tail and legs. The kind that picked up ducks, whatever kind that was. Otho looked as if ducks might pick him up instead. "Is it going to get bigger? Or grow hair? Where did it come from?"

"I ordered it."

"From the *Internet*?"

Piper rolled her eyes at his innocence. "Why is it you're having a creative block again?"

"I need to find Mr. Gray's psychic girlfriend, but it turns out no one knows where she is. She disappeared right when he screwed me over." Greenmantle slid off the car. Carefully. He was stiff from his aerial burial. "How am I supposed to destroy what he needs when it's already gone? They reported her missing and everything. I stole the report and it said that apparently she told her family she was 'underground.'"

He had not stolen the report. He had paid someone to steal the report. But the story sounded better with him as the hero.

Piper said, "Underground? Psychic? That is relevant to my interests."

"Why?"

"While you were out frittering, I did things," she said. "Follow me."

She led him through the garage and through a door that he had been unaware existed and up into the house itself. The stairs emerged in the hallway by the bedroom. She asked, "Didn't you read any of Mr. Gray's reports?"

He stared at her to indicate that he didn't understand the question.

She said, slowly, as if he was an idiot, "When he was here looking for this stupid thing for you. Did you read what he wrote back to you? About tracking it?"

"Oh, those. Of course not."

"Then why did you ask him to send them? There were a million."

"I just wanted him to feel busy and watched. There's nothing like paperwork to make a man feel oppressed. Why?"

Piper opened a closet door to reveal a collection of parcels branded with shipping labels bearing her name. Presumably Otho had arrived in one of them. "I read them in the bath. Then I read those other reports from the other barely literate thugs you hired. And then I read the news."

Greenmantle didn't care for the concept of her reading the Gray Man's letters while naked. He opened one box and peered inside. "What are these?"

"Knee pads," she said, and put them on to demonstrate. She was obnoxiously pleased with herself. "That horrible man talked about these underground psychic energy lines here that were interfering with his search because they were so strong. I thought, stronger is better. I thought, I would like to see whatever this is that is so strong because I am bored out of my mind. And how hard can they be to find? So I ordered these things."

"Knee pads?"

"I'm not interested in cracking a patella while wandering around underground. Doesn't it seem to you, Colin, like the Gray Man's crazy psychic bimbo might be in the same place as these crazy psychic lines? Lucky for you, I bought some knee pads for you, too."

He was so impressed with her ingenuity. He should not have been, really, because Piper was a very ingenious creature. It was just that she didn't normally use her powers for good, and when she did, they usually weren't pointed at him. It was just, he hadn't thought she really liked him.

Because she was so saucily pleased with herself, he didn't have the heart to tell her that he would have rather paid someone else to go underground to look for the Gray Man's girlfriend. And the dress, it turned out, had a hidden zipper, and came off very easily. Piper left the knee pads on.

Afterward, Greenmantle realized he had forgotten the dog was there, which seemed vaguely distasteful.

"So you're going to be a spelunker," he said.

"I don't know what that means."

"Cavewoman. In the most basic linguistic sense, you're going to be a cavewoman."

"Whatever. You're coming with me."

23

B lue was not so much a terrible driver as a terrified one. Because she had not, as Jesse Dittley pointed out, eaten her greens, she had to adjust the seat as close to the pedals as possible. She clutched the steering wheel with the grace of a performing bear. Everything on the dash shouted for her attention. Lights? Speed! Air on face? Air on feet! Fuel-oil-engine! Strange bacon symbol?

She drove very slowly.

The worst part of her terror was how *angry* it made her. There was nothing about the process of driving that seemed confusing or unfair to her. She'd aced her driver's test. She knew what everything apart from the bacon symbol did. Road signs never perplexed; right of way was logical. She was a champion yielder. Give her forty minutes and she could parallel park the Fox Way Ford in any place you liked.

But she could never forget that she was a tiny pilot in a several-thousand-pound weapon.

"It's just because you haven't practiced enough," Noah said generously, but he was gripping the door handle in a way that seemed redundant for the already dead.

Of *course* she hadn't practiced enough. There was only one car at 300 Fox Way, and so it was in high demand. Blue could bike to school, work, and Monmouth Manufacturing, so the car generally fell to people who worked outside of the house or were running errands. At her current rate of practice-acquisition, Blue imagined she would be comfortable behind the wheel of a car sometime in her forties.

This afternoon, however, she'd managed to stake a claim on the car for a few hours. Noah was her only companion on this field trip: Gansey had some raven boy activity, Adam was working or sleeping off work, and Ronan had vanished into the ether as per usual.

They were headed to Jesse Dittley's.

"We are going so slow," Noah said, craning his neck to observe the inevitable queue behind them. "I think I just saw a tricycle pass us."

"Rude."

After a protracted journey, Blue pulled into Jesse Dittley's rutted driveway. The farm looked less mystical in the sun, less gloomy and cursed, and more grubby and rusted. Engaging the parking brake ("We're not even on a *hill!*" protested Noah), she got out, and headed onto the porch. She pounded on the door.

It took a few attempts before he opened it. When he did, she was shocked by the height of him again. He was wearing another white tank top, or perhaps it was the same one. Their height difference made it difficult to discern his expression.

"OH, YOU."

"Yep," Blue reported. "Here is my bargain: You let us explore your cave, and I'll clean up your yard. I have good credentials."

He leaned and she stretched and he accepted the business cards she'd made and cut herself to convince old ladies in her neighborhood to pay her for putting in bedding plants. While he read it, she studied his face and his body, searching for signs of underlying illness, some preexisting condition that might strike him down later. Something besides a cursed cave. She saw nothing but height, and more height.

Finally, he replied, "ARE YOU TRYING TO TELL ME YOU DON'T LIKE WHAT I'VE DONE WITH THE PLACE?"

"Every yard can use some flowers," Blue replied.

"DAMN STRAIGHT." He shut the door in her face.

Noah, who had been standing unobserved beside her, said, "Is that what you meant to happen?"

It wasn't, but before she had a chance to formulate her next plan, he re-opened the door, but this time he was wearing some camouflage-printed rubber boots. He stepped out onto the porch.

"HOW LONG WILL IT TAKE YOU?"

"Today."

"TODAY?"

"I'm super fast."

He stepped off the stairs and surveyed the yard. It was hard to tell if he was analyzing if Blue could accomplish it in an afternoon or contemplating if he would miss the ruin once it was gone.

"YOU CAN PUT THE THINGS IN THE BACK OF THAT TRUCK OVER THERE."

Blue followed his gaze to a rusted brown truck that she'd mistaken for yet more junk.

"Great," she said, and meant it. It would save her time if she didn't have to slowly drive the car to the dump four times. "So, it's a deal?"

"IF YOU GET IT DONE TODAY."

She gave him a thumbs-up. "Okay, then. I'm going to get to work. Time's wasting."

Jesse sort of seemed to look at Noah, but then his eyes slid off and back to Blue. He opened his mouth, and for a moment, she thought he *had* seen Noah and was going to say something about him, but in the end, he just said, "I'M PUTTING WATER ON THE PORCH FOR YOU. MIND THE DOGS DON'T DRINK IT."

There were no dogs in evidence, but it was possible they were hiding behind one of the discarded sofas in the yard. In any case, she was touched by the gesture.

"Thanks," she said. "That's kind of you."

This gratitude apparently gave Jesse the confidence he needed to say what he'd been thinking before. Scratching his chest, he squinted at her in her shredded T-shirt and bleached jeans and combat boots.

"YOU'RE A TINY THING. YOU SURE YOU CAN DO THIS?"

"It's forced perspective. It's because you ate your greens. I'm larger than I look to you. Do you have a chain saw?"

He blinked. "YOU'RE CUTTING DOWN TREES?"

"No. Sofas."

While he went looking for a chain saw within his house, Blue pulled on her gloves and got to work. She did the easy bits first, picking up bits of scrap metal the size of puppies and cracked plastic buckets with weeds growing through them. Then she dragged timbers with nails jutting from them and broken sinks with rainwater film in their basins. When Jesse Dittley appeared with a chain saw, she produced oversized rose-tinted sunglasses from the car to serve as eye protection and began to hack the larger things in the yard into more manageable pieces.

"MIND SNAKES," Jesse Dittley warned from the porch as she paused to catch her breath. Blue didn't understand what he meant until he gestured toward the weeds around the porch with an ominous shake of his hand.

"I get along with snakes," Blue said. Most animals weren't dangerous if you knew how to give them safety margins. She dragged the back of her hand over her sweaty forehead and accepted the glass of water he gave her. "You don't have to babysit me, you know. I can manage this."

"YOU'RE A QUEER LITTLE THING," Jesse Dittley decided. "LIKE ONE OF THEM ANTS."

She tipped her head back to look at him. "How do you reckon?"

"THEM ANTS THAT WAS ON THE TELEVISION. IN SOUTH AMERICA OR AFRICA OR INDIA. CARRY TEN TIMES THEIR OWN WEIGHT."

Blue was flattered, but she said sternly, "All ants can carry ten times their own weight, can't they? Normal ants?"

"THESE DID BETTER THAN NORMAL ANTS. WISH I COULD REMEMBER HOW THEY DID BETTER. SO I COULD TELL YOU."

"Are you trying to say I'm a better sort of ant?"

Jesse Dittley blustered. "DRINK YOUR WATER."

He retreated indoors. With a grin, Blue got back to work. Noah mucked about in the trunk of the car; she'd put a few bags of mulch and some bedding plants in there, and some more in the backseat. He pulled a bag of mulch out halfway, tore it, and exploded wood chips across the driveway.

"Whoopsie."

"Noah," Blue said.

"I know." He began to painstakingly pick up each sliver of mulch as she continued tidying the junk.

It was hard work, but satisfying, a little like vacuuming. It was nice to be able to see the effect right away. Blue was good at sweating and ignoring singeing muscles.

As the sun lowered, the yard darkened, and the sparse trees seemed closer. She couldn't help but feel *watched* in their presence. Most of this, she knew, was because of Cabeswater. She would never forget the sound of a tree speaking, or that day when she'd discovered that intelligent, alien creatures completely surrounded her. These trees were probably just ordinary trees.

Only she wasn't sure anymore if there was such a thing as an ordinary tree. Perhaps in Cabeswater they were able to be heard because of the ley line. Perhaps out here, trees were robbed of their voices.

But I am a battery, she thought. She considered how she'd pulled the plug on Noah before. She wondered if it was possible to do it the other way.

"Sounds tiring," Noah commented.

He wasn't wrong. Blue had been exhausted after the church watch in April, when dozens of spirits had drawn from her. Maybe a middle ground, then.

So were these trees speaking, or was that just the wind?

Blue paused in her patting of mulch and rocked back on her heels. She lifted her chin to look at the trees that enclosed the Dittley property. Oaks, thorns, some redbuds, some dogwoods.

"Are you speaking?" she whispered.

There was precisely no more or no less than what she'd felt and heard before: a rustle in the leaves, a movement in her feet. As if the grass itself was shifting. It was hard to tell precisely where it was coming from.

She thought she heard, faint and thin . . .

tua tir e elintes tir e elintes

. . . but maybe it was just the wind, high and impending between slivers of branches.

She tried to hear it again, to no avail.

They were going to lose light soon, and Blue wasn't thrilled about the idea of driving slowly back in the dark. At least they were finally doing the truly pleasant part — the planting of the flowers, making it look done. Noah had enough strength to help with this, and he knelt beside her in a friendly way, pawing holes in the dirt for the root balls.

At one point, though, she glanced over in the failing light and caught him placing an entire plant into the hole and knocking dirt over all of it, blossoms included.

"Noah!" she exclaimed.

He looked at her, and there was something quite blank about his face. His right hand swept another clump of dirt over petals. It was an automatic gesture, like his hand was disconnected from the rest of him.

"Not that," Blue said, not sure what she was saying, only that she was trying to sound kind and not horrified. "Noah, pay attention to what you're doing."

His eyes were infinity black, and fixed on her face in a way that rose hair on her neck. His hand moved again, crushing more dirt over the flowers.

Then he was closer, but she had not seen him move. His black eyes were locked on hers, his head twisted in a very unboy-like way. There was something altogether Noah-less about him.

The trees shivered overhead.

The sun was nearly gone; the most visible thing was the dead white of his skin. The crushed hole in his face where he had first been hit.

"Blue," he said.

She was so relieved.

But then he added, "Lily."

"Noah —"

"Lily. Blue."

She stood up, very slowly. But she was no farther from him. Somehow he had stood at the same moment as her, perfectly mirroring, eyes locked on her still. Her skin was freezing.

Throw up your protection, Blue told herself. And she did, imagining the bubble around herself, the impenetrable wall —

But it was as if he were inside the bubble with her, closer than before. Nose to nose.

Even malice would be easier to handle than his empty eyes, mirror black, reflecting only her.

Suddenly, the porch light came on, flooding light over and through Noah's body. He was a shadowed, checkered thing.

The front door banged open. Jesse Dittley slammed down the stairs, porch thundering, and strode hugely up to them. His hand shot out — Blue thought he was going to strike her, or Noah — and then he held up something flat between her face and Noah's.

A mirror.

She saw the pebbled back of it; Noah was looking into the reflective side.

His eyes darkened, hollowed. He threw his hands up over his face.

"No!" he shouted. It was like he had been scalded. *"No."*

He stumbled back from Jesse, Blue, and the mirror, his hands still pressed over his eyes. He was making the most terrible wailing sound — more terrible because now it was beginning to sound like Noah again.

He tripped backward over one of the empty pots, landing hard, and he stayed where he fell, his hands over his face, his shoulders shaking. *"No."*

He didn't remove his hands from his eyes, and Blue, with some shame, realized she was glad he didn't. She was quivering, too. She looked up (and up, and up) at Jesse Dittley, who loomed beside her with the mirror, the object looking small and toylike in his hand.

He said, "DIDN'T I TELL YOU THERE WAS A CURSE?"

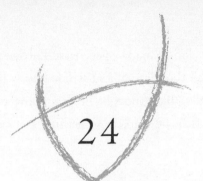

24

Jesse heated up two bowls of SpaghettiOs in the small kitchen while Blue sat on a piece of old furniture that was both a stool and a chair. He seemed even more like a giant in this small room; all of the furniture was doll furniture beside him. Behind him, the malevolent dark pressed against the window above the kitchen sink. Blue was glad of this yellow-toned oasis. She wasn't ready to drive home through this night, especially now that she'd be doing it alone. Noah had vanished, and she wasn't honestly certain if she was ready for him to reappear again.

The microwave beeped. Jesse explained as he placed the bowl in front of her that it wasn't really the cave that was cursed; it was something in the cave.

"And it kills Dittleys," Blue said, "and does terrible things to my friend."

"YOUR DEAD FRIEND," Jesse noted, sitting down opposite her at the tiny drop-leaf table. The mirror lay between them, facedown.

"That's not his fault. Why didn't you say you could see him?"

"I DIDN'T SAY I COULD SEE YOU, EITHER."

"But I'm not dead," Blue pointed out.

"BUT YOU ARE PRETTY SHORT."

She let it pass. She ate a SpaghettiO. It wasn't great, but it was polite to eat it. "What's in the cave that makes it cursed?"

"SLEEPERS," he replied.

This was relevant to Blue's interests.

"THERE ARE THINGS SLEEPING UNDER THESE MOUNTAINS. SOME OF THEM YOU WANT TO STAY SLEEPING."

"Do I?"

He nodded.

"Why would I want such a thing?"

He ate his SpaghettiOs.

"Don't tell me I'll understand when I'm older. I'm old already."

"DIDN'T YOU SEE YOUR FRIEND?"

She had. She had indeed.

With a sigh, he fetched a big book of photographs — the Dittley family album. It was the kind of experience Blue always suspected would be charming and intriguing, an insightful and secret peek into another family's past.

It was not that. It was very boring. But in between the stories of birthdays that went as you'd imagine and fishing trips that happened as fishing trips do, another story appeared: a family living at the mouth of a cave where something slept so restlessly that it peered out through mirrors and through eyes and fuzzed through speakers and sometimes made children tear wallpaper off the walls or wives rip out handfuls of their own hair. This restless sleeper got louder and louder through a generation until finally, a Dittley went into the cave and gave himself to the dark.

Later, the rest of the family took out his bones and enjoyed another few decades of peace and quiet.

And then there were some more photos about the Dittleys building a car port.

"And you're supposed to be next?" Blue asked. "Who will take over after you?"

"MY SON, I RECKON."

Blue didn't mention there was no evidence of anyone else in the house, but he must've picked up on it, because he added, "WIFE AND THE KIDS LEFT FIVE YEARS AGO, BUT THEY'LL BE BACK AFTER THE CURSE IS FED."

She was so startled by all of this that she ate all of the SpaghettiOs without thinking too hard about it. "I've never met someone else with a curse."

"WHAT'S YOURS?"

"If I kiss my true love, he'll die."

Jesse nodded as if to say *yep, that's a good one.*

"Okay, but why don't you just go? Sell this house and someone else can deal with the wallpaper and stuff?"

He shrugged — it was a mighty shrug. "THIS IS HOME."

"Right, but home could be on the other side of Henrietta," Blue persisted. "You could always just drive by this place and say *whoo hello house with bleeding walls see ya later!* Problem solved."

He took her bowl and dumped it in the sink. He didn't seem offended, but he also clearly didn't agree with her, so he wasn't going to comment on it any further.

"Also, when w —" Blue began, only to be interrupted by a furious pounding. It sounded like it was coming from everywhere. Curse? Noah? She pointed at the mirror in a questioning way.

Jesse shook his head and said, "FRONT DOOR."

He wiped his hands on a dish towel that looked like it needed to be wiped on something else, before heading to the front door. Blue heard it open, and then a murmur of voices that rose and fell.

Two people appeared in the doorway to the kitchen, with Jesse behind them. Bizarrely, it was Gansey and Calla. It was strange to imagine the two of them traveling anywhere together, and even stranger to wrap her mind around the two of them standing here in the Dittley kitchen. They were very focused on Blue.

Jesse gestured to her in a demonstrative fashion. "SEE?"

Bursting over the threshold, Calla threw out her hand to Blue, palm up. She was spitting acid. "The car keys. Right now. You are not driving that car again until you are eighty and graying. Right now. Hand them over."

Blue stared. "What? What?"

"You think you can just *go* and not call?"

"You told me no one else needed the car today!"

"And so you thought this meant you didn't have to call?"

Blue was about to retort about how she was a responsible human being and they didn't have any reason to be concerned for her whereabouts, but then she saw Gansey's expression just behind Calla. His fingers lightly touched his temple and his cheekbone, and his eyes looked off at nothing. Blue wouldn't have been able to interpret it a few months ago, but now she knew him well enough to realize that this meant relief: the unwinding of an anxious spring. He looked genuinely ill. She had worried both of them, badly.

"— half a dozen people looking everywhere for you and had begun to assume you were just dead in a ditch somewhere," Calla was saying.

"Wait, what? You were *looking* for me?"

"It's ten P.M.! You left six hours ago, and it wasn't as if you were going to work, was it? We had no idea! I was this close to calling the police again."

She let the *again* hang meaningfully. Blue didn't look at Gansey or Jesse.

"I'm going to call Ronan," Gansey said quietly, "and tell him he can go back to Monmouth."

Ronan had been looking for her, too? It would have been heartwarming, if she'd been in any danger whatsoever.

"I —" Blue realized before she finished the sentence that there was no argument: They were right, and she was wrong. Lamely, she ended, "I didn't think anyone would notice."

"Car," Calla said, "keys."

Blue meekly handed them over.

"Also, I never want to ride in that boy's horrible car ever again," Calla said. "You can ride back with him because I'm too angry to look at your *face*. I will say things I will regret." She started to storm back out, and then she stopped by Jesse, her nose curled. Their arms had touched; clearly she had just gotten some psychometric impression.

She said, "Oh, it was *you*."

He tilted his head down to observe her without malice. She stomped around the corner without further niceties or explanation.

"Er," said Blue, pushing to her feet. "Sorry about this."

"DON'T MENTION IT."

"Thanks for the SpaghettiOs. So, about the cave?"

"YOU STILL WANT TO GO IN IT AFTER THAT?"

"Like you said, it only kills Dittleys."

"THE *CURSE* ONLY KILLS DITTLEYS. THE CAVE MIGHT KILL OTHERS."

"I'm willing to take my chances, if you're willing to let us."

Jesse scratched his chest again. "FAIR IS FAIR, I GUESS."

They shook on it, Blue's hand minuscule in his.

"YOU DID GOOD WORK, ANT," he said.

Gansey stepped in then, putting his phone neatly into his pocket, fetching out his keys instead. There was still something stretched thin about his expression. He looked, in fact, like he had in the cave, his face streaked and unfamiliar. It was so strange to see him without his Richard Campbell Gansey III guise on in public that Blue couldn't stop staring at his face. No — it wasn't his face. It was the way he stood, his shoulders shrugged, chin ducked, gaze from below uncertain eyebrows.

"SHE WAS ALL RIGHT," Jesse assured him.

"My head knew that," Gansey said. "But the rest of me didn't."

25

I can't believe you aren't dead somewhere," Ronan told Blue. "You should be dead somewhere."

It was perhaps a sign of Gansey's irritation over the situation that he didn't correct Ronan on this front.

"Thanks for your concern," she replied.

The kitchen at 300 Fox Way seethed with bodies. Malory, Gansey, Ronan, and Adam were at the kitchen table. Persephone floated near the sink. Calla leaned broodily on the counter. Orla kept appearing in a doorway to steal peeks at Ronan before being shooed away. This claustrophobic, urgent night reminded Adam instead of a night many months before, after Gansey had broken his thumb and nearly gotten shot, after they'd discovered Noah was dead. Things had only just begun to change.

Adam discreetly checked the oven clock. He'd asked to come into the trailer factory two hours late in order to meet with the others tonight, and he wanted to make sure he didn't go over.

Blue asked, "Professor Malory, would you like some tea?"

Malory looked relieved. "I would love a cup of tea."

"Do you prefer, er, fruity or footy?" she asked. "If you were to have one or another in tea form?"

He considered. "Footy."

"Bold choice," Blue said. "Anyone else?"

Several heads shook. Adam and Gansey had both been vic-timized by the beverages of 300 Fox Way. The teas here were harvested from the yard or collected from the farmers' market, chopped and mixed by hand, and then placed in bags labeled with either the predominant ingredient or the intended effect. Some of them were easier to drink recreationally than others.

Calla said, "I went straight to bourbon."

She and Persephone toasted.

As Blue prepared tea and brought water to the Dog, Gansey said, "All right, here's the deal. We've found another cave, and anecdotally, someone is sleeping in it. It's time to decide what to do."

"There's no decision," Ronan said. "We go in."

"You say that because you didn't see Noah today," Blue told him as she set a mug down in front of Malory. "That one doesn't have any hallucinogenic effects, but you might experience some euphoria."

Gansey said, "Nothing I have ever drank here has ever made me experience anything close to euphoria."

"You've never had that one," she said. "Anyway, Noah was a pretty scary thing. Jesse, the man who owns the cave, says there's a curse." She outlined the curse.

"Why doesn't he just move?" Adam asked.

"Out of his family *home*?" Ronan asked, sounding both shitty and earnest.

"*Home* is putting it strongly," Gansey said. "I saw this place."

"You." Blue pointed at him. "Shut up before you say some-thing offensive. There's something else you should know. One of the women here foretold Jesse's death earlier this year. She didn't know him, but she knew his name."

Adam's head jerked up. Not because this was shocking information, but because Blue's voice had changed just a little bit, and Persephone and Calla were busily knocking back their drinks and not looking at each other all of a sudden. Adam, a secretive animal, was acutely tuned to other people's secrets. So he wasn't sure why there would be anything clandestine about the foretold death of a stranger, but he knew that Blue Sargent was telling a partial truth.

"Wait, wait," Gansey said. "So you're telling me that not only does this Jesse Dittley believe there's a curse on this place, but actually, he is right, and he's going to die."

"*Or* he's going to die because of something we do," Blue insisted. "That's why I brought it up. I feel we should make decisions responsibly."

"You guys have a death list?" Ronan broke in. "That is fucking dark. Am I on it?"

"Some days, I wish," Blue said.

"Can I see it?" Adam asked.

"What?"

"Can I see the list?"

Blue turned away to make herself a cup of tea. "I don't have it. Mom took it with her. I just remembered his name. I mean, I thought it was a girl, with an *ie* at the end, but the Dittley part was memorable."

Calla raised one sharp eyebrow, but said nothing.

Ah, Adam thought with grim and sudden certainty. *Here it is. So one of us is on it.*

"Never mind that," Gansey said. "Time's wasting and Adam has to go soon. The point is, are we going into this cave tomorrow?"

Which one of us?

Malory perked up. "Now would be a good time to point out that I will not be going into any caverns. I am happy to lend support from a location the sun is able to reach."

"Of course we're going in," Ronan said. "Why wouldn't we?"

"Risk," Gansey replied. "I can't stress how strongly unwilling I am to put anyone in this room in danger."

"Also, rabbits, remember there's more than one sleeper," Calla pointed out. "Three of them. One is for you to wake, and one is for you to *not* wake."

"And the one in the middle?" Ronan asked.

In her small voice, Persephone said, "These things just really always sound better in threes."

"Jesse also said that some things shouldn't be woken," Blue added, discreetly not allowing Adam to catch her eye. "So, yes, risk."

More than one of us?

"We went into the cave in Cabeswater," Ronan said. "The risk was the same. Maybe worse because we were clueless going in."

Maybe, Adam thought, it was Blue herself on the list. Maybe that was why she hid it from them all.

"Well, I agree with Ronan," Blue said, "but I'm also biased, because I want to find Mom and that's worth the risk for me."

Adam thought about his sessions with Persephone. Would she have bothered to teach him if she knew he was going to die?

She was looking at him now, black-eyes solid, as if challenging him to call out the secrets.

"There's something else we should talk about," Gansey began, hesitant. "And that's what we'll do if this *is* Glendower. If there's a favor when we wake him. I don't know for sure if there's only one, or multiple, and we should know what we're going to say in either scenario. You guys don't have to answer now, but think about it."

There had been a time when all Adam had thought about was the promise of that favor. But now he had only a year of school ahead of him and he was no longer under his father's roof and he could see a way out without Glendower's help. All that was left was to be asked to be free of Cabeswater.

And he wasn't sure he wanted that.

Gansey and Ronan were muttering about something else, Malory pitching in, but Adam couldn't focus on it anymore. He knew he wasn't wrong about Blue's caginess. He knew it in the same way that he knew when it was Cabeswater who woke him from his sleep and when he knew where he needed to go to repair the ley line. He knew it like truth.

He looked at his watch. "If we've decided, I have to go."

He did not. He had a little bit of time. But this couldn't wait. The supposition was growing inside him.

"Already?" Gansey asked, but not disbelievingly. "How rotten. Oh well."

"Yeah," Adam said. "But I've got this weekend and a bunch of days off after. Blue, could you help me get this thing out of the car?"

"What thing?"

He lied swiftly and proficiently. "The stuff you wanted. I can't believe you don't remember. The, the — fabric."

Persephone was still looking at him.

Blue shook her head, but at herself, not at him; rueful at her own lack of memory. She pushed off the counter as he fist-bumped Gansey and nodded to Malory and Ronan. He did his best throughout the parting to hold himself casually, though he felt charged with the unspoken secret. Together they headed back out the front door and down the dark walk to where his car was parked on the curb behind the glorious Camaro.

Out here, it was quiet and cool, the dry leaves rattling together like someone shushing a crowd.

"I don't remembe—" began Blue, and then broke off when Adam grabbed her arm and pulled her close.

"Which one of us, Blue?"

"Hey, don't —!" She wrenched her arm free, but she didn't step back.

"Which of us is on that list?"

She gazed studiously off into the distance, her eyes on a car on a far-off cross street. She didn't answer, but she didn't insult him by saying he was wrong, either.

"Blue."

She didn't look at him.

He stepped around her so that she couldn't *not* look at him. "Blue, which one of us?"

Her face was unfamiliar, all mirth scrubbed from it. She wasn't crying. Her eyes were worse than crying, though. He wondered how long she had been carrying this. His heart was thudding. He'd gotten it right. One of them was supposed to die.

I don't want to die, not now —

"Blue."

She said, "You won't be able to unknow it."

"I have to know," Adam said. "Don't you get it? That will be the favor. That's what I'll ask for. I need to know so we can make that what we ask, if there's only one."

She merely held his gaze.

"Gansey," Adam said.

She closed her eyes.

Of course. Of course he would be taken from them.

His mind supplied the image: Gansey convulsing on the ground, covered in blood, Ronan crumpled beside him in grief. It had been months since Cabeswater showed him the vision, but he had not forgotten it. Nor had he forgotten how, in the vision, it had been Adam's fault.

His heart was a grave.

If it's your fault, Adam thought, *you can stop it.*

26

Blue woke up angry.

She didn't remember what she dreamt, only that it was about her mother, and when she woke up, she could have hit something. She remembered when she had visited Adam one afternoon that summer and he'd kicked a box — that was how angry she was. Only it didn't seem to be worth kicking anything when there wasn't anyone around to see her do it.

She lay there and told herself to go back to sleep, but instead, she got angrier. She was tired of Persephone and Calla and her mother withholding information because Blue wasn't psychic. Of not being able to daydream of fancy colleges because she wasn't rich. Of not being able to hold Gansey's hand because they couldn't hurt Adam's feelings and not being able to kiss Gansey's mouth because she didn't want to kill him. She was tired of knowing that he was going to die and being afraid that her mother would, too.

Over and over, she heard Adam guess the truth: *Gansey.*

She threw off her blankets and angrily got dressed and angrily stormed into the phone room.

Orla sat there, painting her nails at one o'clock in the morning.

Blue froze in the doorway, intention written on her face.

"What?" Orla said. "Go ahead."

Blue didn't move.

"Oh, please. I'm not going to stop you. I was just trying to keep you from breaking your heart, but whatever, go do it," Orla said.

Blue stepped across the room and picked up the phone, glancing at Orla again suspiciously. Her cousin had returned to painting tiny mandalas on her nails. She didn't pretend not to be listening, but looked otherwise untroubled.

Blue called Gansey.

He picked up at once. "I wasn't sleeping."

"I know," she replied. "Come get me."

There was something unfamiliar about him when he arrived in the Pig. Something ferocious about his eyes, some sort of bite in his faint smile. Something altogether hectic and unsettled. She stood on the ledge of his smile and looked over the edge.

This wasn't the Gansey she'd seen in the kitchen earlier; this was the Gansey she secretly called at night.

He didn't ask where she wanted to go. They were not allowed to speak of this, so they said nothing at all.

The Camaro idled on the silent late-night street. She climbed in and slammed the door.

Gansey — heedless, wild Gansey — tore into another gear as soon as they were out of the neighborhood. He sent the car hurtling from stoplight to stoplight and then, when he got to the empty highway, he let the car frantically climb in speed, his hand a fist over the gearshift.

They were driving east, toward the mountains.

Blue turned on the radio and messed with Gansey's music until she found something worth playing loudly. Then she wrestled down her window so that the air screamed over her. It was too cold for that, really, but Gansey reached in the backseat without taking his eyes off the road and dragged his overcoat to the front. She put it on, shivering when the silk lining chilled her bare legs. The collar smelled of him.

They didn't speak.

The radio tripped and waltzed. The car roared. The wind buffeted inside the cab. Blue put her hand on top of Gansey's and held it, white-knuckled. There wasn't another soul on the road but them.

They drove to the mountains — up, up, and through the pass.

The peaks were black and forbidding in the half-light of the headlights, and when they reached the very highest point in the pass, Gansey's fingers tightened beneath hers as he downshifted and hurtled the car around a U-turn back the way they had come.

They sped back to Henrietta, past eerily vacant parking lots of shops, past silent townhomes, past Aglionby, past downtown, past Henrietta. At the other side of town, he slid around a corner to the new, unused bypass: four pristine lanes of streetlight-lined road from nowhere to nowhere.

He pulled over here, and he took his coat from her, and they switched places. She slid the seat up as close to the wheel as it would go and stalled the car, and stalled it again. He put his hand on her knee, fingers on skin, lifeline touching bone, and kept her from letting the clutch out too quickly. The engine revved, strong and sure, and the car surged forward.

They didn't speak.

The streetlights striped through the windshield as she made a pass up one side of the road, then turned and went the other way, again and again. The car was fearsome and willing — too much, too fast, everything all at once. The gearshift knocked under her fist when they were still and the gas pedal stuck and then surged when they were moving. Cool air from an under-dash vent whispered night air over her bare legs; heat from the thrumming engine burned the tops of her feet.

The sound: The sound alone was a monster, amplified when she could feel it vibrating in the gearshift, tugging at the steering wheel, roaring through her feet.

She was afraid of it until she hit the gas, and then her heart was pounding too hard to remember being afraid.

The Camaro was like Gansey tonight: terrifying and thrilling, willing to do whatever she asked.

She was bolder with each turn. For all its noise and posturing, the Pig was a generous teacher. It did not mind that Blue was a very short girl who had never driven a stick before. It did what it could.

She could not forget Gansey's hand on her knee.

She pulled over.

She had thought it was such a simple thing to avoid kissing someone when she'd been with Adam. Her body had never known what to do. Now it knew. Her mouth didn't care that it was cursed.

She turned to Gansey.

"Blue," he warned, but his voice was chaotic. This close, his throat was scented with mint and wool sweater and vinyl car seat, and Gansey, just Gansey.

She said, "I just want to pretend. I want to pretend that I could."

He breathed out.

What was a kiss without a kiss?

It was a tablecloth tugged from beneath a party service. Everything jumbled against everything else in just a few chaotic moments. Fingers in hair, hands cupping necks, mouths dragged on cheeks and chins in dangerous proximity.

They stopped, noses mashed against each other in the strange way that closeness required. She could feel his breath in her mouth.

"Maybe it wouldn't hurt if I kiss you," he whispered. "Maybe it's only if you kiss me."

They both swallowed at the same time, and the spell was broken. They both laughed, again at the same time, shakily.

"And then we never speak of it again," Gansey said, mocking himself softly, and Blue was so glad of it, because she had played the words from that night over and over in her mind and wanted to know he had, too. Gently he tucked her hair behind her ears — this was a fool's errand, because it had never been behind her ears to begin with and wouldn't stay. But he did it again and again, and then he took out two mint leaves and put one in his mouth and one in hers.

She couldn't tell if it was very late or if it had become very early.

And now the catastrophic joy was wearing off and reality was sinking back in. She could see now that he was very nearly that boy that she'd seen in the churchyard.

Tell him.

She rolled the mint leaf over and over her tongue. She felt shivery with cold or fatigue.

"Did you ever think of stopping before you found him?" she asked.

He looked bemused.

"Don't give me that face," she said. "I know that you have to find him. I'm not asking you to tell me why. I get that. But as it gets riskier, have you ever thought of stopping?"

He held her gaze, but his eyes had gone far away, pensive. He was weighing it, maybe, the cost of this quest versus his undying need to see his king. Then he was focused on her again.

He shook his head.

She slouched back and sighed big enough to make her lips go *blbbphhbbbt*. "Well, okay."

"Are you afraid? Is that what you're asking?"

"Don't be stupid," she replied.

"It's okay if you are," Gansey said. "This is only mine, in the end, and I don't expect anyone else —"

"Don't. Be. Stupid." It was ridiculous; she didn't even know if it was the search for Glendower that would kill him — any old hornet would do. She couldn't tell him. Maura was right — it would just ruin the days he had left. Adam was right, too. They needed to find Glendower and ask for Gansey's life. But how could she know this huge thing about him and not *tell* him? "We should go back."

Now he exhaled, but he didn't disagree. The clock in the Camaro didn't work, but it had to be dangerously close to morning. They switched places; Blue curled again in his coat, feet up on the seat. As she tugged the collar up to cover her mouth and nose, she let herself imagine that this place was rightfully hers. That somehow Adam and Ronan already knew and were already okay with it. That her lips carried no threat. That Gansey was not going to die, that he wasn't going to leave for Yale or Princeton, that all that mattered was that he had given her his coat with its wheatgrass and mint on the collar.

As they headed back into downtown, they spotted a shiny vehicle, undoubtedly a raven boy car, pulled over by the side of the road. It was glittering and astronomical in the streetlights.

The ugly feeling of reality nudged Blue again.

"What's this —?" Gansey said.

"One of yours," she replied.

Gansey pulled up alongside and motioned for Blue to roll down her window.

An equally astronomical and glittering black-haired boy sat behind the wheel of the other car.

"You're a chick," he said to her, puzzled.

"Twenty points!" Blue replied tensely. "Heck, have thirty, because it's late and I'm feeling generous."

"Cheng. What's going on?" Gansey said, leaning forward to see past her. His voice had changed immediately to his raven boy one, which made Blue suddenly annoyed to be seen in a car with him. It was like her anger from before had not been properly extinguished and now it only took the knowledge that she was a girl in a car with an Aglionby prince to reignite it.

Henry Cheng leapt out of his car to lean in the passenger window. Blue was distinctly uncomfortable to be this close to his sharp cheekbones.

He said, "I don't know. It stopped."

"Stopped how?" Gansey asked.

Henry replied, "It made a noise. I stopped it. It seemed angry. I don't know. I don't want to die. I have my whole future ahead of me. Do you know anything about cars?"

"Not electric ones. What kind of noise did you say it made?"

"One I don't want to hear again. I can't break it. I broke the last one and my father was *pissed*."

"Do you want a ride back?"

"No, I want your phone. Mine's dead and I can't walk by the road or I'll get raped by the locals." Henry kneed the side of the Camaro and said, "Man, this is the way to do it. American muscle you can hear from a mile away. I'm not very good at this WASP thing. You, on the other hand, are a champion — only I think you have it backward. It's supposed to be hanging with chicks during the day, boys at night. That's what my *halmeoni* used to say, anyway."

There was something terrible about the entire exchange. Blue couldn't decide if it was because it didn't require her, or because it was between two extremely rich boys, or because it was a concrete reminder that she had broken one of her most important rules. (Stay away from Aglionby boys.) She felt like a dusty and ordinary accessory. Or worse. She just felt — bad.

She mutely passed Gansey's phone to Henry.

As the other boy returned to his shiny spacecraft to place the call, she said to Gansey, "I don't like when your voice sounds like that, FYI."

"Like what?"

She knew it wasn't nice to say it, but her mouth said it anyway. "Your fake voice."

"I beg your pardon?"

"The one you do with them," she said. "With the other Aglionby bastards."

"Henry's all right," Gansey said.

"Oh, whatever, 'raped by the locals'?"

"That was a joke."

"Ha ha ha. Ha. Ha. Ha. It's a joke when someone like *him* says it, because he doesn't have to actually worry about it. It's just so typical."

"I don't understand why you're being this way. He's actually a little like you —"

Blue scoffed. "Oh *ho!*" She knew she was being over the top, but she couldn't seem to stop. It was just something about their handsome faces and handsome hair and handsome cars and easy confidence with one another.

"I just think it's probably a good thing that we can't really — we'll never —"

"Oh, is it?" Gansey asked, dangerously polite. "Why is that?"

"We're just not in the same place, is all. We have very different priorities. We're too far apart. It wouldn't actually work."

"Two seconds ago we were nearly kissing," he said, "and now it's all off because we stopped to let a guy use my phone?"

"It was never *on!*" She felt as furious as she had when she first woke up. More.

"Is this because I didn't agree that Henry was a bastard? I'm trying to see things from your point of view, but I am having a very difficult time. Something about my voice?"

"Never mind. Forget it. Just take me home," Blue said. Now she was really regretting — everything. She wasn't even sure where her argument had taken her, only that now she couldn't back down. "After he gives your phone back."

Gansey studied her. She expected to see her anger mirrored on his face, but instead, his expression had cleared. It wasn't happy, exactly, but he no longer looked confused. He asked, "When are you going to tell me what this is really about?"

This made her heave a great shuddered breath that was close to tears. "Never."

27

Gansey woke up in a terrible mood. He was still tired — he had lost hours of sleep to playing and replaying the events inside the car, trying to decide if he had been wrong or right or if it even mattered — and it was drizzling, and Malory was whistling, and Noah was cracking pool balls against each other, and Ronan was pouring breakfast cereal from the box into his mouth, and Gansey's favorite yellow sweater smelled too doggy to bear another wearing, and the Pig flooded and wouldn't start, and so now they were headed off to get Blue and Adam in the soulless Suburban and a brown sweater that looked exactly on the outside like Gansey felt on the inside.

This cave wasn't going to be anything but a cave, like they always were, so Gansey would have been fine staying in Monmouth for another four hours of sleep and doing it another day.

"It might as well be Wales out there with all this rain," Malory said, not sounding very pleased about it. Beside him, Adam was silent, expression troubled in a way Gansey hadn't seen in a while.

Blue, too, was sullenly quiet, with bags under her eyes to match Gansey's. Last night his coat collar had still been scented with her hair; now, he kept turning his head in hopes of catching it, but like everything else in the wretched day, it had gone muted and dusty.

At the Dittley farm, Malory, the Dog, and Jesse settled in the house (Malory, unhopeful: "I don't suppose you have any tea?" Jesse: "DO YOU WANT EARL GREY OR DARJEELING?" Malory: "Oh, sweet heavens!") and the teens trekked across the damp field to the cave.

Adam asked, "Are you really bringing that bird into a cave?"

"Yes, Parrish," Ronan replied, "I believe I am."

There was no way to ask Blue about the night before.

He was too dull-edged to analyze it anymore. He just wanted to *know.* Were they still fighting?

Gansey remained in a bad mood as they applied their caving equipment and checked and double-checked their flashlights. Blue had acquired a used set of coveralls from somewhere and the sheer effort of not looking at her in them was taking what little concentration he could dredge up.

This wasn't the way it was supposed to be, he thought. It wasn't supposed to be crammed in between school events and Congressional tasks. It shouldn't have been a murky fall day, too humid for the season. It should have been a day where he had slept enough to properly *feel* things. It wasn't supposed to be any of the things that it was, and instead, it was all of them.

This was not, he thought as they descended, even how the cavern was supposed to look. Of course Glendower was under-ground — of course Gansey had known that he would have to be *buried* — but somehow he had imagined it lighter. This was just a hole in the ground like the rest. Dirt walls pressing in close, clawed and chiseled out when they grew too narrow to admit a coffin. A rabbit hole, down and down.

This was not how it had looked in his vision, back when he'd stood in Cabeswater's vision tree. But perhaps that hadn't been the truth.

Here was the truth. They were looking right at it.

"Stop it, Lynch," Adam said. He was at the back of the line; Ronan was right in front of him.

"Stop what?"

"Oh, come on."

Ronan didn't reply; they kept walking. They had only made it a few more yards, though, when Adam said, "*Ronan*, come on!"

They came to a slow and stuttering halt. Adam had stopped, and that had jerked Ronan to a stop, which had stopped Blue, and then, finally, Gansey. Chainsaw flapped up, wings grazing the close cavern walls. She came to rest on Ronan's shoulder again, her head pitched low and wary. She frantically cleaned her beak on his shirt.

"*What?*" Ronan demanded, flicking thumb and finger in the raven's direction.

"Singing," Adam said.

"I'm not doing anything."

Adam had his fingers pressed against one of his ears. "I know now — I know it's not you."

"You *think?*"

"No," Adam said, voice thin. "I know it's not you because I'm hearing it in my deaf ear."

A little chill scurried across Gansey's skin.

"What is it singing?" Blue asked.

Chainsaw's beak parted. In a trilling, sideways little voice completely unlike her coarse raven voice, she sang, "All maidens young and fair, listen to your fathers —"

"Stop that," Ronan shouted. Not to Chainsaw, but to the cave.

But this was not Cabeswater, and whatever it was did not attend to Ronan Lynch.

Chainsaw kept singing — a feat made more terrible because she never closed her beak. It was as if she was merely a speaker for some sound inside herself. "The men of all his land, they listened to their fathers —"

Ronan shouted again, "Whoever you are, stop that! She's *mine*."

Chainsaw broke off to laugh.

It was a high, cunning laugh, as much a song as the song.

"Jesus Christ," Gansey said, to hide the sound of every hair on his body standing up and both of his testicles retreating.

"Chainsaw," Ronan snapped.

Her attention darted to him. She peered at him, head cocked, something unfamiliar and intense about her. She had gotten large, her inked feathers ruffled round her throat, her beak savage and expressive. Right then, it was impossible to forget that she was actually a dream creature, not a true raven, and that the workings of her mind were the same mysterious stuff of Ronan Lynch, or of Cabeswater. For a dreadful second, too fast for Gansey to say anything, he thought she was about to stab at Ronan with that fierce beak of hers.

But she merely clicked her beak, and then she took flight down the passage ahead of them.

"Chainsaw!" Ronan called, but she disappeared into the black. "*Damn* it. Untie me."

"No," Adam and Blue said at once.

"No," agreed Gansey, firmer. "I don't even know if we should keep going. I'm not interested in feeding ourselves to a cave."

Chainsaw's defection felt wrong, too. Turned sideways, somehow, or inside out. Everything seemed *unpredictable* — which was in itself strange, because it had to mean that everything to this point had been predictable. No — inevitable.

Now it felt like anything could happen.

Ronan's gaze was still focused down the dark passage, his eyes searching for Chainsaw and not finding her. He sneered, "You can stay if you're too afraid."

Gansey knew Ronan too well to let the barb sting. "It's not myself I'm afraid for, Lynch. Reel it in."

"I think it's just trying to frighten us," Blue pointed out, quite sensibly. "If it really wanted to hurt us, it could have."

He thought of Chainsaw's beak, poised so close to Ronan's eye.

"Adam?" Gansey called down to the end of the line. "Verdict?"

Adam was quiet as he weighed the options. His face was strange and delicate in the sharp light of Gansey's head beam. Swiftly, and without explanation, he reached out to touch the cavern wall. Although he was *not* a dream thing, he was now one of Cabeswater's things, and it was hard not to see it in the way his fingers spidered across the wall and in the blackness of his eyes as they gazed at nothing.

Blue said, "Is he also . . ."

Possessed.

None of them wanted to say it.

Ronan lifted a finger to his lips.

Adam seemed to *listen* to the walls — *who is this person, is he still your friend, what did he give to Cabeswater, what does he become, why does terror grow so much better away from the sun* — and then he said, cautiously, "I vote we go on. I think the frightening is a side effect, not the intention. I think Chainsaw is meant to lure us in."

So they went on.

Down, and down, a more crooked path than the cavern in Cabeswater. That passage had clearly been worn by water, while this one seemed unnatural, clawed out instead of formed. Ahead of them, Chainsaw cawed. It was a strange, daytime sound to hear from the blackness ahead.

"Chainsaw?" Ronan called, voice rough.

"Kerah!" came the reply, from not too far away. This was the bird's special name for Ronan.

"Thank goodness," Blue said.

Gansey, at the head, spotted her first, clinging to a ledge in the rock wall, scrabbling with one foot and flapping a little to keep her position. She didn't flee as he approached, and when he held out his arm to her, she flew to him, landing heavily. She seemed no worse the wear for her possession. He half-turned. "Here's your bird, Lynch."

Ronan's voice was odd. "And there's your tomb, Gansey."

He was looking past Gansey.

Gansey turned. They stood at a stone door. It could have been a door to many things, but it was not. It was a carved tomb door — a stone armored knight with hands crossed over his breast. His head rested on two ravens, his feet, on fleurs-de-lis. He held a shield. Glendower's shield, with three ravens.

But this was wrong.

It was not wrong because this was not how Gansey would have expected Glendower's tomb to look. It was wrong because it was not supposed to happen this way, on this day, when his eyes hurt from sleeplessness and it drizzled outside and it was a cave they had only found a few days before.

It was supposed to be a clue, and then another clue, and then another clue.

It was not supposed to be thirty minutes of walking and a tomb door, just like that.

But it was.

"It can't be," Adam said, finally, from the back.

"Do we just — push it open?" Blue asked. She, too, sounded uncertain. This was not how it worked. It was the looking, not the finding.

"I feel peculiar about this," Gansey said finally. "It feels wrong for there to be no . . . ceremony."

Be excited.

He turned back to the tomb door as the others drew close. Withdrawing his phone, he took several photos. Then, after a pause, he typed in some location notes as well.

"God, Gansey," Ronan said, but it had made Gansey feel a little better about himself.

Carefully, he touched the seam around the effigy of the

knight. The rock was cool, solid, real; his fingers came away dusted. This was happening. "I don't think it's sealed. I think it's just wedged in. Leverage, maybe?"

Adam ran a finger along the edge. "Not much. It's not in very tightly."

He thought about the fact of the three sleepers, one to be woken, one to stay asleep. Would they know if this was the one to leave undisturbed? Surely — because if it was Maura's job to not wake this sleeper, there would be signs of her here.

But he didn't know. There wasn't a way to know.

Everything about this day was tinged by indecision and uncertainty.

Suddenly, the wall exploded in.

As dust swirled in the air and they fell back, coughing, Blue said, *"Ronan Lynch!"*

Ronan rebalanced in the midst of the slowly clearing cloud; he had kicked the tomb door in.

"That," he said thinly, to no one in particular, "was for taking my bird."

"Ronan, tell me now if I have to leash you, because I will," Gansey said. Ronan immediately scoffed, but Gansey pointed at him. "I'm serious. This is not yours alone. If this is a tomb, someone has been buried here, and you're going to give that person respect. Do not. Make me. Ask you. Again. For that matter, if any of us thinks they won't be able to contain themselves going forward, I suggest we turn around and come back another day or the party in question waits out here."

Ronan simmered.

"Don't, Lynch," Gansey said. "I've done this for seven years, and this is the first time I'll have to leave a place looking worse because I've been there. Don't make me wish I'd come without you."

This, finally, made it through the steel to Ronan's heart. His head ducked.

In they went.

It was like they had walked back into the past.

The entire room was carved and painted. The colors were unfaded by the sun: royal blue; berry purple; ruddy, bloody red. The carvings were sectioned into windows or arcades, bounded by lilies and ravens, columns and pillars. Saints looked down, watchful and regal. Martyrs were speared and shot, burned and impassioned. Carved hounds chased hares chased hounds again. On the wall hung a pair of gauntlets, a helmet, a breastplate.

It was too much.

"Jesus," breathed Gansey. He stretched his fingers to touch the breastplate and then found he couldn't. He drew his hand back.

He was not ready for it to be over.

He was ready for it to be over.

In the middle of the tomb was a stone coffin, waist-high, the sides heavily carved. A stone effigy of Glendower lay on top, his helmeted head pillowed on three carved ravens.

Do you remember saving my life?

Blue said, "Look at all the birds."

She trailed her flashlight over the walls and coffin. Everywhere, the beam found feathers. Wings garnishing the coffin. Beaks plucking fruit. Ravens sparring over shields.

The light landed on Adam's face. His eyes were narrowed and wary. Beside him, Ronan looked strangely hostile, Chainsaw hunched down on his shoulder. Blue took Gansey's phone from his pocket and took photos of the walls, the coffin, Gansey.

Gansey's eyes dragged back to the coffin. Glendower's coffin.

Is this really happening?

Everything was sideways, mirrored, not exactly as he'd imagined it.

He said, "What are we doing?"

"I think between all of us, we should be able to leverage the lid off," Adam replied.

But that wasn't what Gansey meant. He meant: *What are we doing? We, of all people?*

With a little, unfunny laugh, Blue said, "My hands are clammy."

They stood shoulder to shoulder. Gansey counted down, a breathless three-two-one, and then they strained. Unsuccessfully. It was like they were trying to shift the cavern itself.

"It's not even wiggling," Gansey said.

"Let's try the other side."

As they moved to the other side and lifted, fingers barely finding purchase, lid unmoving, Gansey could not help but think of the old fairy tales. He imagined this wasn't an ordinary weight holding the lid down; rather, it was unworthiness. They had not proven themselves in some way, and so Glendower was barred from them still.

He was relieved, somehow. That, at least, felt right.

"They didn't have heavy lifting equipment," Ronan said.

"But they could've had ropes and pulleys," Blue noted. "Or more people. Move over, I can't get my other hand on it."

"I'm not sure it'll make a difference," Gansey said, but they all pushed closer together. Her body was crushed against his. Ronan was crushed against Adam on the other side of him.

There was silence except for their breathing.

Blue said, "Three, two —" and they lifted as one.

The lid came off, suddenly weightless in comparison. It shifted and slid rapidly away.

"Grab it!" Blue gasped. Then, as Gansey started forward, "No, wait, don't!"

There was a sick, wrenching sound as the lid scraped diagonally off the opposite side of the coffin and careened to the floor. It came to rest with a smaller but more destructive sound, like a fist hitting bone.

"It's cracked," Adam said.

They drew closer. A coarse cloth hid the interior of the coffin from view.

This is not right.

Suddenly, Gansey felt deadly calm. This moment was so opposite to how his vision had portrayed it that his anxiety vanished. In its wake was nothing at all. He whisked the cloth free.

None of them moved.

At first he didn't understand what he was looking at. The shape of it was alien; he couldn't put it together.

"He's facedown?" Blue suggested, but hesitantly.

Because of course that was what it was, now that she'd said it. A figure in a dark surcoat, purple or red, shoulder blades jutted toward them. A mass of dark hair, more than Gansey had expected, darker than he would've expected. His hands were bound behind his back.

Bound?

Bound.

Something uneasy spasmed inside Gansey.

Wrong. Wrong, wrong, wrong.

Adam flicked the flashlight over the length of the coffin. Glendower's surcoat was hitched, exposing pale legs. Bound at the knee. Facedown, hands tied, knees tied. This was how they buried witches. Suicides. Criminals. Prisoners. Gansey's hand hovered, pulled away. It wasn't that his courage had left him; his certainty had.

This wasn't how it was supposed to be.

Adam swept the flashlight again.

Blue said, "Ah . . ." and then changed her mind.

The hair moved.

"Jesus shit *Mary fuck*," said Ronan.

"Rats?" Adam suggested, a suggestion so hideous that both Gansey and Blue recoiled. Then the hair moved again, and a terrible sound issued from inside the coffin. A scream?

A *laugh.*

The shoulders jerked, shifting the body in the coffin so that the head could turn to see them. As Gansey caught a glimpse of the face, his heart sped and then stopped. He was relieved and horrified.

It wasn't Glendower.

He said, "It's a woman."

28

The woman didn't wait for them to free her.

She wriggled and shimmied as they leapt back, and then she crashed down onto the floor, her hands and legs still bound. She landed right by Ronan's feet and snapped at his toes with a wild laugh.

He and Chainsaw both flapped back.

Blue exchanged a hectic look with Adam.

And now the woman was singing:

"Queens and kings
Kings and queens
Blue lily, lily blue
Crowns and birds
Swords and things
Blue lily, lily blue"

She broke off with a hysterical laugh that perfectly matched the one that had come out of Chainsaw earlier. Rolling onto her back so that she was looking straight up at Ronan's disgusted features, she cooed, "Cut me free, raven prince."

"God," he said, "what are you?"

She laughed again. "Oh! My rescuer came riding on a

milk-white steed and he said fair lady I can bring you what you need —"

Ronan wore an expression nearly identical to the one he'd worn when they picked up Malory. "She's crazy."

Gansey said, very calmly, "Don't touch her." Before, when they'd thought it was Glendower, he'd seemed badly shaken, but now he had more than recovered. Blue's heart was still charging from when the coffin lid had fallen and when the woman had slithered out. It wasn't that she wanted Gansey to be the boss of her, but she was relieved that he was going to at least be the boss of this moment, while she convinced her pulse to slow.

He made his way around the coffin to where the woman lay.

Now that she was faceup, Blue could see that she was young, in her twenties, perhaps. Her hair was enormous, raven black and wild, and her skin was as pale as the dead. Her surcoat was possibly the most incredible thing about her, because it was *real*. It did not look like a medieval costume. It looked like a real piece of clothing, because it was a real piece of clothing.

Gansey leaned over her and asked, in his polite, powerful way, "Who are you?"

"One wasn't enough!" she shrieked. "They sent another! How many young men are in my chamber? Please tell me it's three, the number of the divine. Are you going to untie me? It's very rude to keep a woman bound for any more than two or three or seven generations."

Gansey's voice was even calmer, or perhaps it was unchanged, and only seemed calmer in comparison to her rising cadence. "Was it you who possessed my friend's raven?"

She smiled at him and sang, "All maidens young and fair, listen to your fathers —"

"That's what I thought," Gansey said, and straightened. He glanced to the others. "I don't think it's a wise idea to untie her."

"Ah! Are you *afraid*?" she jeered. "Did you hear that I'm a *witch*? I have three breasts! I have a tail, and horns! I am a giant down below. Oh, I'd be afraid of me, too, young knight. I could get you pregnant! Run! Run!"

"Let's leave her," Ronan said.

Gansey replied, "If we abandoned people in caves because they were crazy, you'd still be back in Cabeswater. Give me your knife."

Ronan said, "I lost it."

"How did you — never mind."

"I have one," Blue said, feeling smug and useful. She produced her pink switchblade as the woman's gray eyes rolled up to look at her. Blue was rather afraid the woman would sing at her, but she just smiled, wide and knowing.

"I thought these were illegal?" Gansey asked, kneeling beside the woman. He seemed so unperturbed now, as if he were calmly dealing with a wild animal. He sliced the straps around the woman's knees, but left her hands bound.

"They are," Blue answered Gansey, but she didn't look away from the woman's eyes. The woman was still smiling, smiling, as if she were waiting for Blue to break and look away. But Blue had good practice with this, thanks to Ronan. So she just kept frowning back. She wanted to ask the woman how she spoke

English, and who she was, and was she okay after being in a box for quite a while, but the woman didn't really seem like a question-answering sort.

"I'm going to help you up," Gansey told the woman, "but if you bite me, I'm putting you back in that coffin. Do you understand?"

"Oh, you little rooster," said the woman. "You remind me of my father. Which is too bad."

Ronan was still staring at the woman, aghast, so Blue hurried forward to help Gansey. The woman was both warmer and realer than Blue had imagined. She was very tall; probably she'd eaten her greens. As Blue lifted her by an elbow, her enormously vertical nest of black hair tickled Blue's face, smelling of dirt and metal. She sang a little song about gifts and kings and internal organs.

"Okay, Gansey," Adam said warily, "what's your plan now?"

"We take her out, obviously," Gansey said. He turned to the woman. "Unless you'd prefer to stay."

She rolled her head back so that her hair crushed down flat upon his shoulder and her face was inches from his. "Does the sun still exist?" the woman asked.

Gansey used her hair to remove her head from his shoulder. "As of a few hours ago."

"Then take me! Take me!"

Adam was just shaking his head.

"I cannot wait," Ronan said, "to hear you explain this to Malory."

The clouds had disappeared when they emerged, replaced by a sky so bright and blue and wind-seared that they all had to duck their heads against the grit hurled through the air. The wind was so ferocious that it snapped Blue's bangs painfully against her cheeks. A flock of crows or ravens flew high overhead, tossed and catapulted. Ronan held Chainsaw to his chest as if she were still a young raven, protecting her from the wind.

As they walked back toward the Dittley house, leaning into the gusts, rain spattered intermittently out of the cloudless sky. Adam reached to wipe it from his cheek, and Blue said, "Adam, your face —"

Adam pulled his finger away; the tip was red. Blue held out her hand to catch another stray drop. Red.

"Blood," Ronan said, sounding factual rather than concerned.

Blue shuddered. "Whose?"

Gansey studied a red spatter on the shoulder of his jacket, lips parted in astonishment.

"Gansey," Adam called, pointing. "Look."

They stopped in the middle of the beaten-down grass to gaze into the bright day sky. On the horizon, something glinted furiously, like the sun off a faraway plane. Blue shielded her eyes and saw that the object had a fiery tail. She couldn't quite imagine what it would be, so visible in this bright daytime.

"A plane crash?" she asked.

"A comet," Ronan said with certainty.

"A *comet*?" echoed Adam.

Blue was more afraid now than when they'd been in possible danger in the cave. What were they *doing*?

"It starts!" the woman shouted. "It starts again! Round and round and round!"

She twirled in the field, her hands still bound behind her back. In the sunlight, the woman's regal beauty was more apparent. She had a rather large nose that was lovely in shape, sloping cheeks and forehead, dark quizzical eyebrows, and of course that impossibly tall hair snarling out above her already tall body. Her purple-red robe was like a smear of paint in the field.

Gansey watched the heavenly body burn a slow trail across the blue. He said, "Signs and portents. A comet was seen in 1402, when Glendower was beginning to rise."

"Ha!" shouted the woman. "Rise, rise, rise! Plenty of blood to be had then, too, plenty of blood to be had by all!"

This last bit had fallen into song once more.

Adam grabbed the woman's shoulder, stopping her from spinning. She rolled her body away from his hand like a drunk dancer and then fixed him with a wild-eyed gaze.

"You," she said, "are my least favorite. You remind me of both a man and a dog that I never liked."

"Noted," he replied. "Do we get a favor? For waking you?"

Of course, Blue thought stupidly. *Of course we should have thought to ask that at once.* It was all sleepers who supposedly granted a favor in the legends, not just Glendower. It seemed impossible that it wouldn't have occurred to all of them, but everything that had seemed obvious in theory was muddy and loud and frightening in practice.

The woman shrieked like the crows overhead, and then she shrieked again, and then Blue realized it was laughter. "A favor! For waking me? Little mongrel, I never *slept*."

Adam stared at her, raw, unmoving. He had let a single word — *mongrel* — slice down to his spine.

Gansey cut in, fearsomely polite. "We've been nothing but kind to you. His name is Adam Parrish, and that's what you can call him."

She bowed cartoonishly to Gansey, stumbling to a knee with her hands still tied.

"Forgive me," she sneered, "*my lord*."

He pursed his lips, dismissive of the gesture. "What do you mean that you didn't sleep?"

"Go to sleep, my little daughter," said the woman sweetly. "Dream of war. Only I didn't. I couldn't. I've always been a restless sleeper!" She cast a dramatic pose, legs spread to balance herself. A drop of blood had peppered her cheek like a tear. In a high-pitched voice, she called, "Help! Help! I'm not asleep! Come back! Come back!" Lower: "Did you hear something? Only the sound of my blood throbbing in my manhood! Let's go!"

Ronan's lip curled.

Blue was pretty sure she'd heard that sound in the halls of her high school. She asked, "Do you mean to say you've been awake for six hundred years?"

She chanted, "Give or take two hundred."

"No wonder she's mad as a cow's tit," Ronan said.

"Ronan," Gansey started, but then he clearly couldn't think of a good rebuke. "Let's go."

Inside the house, Jesse Dittley peered at the woman. She was nearly as tall as he was. "WHAT'S THIS?"

"Your curse," Gansey replied.

Jesse looked dubious. He asked her, "NOW TELL ME THIS: DID YOU EVER MAKE MY WALLS WEEP?"

"Only three or five times," she said. "Was it your father's blood that choked me to silence?"

"DID YOU KILL MY WIFE'S CAT?"

"That," she sang, "was an accident. Was it your grandfather's blood before that?"

"TAKE HER OUT OF MY HOUSE," Jesse said. "PLEASE."

As the boys bundled the woman out the other side of the house, Malory and the Dog hurrying after, Blue stayed behind. She stood by Jesse as he drew aside a shabby curtain to watch the boys persuading the woman to get into the Suburban. Blue got a good glimpse of her biting the Dog.

She felt a little less afraid now that she was no longer standing right next to the woman, although she couldn't stop seeing Chainsaw's beak eerily parted in false song, or forget the jump of her heart when the body first moved within the coffin. This crooked enchantment felt nothing like Cabeswater's organic magic.

"THAT ONE'S NOT ALL THERE."

Blue said, "She's been awake for hundreds of years. Somehow, when a Dittley died in the cave, it must've shut her up for a little bit. But we have her now. She was the curse. You don't have to go into the cave and die now."

Jesse let the curtain fall back into place. "DO YOU RECKON YOU CAN LOSE A CURSE AS EASY AS THAT?"

"Maybe. Probably! She's been in there for a really long time," Blue said. "As long as there have been Dittleys here. You heard her say she did those things."

"BUT WHAT ARE YOU GOING TO DO WITH HER?"

"I dunno. Something." She patted his arm. "You should call your wife, or your dog."

Jesse scratched his chest. "YOU REALLY ARE A VERY GOOD KIND OF ANT."

They shook hands.

Blue saw him watching out the window as they left.

They took the woman to 300 Fox Way, of course, where they found an extremely unimpressed Calla and a rather alarmed-looking Jimi and a fascinated Orla. Persephone took one look at the woman, nodded firmly, and then disappeared upstairs. Malory drank footy tea in the reading room. Adam and Ronan lurked in the hall, eavesdropping, too cowardly to face Calla's wrath.

And Calla was indeed in fine form. She barked, "Do you remember how I said that there were three sleepers, and Maura's job was to not wake one of them, and your job was to wake one of the others? Remember how I didn't say anything about the other one? *I did not mean bring her to my kitchen.*"

Blue felt equal parts relief and annoyance. The former because she had been worried that the woman might have been the sleeper that was not to be woken. The latter because they were in trouble.

She demanded, "Where else are we supposed to take her? Mom would've said to bring her here."

"Your mother has no common sense! We're not a halfway home." Calla walked right up to the woman, who gazed around the kitchen with something between bewilderment and regal insanity. "What's your name?"

"My name is that of all women," the woman replied. "Sorrow."

One of Calla's eyebrows momentarily considered punching the woman. She said, "Why didn't you just leave her?"

From the hall, Ronan shot a superior look at Gansey.

"Look, I understand she can't stay here," Gansey said. "But she's clearly more like you than like . . ."

Calla's expression turned volcanic. "Like what, sir? Like *you*, Richard Gansey? Is that what you were going to say? You think she's going to get her crazy on you but we're immune? Well, you've got another think coming, mister."

Gansey blinked rapidly.

A slow smile spread over the woman's face. "He's not wrong, witch."

Lava spilled over Calla's eyelids. "*What* did you just call me?"

The woman laughed and sang, "Blue lily, lily blue, you and I."

Both Blue and Calla scowled at the eerily familiar words. This woman must have been the one who had possessed Noah, just as she had possessed Chainsaw. Blue hoped this skill didn't extend beyond dream birds and dead boys.

"It's not too late to put her back," Ronan said.

"YOU TWO," roared Calla. Both Adam and Ronan winced. "Go to the store and get some supplies for her."

Adam and Ronan exchanged a wide-eyed look. Adam's look said, *What does that mean?* and Ronan's said, *I don't care; let's get out of here before she changes her mind.* Gansey frowned after them as they scrambled to the front door.

Persephone reappeared then, holding the sweater with mismatched arms. She peered at the woman in an appraising sort of way; it would have seemed rude if it hadn't been Persephone. The woman appraised her back, with a lot more of the whites of her eyes showing.

Finally, Persephone seemed satisfied. She offered up the sweater. "I made you this. Try it — oh! Why haven't they untied you yet?"

"We thought she might be . . . dangerous?" Gansey answered lamely.

Persephone cocked her head at him. "And you thought tying her hands would change that?"

"I . . ." He turned to Blue for help.

"She's an uncooperative witness," Blue provided.

"This isn't how we treat guests," Persephone said, faintly chastising.

Calla retorted, "*I* was unaware she was a guest."

"Well, *I* was expecting her," Persephone said. She paused. "I think. We'll see if the sweater fits."

Gansey cut his eyes over to Blue; she shook her head.

"You should untie me, little lily," the woman said to Blue. "With your little lily knife. It would be very fitting and circular."

"Why would it be fitting and circular?" Blue asked warily.

"Because your father is the one who tied me in the first place. Oh, *men*."

Blue was abruptly awake. She had been awake *before*, but she was now so much more than she had been the second before, that she felt as if she had been sleeping.

Her father.

The woman was suddenly in her face, hands still tied behind her back.

"Oh, yes. *Suitable punishment*, he said. Artemusssssssss." She laughed at the shocked faces in the room. "Oh, the things I know! Behold the way in which it glows, within a ring of water, within a moat, upon a lake, all in a ring of water!"

Earlier that year, when Blue had first met the boys, there had been a moment when she had been suddenly struck by how she was being drawn into their tangled lives. Now she realized that she had never been *drawn in*. She had been there all along, together with this woman, and all the other women at Fox Way, and maybe even Malory and his Dog. They were not creating a mess. They were just slowly illuminating the shape of it.

With a frown, Blue took out the switchblade. Taking care not to cut herself or the woman's pale white skin, she sliced the worn bonds at her wrists. "Okay, talk."

The woman stretched her arms up and out, her face rapturous. She spun and spun, knocking glasses off the table and smashing her hands into the complicated light fixture hanging over the kitchen table. She tripped over shoes and kept going, laughing and laughing, ever more hysterical.

When she stopped, her eyes were electric and unhinged.

"My name," she said, "is Gwenllian."

"Oh," said Gansey, in a very small voice.

"Yes, little knight, I thought you knew."

"Knew what?" Calla asked suspiciously.

Gansey's expression was troubled. "You're Owen Glendower's daughter."

29

"I don't even know what to get. A kennel?" Ronan asked.

Adam didn't reply. They were in a large, glowing big box store looking at toiletries. He picked up a bottle of shampoo and put it back down. His clothing was still flecked with blood from the apocalyptic drizzle and his soul still smarted from the mongrel comment. Gwenllian — Gansey had texted Ronan her identity — had been in a cave for six hundred years and had gotten his number at once. How?

Ronan picked up a bottle of shampoo and tossed it in the cart Adam pushed.

"That one's fourteen dollars," Adam said. He found it impossible to turn off the part of his brain that added up the sum of groceries. Perhaps this was what Gwenllian could see in the furrow of his eyebrows.

The other boy didn't even turn around. "What else? Flea collar?"

"You already did a dog joke. With 'kennel.'"

"So I did, Parrish." He continued down the aisle, shoulders square, chin tilted haughtily. He did not look like he was shopping. He looked like he was committing larceny. He swept some toothpaste into the basket. "Which toothbrush? This one looks fast." He sent it plummeting in with the other supplies.

The discovery of Gwenllian was doing odd things to Adam's brain. Disbelief shouldn't have been an option after all of the things that had happened with the ley line and Cabeswater, but Adam realized that he still hadn't truly believed that Glendower might still be sleeping under a mountain somewhere. And yet here was Gwenllian, buried in the same legendary way. His final skepticism had been taken from him.

"What do we do now?" Adam asked.

"Get a doghouse. Damn. You're right. I really can't think of another joke."

"I mean now that we have Gwenllian."

Ronan made a sound that indicated he didn't find this line of thought interesting. "Do what we were doing before. She doesn't matter."

"Everything matters," Adam replied, recalling his sessions with Persephone. He contemplated adding deodorant to the cart, but he wasn't sure if there was any point getting it for someone who had been born before it was invented.

"Gansey wants Glendower. She's not Glendower." Ronan started to say something and then didn't. He hurled a bottle of shave cream into the cart, but no razor. It was possible it was for him, not Gwenllian. "I'm not sure we shouldn't stop while we're ahead, anyway. We have Cabeswater. Why do we need Glendower?"

Adam thought of the vision of Gansey dying on the ground. He said, "I want the favor."

Ronan stopped so abruptly in the middle of the aisle that Adam nearly ran the cart into the back of his legs. The six items in the bottom skittered forward. "Come on, Parrish. You still think you need that?"

"I don't question the things that moti —"

"Blah blah blah. Right, I know. Hey, look at that," Ronan said.

The two of them observed a beautiful woman standing by the garden section, attended by three male store workers. Her cart was full of tarps and hedge trimmers and various things that looked as if they might be easily weaponized. The men held shovels and flagpoles that didn't fit in the cart. They seemed very eager to help.

It was Piper Greenmantle. Adam said wryly, "She doesn't strike me as your type."

Ronan hissed, "That's Greenmantle's wife."

"How do *you* know what she looks like?"

"Oh, please. Now *that's* what we should be thinking about. Have you researched him yet?"

"No," Adam said, but it was a lie. It was difficult for him to ignore a question once it had been posed, and Greenmantle was a bigger question than most. He admitted, "Some."

"A lot," Ronan translated, and he was right, because, strangely enough, Ronan knew a great deal about how Adam worked. It was possible Adam had always been aware of this but had preferred to consider himself — particularly the more unsightly parts of himself — impenetrable.

With a last glance at the blonder Greenmantle, they made their way through the checkout line. Ronan swiped a card without even looking at the total — *one day, one day, one day* — and then they headed back out into the bright afternoon. At the curb, Adam realized he was still pushing the cart with its single bag nestled in the corner. He wondered if they were supposed to have gotten more things, but he couldn't imagine what they would have been.

Ronan pointed at the cart. "Get in there."

"What?"

He just continued pointing.

Adam said, "Give me a break. This is a public parking lot."

"Don't make this ugly, Parrish."

As an old lady headed past them, Adam sighed and climbed into the basket of the shopping cart. He drew his knees up so that he would fit. He was full of the knowledge that this was probably going to end with scabs.

Ronan gripped the handle with the skittish concentration of a motorcycle racer and eyed the line between them and the BMW parked on the far side of the lot. "What do you think the grade is on this parking lot?"

"C plus, maybe a B. Oh. I don't know. Ten degrees?" Adam held the sides of the cart and then thought better of it. He held himself instead.

With a savage smile, Ronan shoved the cart off the curb and belted toward the BMW. As they picked up speed, Ronan called out a joyful and awful swear and then jumped onto the back of the cart himself. As they hurtled toward the BMW, Adam realized that Ronan, as usual, had no intention of stopping before something bad happened. He cupped a hand over his nose just as they glanced off the side of the BMW. The unseated cart wobbled once, twice, and then tipped catastrophically onto its side. It kept skidding, the boys skidding along with it.

The three of them came to a stop.

"Oh, God," Adam said, touching the road burn on his elbow. It wasn't that bad, really. "God, God. I can feel my teeth."

Ronan lay on his back a few feet away. A box of toothpaste rested on his chest and the cart keeled beside him. He looked profoundly happy.

"You should tell me what you've found out about Greenmantle," Ronan said, "so that I can get started on my dreaming."

Adam picked himself up before he got driven over. "When?"

Ronan grinned.

30

"This house is lovely. So many walls. So, so many walls," Malory said as Blue entered the living room a little later. The cushions of the couch ate him gratefully. The Dog lay stiffly on the floor beside the couch, crossing his paws and looking generally judgmental.

Behind the closed door of the reading room, the murmur of Gansey's voice rose briefly before being buried by Calla's. They were fighting with Persephone, or talking while she was in the same room with them. It was hard to tell the difference.

"Thanks," said Blue.

"Where is that insane woman?"

Blue had just finished hauling all Neeve's things off the mattress in the attic so that Gwenllian could stay up there. Her hands still smelled like the herbs Neeve had used for her divination and the herbs Jimi had used to try to vanquish the herbs Neeve had used for divination. "She's up in the attic, I guess. Do you really think she's Glendower's daughter?"

"I see no reason to disbelieve," Malory said. "She does seem to be outfitted in a period dress. It's rather a lot to take in. It's a pity one can't publish it in a journal. Well, I suppose one could, if one wanted his career to be over in a conclusive way."

"I wish she would just talk straight," Blue said. "She says my father was the one who tied her up and put her to sleep, only she told us that she never slept. But that's impossible, isn't it? How can you just be alive and awake for six hundred years?"

The Dog gave Blue a thin, wry look that indicated he believed that was how Gwenllian had come to be the way that she was.

"It seems likely that this Artemus was also the individual who sent Glendower to sleep," Malory observed. "I don't mean to be rude, but the idea that he also fathered you strains the credulity rather."

"Rather," Blue echoed. She didn't have an emotional stake in it either way: Her father had always been a stranger to her, and whether or not he also turned out to be a six-hundred-year-old crazy person didn't change that. It was interesting that Gwenllian had been tied up and sent to sleep by someone named Artemus, and interesting that this Artemus person apparently looked a lot like Blue, and interesting that Maura had also said that Blue's father was named Artemus, but *interesting* wouldn't find Maura.

"Although one considers that tapestry," Malory said.

The old tapestry from the flooded barn. Blue saw it again — her three faces, her red hands. "What does one consider about it?"

"One doesn't know. Is she staying here?" Malory asked.

"I guess. For now? Probably she'll kill us all in our beds, no matter what Persephone says."

"I think it's wise that she stays here," Malory said. "She belongs here."

Blue blinked at him. Although the crotchety professor had grown on her since she'd first met him, she certainly wouldn't have pegged him for the sort to consider other people enough to be able to offer interpersonal insight.

"Would you like to know what service the Dog provides?" he asked.

This didn't seem to have any bearing on his previous statement, but Blue's curiosity devoured her. With restraint, she replied, "Oh, well. I don't want you to feel uncomfortable."

"I feel uncomfortable all the time, Jane," Malory said. "That's what the Dog is for. The Dog is a psychiatric dog. The Dog is trained so that if the Dog senses I am having anxiety, he does something to improve the situation. Such as sit beside me, or lie on my chest, or place my hand in his mouth."

"Are you anxious a lot?"

"It's a terrible word, *anxious*. It makes one think of wringing hands and hysteria and bodices. Rather I simply don't care for people because people — my, they are going at it, aren't they?"

This was because Calla had just shouted in the other room, "DON'T GIVE ME THAT VACUOUS PREP BOY STARE."

Blue had previously been pleased to not be looped into the serious discussion in the reading room, but now she was reconsidering.

Malory continued, "I was paired with the Dog directly before this trip, and I must say I did not imagine it would be so challenging to travel with a canine. Not only was it quite a thing to find a place for the Dog to relieve himself, the Dog was constantly trying to lie on my chest while I was standing in that dreadful security line."

The Dog did not look sorry.

Malory continued, "It is not the outside of people that bothers me, but the inside. Ever since I was a child, I have been able to see auras, or what-have-you. Personhood. And if the person —"

"Wait, did you say you could see *auras?*"

"Jane, I didn't expect you to be judgmental, of all people."

Blue was well familiar with the idea of auras — energy fields that surrounded all living objects. Orla had gone through a period in her teens of telling everyone what their auras said about them. She had told Blue that her aura had meant she was short. She had been a pretty awful teenager.

"I wasn't judging!" she assured Malory. "I was clarifying. This relates to the Dog because . . . ?"

"Because when people are too close to me, their auras touch me, and if too many auras touch me, it confuses me and makes me what doctors have foolishly called anxious. Doctors! Fools. I don't know if Gansey ever told you how my mother was murdered by the British healthcare system —"

"Oh, yes," Blue lied swiftly. She was very interested in hearing about how Malory saw auras, which was firmly in her circle of interests, and less interested in hearing about deaths of mothers, which was decidedly outside of her circle of interests.

"It's a shocking story," Malory said, with some relish. Then, because of Blue's face or stature, he told her the story. He finished with, "And I could see her aura slowly vanish. So you see, this is how I know that Gwenllian belongs in a place like this."

Blue dragged an expression back onto her face. "Hold on. What? I missed something in here."

"Her aura is like yours — it's *blue*," he said. "The clairvoyant aura!"

"Is it?" She was going to be extremely annoyed if this was how she had gotten her name — like naming a puppy *Fluffy*.

"That color of aura belongs to those who can pierce the veil!"

She decided that telling him that she couldn't, in fact, pierce the veil would only prolong the conversation.

"It's why I was originally drawn to Gansey," Malory continued. "Despite his mercurial personality, he has a very pleasant and neutral aura. I don't feel like I am with another person when I am with him. He doesn't take from me. He is a little louder now, but not very much."

Blue had only a very limited understanding of what mercurial meant, and that limited understanding was having a very bad time of trying to apply it to Gansey. She asked, "What was he like, back then?"

"They were glorious days," Malory replied. Then, after a pause, he added, "Except for when they weren't. He was smaller then."

The way he said *smaller* made it seem as if he wasn't talking about height, and Blue thought she knew what he meant.

Malory continued, "He was still trying to prove that he hadn't just hallucinated. He was still quite obsessed with the event itself. He seems to have grown out of that, fortunate for him."

"The event — the stinging? The death, I mean?"

"Yes, Jane, the death. He puzzled it over all the time. He was always drawing bees and hornets and stuff-and-such. Got screaming nightmares over it — he had to get his own place, since I couldn't sleep with it, as you might well imagine. Sometimes these fits would happen during the day, too. We'd just be toddling through some riding path in Leicestershire and next thing I knew he'd be on the ground clawing his face like a mental patient. I let him be, though, and he'd run his course and be fine like nothing had happened."

"How terrible," whispered Blue. She imagined that easy smile Gansey had learned to throw up over his true face. With shame, she recalled how she had once wondered what would have made a boy like *him*, a boy with everything, ever learn such a skill. How unfair she'd been to assume love and money would preclude pain and hardship. She thought of their disagreement in the car the night before with some guilt.

Malory hadn't seemed to hear her. "Such a researcher, though. Such a keen nose for hidden things. You can't train that! You have to be born with it."

She heard Gansey's voice in the cave, hollow and afraid: *"Hornets."*

She shivered.

"Of course, then he just went one day," Malory mused.

"What?" Blue focused abruptly.

"I should not have been surprised," the professor said in an offhand voice. "I knew he was a great traveler. But we were not truly done researching, I thought. We had a bit of a toss-up, patched it up. But then, one morning, he was just gone."

"Gone how?"

The Dog had climbed onto Malory's chest and now licked his chin. Malory didn't push him away. "Oh, gone. His things, his bags. He left much of it behind, what he didn't need. But he never returned. It was months before he called me again, like nothing had happened."

It was hard to imagine Gansey abandoning anything that way. All around him were things he clung to ferociously. "He didn't leave a note, or anything?"

"Just gone," Malory said. "After that, his family called me sometimes, trying to find out where he'd gone."

"His *family?*" She felt like she was being told a story about a different person.

"Yes, I told them what I could, of course. But I didn't really know. It was Mexico before he came to me, then Iceland after, I think, before the States. I doubt I know the half of it still. He picked himself up and moved so easily, so quickly. He had done it so many times before England, Jane, and it was old hat to him."

Past conversations were slowly realigning in Blue's head, taking on new shades of meaning as they did. She recalled one charged night on the side of a mountain, looking down at Henrietta lit like a fairy village. *Home,* he'd said, like it pained him. Like he couldn't believe it.

It wasn't exactly like the story Malory had just told conflicted with the Gansey she knew. It was more like the Gansey she'd seen was a partial truth.

"It was cowardice and stupidity," Gansey said from the doorway. He leaned on the doorjamb, hands in pockets, as he often did. "I didn't like good-byes, so I just abstained, and I didn't think about the consequences."

Blue and Malory both peered at him. It was impossible to tell how long he'd been standing there.

"It's very decent of you," he continued, "to not say anything about it to me. It's more than I deserved. But know that I've regretted it, a lot."

"Well," said Malory. He seemed profoundly uncomfortable. The Dog looked away. "Well. What is the verdict on your cavewoman?"

Gansey put a mint leaf in his mouth; it was impossible to not think of the night before, when he'd put one in hers. "She stays here, for now. That wasn't me, that was Persephone. I offered to fix the first floor of Monmouth. That might still end up being what happens."

"Who is she?" Blue asked. She tried the name: "Gwenllian." She wasn't saying it right — the double *lls* were not said anything like they looked.

"Glendower had ten children with his wife, Margaret. And at least four . . . not with her." Gansey said this part with distaste; it was clear that he didn't find this fitting for his hero. "Gwenllian is one of the four illegitimate on record. It's a patriotic name. There were two other very famous Gwenllians who were associated with Welsh freedom."

There was something else he wanted to say, but he didn't. It meant it was unpleasant or ugly. Blue said, "Spit it out, Gansey. What is it?"

He said, "The way she was buried — the tomb door had Glendower on it, and so did the coffin lid. Not an image of her. We can ask her, though getting real information out of her is quite a thing, but it seems likely to me that she was buried in a shill grave."

"What's that?"

"Sometimes when there's a very rich grave, or a very important one, they'll put a duplicate grave somewhere nearby, but easier to find, to give grave robbers something to find."

Blue was scandalized. "His own daughter?"

"Illegitimate," Gansey said, but he was unhappy as he did. "You heard her. As punishment for something. It is all so distasteful. I am starving. Where did Par — Adam and Ronan go?"

"To get supplies for Gwenllian."

He looked at his enormous and handsome watch with an enormous and puzzled frown. "Has it been long?"

She made a face. "Ish?"

"What do we do now?" Gansey asked.

From the other room, Calla bellowed, "GO BUY US PIZZA. WITH *EXTRA CHEESE*, RICHIE RICH."

Blue said, "I think she's starting to like you."

31

Ronan drove back to St. Agnes. Adam thought he meant to go to Adam's apartment above the church office, but when they got out at the street, Ronan veered off and headed to the main entrance of the church itself.

Although Adam lived above the church, he had not been inside it since he'd moved into his apartment. The Parrishes had never been churchgoers, and although Adam himself suspected there might be a God, he also suspected it didn't matter.

"Lynch," he said as Ronan opened the door to the dusky sanctuary. "I thought we were going to talk."

Ronan dipped his fingers into the holy water and touched his forehead. "It's empty."

But the church didn't feel empty. It was claustrophobic with the scent of incense, vases of foreign lilies, reams of white cloth, the broken gaze of a sorrowing Christ. It bled with stories Adam didn't know, rituals he would never do, connections he would never share. It was dense with a humming sort of history that made him feel light-headed.

Ronan hit Adam's arm with the back of his hand. "Come on."

He walked along the back of the dim church and opened a door to a steep staircase. At the top, Adam found himself on a hidden balcony populated by two pews and a pipe organ. A statue of Mary — probably Mary? — held its hands out to him, but that was because she didn't know him. Then again, she entreated Ronan, too, and she probably *did* know him. A few small candles burned at her feet.

"The choir sits up here," Ronan said, sitting at the organ. Without warning, he played a terrifically loud and shockingly sonorous fragment.

"Ronan!" hissed Adam. He looked at Mary, but she didn't seem bothered.

"I told you. No one's here." When Ronan saw that Adam still did not believe, he explained, "It's confession day up in Woodville, and they share our priest. This is when Matthew used to have his organ lessons because no one would be around to care how bad he sucked."

Adam finally sat down on one of the pews. Laying his cheek against the smooth back of it, he looked at Ronan. Strangely enough, Ronan belonged *here*, too, just as he had at the Barns. This noisy, lush religion had created him just as much as his father's world of dreams; it seemed impossible for all of Ronan to exist in one person. Adam was beginning to realize that he hadn't known Ronan at all. Or rather, he had known part of him and assumed it was all of him.

The scent of Cabeswater, all trees after rain, drifted past Adam, and he realized that while he'd been looking at Ronan, Ronan had been looking at him.

"So, Greenmantle," he said, and Ronan looked away.

"Fucker. Yeah."

"I looked up all the public stuff that first night." It would have been easy enough for Ronan to do it himself, but perhaps he had known that Adam would like the mind-occupying puzzle of it. "Double PhD, home in Boston, three speeding tickets in the last eighteen months, blah blah blah."

"What about the spider-in-web stuff?"

"Doesn't matter," Adam replied. It had taken him only a little bit of time to get the readily available version of Colin Greenmantle's life story. And only a little bit more time to realize that it wasn't really the life story he needed. He didn't need to undo the web — probably *couldn't* undo the web. He needed to spin a new web.

"Of course it matters. It's all that matters."

"No, Ronan, look — come here."

Adam began to write in the dust on the pew beside him. Ronan joined him, crouching to read it.

"What's that?"

"The things we would put into place," Adam said. He'd worked it all out in his head. Though it would have been easier to write it down, he'd thought better of it. Better to have no paper trail or electronic record. Only Cabeswater could hack into the record of Adam's mind. "This is all of the bits of evidence you'd need to dream and how we'd need to bury them."

Some of the things needed to be literally buried. The plan was tidy in conception but not in execution; it was filthy business framing someone, and murders required bodies. Or at least parts of bodies.

"It looks like a lot," Adam admitted, because it did, once he had written it all down in the dust. "I guess it kind of is. But it's mostly small things."

Ronan finished reading Adam's plan. He had his face slightly turned away from the horror of it, just as he had turned his face away from his dream object. He said, "But — this isn't what happened. This isn't what Greenmantle *did*."

Ronan didn't have to say it: *This is a lie.*

Adam should have known this would be a problem for him. He struggled to explain. "I know it's not. But it's too hard to frame him for having your father killed. It's too subtle and it has too many pieces I don't know. He could refute one of our pieces with a real piece, or something real, like the real timeline of what he actually did, could ruin something we'd come up with. But if I invent the crime, I can control all the pieces."

Ronan just stared at him.

"Look, and it has to be something really horrible, something he wouldn't want to go to prison for," Adam said. Now he was feeling a little dirty; he couldn't tell if Ronan's visible distaste was just from the nature of the crime Adam had suggested, or from Adam being able to contemplate such a crime at all. But he persisted, because it was too late to back out now. "We want him too threatened to even think about opening his mouth or countering. If he was even accused of this, he'd be ruined, and he'll know that. And if he did get nailed for it, people who commit crimes against children are treated badly in jail, and he'll know that, too."

Adam could see the two sides of Ronan warring. Could see, unbelievably, that the lie was going to lose.

"Only once," Adam said quickly. "It's just this once. I could redo it to actually be about your father, but it wouldn't be as bulletproof. And then you'd have to deal with court cases. So would Matthew." He felt bad about that last part, even though it was true. Because he knew it would sway Ronan, and it did.

"Okay," Ronan said unhappily. He looked at the plan written in the dust, and his eyebrows furrowed. "Gansey would hate this."

Because it was the worst kind of filth. Kings were not meant to drag their hems in this.

"That's why we're not going to tell him."

He expected Ronan to balk on this point, too, but he just nodded. Two things they agreed on: protecting Gansey's crumbling feelings, and lying by omission.

"Do you think you can do it?" Adam asked. "It's a lot of specifics."

It should have been impossible. No one should have been able to dream any of these things, much less all of them. But Adam had seen what Ronan could do. He'd read the dreamt will and ridden in the dreamt Camaro and been terrified by the dreamt night terror.

It was possible that there were two gods in this church.

Ronan crouched by the pew again, studying the list, his fingers running idly over his stubble as he thought. When he wasn't trying to look like an asshole, his face looked very different, and for a tilting moment, Adam felt the startling inequality of their relationship: Ronan knew Adam, but Adam wasn't sure he knew Ronan, after all.

"I'll do it now," Ronan said finally.

"Now?" Adam asked incredulously. "Here? *Now?*"

Ronan flashed a cocky grin, pleased to have gotten a reaction. "No time like the present, Parrish. Now. Everything but the phone. I have to see what kind he has before I can dream that."

Adam glanced around the still church. It still felt so *inhabited.*

Even though he intellectually believed Ronan that the church would stay empty, in his heart, he felt crowded by . . . possibilities. But Ronan's face held a challenge and Adam wasn't going to back down. He said, "I know what kind of phone he has."

"Telling me a model isn't good enough. I need to *see* it," replied Ronan.

Adam hesitated, and then asked, "What if I asked Cabeswater to show you his phone in the dream? I know what kind it is."

He waited for Ronan to falter or wonder over Adam's strangeness, but Ronan just straightened and rubbed his hands together. "Yeah, good. Good. Look, maybe you should go, though. To the apartment, and I'll meet you after I'm done."

"Why?"

Ronan said, "Not everything in my head is a great thing, Parrish, believe it or not. I told you. And when I'm bringing something back from a dream, sometimes I can't bring back only one thing."

"I'll risk it."

"At least give me some room."

Adam retreated to sit beside Mary as Ronan stretched out on the pew, rubbing out the dingy plan with the legs of his jeans. Something about his stillness on the pew and the funereal quality of the light reminded Adam of the effigy of Glendower they'd seen at the tomb. A king, sleeping. Adam couldn't imagine, though, the strange, wild kingdom that Ronan might rule.

"Stop watching me," Ronan said, though his eyes were closed.

"Whatever. I'm going to ask Cabeswater for the phone."

"See you on the other side."

As Ronan fidgeted, Adam flicked his eyes over to the candles at Mary's feet. It was harder to look into a flame than a pool of black water, but it served the same purpose. As his vision whited out, he felt his mind loosen and detach from his body, and just before he fell out of himself, he asked Cabeswater to give Ronan the phone. *Asking* was not quite the right word. *Showing* was better, because he showed Cabeswater what he needed: the image of the phone presenting itself to Ronan.

Time was impossible to judge when he scryed.

Nearby — what was nearby? — he heard a sharp sound, like a caw, and he suddenly realized that he wasn't sure if he'd been staring into the light for a minute or an hour or a day. His own body felt like the flame, flickering and fragile; he was getting in too deep.

Time to go back.

He waded back, retreating into his bones. He felt the moment his mind clung to his body once more. His eyes flickered open.

Ronan was convulsing in front of him.

Adam jerked his legs in toward his body, out of reach of the disaster just in front of him. Ronan's arms were streaked with blood and his hands were pinpricked with visceral, juicy wounds. His jeans were soaked black. The church carpet glistened with it.

But the horror was his spine, bent back on itself. It was his hand, pressed to his throat. It was his breath — a gasp, a gasp, a choked-off word. It was his fingers, shaking as he held them to his mouth. It was his eyes, open too wide, too bright, cast up to the ceiling. Seeing only pain.

Adam didn't want to move. He couldn't move. He couldn't do this. This wasn't happening.

But it was, and he could.

He scrambled forward. *"Ronan —* Oh, God."

Because now that he was closer, he could see what a ruin Ronan's body was. Beyond repair. He was dying.

I did this — this was my idea — he didn't even really want to —

"Are you happy now?" Ronan asked. "Is this what you wanted?"

Adam started violently. The voice had come from somewhere else. He looked up and found Ronan sitting cross-legged on the pew above them, his expression watchful. One of this Ronan's hands was bloody, too, but it was clearly not his own blood. Something dark flickered across his face as he cast his eyes down to his dying double. The other Ronan whimpered. It was a hideous sound.

"What — what's happening?" Adam asked. He felt light-headed. He was awake; he was dreaming.

"You said you wanted to stay and watch," Ronan snarled from the bench. "Enjoy the show."

Adam understood now. The real Ronan had not moved; he'd woken exactly where he had fallen asleep. This dying Ronan was a copy.

"Why would you dream this?" demanded Adam. He wanted his brain to believe that this agonized Ronan wasn't real, but the duplication was too perfect. He saw at once a Ronan Lynch violently dying and a Ronan Lynch watching with cool remove. Both were true, though both should have been impossible.

"I tried for too much at once," Ronan said from the pew. His words were short, clipped. He was trying not to look like he cared about watching himself die. Maybe he didn't. Maybe this happened all the time. What a fool Adam was to think he knew anything about Ronan Lynch. "It wasn't the sort of thing — the sort of things I normally dream about, and everything got agitated. The night horrors came. Then the wasps. I could tell I would bring them back with me. That I'd wake up like *that*. So I dreamt another me for them to have and then — I woke up. And here I am. And here I am, again. What a cool trick. What a damn cool trick."

The other Ronan was dead.

Adam felt the same way he had when he had seen the dream world. Reality was twisting in on itself. Here was Ronan, dead, and ungrievable, because there was Ronan, alive and unblinking.

"Here —" said Ronan. "Here's your shit. The lies you wanted."

He thrust a bulging, oversized manila envelope at Adam, full, presumably, of the evidence to frame Greenmantle. It took Adam too long to realize that Ronan wanted him to take it, and then a second longer to shift his mind to the mechanics of taking it. Adam told his hand to reach out, and reluctantly it did.

Get it together, Adam.

There was blood on the envelope, and now, on Adam's hand. He asked, "Did you get everything?"

"It's all there."

"Even the —"

"*It's all there.*"

What an impossible and miraculous and hideous thing this was. An ugly plan hatched by an ugly boy now dreamt into ugly life. From dream to reality. How appropriate it was that Ronan, left to his own devices, manifested beautiful cars and beautiful birds and tenderhearted brothers, while Adam, when given the power, manifested a filthy string of perverse murders. Adam asked, "What now? What do we do with . . ."

"Nothing," growled Ronan. "You do nothing. No, you do what I asked before. Go."

"What?"

Ronan was quivering. Not from venom, like the other Ronan, but from some chained emotion. "I said I didn't want you here in case this happened, and now it has, and look at you."

Adam thought he'd taken the whole thing pretty well, considering. Gansey would have swooned by this point. He certainly couldn't see how his presence had made the situation any worse. He *could* see, however, that Ronan Lynch was angry because he wanted to be angry. "Way to be an asshole. This wasn't my fault."

"I didn't say it was your fault," Ronan said. "I said *get the hell away from me.*"

The two boys stared at each other. Insanely, it felt like every other argument they'd ever had, even though this time there was a Ronan-shaped body curled between them covered in gore. This was just Ronan wanting to shout where someone could hear him. Adam felt it whittling away at his temper, not because he believed

Ronan was angry at *him*, but because he was tired of Ronan thinking *this* was the only way to show he was upset.

He said, "Oh, come on. What now?"

Ronan said, "Bye. That's what."

"Whatever," Adam said, heading for the stairs. "Next time you can die alone."

32

Back at the apartment, Adam stood in the shower for a very long time. For once, the part of his brain that calculated how much a long, hot shower might cost was silent. He stood in the water until it had gone tepid. After he got out and dressed, it occurred to him, belatedly, that Ronan might have been upset by the dream itself, not by watching himself die. He had gone to sleep intending to get evidence of murder, and had woken with blood on his hands. Adam knew that the night horrors only came to Ronan when he had a nightmare. Ronan must have known what would be waiting for him, but still, he'd charged in willingly when Adam had asked him.

Probably Adam should see if he was all right. Surely he would still be there.

But Adam stayed where he was, thinking about the other Ronan. The dead one. The strangest part was that the moment had been Adam's vision from the tree in Cabeswater, but turned inside out. Not Gansey dying, but Ronan. So had that vision been wrong? Had he changed his future already? Or was there more to come?

There was a knock on the apartment door.

Probably Ronan. Although, it would be uncommonly unlike him to be the first to admit wrongdoing.

The knock came again, more insistent.

Adam checked to make sure his hands were no longer bloody, and then he opened the door.

It was his father.

He opened the door.

It was his father.

He opened the door.

It was his father.

"Aren't you going to ask me to come in?" his father was saying.

Adam's body wasn't his, and so, with a little wonder, he watched himself step back to allow Robert Parrish to enter his apartment.

How narrow-shouldered he was beside this other man. It was hard to see where he'd come from without a close look at their faces. Then one could see how Robert Parrish wore Adam's thin, fine lips. Then it wasn't hard to see the same fair hair, spun from dust, and the wrinkle between the eyebrows, formed by wariness. It was actually not a difficult thing at all to see that one had sired the other.

Adam couldn't remember what he had been thinking about before he opened the door.

"So this is where you're keeping yourself," said Robert Parrish. He peered at the thrift-store shelf, the makeshift night-stand, the mattress on the floor. Adam was a thing standing out of the way.

"It seems like you and I have a date together soon," added his father. He stopped to stand directly in front of Adam. "You gonna look in my face when I talk to you, or you gonna keep looking at that shelf?"

Adam was going to keep looking at that shelf.

"Okay, then. Look, I know we had some words, but I think you might as well call this thing off. Your mother's real upset, and it's going to look pretty ridiculous on the day of it."

Adam was pretty sure that his father was not allowed to be here. He didn't remember everything that had happened after he'd pressed charges, but he did think it had involved a temporary restraining order. At the time, he thought he remembered finding it comforting, a memory that seemed foolish now. His father had beaten him for years before being caught, and a punch was a bigger act than a trespass. He could call the police afterward, of course, and report his father's violation; he wasn't certain if they would penalize his father, but the adult side of Adam thought that it seemed like a good thing to get on the record. All of that, though, would come after these minutes that he still had to live through.

He did not want to get hit.

It was a strange realization. It wasn't that Adam had ever gotten used to being struck. Pain was a wondrous thing that way; it always worked. But back when he'd lived at home, he'd gotten used to the *idea* of that sort of intimate violence. Now, though, enough days had passed that he had stopped expecting it, which made the sudden possibility of it somehow more intolerable.

He did not want to get hit.

He would do what he needed to do to not get hit.

Anticipation trembled in his hands.

Cabeswater is not the boss of you, Persephone's voice said.

"Adam, I'm being real decent here, but you're trying my patience sorely," his father told him. "At least pretend like you heard what I said."

"I heard," Adam replied.

"Sass. Nice."

Just because it tantrums doesn't mean it's more right than you.

To the shelf, Adam said, "I think you should go."

He felt cowardly and boneless.

"So that's how it's going to be?"

That was how it was going to be.

"You should know, then, that you're going to look like a fool in that courtroom, Adam," Robert Parrish said. "People know me and they know what kind of man I am. You and I both know this is just a pathetic cry for attention, and everyone else will, too. It's too easy to look at you and see what kind of shit you've become. Don't think I don't know where this comes from. You prancing around with those entitled bitch-boys."

Part of Adam was still there with his father, but most of him was retreating. The better part of him. That Adam, the magician, was no longer in his apartment. That Adam walked through trees, running his hand along the moss-covered stones.

"Court's gonna see right through that. And you know what you're going to be then? In the papers as that kid who wanted to put his hardworking daddy in jail."

The leaves rustled, close and protective, pressing up against his ears, curled in his fists. They didn't mean to frighten. They only ever tried to speak his language and get his attention. It was not fearsome Cabeswater's fault that Adam had already been a fearful boy when he'd made the bargain.

"You think they're really gonna look at you and see an abused kid? Do you even know what abuse is? That judge will've heard enough stories to know a whopper. He's not gonna blink an eye."

The branches leaned toward Adam, curling around him protectively, a thicket with thorns pointed outward. It had tried, before, to cling to his mind, but now it knew to surround his body. He'd asked to be separate, and Cabeswater had listened. *I know you are not the same as him*, Adam said. *But in my head, everything is always so tangled. I am such a damaged thing.*

"So we're back where we started, you and me, when I came here. You can call off that hearing quick as you please, and this all goes away."

The rain splattered down through the leaves, turning them upside down, trickling onto Adam.

"And look at you, and I've just been *talking* to you. Practicing for your day in court? At least pretend like I haven't been talking to a wall. What the *hell* —?"

The braying note in his father's voice brought Adam rushing back to himself. One hand was poised in the air, as if he had meant to touch Adam, or had already, and was withdrawing.

In the meat of his palm, a small thorn protruded. A thread of blood trembled from the wound, bright as a miracle.

Plucking the thorn free, his father regarded Adam, this thing he had made. He was silent for a long moment, and then something registered in his face. It wasn't quite fear, but it was uncertainty. His son was before him, and he did not know him.

I am unknowable.

Robert Parrish began to speak, but then he didn't. Now he had seen something in Adam's face or eyes, or felt something in that thorn that pricked him, or maybe, like Adam, he could now smell the scent of a damp forest floor in the apartment.

"You're going to be a fool in that courtroom," his father said finally. "Are you going to say anything?"

Adam was not going to say anything.

His father slammed the door behind him as he left.

Adam stood there for a long moment. He wiped the heel of his hand over his right eye and cheek, then dried it on his slacks.

He climbed back into his bed and closed his eyes, hands balled to his chest, scented with mist and with moss.

When he closed his eyes, Cabeswater was still waiting for him.

33

The thing that amazes me," Greenmantle mused aloud, "is that there are some people who actually do this as a form of leisure. People who trade vacation days for this experience. It dazzles, really. I have absolutely no idea where we are. I'm assuming you'd have said something if we were lost and/or were going to die down here."

The Greenmantles were in a cave: wife, husband, dog, an American cave family. Piper had discovered that Otho, when left alone, ate through the bathroom doors of rental homes, so he now minced ahead of her. The cave was dark and armpit-scented. Greenmantle had done a perfunctory amount of research on caving before setting out this afternoon. He'd discovered that caves were supposed to be vessels of natural untouched beauty.

It turned out they were just holes in the ground. He felt caves had been extremely oversold.

"We're not going to die down here," Piper said. "I have book club on Tuesday."

"Book club! You've only been here two weeks and you're in a book club."

"What else am I supposed to do while you're out finding yourself? Just *hang around* the house, getting fat, I suppose? Don't say 'talk to your little friends on the phone' because I'll put this pickax through your right eye."

"What's the book?"

Piper pointed the flashlight at the ceiling and then the damp floor. Both the flashlight beam and Piper's lip curled in disgust. "I don't remember the title. Something about citrus. It's a literary memoir of a young woman coming of age on an orange plantation set against a backdrop of war and subversive class struggle with possible religious undertones or something like that. Don't say 'I'd rather die.'"

"I didn't say anything," Greenmantle replied, although he had indeed been considering "I'd rather die" as a candidate to further the conversation. He preferred spy thrillers that involved dashing men who were slightly over thirty darting in and out of high-technology shadows while driving fast cars and making important phone calls. He held up the EMF reader in his hand to see if he could vary the degree of flashing going on across its face. He could not.

Otho had stopped to relieve himself; Piper flicked out a plastic baggie.

"This is pointless. Did you just put that shit in your bag?"

"I saw a spot on ABC about how ecotourism is denuding caves," she informed him. "That face? The one you're wearing now? Is part of the problem. You are part of the problem."

Holes in the ground were, in Greenmantle's opinion, the very best place to throw dog crap into. He swiped the EMF reader across the wall with one hand and a geophone with the other. He would have gotten an identical amount of insight if he'd been holding a flare and a ukulele. "What I'm going to do is hire a billion million minions to come look in caves for this woman, and if that doesn't work, I'll just eviscerate her daughter in front of the Gray Man instead."

"Minions! I don't want a million minions tramping around down here. I want to explore my psychic connections without all that grunting going on."

"Your psychic connections!" He felt her glaring at him; the skin on the back of his neck was melting. "Fine, I'll tell them to be tactful."

"You know what? You should let me have two of them, to help me in my life goals."

"What?"

"I could call them and pretend to be you. *Hi, thugman, this is Colin, could you do me a solid?*" She did a passable job of his voice, if slightly too nasal and in love with itself. She stopped short, legs apart, blond hair billowing around her like a caving photo shoot. For a strange, slipping moment, Greenmantle thought that he'd found her in the cave and was bringing her back to the light, and then he remembered the bag of dog shit and how they'd gotten here. He thought that this cave was probably full of carbon monoxide. He was probably dying.

Piper asked, "Did you hear that?"

"The sound of you mocking me?"

She didn't reply. She was frowning down the tunnel, her chin lifted, her eyebrows pushed together as if she were listening. He thought about someone sleeping. He thought about waking them up.

"The sound of my love?" he tried.

She still didn't reply. She was still listening.

"The sound of you creeping me the hell out?"

But really he was creeping himself out.

Finally, she turned back to him. She did not look as if she had heard the sound of his love. She said, "I definitely need two of your minions. Let's get back to a cell phone signal."

He was very happy to oblige. He never wanted to see a cave again.

34

Gansey might have found Gwenllian, but Blue had to live with her. All of the women of 300 Fox Way had to, actually. It was like living with a natural disaster, or a feral child, or a feral natural child disaster.

For starters, she didn't sleep. She shouted at Calla that she had had enough sleep for one thousand lifetimes and that she intended to spend the rest of this one awake, and then proceeded to do just that. At small hours of the morning, Blue would wake and hear her clogging around in the attic above her room.

Then there was her manner of dress. Her supernatural awareness inside the tomb had given her just enough exposure to the changing outside world to not be shocked by the existence of cars or befuddled by the English language, but not enough to award her any social customs. So she wore what she wanted to wear (Blue could at least respect the motivation, if not the outcome), which was always a dress, sometimes two or three on top of each other, sometimes backward. This often involved stealing clothing from other people's closets. Blue was spared only because she was so much shorter.

There were problems with mealtimes, too: For Gwenllian, every time was mealtime. She seemed to have neither sense of fullness nor taste, and would often combine foods in manners that struck Blue as problematic. She didn't believe in telling people how to live their lives (well, maybe a little), but it was hard to stand by and watch Gwenllian spread peanut butter on a cold hot dog.

And there was the crazy part. Forty percent of what came out of her mouth came out in song, and the rest was a varied mixture of chanting, screaming, mocking, and creepy whisper. She climbed on the roof, she talked to the tree in the backyard, and she stood on furniture. She often put things in her hair for later retrieval, and then seemed to forget they were there. In very short order, her enormous tangle of hair became a vertical repository for pencils, leaves, tissues, and matches.

"We could cut it," Orla suggested at one point.

Persephone said, "I do not think that is a decision one human can make for another human."

Orla asked, "Even if that other human looks like a hobo?"

It was a point on which Blue and Orla agreed.

The worst part of it was that Gansey had offered to take her away — *kept* offering to take her away — and Persephone insisted Gwenllian stay with them.

"It takes longer than a weekend to undo centuries of damage," Persephone said.

"Centuries of damage are being incurred in just a weekend," Calla replied.

"She's a very gifted psychic," Persephone said mildly. "Eventually she will earn her keep."

"And pay for my therapy," Blue added.

"Good one," Orla said. To reward Blue for her excellent comeback, she painted Blue's fingernails to match the Pig, a polish color, she informed Blue, that was called *Belligerent Candy*.

Gansey kept trying to talk with Gwenllian, but she was always sassily deferential when he came to the house.

On top of that, Gansey had some sort of school commitment that he was cagey about, Ronan and Adam kept vanishing places together, and Noah couldn't or wouldn't come into 300 Fox Way.

Blue was feeling a little as if she had been locked into a madhouse.

Mom, it's time for you to come home.

The Gray Man came over midweek, much to her gratitude.

"It's me," he called down the hallway as he stepped inside. Blue could see him from her homework post at the kitchen table; he was tidy and dangerous looking in a gray shirt and slacks. He looked more optimistic than the last time she had seen him.

Gwenllian, who was examining the roaring vacuum cleaner but not vacuuming with it, spotted him, too. "Hello, handsome sword! Have you killed anyone today?"

"One sword knows another," he told her mildly, placing his car keys in his pocket. "Have *you* killed anyone?"

She was so delighted that she turned off the vacuum cleaner so that her insane smile could be the loudest thing in the hall.

"Mr. Gray, leave her alone and come get a cup of tea," Blue called from the kitchen table. "You'll make her start singing again."

The Gray Man glanced over his shoulder at Gwenllian as he came into the kitchen and did as Blue instructed, taking a few minutes to find a tea more likely to provoke sanguinity than loose stools.

"I have been employed by your friends Mr. Parrish and Mr. Lynch," he said as he sat down opposite Blue. *So this is where those two were going!* He tapped one of her algebra problems until she dragged it back to her and reworked it correctly. "They have a plan for Greenmantle, and it seems quite promising."

"What is it?"

"I would rather not tell you, as it is better the fewer people know it. Also, it is not polite table conversation," Mr. Gray said. "I have a question for you. Your cursed cave. Do you think it is the sort of place you could hide a body? Or at least part of one?"

Blue narrowed her eyes. "There was lots of room in that cave for lots of things. Whose body? Which part?"

Gwenllian instantly manifested in the kitchen, dragging the vacuum cleaner behind her like a reluctantly walked dog. "What about the curse, lily?"

"I thought *you* were the curse," Blue replied.

"Probably," Gwenllian said carelessly. "What else is there but I? I'm known to Welshmen free, lovely Gwen, lovely Gwen, from Gower to Anglesey, lovely Gwen, oh Gwen the dead!"

Blue said, "I told you she would start singing."

But the Gray Man just raised his eyebrows. "Weapons and poetry go hand in hand."

Gwenllian drew herself up. "What a *cunning* weapon you are. A poet is how I ended up in that cave."

"Is it a good story?" the Gray Man asked.

"Oh, it is the finest."

Blue watched the exchange with a bit of awe. Somewhere there was a lesson in this.

The Gray Man took a sip of his tea. "You should sing it for us."

And unbelievably, she did.

She sang a furious little song about Glendower's poet Iolo Goch, and how he whispered war in her father's ear (she whispered this part into Blue's ear) and so, as blood soaked into the ground of Wales, Gwenllian did her level best to stab him to death.

"Was he sleeping?" the Gray Man asked with professional interest.

Gwenllian laughed for about a minute. Then she said, "It was at dinner. What a lovely meal he would've been!"

Then she spit in the Gray Man's tea, but it seemed to have more to do with Iolo Goch than Mr. Gray.

He sighed and pushed the cup away. "So they sentenced you to that cave."

"It was that or hanging! And I chose hanging, so they gave me the false grave instead."

Blue squinted at Gwenllian, trying to imagine her as she had been six centuries before. A young woman, Orla's age, the daughter of a nobleman, a witch in an age when witches were not always the best thing to be. Surrounded by war, and doing her best to stop it.

Blue wondered if she would have the courage to stab someone if she thought it would save lives.

Gwenllian dragged the vacuum cleaner back into the hall without any sort of good-bye.

"Gwenllian and vacuum, exit stage right," Blue said.

The Gray Man pushed his tea even farther away. "Do you

think you might have time to show me this cave you pulled her from? Just so I know where it is, as an option?"

The idea of leaving the house was incredibly appealing. It wouldn't be a bad thing to see Jesse again, either. And although she was annoyed that Adam and Ronan hadn't trusted her with whatever their Greenmantle plan was, she wanted to be helpful anyway. "Possibly. Will you feed me?"

"I won't even spit in it."

Blue warned Calla that she was leaving the house with a hit man, and then Mr. Gray took her to the downtown drugstore for a tuna fish sandwich (BEST TUNA FISH IN TOWN!) before driving out of Henrietta. The car zoomed and darted through the darkness in a way that seemed slightly out of the Gray Man's control.

"This car is really terrible," Blue said.

This was allowed, as the car was not really Mr. Gray's. It was a hand-me-down white Mitsubishi of the sort that young men with big dreams and egos normally drove. It sported a custom license plate that read THIEF.

"It grows on you," Mr. Gray said. He paused. "Like a cancer."

"Buh dum *pa*."

Both Blue and Mr. Gray enjoyed a laugh, and then were briefly silent as they realized it had been too long since they had been in the company of someone with their precise sense of humor, i.e., Maura Sargent. In the background, the Kinks played gently, the sound of Mr. Gray's soul.

"I keep waiting for things to go back to normal," Blue admitted. "But I know now that that's not going to happen, even when Mom comes back." She meant *if*, but she said *when*.

"I wouldn't have pegged you for a fan of normal," the Gray Man said. He slowed slightly as the headlights illuminated the eyes of three deer standing by the side of the road.

It was warming to be so *known*. She said, "I'm not, really, but I was used to it, I guess. It's boring, but at least it's not scary. Do you ever get scared? Or are you too badass for that?"

He looked amused, but also like a badass, sitting quietly and efficiently behind the wheel of the car.

"In my experience," the Gray Man said, "the badasses are the most scared. I just avoid being *inappropriately* frightened."

Blue thought this seemed like a reasonable goal. After a pause, she said, "You know, I like you."

He glanced over at her. "I do, too."

"Like me or like you? The grammar was unspecific."

The two of them enjoyed another laugh and the presence of someone else with their precise sense of humor.

"Oh, here it is," Blue said. "Don't pass it."

The Dittley farm was mostly dark as they pulled down the driveway, with only the kitchen window lit up. For a moment, Blue thought perhaps Jesse had left to win back his wife and son and dog. But then she saw his big silhouette pull aside the curtain to observe their headlights pulling up to the house.

He came to the door at once.

"Howdy," Blue said. "I came to impose on you and maybe show Mr. Gray your cave, if that's okay."

He let them in. "YOUR BREATH SMELLS LIKE TUNA FISH."

"Should I have brought you some?" she asked.

"I ONLY EAT SPAGHETTIOS." He shook hands with

the Gray Man, who introduced himself as Mr. Gray. Then Jesse leaned and Blue stood on tiptoes and they hugged, because that seemed right.

"I JUST TOOK SOME GIRL SCOUT COOKIES OUT OF THE FREEZER."

"Oh, that's okay," Blue said. "As you smelled, we just ate."

"I'll take one," the Gray Man interjected. "If they're Thin Mints."

Jesse fetched them. "NOTHING FOR YOU, ANT?"

She said, "How about a glass of water and an exciting update about how great your life is now that we've taken the crazy person out of your cave?"

"LIFE IS GREAT," Jesse admitted. "BUT THE CAVE — ARE YOU WEARING BOOTS? BECAUSE IT IS MUDDY."

Blue and Mr. Gray assured him they were fine with their current footwear. Retrieving a flashlight for Blue and a floodlight and a shotgun for himself, Jesse led the three of them across the dark field to the building that housed the cave. As they grew closer, Blue thought she smelled something familiar. It was not the earthy scent of the wet field or the smoky scent of the fall night. It was metallic and close, damp and stagnant. It was the smell, Blue realized, of the cave of ravens.

"WATCH YOUR STEP."

"What am I watching for?" Mr. Gray asked.

"THAT IS THE RIGHT QUESTION."

Jesse minced as best a Dittley could mince to the door. He handed the floodlight to Blue as he unlocked the padlock.

"STAND BACK."

She stood back.

"BACKER THAN THAT."

She stood back farther. The Gray Man stepped in front of her. Only enough to block an assault, not her view.

Jesse Dittley kicked in the door. It was a slow-motion kick because his leg was so long — there was a considerable lag between when he began to swing his leg and when his foot actually hit the door. Blue wondered what that was called. A leg roundhouse, or something.

The door opened.

"YUP," said Jesse as *something* shot toward him.

It was a terrible something.

Blue was a fairly open-minded human, she thought, willing to accept that there was a good bit of the world that was outside her understanding and knowledge. She knew, academically, that just because something looked scary didn't mean that it wanted to hurt you.

But this *something* wanted to hurt them.

It wasn't even malevolence. It was that sometimes something was on your side, and sometimes it was not, and this was not. Whatever humans were, this was against.

The sensation of being *undone* buffeted them, and then something charged through the doorway.

The Gray Man took an enormous black handgun from his jacket and shot the thing three times in each of its heads. It fell to the ground. There was not much in the way of heads left.

"THAT SEEMED EXCESSIVE," Jesse said.

"Yes," agreed the Gray Man.

Blue was glad that it was dead and then felt bad that she felt glad that it was dead. It was easier to be generous about it now that it wasn't trying to unwind the core of her existence.

Jesse closed the door and locked it again.

"THAT HAS BEEN MY WEEK."

She looked at the strange, jointless body, vaguely wormish, glittering rainbow scales in the beam of her flashlight. She couldn't decide if it was ugly or beautiful or just unlike anything she had seen before. "Have there been a lot of them?"

"ENOUGH."

"Have you seen any of these before?" Mr. Gray asked.

"NOT TILL NOW. DON'T ALWAYS LOOK THIS WAY, EITHER. SOME OF THEM DON'T WANT TO KILL YOU. SOME OF THEM ARE JUST OLD THINGS. THEY DO GET IN THE HOUSE, THOUGH."

"Why are they coming out?" Blue asked.

"TOLD YOU THE CAVE WAS CURSED."

"But we took her out!"

"RECKON SHE WAS THE ONE KEEPING THEM DOWN. CAVE LOVES A SACRIFICE."

They all regarded the body for several long minutes.

Mr. Gray said, "Shall we dispose of it?"

"NAH. CROWS WILL EAT WHAT'S LEFT."

Blue said, "This seems pretty bad." She wanted to offer to help, but what could they do? Put Gwenllian back?

The Gray Man tucked his gun away. He looked displeased by this entire turn of events. Blue wondered if he was thinking about hiding body parts in a cave that already seemed to be full of bodies, and then she wondered if he was thinking about

Maura in a cave with these creatures, and as soon as she thought about it herself, her expression mirrored the Gray Man's.

"THERE, THERE, LITTLE ANT," Jesse said. "RECKON SHE GUARDED THE CAVE FOR HER TIME. NOW IT'S MY TURN."

35

That night, Gwenllian's laugh announced her presence at the doorway to Blue's bedroom. It was poor timing; Blue was in a terrible mood because it was time for Maura to come back or for her to go find Maura or *something*. She would go to the cave of ravens herself. She would battle monsters in Dittley's cave and charge to the middle of the earth looking for her. She made plans and broke them and rewrote them, a new one every second.

Gwenllian laughed again, meaningfully. It was her version of clearing her throat. With a sigh, Blue rolled over. She found the other woman treasuring a spoon of something that looked terribly like it might be mayonnaise.

"Are you running away, little blue lily?"

"Not yet," Blue replied, narrowing her eyes at Gwenllian to see if there was a deeper meaning. In the background, she heard Calla and Persephone fighting in Persephone's room. Well, really, Calla was fighting, and Persephone was saying nothing. She continued, "Look, there's no nice way to ask this, so I'm just going to put it out there: Do you think you might grow out of the crazy any time soon? Because I have a lot of questions about my father, and my mother's missing, and trying to do crime scene via sing-along is starting to stress me out."

"You begin to sound like your princeling, little lily,"

Gwenllian said. "And I'm not sure that's your place. Which is to say, carry on. I'm all for ranks of usurping women."

Blue let this pass. Gwenllian had already proven herself extremely gifted at finding each person's one weakness and then leaning on it casually. "I just want my mother back. And please stop calling me that. My name's Blue."

"Lily," Gwenllian added.

"Please —"

"Lily."

"— stop."

"Blue," Gwenllian finished with some triumph. She finished whatever was left on the spoon. Possibly it was hair conditioner. "Come to my room and I will show you how we're the same, you and I and I and you."

With a sigh, Blue rolled out of her bed and followed Gwenllian up to the dim attic. Even now, after the sun had gone down, it was several degrees warmer than the house, which made it feel small and close, like a jacket.

Blue had cleaned up nearly all of the evidence Neeve had left behind, and Persephone and Calla had picked over the rest. The only sizable remains were two large mirrors that stood facing each other in the dormer.

Gwenllian led Blue directly to them, careful not to stand between them. She pet Blue's hair with both hands, like she was smoothing a wig, and then used her hands to turn Blue's head to the mirror on the left.

"That is I," she said. She turned Blue's head to the mirror on the right. "That is *vous*."

"Explain."

"I have been a sword and I have been a thunderclap, and I have been a burned-out comet and I have been a word and I have been a mirrrrror!"

Blue waited until the song was done. "So you're saying you're a mirror."

"Of the deepest blue," Gwenllian whispered in Blue's ear. She leapt back so that she could trace the shape of Blue in the air with her fingers. "Blue. Blue. Blue. Blue. All around. And me. It's what we do."

"Oh. Our auras? Okay, sure. But Persephone says that you're psychic, and I am definitely not."

Very bored, Gwenllian spread her arms out dramatically. Both hands once again pointed at the mirrors. "Mirrors! I am telling you, that is what we do."

Something prickled in Blue, uncomfortably. She eyed the mirrors; Neeve had used them for divination, Calla said. She'd stood between them and seen endless possibilities for herself stretched out on either side, in either mirror.

Maura was always shuffling the page of cups out of her tarot deck and showing it to Blue: *Look, it's you! Look at all the potential she holds!*

"Yes," Gwenllian said, shrill. "You're getting it. Do they *use* you, blue lily? Do they ask you to hold their hands so they can better see their future? Do you make them see the dead? Do you get sent from the room when things get too loud for them?"

Blue nodded dumbly.

"Mirrors," Gwenllian cooed. "That is what we are. When you hold a candle in front of a glass, doesn't it make the room twice as bright? So do we, blue lily, lily blue."

She leapt onto her mattress. "How useful! A wonderful addition to the stables. Like the steed of *Gwythur* and *Gwarddur* and *Cunin* and *Lieu*." She broke from her song to shake her head and say, in a more normal voice, "No, not of Lieu. But the others."

Blue couldn't quite believe that she had finally met someone who was like her. She hadn't known it was possible. "What is blue lily, then? Where is that name from?"

Gwenllian charged the mirrors, stopping just short of going between them. She flung herself around to stand an inch in front of Blue. "*Witches*, my little floral cushion. That's what we are."

A delicious and wicked thrill went through Blue at the word. It was not that she had aspirations of being a witch; it was that she had been a nameless accessory for so long that the idea of having a title, or being *anything*, was a delicious one.

But misguided.

"Maybe you," Blue said. "But the best I can do is *not* help people. Sometimes." She thought about how she had pulled the plug on Noah in Monmouth but had been unable to at Jesse Dittley's. That, she realized, had been Gwenllian.

"People!" Gwenllian laughed gloriously. "*People! Men?* What makes you think you are a friend to *men*?"

It could be argued, Blue thought, that Blue was *only* a friend to men, but she didn't feel it was useful to bring it up.

"Whoever wants to talk to people!" Gwenllian gestured grandly to the two mirrors. "Go! Stand in there! Stand!"

Calla had previously made it quite clear that she didn't want to stand between Neeve's two mirrors. And she'd also implied that doing so might have had something to do with how Neeve had disappeared.

Blue did not want to stand between them.

Gwenllian shoved.

Blue hurtled toward them, arms wheeling. She could see the light flashing off their surfaces. She teetered. She stopped short.

"Okay, I —" she said.

Gwenllian shoved her again.

Blue only stepped back once, but that was enough to put her squarely between the two mirrors.

She waited to be vaporized.

She waited for monsters to appear.

Neither thing happened.

Instead, she peered slowly to her left and then to her right, and then she looked at her hands. They were still visible, which was notable because her reflection was in neither mirror. The mirrors merely reflected each other, again and again. There was something a little dark and troubling about the images inside them, but nothing more.

"Where am I?" Blue asked Gwenllian.

Gwenllian laughed and sprang about, clapping gleefully. "Grieve not for your stupidity! Mirror magic is nothing to mirrors."

Blue took the opportunity to step out quickly, back into the middle of the room. "I don't understand."

"Nor I," said Gwenllian carelessly. "And I starve from this idle talk."

The woman started down the attic stairs.

"Wait!" called Blue. "Will you tell me about my father?"

"No," Gwenllian replied. "I will get mayonnaise."

36

The very first supernatural artifact Greenmantle had acquired had been a haunted doll. He'd bought it on eBay for $500 (the price included two-day shipping). The auction listing had promised that the doll had spent the last two weeks in the seller's basement growling and rolling its eyes into its head. Sometimes, the listing noted, a scorpion would crawl out of the doll's ears. The listing warned that this was not a child's toy and indeed was only being offered to augment Satanic or left path rituals.

Greenmantle had purchased it with equal parts skepticism and hope. To his annoyance but not surprise, the doll was unremarkable upon arrival. It did not growl. Its eyes closed and opened only when the doll was tipped. There was no sign of any insect life.

Piper — his girlfriend at the time — and he had spent the evening eating take-out sushi and throwing edamame beans at the doll in an attempt to provoke some demonic activity.

Afterward, Piper said, "If we had a puppy, it could pick up those beans for us."

Greenmantle had replied, "And then we could sacrifice it and use its blood to activate the doll."

"Will you marry me?" she asked.

He thought about it. "I love myself the most, though. Are you okay always coming in second?"

"Samesies," she replied. Then she cut herself and smeared her blood on the doll's forehead, a level of personal involvement that Greenmantle had yet to achieve.

The doll still never growled or bit anyone, but that night, Greenmantle put it in a box in the spare bedroom, and in the morning it was lying on its face by the front door. He felt the appropriate level of thrill and fear and delight.

"Lame," Piper said, stepping over it on her way to her ladies' fencing class or her naked baking club. "Find me something better."

And he had.

Or rather, he had hired people to find something better. Now, years later, he had loads of supernatural artifacts, nearly all of them more interesting than the occasionally moving doll. He still preferred his artifacts to be mildly atmospheric. Piper liked hers dark.

Something was happening to her here in Henrietta, and it wasn't just her yoga class.

He shouldn't have brought her.

Greenmantle stepped into the rental house.

"Piper," he called. There was no response. He paused in the kitchen to get himself a bite of cheese and a grape. "Piper, if you are being held up by Mr. Gray, bark once."

She was not being held up by anything except the mirror. She was in the hall bathroom staring at herself, and she didn't answer when he called her name. This wasn't particularly unusual, as Piper was easily entranced by her own reflection. He returned to the kitchen to get himself a glass of wine. Piper had used all the wineglasses and not washed them, so he poured a nasty little Pugnitello into an Aglionby Academy mug.

Then he returned to the bathroom. She was still gazing intently at herself.

"You're cut off," he said, pulling her away. He noticed a tarot card — the three of swords — sitting on the edge of the bathroom sink. "It's time to stare at me now."

She was still looking off into nowhere, so he snapped his fingers rudely in front of her for a few minutes, and then after he began to get a little creeped out, he dipped her fingers into the mug and then placed the wine-covered fingertips in her own mouth.

Piper came to.

"What do you want? Why are my fingers in my mouth? You are such a perversion."

"I was just saying hello. Hello, honey, I'm home."

"Great. You're home. I'm busy." And she slammed the bathroom door in his face. From inside the bathroom, he heard humming. It didn't sound like Piper, even though it had to be.

Greenmantle thought it was probably time to finish this job and get the hell out of this place.

Or maybe just get the hell out of this place.

37

Sometimes, Gansey forgot how much he liked school and how *good* he was at it. But he couldn't forget it on mornings like this one — fall fog rising out of the fields and lifting in front of the mountains, the Pig running cool and loud, Ronan climbing out of the passenger seat and knocking knuckles on the roof with teeth flashing, dewy grass misting the black toes of his shoes, bag slung over his blazer, narrow-eyed Adam bumping fists as they met on the sidewalk, boys around them laughing and calling to one another, making space for the three of them because this had been a thing for so long: Gansey-Lynch-Parrish. Mornings like this one were made for memories.

There would be nothing to ruin the crisp perfection of it if not for the presence of Greenmantle somewhere and the non-presence of Maura. If not for Gwenllian and Blue's hands and looming caves full of promises and threats. If not for everything. It was so difficult for these two worlds to co-exist.

Morning crows and workmen on scaffolding called to one another over the campus as the boys walked across the school green together. The sound of hammers echoed off the buildings; they were replacing part of the roof. The scaffolding was piled with slate tiles.

"Look at this," Ronan said. With a jerk of his chin, he indicated Henry Cheng, who stood with a placard on the corner of the school green.

"'Make a difference: *After* you graduate,'" Gansey read as they approached him. "Jesus, have you been out here all night?"

Henry's shoes were slick with condensation, and his shoulders were shrugged up against the cold. His nose was extremely pink. His usually gloriously and enormously spiked hair, however, was still glorious and spiked; he clearly had his priorities. He'd planted another sign into a pot behind him; that one read THINK DEEPLY . . . *but not about Aglonby.* "No way. Only since six. I wanted them to *think* I'd been here all night."

Adam raised a diffident eyebrow at the scene. "Who's 'them'?"

"The faculty, obviously," Henry replied.

Gansey removed a pen from his bag and carefully added an *i* to *Aglonby.* "Is this still about the student council?"

"They totally ignored my petition," Henry said. "Fascists. I had to do something. I'm standing here until they agree to start one."

"Looks like you've hit on a good way to get expelled," Ronan observed.

"*You* should know."

Adam narrowed his eyes. There was something different about him. Or maybe there was just something different between him and Henry. Henry was a boy. Adam was a —

Gansey didn't know.

Adam asked, "On what grounds did they ignore the petition?"

Henry paused to shout across the green: "ChengTwo — if that coffee isn't for me, get me another! Please! Thank you! Please!"

The other Cheng distantly lifted the coffee cup in salute and shouted, "Sorry! Sorry!" before disappearing into one of the academic buildings.

"No honor," muttered Henry. To Adam, he said, "They said it would be too much of a drain on the administration's resources to set it up and monitor it."

"That seems like a reasonable reason," Adam replied, his eyes already on the class buildings. "What are you even going to council about? The lunch menu?"

Ronan smirked in an unpleasant way.

Cheng shivered and said, "You, Parrish, are part of the problem."

"I'll get you a coffee." Gansey eyed his watch. "I've got time."

"Gansey," complained Ronan.

"I'll meet you in there."

Cheng said, "You're a prince among men, Dick Gansey."

"More like a man among princes," muttered Adam. "You've got seven minutes, Gansey."

Gansey left them talking to Cheng and headed to the faculty room. Broadly speaking, students were not supposed to come and go freely through the faculty room, but narrowly speaking, Gansey was exempt by virtue of gross favoritism. He scuffed the damp cut grass off his shoes on the mat by the entrance and shut the door behind himself. The old floor by the door was buckled by the weight of tradition and required a hefty, familiar shove to close it; Gansey did it without thinking.

Inside, the room was spare and drafty and smelled of woodsmoke and bagels. It had all of the comforts of a quaint prison: wooden benches on the walls, historic mural on the plaster, spidery chandelier overhead, gaunt spread of breakfast foods on a warped old table. Gansey stood in front of the coffeepot. He was getting that odd time-slipping feeling that the campus often gave him: the sense that he had always been standing in this old room in this old building, or *someone* had, and all times and all people were the same. In that formless place, he found himself intensely grateful for Ronan and Adam waiting outside for him, for Blue and her family, for Noah and for Malory. He was so grateful to have found all of them, finally.

He thought about that pit in the cave of ravens.

For the barest second, he thought he knew — something. The answer.

But he hadn't asked a question, and then it was gone, anyway, and then he realized that he was hearing something. A shout, a crash, Adam's name —

He didn't remember the decision to move, only his feet already running to the door.

Outside, the courtyard looked like a set piece for a play: Two dozen students dotted the green, but none of them were moving. A slow, pale cloud moved among them, slowly settling. Everyone's attention was turned toward the corner of the green where Henry had been standing.

But it was Adam's name he'd heard.

He saw that the topmost area of the scaffolding hung crookedly, the workmen staring down from their positions on the roof.

Dust. That's what the cloud was. From whatever had fallen from the scaffolding. The slate tiles.

Adam.

Gansey shoved through the students. He saw Henry first, then Ronan, unharmed, but powdered like Pompeii corpses. He made eye contact with Ronan — *Is it all right?* — and he didn't recognize Ronan's expression.

There was Adam.

He was standing, very still, his hands by his sides. His chin was tilted up in a wary, fragile sort of way, and his eyes narrowed at nothing. Unlike Ronan and Henry, he was dustless. Gansey saw the jerk of his chest as it rose and fell.

Around him lay hundreds of shattered slate tiles. The pieces exploded out for a dozen yards, dug into the grass like missiles.

But the ground around Adam was bare in a perfect circle.

It was this circle, this impossible circle, that the other students stared at. Some of them were taking photos on their phones.

No one was talking to Adam. It wasn't difficult to understand this: Adam didn't look like someone you could talk to, just then. There was something more frightening about him than there was about the circle. Like the bare ground, there was nothing inherently unusual about his appearance. But in context, surrounded by these brick buildings, he didn't . . . *belong.*

"Parrish," Gansey said when he got close. "Adam. What happened?"

Adam's eyes slid over to him but his head didn't turn. It was the stillness that made him seem so *other.*

Behind him, he heard Ronan say, "I like the way you losers thought Instagram before first aid. Fuck off."

"No, don't fuck off," Henry corrected. "Notify a teacher that there's some men on the roof who are about to be sued."

"Scaffolding failed," Adam said in a low voice. An expression was now appearing on his face, but it, too, was unfamiliar: wonder. "Everything fell."

"You are the luckiest man in this school," Henry said. "How are you not dead, Parrish?"

"It's your bullshit signs," Ronan suggested, looking vastly less concerned than Gansey felt. "They created a bullshit force field."

Gansey leaned and Adam pulled him in even closer, gripping his shoulder tightly. Right into Gansey's ear, he whispered, voice tinged in disbelief, "I didn't — I just asked — I just *thought* —"

"Thought what?" Gansey asked.

Adam released him. His eyes were on the circle around him. "I thought *that*. And it happened."

The circle was absolutely perfect: dust without, dustless within.

"You marvelous creature," Gansey said, because there was nothing else to say. Because he had just thought that these two worlds could not co-exist and yet here was Adam, both at once. Alive because of it.

This *thing* they were doing. This thing. Gansey's heart was a gaping chasm of possibilities, fearful and breathless and awed.

Ronan's smile was sharp. Now Gansey recognized the expression on Ronan's face: arrogance. He had not been afraid for

Adam. He had known Cabeswater would save him. Been certain of it.

Gansey thought of how strange it was to know these two young men so well and yet to not know them at all. Both so much more difficult and so much better than when he'd first met them. Was that what life did to them all? Chiseled them into harder, truer versions of themselves?

"I told you," Ronan said. "Magician."

38

It was finally here.

After all of the continuances, after months of waiting, it was the day of the court case.

Adam got up as he would normally for school, but instead of putting on his uniform, he put on the good suit he'd bought on Gansey's advice the year before. He had not permitted Gansey to pay for any of it, back then. The tie he tied on now, though — the tie was a Christmas gift from Gansey, permitted because Adam had already had a tie when Gansey bought it, so it couldn't be charity.

It seemed like a silly bit of principle now, completely divorced from the point of anything. He wondered if he was going to go through each year of his life thinking about how stupid he'd been the year before.

He thought about waiting until after breakfast to get dressed, to keep from spilling anything on his suit, but that was foolish. He wouldn't be able to eat anything.

His case was at ten A.M., hours after school began, but Adam had asked permission to take the entire day off. He knew it would be impossible to hide the reason for his absence from Gansey and Ronan if he had to leave midmorning, and equally difficult to disguise where he'd been if he returned right after court.

Part of him wished that he wasn't doing this without the others — a shocking wish in light of the fact that only a few weeks before, the very idea that Gansey might even know about the court case had troubled Adam.

But now — no. He still didn't want them to remember this part of him. He only wanted them to see the new Adam. Persephone had told him that no one had to know his past if he didn't want them to.

He didn't want them to.

So he waited, while Gansey and Ronan and Blue went off to school and had ordinary days. He sat on the edge of his mattress and worked on the plan to blackmail Greenmantle as first period happened. He stared at his biology text and thought about a dustless circle around his feet for second period. Then he drove to the courthouse.

Cabeswater beckoned him, but he couldn't retreat. He had to be here for this.

Every step before the courthouse was an event forgotten as soon as it had happened. There was parking, a metal detector, a clerk, a back staircase instead of the elevator, another clerk, a glimpsed low-ceilinged room with pews like a church on either side of an aisle, a church for the mundane, a service for those who claimed not guilty.

Adam tried to soothe himself by telling himself that people worked here every day, this was nothing extraordinary to them, there was nothing special about this building. But the old, mold-and-glue smell of it, the feeling of threadbare carpet beneath his feet, the sickly, uneven light of the fluorescents overhead — all of it felt alien. All of it burdened his senses with how this day was like no other. He was going to be sick. Or faint.

Was his father in the building yet?

It was a closed courtroom for juvenile cases, so the only people in the room so far were the staff: clerks, lawyers, bailiffs.

Adam turned over the possible outcomes in his head. If he lost, he knew academically that the court couldn't make him return home. He was eighteen and free to go and fail or succeed in life apart from his family. But would this linger on his record then: a boy who had spuriously taken his father to court? How ugly that would look. How base. He imagined Gansey's father interpreting: familial squabbling of the lower classes. This is how the low stayed low, he would say. Infighting and drinking, daytime TV and Walmart everyday low prices.

He couldn't quite feel invested in winning, either, because he wasn't sure what it would look like. It was possible that his father would go back to jail. If he did, could his mother pay the bills?

He shouldn't care. But he couldn't make himself stop.

Adam felt as if he were playing pretend in his good suit.

But you are just one of them, white trash in diamonds.

There was his father.

He was in a jacket with some local company's logo on the back and his company polo shirt. Adam prayed for some sort of clarity, to see his father as everyone else saw him, instead of as *Dad? It's Adam —*

"There's still time for you to tell the truth," Robert Parrish said.

Adam's mother had not come.

Adam's fingers were numb.

Even if I lose, he thought weakly, *he can't have me back, so it won't matter. It will only be this hour of humiliation and then it will be over.*

He wished he had never done this.

"All right, then," said the judge. His face was a memory that vanished the minute Adam blinked.

Cabeswater stole him away for a blissful second, leaves curled against his throat, and then released him. How desperately Adam wanted to cling to Cabeswater. Strange as it was, it was familiar, and on his side.

He had been wrong to come here alone. Why did he care if Gansey and Ronan saw this? They already knew. They knew everything about him. What a lie *unknowable* was. The only person who didn't know Adam was himself.

What a proud idiot you have been, Adam Parrish.

"Are there any witnesses for this case?" the judge asked.

There were not.

Adam didn't look at his father.

"Then I guess we shall begin."

A hissing sound came from the bailiff beside the judge: a voice through his radio. The bailiff leaned his head to listen, then muttered something back to the speaker. Coming close to the judge, he said, "Your Honor, Bailiff Myley says there are some witnesses for the case outside if it's not too late for them to come in."

"The door's already closed, is it not?"

"It is."

The judge peered at his watch. "They are certainly for the Parrish case?"

"Bailiff Myley seems to think they are."

The judge smiled with some private humor; this was some long-running joke the others weren't privy to. "Far be it from me to doubt him. Send them in, and I'll decide whether to allow them."

Adam miserably wondered which of the neighbors were coming to his father's defense.

In an hour, this will be over. You will never have to do it again. All you have to do is survive.

The door cracked open. Adam didn't want to look, but he did anyway.

In the hall stood Richard Campbell Gansey III in his school uniform and overcoat and scarf and gloves, looking like someone from another world. Behind him was Ronan Lynch, his damn tie knotted right for once and his shirt tucked in.

Humiliation and joy warred furiously inside Adam.

Gansey strode between the pews as Adam's father stared at him. He went directly to the bench, straight up to the judge. Now that he stood directly beside Adam, not looking at him, Adam could see that he was a little out of breath. Ronan, behind him, was as well. They had run.

For him.

Removing his right glove, Gansey shook hands with the judge.

"Judge Harris," he said warmly.

"Mr. Gansey," said Judge Harris. "Have you found that king of yours yet?"

"Not just yet. Have you finished that terrace yet?"

"Not just yet," Harris replied. "What's your business with this case?"

"Ronan Lynch here was at the incident," Gansey said. "I thought his side of the story might be worthy. And I've been friends with Adam since day one here in Henrietta, and I'm glad to see this miserable business over. I'd like to be a character witness, if I could."

"That sounds reasonable," Harris said.

"I object," Robert Parrish exclaimed.

Gansey turned to Adam, finally. He was still wearing his glorious kingly face, Richard Campbell Gansey III, white knight, but his eyes were uncertain. *Is this okay?*

Was it okay? Adam had turned down so many offers of help from Gansey. Money for school, money for food, money for rent. Pity and charity, Adam had thought. For so long, he'd wanted Gansey to see him as an equal, but it was possible that all this time, the only person who needed to see that was Adam.

Now he could see that it wasn't charity Gansey was offering. It was just *truth*.

And something else: friendship of the unshakable kind. Friendship you could swear on. That could be busted nearly to breaking and come back stronger than before.

Adam held out his right hand, and Gansey clasped it in a handshake, like they were men, because they *were* men.

"All right," Harris reported. "Let's get this case under way."

39

Adam didn't normally take anyone with him when he did Cabeswater's work. He trusted his skills on his own. His *emotions* he trusted on his own. He could hurt no one in an empty room. No one could hurt him.

He was unknowable.

Except that he wasn't.

So he asked Blue Sargent to come with him when he finally went to do what Cabeswater had asked him to do weeks before. He didn't tell her, in case it didn't work, but he thought that if he brought her with him, Cabeswater might help them find Maura.

Now he waited in the car at a faded gas station outside of Henrietta. He couldn't tell if the pulse in his palms was his heartbeat or the ley line.

"I know what you mean," Noah said from the backseat. He was draped over the passenger headrest like a sweater with a body still in it. Adam had nearly forgotten he was there, because he hadn't been invited. Not because he was unwanted, but because he was dead, and the deceased couldn't be counted on to show up at specific times.

"Did you just reply to my thoughts?"

"I don't think so."

Adam couldn't remember if he'd spoken out loud. He didn't think he had.

The car rocked as a farm truck trundled by on the highway. Everything about this area was worn. The gas station was a survivor from decades past, with tin signs in the window and chickens for sale behind it. The farm across the road was faded but charming, like a yellowed newspaper.

He turned Greenmantle's blackmail over in his mind. It had to be bulletproof. He hadn't told Gansey; he hadn't told Blue. He'd convinced Ronan of it and brought the Gray Man into it, but in the end, it was all on him if Greenmantle exploded in their faces.

"I think it's ready," Noah said.

"Stop that. Stop. It's creepy."

He shot a glance to Noah in the rearview mirror and regretted it; the dead boy was more frightening in reflections. Much less living.

Noah knew it; he ducked out of the mirror's view.

From outside the car, Blue's voice rose. "How would you feel if I reduced *you* to your legs?"

Adam and Noah craned to look out the back window.

Blue's voice came again. "No. No. How about you see it *my* way? How about you don't reduce me to a commodity and then, when I ask you not to, tell me it's a compliment and I should be *glad* for it?"

Noah's mouth made an *oooo* shape.

"Yeah," Adam agreed, climbing out.

Blue stood a few feet away. She wore a big boxy T-shirt, teal shorts, combat boots, and socks that came up over her knees. Only four inches of bare skin were visible, but they were a really nice four inches.

An old man wearing a seed cap was saying, "Little lady, one day you'll remember the days people told you that you had nice legs as a good memory."

Adam braced for the explosion.

It was nails and dynamite. "Good — memory? Oh, I *wish* I were as ignorant as you! What happiness! There are girls who *kill* themselves over negative body image and *you* —"

"Is there a problem here?" Adam broke in.

The man seemed relieved. People were always pleased to see clean, muted Adam, the deferential Southern voice of reason. "Your girlfriend's quite a firecracker."

Adam stared at the man. Blue stared at Adam.

He wanted to tell her it wasn't worth it — that he'd grown up with this sort of man and knew they were untrainable — but then she'd throw the thermos at Adam's head and probably slap that guy in the mouth. It was amazing that she and Ronan didn't get along better, because they were different brands of the same impossible stuff.

"Sir," Adam started — Blue's eyebrows spiked — "I think maybe your mama didn't teach you how to talk to women."

The old man shook his head at Adam, like in pity.

Adam added, "And she's not my girlfriend."

Blue flashed him a brilliant look of approval, and then she got into the car with a dramatic door slam Ronan would have approved of.

"Look, kid," the old man started.

Adam interrupted, "Your fuel door's open, by the way."

He climbed back into his little, shitty car, the one Ronan called the Hondayota. He felt heroic for no good reason. Blue simmered righteously as they pulled out of the station. For a few moments, there was nothing but the labored sound of the little car's breathing.

Then Noah said, "You do have nice legs, though."

Blue swung at him. A helpless laugh escaped Adam, and she hit his shoulder, too.

"Did you get the water at least?" he asked.

She sloshed the thermos to demonstrate success. "I also brought some jet. It's supposed to be good protection while you're scrying."

"We're *scrying*?" Noah sat up straight.

Adam struggled to explain. "Cabeswater speaks one language, and I speak another. I can get the broad idea from reading the cards. But it's harder to get the specifics of how to fix the alignment. So I'm scrying. I do it all the time. It's just efficient, Noah."

"An efficient way to get your naked soul stolen by forces of *raw evil*, maybe," Noah said.

Blue exchanged a look with Adam. "I don't believe in raw evil."

Noah said, "It doesn't care if you believe in it."

She turned in her seat to face him. "I don't normally like to point out when you're being creepy. But you are."

The dead boy retreated farther into the backseat; the air warmed marginally as he did. "*He* already called me creepy today."

"Tell me more about the aligning stuff," Blue said to Adam. "Tell me *why* it wants you to."

"I don't understand how it matters."

She made a noise of profound exasperation. "Even putting aside every single spiritual consideration, or, or, mythological consideration, or anything that actually means anything, you're manipulating this massive energy source that seems to communicate directly into your head in a different language, and that, to me, seems like something I would have a lot of questions about if I were you!"

"I don't want to talk about it."

"But I do. You're driving all the way out here, and you don't even ask why?"

Adam didn't reply, because his reply wouldn't have been civil.

His silence, however, seemed to be worse. She snapped, "If you didn't want to talk, I don't know why you asked me if I wanted to come!"

"Maybe I shouldn't have."

"Right, who wants someone who *thinks* along with them!"

He reined himself in, with effort. With only a little barbed wire in his tone, he said, "I just want to get this *done*."

"Just put me out here. I'll *walk back*."

He slammed on the brakes. "Don't think I won't."

"Do it, then!" She already had her hand on the door handle.

"*Guys,*" Noah wailed.

The best and worst thing about Blue Sargent was that she meant what she said; she really would walk herself back to Henrietta if he stopped now. He grimaced at her. She grimaced back.

Don't fight with Blue. Don't fight with Gansey.

With a sigh, he sped up again.

Blue got herself back together and then turned on the radio.

Adam hadn't even realized the ancient tape deck worked, but after a hissing few seconds, a tape inside jangled a tune. Noah began to sing along at once.

"Squash one, squash two —"

Adam pawed for the radio at the same time as Blue. The tape ejected with enough force that Noah stretched a hand to catch it.

"That *song*. What are you doing with *that* in your player?" demanded Blue. "Do you listen to that recreationally? How did that song escape from the Internet?"

Noah cackled and showed them the cassette. It boasted a handmade label marked with Ronan's handwriting: PARRISH'S HONDAYOTA ALONE TIME. The other side was A SHITBOX SING-ALONG.

"Play it! Play it!" Noah said gaily, waving the tape.

"Noah. Noah! Take that away from him," Adam said.

Ahead of them, the entrance for Skyline Drive loomed. Adam was ready this time; he opened his wallet as they coasted closer. Inside nestled precisely fifteen dollars.

Blue handed over a five. "My contribution."

There was a pause.

He took it.

At the window, he exchanged their combined funds for a map, which he gave back to Blue. As he headed into a slanted parking area shortly beyond the entrance, he uncertainly examined his pride for damage and was surprised to find none.

"Is this the right place?" she asked. "Do you need our fifteen-dollar map?"

Adam said, "I'll know in a second. We can get out."

Before them, the ground dropped sharply into a bottomless ravine; behind them, the mountains ascended darkly. The air was clouded with the pleasant and dangerous scent of wood-smoke: Somewhere, one of these autumn mountains was on fire. Adam squinted until he found its source, smoke shrouding a distant peak. From this far away, it seemed more magical than threatening.

Blue and Noah horsed around as Adam retrieved his tarot cards. Squaring his feet so that he could better feel the line's pulse, he placed a random card on the warm hood. His unfocused eyes skipped over the image — a black-smudged knight on horseback carrying a vine-wrapped staff — and began to remake it into something wordless and dreamy. Sight was replaced with sensation. A vertiginous feeling of travel, climbing, rightness.

He covered the image with his hand until he got his eyes back, and then he put the card away.

"Knight of wands?" Blue asked him.

Already Adam couldn't remember what the card had *really* been. "Was it?"

"Now who's creepy?" Noah asked.

Adam shouldered his backpack and headed toward the trail-head. "Come on. It's this way."

The rocky, narrow trail was dusted with crumbled leaves. The ground fell away abruptly on one side and rose as precipitously on the other. Adam was hyperaware of the massive boulders that jutted into the trail. Beneath a furring of mint-green lichen, the stones felt cool and alive, wild conductors of the ley line. He led Noah and Blue upward until they came to a confusion of boulders. Stepping off the trail, Adam climbed alongside them, finding footholds on jutting stones and exposed tree branches. The big, blue stones were tumbled onto one another like a giant's playset.

Yes, this is it.

He peered into a man-sized crevice.

Blue said, "Snakes? Nests? Bears?"

"Protected national park," Noah said, darkly funny. And then, with unexpected valiance, "I'll go in first. They can't hurt me."

He looked smudgy and insubstantial as he slid inside. There was silence, silence.

Blue squinted. "Noah?"

From inside the crevice came a great rustling flurry. All at once, a large puff of oak leaves exploded from the opening, startling both Blue and Adam.

Noah reappeared. He plucked four and a half oak leaves out of Blue's spiky hair and blew some leaf crumbs from the bridge of Adam's nose. "It's safe."

Adam was glad to have them with him.

Inside was dim but not dark; light came from the entrance, and also from below, where the rocks were stacked imperfectly. In the middle of the small space was a large boulder the size of a desk or an altar. The surface was worn and cupped.

He remembered or recognized it from his insight in the garage.

He felt a little shake of nerves, or anticipation. It was strange to do this with an audience. He didn't quite know what he looked like from the outside.

"Pour the water in there, Blue."

Blue ran a hand over the stone to clear out debris. "Oh!" Retrieving a black stone from her pocket, she placed it by the indentation. Then she slowly filled it with water.

The shallow pool reflected the dark ceiling.

Noah backed well away from it, making sure he wasn't reflected. His fear sucked the warmth from the space. Blue stretched a hand to him, but he shook his head.

So she stayed by Adam, shoulder pressed to his, and Adam found he was glad for this, too. He couldn't remember the last time someone had touched him, and it was strangely grounding. After a second, he realized that part of it was probably the fact of Blue's ability, too, amplifying whatever part of Cabeswater he was tied to.

They eyed the water. He had done this before, but never like this, surrounded by rock. It felt like there was someone else in the room with them. He didn't want to admit that he was already intimidated by the dark pool even before anything supernatural had happened. Neither of them said anything for a few minutes.

Finally, Blue whispered, "It's like, if someone said to you, 'Nice sweater, dude!' when you were in your Aglionby uniform."

"*What?*"

"I wanted you to know why I got so angry at that old guy. I've been trying to think of a way to explain it. I know you don't get it. But that's why."

It was true that he hadn't understood the fuss at the gas station, really, beyond the fact that she was bothered, and he didn't like for her to be bothered. But she was right about the sweater, too. People assumed things based on the Aglionby sweater or blazer all the time; he'd done it himself. Still did it.

"I get it," he whispered back. He wasn't sure why they were whispering, but he did feel better now. More normal. They were in control here. "It's simplifying."

"Exactly." She took a deep breath. "Okay. What now?"

"I'm going to look in and focus," Adam said. "I might zone out."

Noah whimpered.

Blue, however, sounded practical. "What do you want us to do if you zone out?"

"I don't reckon you should do anything. I don't really know what it will look like from the outside. I guess, use your judgment if something seems wrong."

Noah hugged his arms around himself.

Leaning over the pool, Adam saw his face. He hadn't noticed that he didn't look like everyone else until he got to high school, when everyone else started noticing. He didn't know if he was good-looking or bad-looking — only that he was different-looking. It was up to interpretation whether the strangeness of his face was beautiful or ugly.

He waited for his features to disappear, to smudge into a sensation. But all he saw was his Henrietta-dirt face with its pulled-down thin mouth. He wished he wouldn't grow up to look like his parents' combined genes.

"I don't think it's working," he said.

But Blue didn't reply, and after half a heartbeat, Adam realized that his mouth hadn't moved in the reflection when he spoke. His face just stared back, eyebrows drawn into suspicion and worry.

His thoughts churned up inside him, silt clouding a pool of water. Humans were so circular; they lived the same slow cycles of joy and misery over and over, never learning. Every lesson in the universe had to be taught billions of times, and it never stuck. *How arrogant we are*, Adam thought, *to deliver babies who can't walk or talk or feed themselves. How sure we are that nothing will destroy them before they can take care of themselves.* How fragile they were, how easily abandoned and neglected and beaten and hated. Prey animals were born afraid.

He had not known to be born afraid, but he'd learned.

Maybe it was good that the world forgot every lesson, every good and bad memory, every triumph and failure, all of it dying with each generation. Perhaps this cultural amnesia spared them all. Perhaps if they remembered everything, hope would die instead.

Outside yourself, Persephone's voice reminded him.

It was difficult to tear himself away; there was a strange, hideous comfort to wearing the edges off his interior.

With effort, he recalled Cabeswater. He felt along the field of the energy in his mind. Somewhere there would be a fray or dispersion, some ailment he could cure.

There it was. Far down the ley line, the energy was fractured. If he concentrated, he could even see why: A highway had been cut into a mountain, gouging out rock and breaking the natural line of the ley. Now it sputtered unevenly as it leapt across and under the highway. If Adam could realign a few of the charged stones at the top of this mountain, it would cause a chain reaction that would eventually make the line dig underground, beneath the highway, joining the frayed ends again.

He asked, "Why do you want me to do this? *Rogo aliquem aliquid.*"

He didn't really expect an answer, but he heard a babble of speech, incomprehensible but for one word: *Greywaren.*

Ronan, who effortlessly spoke Cabeswater's language. Not Adam, who struggled.

But not in the Aglionby courtyard. He hadn't struggled then. There hadn't *been* a language. Just him and Cabeswater.

"Not Ronan," Adam said. "Me. I'm the one who's doing this for you. Tell *me.* Show *me.*"

Images barraged him. Connections darted electric. Veins. Roots. Forked lightning. Tributaries. Branches. Vines snaked around trees, herds of animals, drops of water running together.

I don't understand.

Fingers twined together. Shoulder leaned on shoulder. Fist bumping fist. Hand dragging Adam up from the dirt.

Cabeswater rifled madly through Adam's own memories and flashed them through his mind. It hurled images of Gansey, Ronan, Noah, and Blue so fast that Adam couldn't keep up with all of them.

Then the grid of lightning blasted across the world, an illuminated grid of energy.

Adam still did not understand, and then he did.

There was more than one Cabeswater. Or more of whatever it was.

How many? He didn't know. How alive was it? He didn't know that, either. Did it *think*, was it an alien, did it die, was it good, was it right? He didn't know. But he knew there was more than one, and this one stretched its fingers out as hard as it could to reach the other.

The enormity of the world grew and grew inside Adam, and he didn't know if he could hold it. He was just a boy. Was he meant to know this?

They had transformed Henrietta already by waking this ley line and strengthening Cabeswater. What would a world look like with more forests woken all over it? Would it tear itself apart with crackling electricity and magic, or was this a pendulum swing, a result of hundreds of years of sleep?

How many kings slept?

I can't do this. This is too big. I was not made for this.

Doubt suddenly tore blackly through him. It was a thing, this doubt, it had weight, and body, and legs —

What? Adam thought he said it out loud, but he couldn't quite remember how *doing* was different than *imagining*. He'd wandered too far from his own body.

Again, he felt that doubtful thing reaching at him, speaking to him. It didn't believe in his power here. It knew he was a pretender.

Adam dragged at words. *Are you Cabeswater? Are you Glendower?* But words seemed like the wrong medium for this place. Words were for mouths, and he didn't have one anymore. He stretched through the world; he couldn't seem to find his way back to the cave. He was in an ocean, sinking, darkly.

He was alone except for this thing, and he thought it hated

him, or wanted him, or both. He longed to see it; seeing it would be the worst thing.

Adam flailed in the black. All directions looked the same. Something was crawling on his skin.

He was in a cavern. Crouched. The ceiling was low and the stalactites touched his back. When he reached to touch the wall, it felt real under his fingers. Or like it was real and he wasn't.

Adam

He turned to the voice, and it was a woman he recognized but couldn't name. He was too far from his thoughts.

Even though he was certain it had been her voice, she didn't look at him. She was crouched in the cavern beside him, eyebrows knitted in concentration, a fist pressed to her lips. A man knelt adjacent to her, but everything about his folded-over, lanky body suggested that he wasn't in communication with the woman. They were both motionless as they faced a door set into the stone.

Adam, go

The door told him to touch it. It described the satisfaction of the handle turning beneath his hand. It promised an understanding of the blackness inside him if he pushed it open. It pulsed in him, the hunger, the ascending desire.

He had never wanted anything so badly.

He was in front of it. He didn't remember crossing the distance, but somehow he had. The door was dark red and carved with roots and knots and crowns. The handle was oily black.

He had come so far from his body that he couldn't imagine how to even begin going back.

The door needs three to open

Go

Adam crouched motionless, fingers braced against the stone, afraid and desirous.

Somewhere far away, he felt his body getting older.

Adam, go

I can't, he thought. *I'm lost.*

"Adam! *Adam. Adam Parrish.*"

He came to in a fury of pain. His face felt wet; his hand felt wet; his veins felt too full of blood.

Noah's voice rose. "Why did you cut him so deep!"

"I didn't *measure!*" Blue said. "Adam, you jerk, say something."

Pain made every possible response meaner than it would have been otherwise. Instead, he hissed and rocked himself upright, gripping one hand with the other. His surroundings were slowly representing themselves to him; he'd forgotten that they'd crawled in between these boulders. Noah crouched an inch away, eyes on Adam's. Blue stood a little bit behind him.

Things were starting to come together. He was very aware of his fingers and mouth and skin and eyes and himself. He couldn't remember ever being so glad to be Adam Parrish.

His eyes focused on the pink switchblade knife in Blue's hand. "You cut me?" he said.

Noah's shoulders slumped in relief at his voice.

Adam studied his hand. A clean slice marred the back of it. It was bleeding like nobody's business, but it didn't hurt badly unless he moved it. The knife must've been very sharp.

Noah touched the edge of the wound with his freezing fingers, and Adam slapped him away. He struggled to remember everything the voice had just said, but already it was sliding out of his head like a dream.

Had there even been words? Why did he think there had been words?

"I didn't know what else to try to get you back," Blue admitted. "Noah said to cut you."

He was confused by the switchblade. It seemed to represent a different side of her; a side that he had not thought existed. His brain wearied when he tried to fit it in with the rest of her. "Why did you *stop* me? What was I doing?"

She said "nothing" at the same time that Noah said "dying."

"Your face went sort of empty," she went on. "And then your eyes just . . . stopped. Blinking? Moving? I tried to get you back."

"And then you stopped breathing," Noah said. He slunk to his feet. "I *told* you. I told you it was a bad idea, and nobody ever listens to me. 'Oh, we'll be fine, Noah, you're such a worrywart' and next thing you know you're in some kind of death thrall. Nobody ever says, 'Noah, you know what you were right thanks for saving my life because being dead would suck.' They just always —"

"Stop," Adam interrupted. "I'm trying to remember everything that happened."

There had been someone important — three — a door — a woman he recognized —

It was fading. Everything except for the terror.

"Next time I'll let you die," Blue said. "You forget, Adam, when you're pulling your special snowflake act, where I grew up. Do you know what the phrase is for when someone helps you during a ritual or a reading? It's *thank you*. You shouldn't have brought us if you wanted to do it alone."

He remembered this: He had been lost.

Which meant that if he had come alone, he would have been dead now.

"Sorry," he said. "I was being sort of a dick."

Noah replied, "We weren't going to say it."

"I was," Blue said.

Then they climbed to the top of the mountain and, as the sun blasted them from above, found the stones Adam had seen in the scrying pool. It took all of their combined strength to shove the rocks just a few bare inches. Adam didn't know how he would have managed this part without help, either. Possibly he was doing it wrong, and there was a better, more proper magician way.

He left bloody fingerprints on the rock, but there was something satisfying about that.

I was here. I exist. I'm alive, because I bleed.

He hadn't stopped being thankful for his body. *Hello, Adam Parrish's formerly chapped hands, I'm happy to have you.*

They knew the precise moment they'd solved the alignment, because Noah said, "Ah!" and stretched his fingers up to the air. For a few minutes, anyway, he was silhouetted against the livid sky, and there was no difference between him and Blue and Adam. There was nothing to say that he was anything less than fully living.

As the winds buffeted them, Noah slung a comradely arm around Blue's shoulders and another around Adam's and pulled them to him. They staggered back toward the trail. Blue's arm was linked around the back of Noah, and her fingers grabbed Adam's T-shirt so that they were one creature, a drunken six-legged animal. Adam's hand was throbbing with the beat of his heart. Probably he was going to bleed to death on the way back down the mountain, but he was okay with that.

Suddenly, with Noah to his side and Blue next to him, three strong, Adam remembered the woman he had seen in the pool.

He knew all at once who she was.

"Blue," he said. "I saw your mother."

40

This is one of my favorite places," Persephone said, tipping her rocking chair to and fro with her bare feet. Her hair cascaded over the arms. "It's so homey."

Adam perched on the edge of the rocking chair beside her. He did not much like the place, but he did not say it. She had asked him to meet her here, and she nearly never made the decision of where to meet; she left it up to him, which always felt like a test.

It was a strange old general store of the sort that had died everywhere else but was not uncommon around Henrietta. The outside usually looked like this one: a sweeping, low porch lined with rocking chairs facing the road, a rutted gravel parking lot, signs for bait and cigarettes in the windows. The inside usually held convenience store foods in brands one had never heard of, T-shirts Adam would not wear, fishing supplies, toys from another decade, and the occasional taxidermied deer head. It was a place that Adam, a hick, found to be populated by people he considered even more hickish.

Gansey would probably like it, though. It was one of those places where time seemed irrelevant, especially on an evening like this: dappled light fuzzing through leaves, starlings calling from the close-strung telephone wires, old men in old trucks driving slowly past, all of it looking like it could have happened twenty years before.

"Three," Persephone said, "is a very strong number."

Lessons with Persephone were an unpredictable thing. He never knew, going in, what he was going to learn. Sometimes he still hadn't figured it, going out.

This evening he wanted to ask her about Maura, but it was hard to ask Persephone a question and get an answer when you wanted it. Usually, it worked best if you asked the question right before she was about to say the answer anyway.

"Like three sleepers?"

"Sure," Persephone replied. "Or three knights."

"Are there knights?"

She pointed, drawing his attention to a large crow or raven hopping slowly on the other side of the road. It was hard to say if she thought it was significant or just funny. "There were, once. Also, three Jesuses."

This took Adam a moment. "Oh, God. You mean God and Jesus and the Holy Spirit?"

Persephone twirled a small hand. "I always forget the names. There's a three-lady-god, too. One's named War, I think, and another one's a baby — I don't know, I forget the details. The three is the important part."

He was better at playing these games than he used to be. Better at guessing the connections. "You and Maura and Calla."

Maybe now was the time to bring it up —

She nodded, or rocked, or both. "It's a stable number, three. Fives and sevens are good, too, but three is the best. Things are always growing to three or shrinking to three. Best to start there.

Two is a terrible number. Two is for rivalry and fighting and murder."

"Or marriage," Adam said, thinking.

"Same thing," Persephone replied. "Here is three dollars. Go inside and get me a cherry cola."

He did so, trying to think, the entire time, how to ask about using his vision to find Maura. With Persephone, it was possible that that was what they had actually been talking about the entire time.

When he returned, he said, suddenly, "This is the last time, isn't it?"

She continued rocking, but she nodded. "I thought, at first, that you might replace one of us if something ever happened."

It took him a long time to make the sentence make sense, and when he finally did, the surprise kept him from answering for another minute longer.

"Me?"

"You're a very good listener."

"But I'm — I'm —" He couldn't think of how to finish the sentence. He finally said, "Leaving."

Even as he said it, he knew it wasn't what he meant.

But Persephone just said, in her tiny voice, "But I see now that it could never be. You're like me. We're not really like the others."

Other what? Humans?

You are unknowable.

He thought of that moment on the mountaintop with him and Blue and Noah. Or in the courtroom, him and Ronan and Gansey.

He wasn't sure anymore.

"We're really better in our own company," Persephone said. "It makes it hard, sometimes, for others, when they can't understand us."

She was trying to get him to say something, to make some connection, but he wasn't sure what. He said, "Don't tell me Maura is dead."

She rocked and rocked. Then she stopped and looked at him with her black, black eyes. The sun eased down behind the tree line, making a black lace of the leaves and a white lace of her hair.

Adam's breath caught. He asked in a low voice, "Can you see your own death?"

"Everyone sees it," Persephone said mildly. "Most people make themselves stop looking, though."

"I don't see my own death," Adam said. But even as he said it, he felt the corner of the knowledge bite into him. It was now, it was coming, it had already happened. Somewhere, some*when*, he was dying.

"Ah, you see," she said.

"That's not the same as knowing *how*."

"You didn't say *how*."

What he wanted to say, but couldn't, because Persephone wouldn't understand, was that he was afraid. Not of seeing things like this. But of one day not being able to see everything else. The real. The mundane. The . . . *human* things.

We're not really like the others.

But he thought that maybe he was. He thought he must be, because he cared deeply about Maura's disappearance, and he cared even more deeply about Gansey's death, and now that he knew about these things, he wanted to do something about them. He needed to. He was Cabeswater, stretching out to others.

He took a shaky breath. "Do you know how Gansey dies?"

Persephone stuck her tongue out, just a little. She didn't seem to notice she was doing it. Then she said, "Here is three more dollars. Go get yourself a cherry cola."

He didn't take the money. He said, "I want to know how long you've known about Gansey. From the beginning? From the beginning. You knew it when he walked in the door for the reading! Were you ever going to tell us?"

"I don't know why I would do such a ridiculous thing. Get your cola."

Adam still didn't take the bills. Bracing his hands on the arms of his rocker, he said, "When I find Glendower, I'm asking him for Gansey's life and that'll be that."

Persephone just looked at him.

In his head, Gansey shook and kicked, covered with blood. Only now it was Ronan's face — Ronan had already died, Gansey was going to die — somewhere, some*when*, was this happening?

He didn't want to know. He wanted to know.

"Tell me, then!" he said. "Tell me what to do!"

"What do you want me to say?"

Adam leapt out of the chair so quickly that it rocked frantically without him. "Tell me how to save him!"

"For how long?" Persephone asked.

"*Stop!*" he said. "*Stop that!* Stop being so — so — zoomed out! I can't look at the big picture all the time, or what's the point? Just tell me how I can keep from killing him!"

Persephone cocked her head. "What makes you think *you* kill him?"

He stared at her. Then went back inside for another cherry cola.

"Thirsty?" asked the clerk as Adam handed over his money.

"The other one was for my friend," Adam said, although he wasn't sure anyone was Persephone's friend.

"Your friend?" asked the clerk.

"Probably."

He went back outside and found the porch empty. His rocker was still rocking, just a little. The other cherry cola was sitting beside it.

"Persephone?"

With sudden misgiving, he rushed to the rocker she had been sitting in. He put his hand on the seat. Cool. He put his hand on the seat of his. Warm.

He craned his neck, looking to see if she was back inside the car. There was nothing. The parking lot was still; even the bird was gone.

"No," he said, though there was no one to hear him. His mind — a mind curiously remade by Cabeswater — frantically pulled from everything he knew and felt, everything Persephone had said, every moment since he had arrived. The sun crept behind the trees.

"No," he said again.

The clerk was at the door, locking it for the night.

"Wait," Adam said. "Did you see my friend? Or did I come here alone?"

She raised one eyebrow.

"I'm sorry," he said. "I know how it sounds. Please. Was it just me?"

The clerk hesitated, waiting for the prank. Then she nodded.

Adam's heart felt bottomless. "I need to use your phone. Please, ma'am. Just for a second."

"Why?"

"Something terrible has happened."

41

I'm here," Blue said, whirling in the door of 300 Fox Way. She was sweaty and irritable and nervous, torn between hoping for a false alarm and hoping it was important enough to justify begging off in the middle of her Nino's shift.

Calla met her in the hall as she dropped her bag by the door. "Come here and help Adam."

"What's wrong with Adam!"

"Nothing," Calla snapped. "Besides the usual. He's looking for Persephone!"

They reached the reading room door. Inside, Adam sat at the head of the reading room table. He was very still, and his eyes were closed. In front of him was the black scrying bowl from Maura's room. The only light was from three flickering candles. Blue's stomach did something unpleasant.

"I don't think this is a good idea," she said. "Last time —"

"I know. He told me," Calla said. "But he's willing to risk it. And it'll be better with three of us."

"Why is he looking for Persephone?"

"He thinks something's wrong with her."

"Where is she? Did she tell you where she went?"

Calla gave Blue a withering look. Of course. Persephone never told anyone anything.

"Okay," Blue said.

Calla closed the reading room doors behind her and pointed for Blue to sit beside Adam.

Adam opened his eyes. She wasn't sure what to ask him, and he just shook his head a little, like he was angry at himself or Persephone or the world.

Calla sat opposite and took one of Adam's hands. She ordered Blue, "You take the other. I'll ground him, and you'll amplify him."

Blue and Adam exchanged a look. They had not held hands since their breakup. She slid her hand across the table and he linked his fingers through hers. Gingerly. Not pushing the issue. Blue closed her fingers around his hand.

Adam said, "I'm . . ."

He stopped. He was looking at the scrying bowl out of the corner of his eye, not dead-on.

"You're what?" Calla said.

He finished, "I'm trusting you guys."

Blue held his hand a little tighter. Calla said, "We won't let you fall."

The bowl shimmered darkly, and he looked into it.

He looked and looked, the candles flickering, and Blue felt the precise moment his body released his soul, because the candles went strange in the reflections and his fingers went limp in hers.

Blue looked sharply to Calla, but Calla merely remained as she was, his light hand lying in her dark one, her chin tilted up, her eyes cut over to Adam watchfully.

His lips moved, like he was mumbling to himself, but no sound came out.

Blue thought of how she amplified his scrying, forcing him

further down into the ether. Adam wandered now, traveling out from his body, unwinding the thread that tied him back to it. Calla hung on to the thread, but Blue pushed on him.

Adam's eyebrows furrowed. His lips parted. His eyes were utterly black — the black of the mirrored scrying bowl. Every so often, the three twisted flames reflected in the bowl appeared in his irises. Only sometimes there were two in one eye and only one in the other, or three in one, and none in the other, or three in both, and then blackness.

"No," whispered Adam. His voice sounded unlike his own. Blue was reminded terribly of the night she had stumbled upon Neeve scrying in the roots of the beech tree.

Again Blue looked to Calla.

Again Calla remained still and watchful.

"Maura?" Adam called. "Maura?"

Only it was Persephone's voice coming out of Adam's mouth.

I can't do this, Blue thought suddenly. Her heart couldn't manage it, being afraid.

Calla's other hand reached across the table to take Blue's. They were joined in a circle around the scrying bowl.

Adam's breathing hitched and slowed.

Not again.

Blue felt Calla's body shifting as she gripped Adam's hand tighter.

"No," he said again, and this was his own voice.

The flames were huge in his eyes.

Then they went back to black.

He didn't breathe.

The room was silent for one beat. Two beats. Three beats.

The candles went out in the scrying bowl.

"PERSEPHONE!" he shouted.

"Now," Calla said, releasing Blue's hand. "Let go of him!"

Blue released his hand, but nothing happened.

"Cut him off," Calla snarled. "I know you can. I'll pull him back!"

As Calla used her free hand to press a thumb to the center of Adam's forehead, Blue frantically imagined what she had done to pull the plug on Noah back in Monmouth. Only it had been one thing to do it while Noah threw things about. It was another thing to do it as she watched Adam's still chest and his empty eyes. Another thing as his shoulders sagged and his face fell into Calla's waiting hands just before he slumped into the scrying bowl.

He's trusting us. He never trusts anyone, and he's trusting us.

He's trusting you, Blue.

She jumped out of her chair and put up her walls. She tried to visualize the white light pouring down to strengthen them, but it was hard when she could see Adam's body sprawled limply across the end of the reading table. Calla slapped his face.

"Come on, you bastard! Remember your body!"

Blue turned her back on the scene.

She closed her eyes.

And she did it.

There was silence.

Then the overhead lights came on and Adam's voice said, "She's here."

Blue spun.

"What do you mean, *here*?" Calla demanded.

"Here," Adam said. He shoved out of his chair. "Upstairs."

"But we checked her room," Calla said.

"Not in her room." Adam waved a hand impatiently. "The highest — where's the highest place?"

"The attic," Blue said. "Why would she be up there? Gwenllian —?"

"Gwenllian's in the tree in the backyard," Calla said. "She's singing at some birds who hate her."

"Are there mirrors?" Adam asked. "Some place she would go to look for Maura?"

Calla swore.

She tore open the attic door and charged up first, Blue and Adam close on her heels. At the top of the stairs, she said, "No."

Blue jumped past her.

In between Neeve's two mirrors was a pile of lace, canvas, and — Persephone.

Adam hurried forward, but Calla seized his arm. "No, you idiot. You can't reach between them! Blue, stop!"

"I can," Blue replied. She slid to kneel beside Persephone. She was collapsed in a way that was clearly unintentional. She was on her knees with her arms bent behind her and her chin hitched up, caught on the feet of one of the mirrors. Her black eyes stared into nothing.

"We'll get her back," Adam said.

But Calla was already crying.

Blue, unconcerned with dignity, dragged Persephone out by her armpits. She was light and unresisting.

They would pull her back, just as Adam said.

Calla sank to her knees and covered her face.

"Stop it," snapped Blue, voice cracking. "Get over here and help."

She took Persephone's hand. It was as cold as the cave walls.

Adam stood with his arms wrapped around himself, a question in his eyes.

Blue already knew the answer, but she couldn't say it.

Calla did: "She's dead."

42

Blue had never believed in death until then.

Not in a real way.

It happened to other people, other families, in other places. It happened in hospitals or automobile crashes or battle zones. It happened — now she remembered Gansey's words outside Gwenllian's tomb — with ceremony. With some announcement of itself.

It didn't just happen in the attic on a sunny day while she was sitting in the reading room. It didn't just *happen*, in only a moment, an irreversible moment.

It didn't happen to people she had always known.

But it did.

And there would now forever be two Blues: the Blue that was before, and the Blue that was after. The one who didn't believe, and the one who did.

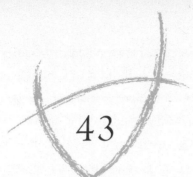

43

Gansey arrived at 300 Fox Way after the ambulance had left, not because of a lack of haste, but because of a lack of communication. It took twenty-four calls from Adam to Ronan's cell phone before Ronan could be persuaded to pick up, and then it took Ronan a bit of doing to track down Gansey on campus. Malory was still out and about with the Dog somewhere, prowling Virginia in the Suburban, but he would be fine not knowing for a while.

Persephone was dead.

Gansey couldn't believe it, not because he could not believe in the nearness of death — he could not *stop* believing in the nearness of death — but because he would not have expected *Persephone* to do something as mortal as dying. There had been something immutable about the three women in 300 Fox Way — Maura, Persephone, and Calla were the trunk from which all of the branches sprang.

We must find Maura, he thought as he climbed from the Camaro and started up the walk, Ronan dogging his steps with his hands shoved in pockets, Chainsaw flapping grimly from branch to branch to follow. *Because if Persephone can die, there is nothing to stop Maura from dying, too.*

Adam sat on the dappled shade of the front step, eyes blank, a wrinkle between his eyebrows. Gansey's mother used to press her thumb to that place between Richard Gansey III's brows and rub the frown out; she still did it to Gansey II. He felt the urge to do it now as Adam tipped his face up.

"I found her," Adam said, "and it didn't do any good at all."

He needed Gansey to say it was all right, and even though it was not all right, Gansey found his voice and said, "You did your best. Calla told me on the phone. She's proud of you. It's not going to feel any better now, Parrish. Don't expect it to."

Adam, freed, nodded miserably and looked at his feet.

"Where's Blue?"

Adam blinked. He clearly didn't know.

"I'm going in," Gansey said as Ronan sat down on the step beside Adam. As Gansey shut the door behind him, he heard Adam say, "I don't want to talk," and Ronan reply, "The fuck would I talk about?"

He found Calla and Jimi and Orla and two other young women he didn't recognize in the kitchen. Gansey had meant to begin with *I'm sorry for your loss* or something polite, something that would make sense outside of this kitchen, but in this context, all of it felt more false than usual.

Instead, he said, "I'm going into the cave. We are."

It was impossible, but it didn't much matter. Everything was impossible. He waited for Calla to say that it was a bad idea, but she didn't.

A small part of him still wished that she would: the part that could feel small legs crawling over the back of his neck.

Coward.

He had spent a long time learning to put that in the back of his mind, and he did it now.

"I'm going with you," Calla said, her knuckles tight around a glass. "Enough of this flying solo nonsense. I'm so angry I could . . ."

She hurled the glass to the kitchen floor; it splintered at Orla's feet. Orla stared at it and then at Gansey, her expression apologetic, but Gansey had lived with Ronan's grief for long enough to recognize it.

"There!" Calla shouted. "That's what it's like. Just destroyed for no purpose!"

"I'll get a vacuum," Jimi said.

"I'll get a Valium," Orla said.

Calla stormed into the backyard.

Gansey retreated and crept up the stairs to the Phone/ Sewing/Cat Room. It was the only place he'd been on the second floor, and the only other place he knew to look for Blue. She was not in there, though, nor in the adjacent room that was clearly her bedroom. He found her instead in a room at the end of the hall that seemed to be Persephone's; it smelled like her, and everything was odd and clever in it.

Blue sat beside the bed, chipping aggressively at the polish on her nails. She looked up at him; the afternoon sunlight came in sharp and strong to land on the side of the mattress behind her, causing her to squint.

"That took forever," she said.

"My phone was off. I'm sorry."

She chipped another bit of polish onto the shaggy rug. "I guess there was no point to hurrying anyway."

Ah, Blue.

"Is Mr. Gray here?" she asked.

"I didn't see him. Look, I told Calla we were going into the cave. To find Maura." He corrected, more formally, "Your mother."

"Oh, seriously! Don't Richard Gansey on me!" Blue snapped, and then, at once, she began to cry.

It was against the rules, but Gansey crouched down beside her, one of his knees against her back, one against her knees, and hugged her. She curled against him, hands balled up against his chest. He felt a hot tear slip into the dip of his collarbone. He closed his eyes against the sun through the window, burning hot in his sweater, foot falling asleep, elbow grinding into the metal bed frame, Blue Sargent pressed up against him, and he didn't move.

Help, he thought. He remembered Gwenllian saying that it was starting, and he could feel it, winding out faster and faster, a ball of thread caught in the wind.

Starting, starting —

He could not tell who was comforting whom.

"I'm part of the useless new generation," Blue said finally, the words right on his skin. Desire and dread lay right next to each other in his heart, each sharpening the other. "The computer generation. I keep thinking that I can hit the reset button, restart things."

He pulled back, wincing through pins and needles, and gave her a mint leaf before sitting back against the bed frame beside her. When he looked up, he realized that Gwenllian stood in the doorway. It was impossible to say how long she'd been there, her arms stretched up above her to the door frame as if she was trying to keep from being pushed into the room.

She waited until she was sure Gansey was looking, and then she sang,

"Queens and kings
Kings and queens
Blue lily, lily blue
Crowns and birds
Swords and things
Blue lily, lily blue"

"Are you trying to make me angry?" he asked.

"*Are* you angry, knightling?" Gwenllian replied sweetly. She leaned her cheek on her arm, rocking back and forth. "I used to dream of death. I had sung every song I knew so many times while I lay in that box on my face. Every eye! Every eye I could reach I asked to look for me. And what did I get but stupidity and blindness!"

"How did you use other people's eyes if you're just like me?" Blue asked. "If you don't have any psychic powers of your own."

Gwenllian's mouth hung in the most dismissive shape possible. "This question! It is like asking how you can smash a nail if you are not a hammer."

"Whatever," Blue said. "It doesn't matter. I don't really care."

"Artemus taught me," Gwenllian said. "When he wasn't working one-two-three-four my father. Here's a riddle, my love, my love, my love, what grows, my love, my love, my love, from dark, my love, my love, my love, to dark, my love, my love, my love."

Blue pushed angrily to her feet. "No more games."

"A tree at night," Gansey said.

Gwenllian stopped rocking on her arms and studied him where he still sat on the floor.

"Much of my father," she replied. "Much of my father in you. That is Artemus, the tree at night. Your mother looks for him, blue lily? Well, then you should seek my father. Artemus will be as near to him as he is able unless something prevents him. The better to whisper."

She spit on the floorboards by Gansey.

"I *am* seeking him," Gansey said. "We're going underground."

"Order me to do something for you, little prince-boy," she told Gansey. "Let's see your king-mettle."

"Is that how your father convinced people to do things for him?" he asked.

"No," Gwenllian said, and looked annoyed about it. "He asked them."

Even through all of this wrongness, this impossibility, this warmed Gansey. This was right: Glendower should have ruled by request, not by command. This was the king he sought.

"Will you go with us?" he asked.

44

W hen Colin Greenmantle went out onto the porch of the historic farmhouse and looked down at the field below, he discovered a herd of cows standing far away and two young men standing very close.

It was, in fact, Adam Parrish and Ronan Lynch.

He looked down at them.

They looked up.

Neither party said anything. Both of the boys were unsettling — Adam Parrish, in particular, had a curious face. Not as in, he was a curious person. But rather that there was something peculiar about his facial features. He was an alien, handsome specimen of this western Virginia species; feather-boned, hollow-cheeked, eyebrows fair and barely visible. He was feral and raw-boned by way of those Civil War portraits. *Brother fought brother while their farms ran to ruins —*

And Ronan Lynch looked like Niall Lynch, which was to say, he looked like an asshole.

Oh, youth.

So Greenmantle broke the ice. He called down, "Are you turning in your exercises?"

They continued standing there, looking like a pair of horror movie twins, one dark, one light.

Adam Parrish smiled a little; it took two years off his age in a second. He had teeth on both his top and bottom jaw. "I know what you are."

This was interesting. "And what am I?"

"Don't you know?" Adam Parrish asked it with bland insouciance.

Greenmantle narrowed his eyes. "Are we playing a game, Mr. Parrish?"

"Possibly."

Games, at least, were one of Greenmantle's specialties. He leaned against the railing. "In that case, I know what you are, too."

Ronan Lynch handed Adam Parrish an oversized, bulging manila envelope.

"Oh, I don't think you do," Adam replied.

Greenmantle disliked the fearlessness in his face. It was not even fearlessness: It was a lack of expression entirely. He wondered what was in the envelope. *Confessions of a Teen Sociopath.*

He said, "Do you know what keeps poor people down, Mr. Parrish? It's not a lack of income. It's a poverty of imagination. The trailer park dreams of the suburbs, and the suburbs dreams of the city, the city dreams of the stars, so on and so forth. The poor can imagine the throne, but not being kingly. Poverty of imagination. But you — you are a cuckoo who sneaks into this nest. You are Mr. Adam Parrish, of twenty-one Antietam Lane, Henrietta, Virginia, and you have a good imagination, but you are a pretender nonetheless."

The kid was good. The skin around his eyes tightened only a tiny bit when Greenmantle read off the trailer park's address.

"And it would be so easy to hurl you to the ground from this tree," Greenmantle said, in case he wasn't nervous yet. "You would long for those days in your trailer park."

Adam Parrish looked at him. Greenmantle realized all at once that he was unsettling in the same way that Piper had been when he caught her looking in the mirror.

Adam turned the bulging envelope around so that Greenmantle could see that it was seeping something red-brown, which was never a good sign. He said, "If you're not out of Henrietta by Friday, everything in that envelope comes true."

Ronan Lynch smiled then, too, and it was a weapon.

They left the envelope there.

"Piper!" Greenmantle called after they had gone. But she didn't answer. It was impossible to know if she was there, but in a trance, or if she was gone, hunting for the thing that she heard humming in mirrors.

This place. This damn place. They could have it.

He climbed down the stairs, finally, and managed to find a door that led outside. He opened the envelope. The seeping was from a rotting, severed hand. It was small. A child's hand. Beneath it was a sealed plastic bag, smeared with gore, containing paperwork and photographs.

Individually, they were distasteful.

Collectively, they were damning.

The envelope contents told a story of Colin Greenmantle, intellectual mass murderer and habitual pervert. It provided evidence of where the bodies, and parts of bodies, could be found. There were screenshots of condemning texts and cell phone photos — and when Greenmantle swiped up his real phone, he discovered that, somehow, they actually were on his phone in all their gruesome glory. There were letters, homemade DVDs, photographs, a mountain of evidence.

None of it was true.

All of it had been dreamt up.

But it didn't matter. It *looked* true. Truer than the truth.

The Greywaren was real, and those two boys had it, but it didn't matter, because they were untouchable, and they knew it.

Damn youth.

On the very bottom of the stack of filth was a single piece of paper with handwriting so similar to Niall Lynch's that it could only belong to his son.

It said, *Qui facit per alium facit per se.*

Greenmantle knew the proverb.

He who does a thing by the agency of another does it himself.

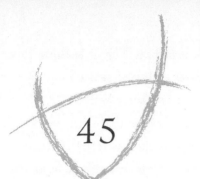

45

Okay, we're going," Greenmantle said. "Family emergency. Back to Boston. Pack your things. Call your friends. You're off the hook for that book club book."

Piper was getting her purse. "No, I'm going out with the men."

"The men!"

"Yes," Piper said. "Does that horrible Gray Man drive a white car? One of those boy racer cars. You know, with the big wing on the back. It's supposed to demonstrate what a big member the driver has? Because I feel like one of those has been following me. I mean, ha, more than usual, because please." She flipped her hair.

"I don't want to talk about the Gray Man," Greenmantle said. "I want to talk about your luggage."

"I'm not packing. I think I've found something," Piper said.

Greenmantle showed her the envelope.

She was not as impressed as he had been. She said, "Oh, please. If I find what I think I'm finding, making that go away will be children's play. No pun intended. Oh, that was distasteful." She laughed. "Okay, I'm out."

With *the men.* Greenmantle got up. "I'll come with you. I'll convince you to come back with me along the way."

There was no chance Piper was finding something to

counteract that envelope. The only thing Piper could find was fad exercise classes and hairless dogs.

"Whatever. Put on some boots."

Piper's destination for that night involved meeting up with two thugs Greenmantle had hired. Actually, they were not as thuggish as Greenmantle would have expected. One of the men was named Morris, and a problem with alimony had driven him to a life of crime. The other seemed to be named Beast, and — well, actually, he was exactly as thuggish as Greenmantle had expected.

They both treated Piper as if she knew what she was talking about.

"Show me what you got," Piper said to them.

Morris and Beast led them to a run-down farm just as the sun set. Even in the car lights, it was easy to tell that the farmhouse had seen better days. The porch sagged. Someone had tried to improve it by planting a cheery row of flowers in front.

Beast and Morris led them past the farmhouse and through a field. They had all kinds of equipment. Piper had all kinds of equipment. Greenmantle had boots. He felt like a fourth wheel on a vehicle that was not, in fact, meant to have four wheels.

He looked over his shoulder to make sure that the Gray Man, ever standing over his shoulder, was not, in fact, standing just over it.

"I'm not experienced with practical crime," Greenmantle said as they walked across the field, "but shouldn't we have parked the cars someplace more clandestine?" He added, "Sneakier?" for Beast.

"No one lives there," grunted Beast. Greenmantle was both horrified and impressed by the subsonic nature of his voice.

Morris, considerably more cultured-sounding, added, "We were here earlier, checking it out."

The two men — thugs — the thug and Morris — brought them to a stone building. Greenmantle thought it didn't have a roof, but then after a second, his eyes adjusted and he saw that it was a stone tower extending up into the night. He wasn't sure why he'd thought it was a ruin at first. He wasn't sure why a tower like this would exist in the middle of redneck Virginia, either, but it was interesting at least, and he liked interesting.

"The cave's in here," said Morris. There was a padlock on the door, but it had already been busted open, presumably by Beast's molars.

"And this cave seems to match the description I gave you?" Piper asked.

"Why do you have a description of a cave?" Greenmantle asked.

"Shut up before you hurt yourself," she told him kindly.

"Yeah," Morris said. "I didn't see any doors like you described, but we didn't go very far in." He pushed open the door as Beast turned on a massive spotlight.

It illuminated an enormous man sitting at the cave entrance. He had a shotgun lying across his knees.

"I'M TELLING YOU NOW THAT THIS CAVE IS CURSED," the man told them. "AND I THINK YOU BEST GO NOW. SHORT WAY'S ACROSS THE FIELD."

Piper looked at Morris and Beast. "Was this guy here the last time you came in?"

"No, ma'am," replied Morris. "Sir, we're headed into that cave, easy way or hard way. Right?"

This was with a glance to Piper.

"Right," she replied. "Thanks for the warning, though."

The man's enormous brow furrowed. "THERE'S THINGS IN THERE YOU SHOULDN'T DISTURB."

Greenmantle, wary of this man identifying him later on, took a tactful step back into the shadows to hide his face.

He backed directly into someone's chest.

"Colin," the Gray Man said. "I'm disappointed. Didn't you read the envelope?"

"Oh, for the love of the saints," Greenmantle wailed. "This was not my idea."

"*You*," Piper said.

"Yes," the Gray Man agreed. He was, strangely enough, as well equipped as Piper, as if he, too, had been about to head into a cave. "Mr. Dittley, how are you?"

"WELL ENOUGH."

The Gray Man said, "It's time for the rest of you to leave."

"No, you know what?" Piper demanded. "I am beyond tired of you showing up and throwing your weight around. I was here first, and I had plans. Men, do man things."

Greenmantle hadn't the faintest idea of what that meant, but Morris and Beast headed immediately for the Gray Man as Dittley rose to his feet.

The Gray Man dispatched Beast to either the grave or the infirmary in a disappointing two seconds. It was Morris who turned out to be a better match. They fought quietly, all bruised breaths and sighed punches, as Jesse Dittley put his gun down and held Greenmantle's wrists like a petulant child.

"Everybody drop everything," Piper said.

She was pointing a gun at the Gray Man's head. A silvery one. Greenmantle still didn't think it looked as dangerous as the black ones, but the others clearly did. The Gray Man narrowed his eyes, but released Morris.

She looked pretty smug about it. To the Gray Man, she said, "Yeah, how does it feel? Great? Remember when you put one of these to my head? Yeah. An asshole thing to do."

The Gray Man's expression didn't change. It was possible he had no fear-face.

"Where did you get that?" Greenmantle asked his wife. "Did you get me one?"

Piper looked at him witheringly and jerked her chin. "You get that one."

She meant Jesse Dittley's shotgun, which he'd put down to hold Greenmantle at bay. It occurred to Greenmantle how pointless a virtue mercy was. If Jesse Dittley had just shot Greenmantle earlier, Greenmantle would not be holding his shotgun now.

Greenmantle pointed the shotgun at Jesse Dittley's chest. He disliked all of this profoundly. He did not like to do things himself. He liked to hire people to do things for him. He liked to keep his fingerprints to himself. He did not like prison.

He blamed Piper for everything.

"Out of the way," he said, then wished he'd thought of something catchier.

"I CAN'T LET YOU DO THAT."

Greenmantle looked at Jesse Dittley. He could not believe they allowed humans to grow so tall. "You're really making this a bigger deal than it needs to be."

Jesse Dittley just shook his head, very slowly.

"Stand down!" Greenmantle tried. In the movies, this worked instantly. You pointed a gun at someone, they scurried out of your way. They didn't just stand there looking at it.

Jesse Dittley said, "THIS IS NOT YOUR CAVE."

Piper shot him.

Three times, fast, black spots appearing on his shirt and head.

By the time they looked back at her, she already had pointed her gun back at the Gray Man.

Greenmantle could not believe how unbelievably dead the giant man was. He was so very, very dead, and punctured. There were holes in him. Greenmantle couldn't stop looking at the holes. They probably went all the way through him.

"Piper," he said. "You just shot that man."

"No one else was doing anything, seriously. All of this dick slinging!" Piper said. To the Gray Man, she said, "Drag him into the cave."

"No," the Gray Man said.

"No?" She had her shooting-people face on — which was to say, the face that she wore all the time.

"Oh, don't shoot him," Greenmantle said. His pulse was feeling rather jittery. All he could think about was how much more plausible the documents in that envelope were going to look when paired with the events of this evening. Didn't Piper know that crime was supposed to involve painstaking planning and cleanup? It wasn't the shooting that was hard, it was the getting away with it.

"I'm not going to move any bodies without gloves," the Gray Man said in a chilly voice, demonstrating clearly why he had been good at this. "I would not have shot him without gloves, either. Prints and gunpowder residue are stupid ways to end up in prison."

"Thanks for the advice," Piper said. "Morris? You're wearing gloves. Drag that dude and let's get going."

"What about *him*?" Morris asked, looking at the Gray Man.

"Tie him up. We'll bring him with. Colin, why are you just standing there?"

"Actually," Greenmantle said, "I think I'm going to sit this one out."

"You have got to be kidding me."

Not only was he not kidding, he was considering vomiting. He should have stayed single. He should have stayed in Boston. He should have been single in Boston. He was part of the way toward the door; he kind of wanted to be sure that he had a bit of cover in case she got pissed and decided to shoot him, too. "I'm just going to . . . head back. Don't get me wrong, I think you look fantastic with the gun, but . . ."

"This is just. So. Typical. You always say, 'We're going to do this together, you and me,' and then who ends up always doing it? Me, while you go start some other new project. Fine. Go on back. Don't expect me to hurry back after you, though."

He met the Gray Man's eyes. The Gray Man was in the process of having his hands tied behind him by Morris. Efficiently, with a zip tie.

The Gray Man looked at Jesse Dittley's body and closed his eyes for a second. Unbelievably, he looked angry, so he must have possessed emotions after all.

Greenmantle hesitated.

"Piss or get off the pot," Piper snapped.

"Just go, Colin," the Gray Man said. "You would have spared us both a lot of trouble if you'd never come."

Greenmantle took the opportunity to go. He got lost heading back across the field — he had such a shit sense of direction — but once in the car, he knew the way. Away. All directions were away.

46

Blue Sargent was afraid.

There are many good words for the opposite of *afraid.* *Unafraid, fearless, unfrightened.*

Some might suggest *courageous* or *brave* as opposites.

But Blue Sargent was brave because she *was* afraid.

If Persephone could die, anyone could die. Maura could die. Gansey could die. There didn't have to be ceremony or portent.

It could happen in a moment.

They went to Cabeswater again. Calla came with, but they were sans Malory, who was still unreachable, and sans Mr. Gray, who had vanished without explanation, and sans Noah, who had appeared only as a brief whisper in Blue's ear that morning.

Again they were prepared with safety equipment and helmets, only this time Adam and Ronan were to lead the way into the pit. This had been Adam's idea, quickly backed up by Ronan. Cabeswater would not let Adam die because of the bargain, and it would protect Ronan for reasons unknown.

It was dark. The headlights of Ronan's BMW and Gansey's Camaro made it only a few feet into the mist rising from the damp field outside of Cabeswater. It seemed impossible that it was the same day Persephone had died. How did some days have so many hours in them?

Outside of the cars, Blue begged Calla, "Please stay here and keep time with Matthew."

"No way, chicken. I'm coming with you," Calla said. "I'm not letting you do this by yourself."

"Please," Blue said again. "I'm not by myself. And I can't take it if —"

She didn't finish. She couldn't say *if you died, too.*

Calla put her hands on either side of Blue's head, smoothing down her unsmoothable hair. Blue knew that she was feeling everything that Blue couldn't say, but she was okay with that. Words were impossible.

Calla studied Blue's eyes. Her fingers studied Blue's soul.

Please trust me please stay here please trust me please stay here please don't die

Finally, Calla said, "Grounding. I'm good for grounding. I will stay here and ground you."

"Thank you," Blue whispered.

Inside Cabeswater was mist and more mist. Ronan greeted the trees as he moved in a pool of muzzy light cast from the dream light he had brought from the Barns. Adam had called it the ghost light, and it seemed appropriate.

Ronan respectfully asked for safe passage.

It reminded Blue of a prayer.

The trees rustled a response, unseen leaves moving in the night.

"What did they say?" Gansey asked suddenly. "Didn't they just say to be careful?"

Ronan said, "The third sleeper. They warned us not to wake him."

They went into the cave.

On the way down the tunnel toward the pit, Gwenllian sang a song about proving oneself worthy for a king.

They went in deeper.

Gwenllian was still singing, now about tasks and trials and pretender knights. Adam's hands fisted and unfisted in the moving headlamp beams.

"Please shut up," Blue said.

"We're here," Ronan said.

Gwenllian shut up.

Adam joined Ronan at the edge of the precipice, both of them peering in as if they might be able to see the bottom. The light around them was curious and golden, thrown not only by the flashlights and headlamps but by the ghost light.

Adam murmured something to Ronan. Ronan shook his head.

"Still bottomless?" Gansey's voice came from far back.

Ronan unslung the ghost light from his shoulder, where it hung like a messenger bag, and tied it to one of the safety ropes.

Blue was more afraid than before. It was easier to be unafraid when you were the one doing the fearful things.

"Lower that in," Ronan directed Adam. "Let's take a look around down there, right?"

The two boys stood for several long minutes, swinging the ghost light in the pit. Swaths of light cut crazily back and forth above the pit as they did. But they seemed unsatisfied with their results. Adam leaned forward — Ronan gripped his arm tightly — and then the two of them turned back to where the others waited.

"Can't see a thing," Adam said. "There's nothing to do but go in."

"Please —" Gansey started, then stopped. "Be careful."

Adam and Ronan regarded each other, and then the pit. They looked winsome and brave, trusting of Cabeswater or of each other. They did not look afraid, so Blue was afraid for them.

"Say it," Ronan told Gansey.

"Say what?"

"Excelsior."

"That's onward and upward," Gansey said. "It means to ascend. That's opposite."

"Oh, well," Ronan said. "Squash one, squash two, squash *three* on and on and on —"

Then he disappeared into the hole, his voice still carrying up.

Adam said, "I'm not singing along!" but he followed Ronan in.

Ronan's voice sang and sang and then suddenly broke off.

There was silence.

A complete silence, the sort one can only achieve in a hole in the ground.

Then there was a skittering sound, like pebbles shimmying over rock.

And more silence.

"Jesus," Gansey said. "I can't take this."

"Worry is weakness, king," Gwenllian piped up.

Silence.

Then a hoarse, cutoff shout in an unrecognizable voice. Adam, or Ronan, or something else entirely.

Gansey made a terrible sound and rested his forehead against the wall. Blue's hand shot out to grab his, tightly. She couldn't bear it, either, but there was nothing to do *but* bear it. Inside her, this new, black fear grew, the knowledge that death happened in a moment and to anyone. Ronan and Adam could be dead and there would be no earthquake. There would be no fanfare.

The dread was like blood filling her stomach.

Did they trust Cabeswater?

That was the question.

Did that pit stretch out of Cabeswater's reach?

That was the second question.

"I can't live with this," Gansey said. "If anything has happened."

"You'll never be a king," Gwenllian said. "Don't you know how war works?"

But her bitterness wasn't really for Gansey; it was a jeer for someone who had buried her or been buried with her long ago.

Suddenly, a voice came from down below.

"Gansey?"

"Adam," Gansey shouted. "Adam?"

The voice came up again. "We're coming back to show you the way down!"

47

They had found a valley of skeletons.

The pit was not bottomless, although it was vast and deep. The bottom had slanted and narrowed, shuttling them away from Gansey and the others, sliding them surprisingly and abruptly away from the surface. Under the diffuse gaze of the ghost light, Adam caught a glimpse of strange nests clinging to the wall. He flung his hands out, trying to slow himself. The holes of the nests heaved with something black and restless, but Adam couldn't see what. They might have been insect nests, but then he heard Ronan, skittering ahead of him, speaking rapidly in Latin, and even as Adam skidded by them, he saw them transmuting to twiggy birds' nests.

This was their job, Adam realized. This was what they had to offer: making it safe for the others. That was what they had promised: to be Gansey's magicians.

So they had slid, and they had whispered, and they had asked, and together they'd convinced Cabeswater to transform the nests to something harmless. At least for a while.

Then they had shot out the bottom of the slope into a cavern.

Now the others had joined them, and they all gazed at the underground valley.

In between them and the faraway opposite wall was a herd of bones, an army of bones, a tragedy of bones. There were horse skeletons and deer skeletons, tiny cat skeletons and sinuous weasel skeletons. Every one of them was caught mid-run, all pointed toward the teens standing by the valley entrance.

Somehow the effect was of awe, not terror.

The room itself was a wonder, too. It was a vast bowl of a cavern room, twice as long as it was wide. Godfingers of light streamed down from holes in the cavern ceiling hundreds of feet overhead. Unlike the cavern they had just left behind, this valley had color: ferns and moss reached for the unreachable sunlight.

"Clouds," whispered Blue.

It was true; the ceiling was so far overhead that mist clung to the roof, pierced by stalactites.

Adam felt as if he'd slid into one of Ronan's dreams.

Gwenllian began to laugh and clap her hands. The laugh, a song itself, echoed off the ceilings.

"Shut her up, someone," Ronan said. "Before I do."

"What is this place?" Blue asked.

Adam was the first to step down.

"Careful —" Gansey warned.

Gwenllian danced ahead. "What are you afraid of? Some *bones?*"

She kicked one of the cat skeletons; bones flew. Adam winced.

"Don't do that!" Blue said.

"The dead stay dead stay dead," Gwenllian replied, and used a femur to crash through another skeleton.

"Not always," Gansey warned. "Have a care."

"Yes, Father!" But she wound up for another great kick.

"Ronan," Gansey said sharply, and Ronan moved to stop her, binding her arms behind her without malice or squeamishness.

Adam stopped by one of the beasts near the front; its shoulder was taller than him, its great skull even higher, and above it all spread a set of antlers that seemed massive in comparison even to the giant skeleton. It was beautiful.

Blue's voice came from very close. "It's an Irish elk."

He turned to find her beside him, touching one of the great white bones. She ran her finger along it so tenderly that it was as if it were alive.

"They're extinct," she added. "I always felt bad that I'd never get to see one. Look how many of them there are."

Adam did look; there were many. But to look at them was to see beyond them, and to see beyond them was to be dazzled again by this spectacle of bones. A thousand animals, suspended on their toes. It was reminding him of something, though he couldn't think what.

He craned to look at the entrance, then at Ronan and Gwenllian. Gansey moved through the skeletons as if in a dream, his face caught with wonder and caution. He touched the arched neck of a skeletal creature with respect, and Adam remembered him telling Ronan that he had never left a place worse for being there. Adam understood, then, that Gansey and Blue's awe changed this place. Ronan and Adam may have seen this place as magical, but Gansey and Blue's wonder made it *holy*. It became a cathedral of bones.

They slowly walked through the valley, searching for answers and clues. There was no other exit to the room. There was only this vast space, and a stream running along its floor, disappearing beneath a rock wall.

"What is the point of this?"

"Tricks and more tricks," Gwenllian snarled. "All brave, young, and handsome — all noble and true —"

"Whosoever pulls this sword from this stone," Gansey muttered. Blue nodded. "This is a test."

"We wake them," Ronan said suddenly. He released Gwenllian. "That's what it is, isn't it?"

"It's not my test, bold sir knight," Gwenllian said. "You're up." She made cowboy shooters at him.

Blue's eyes were on the Irish elk; she was quite taken by it. "How do you wake bones?"

"Same as you'd wake a dreamer," Gwenllian cooed, her words for Ronan. "If you cannot wake these bones, how can you expect to raise my father? But what do I see on your shoulders? Oh, failure is what you're wearing these days, I see — it matches your eyes. You've tried this before, faulty dreamer, but you've got more passion than accuracy, don't you?"

"Stop," Gansey said.

He said it in such a way that they all stopped and looked at him.

There was no anger in his voice, no unfairness. He stood beside a brace of massive skeletal stags, his shoulders square and his eyes serious. For a moment, Adam saw the present, but he also saw the past, and the future, stretched out as when Persephone had inspired him to see his own death. He saw Gansey here now, but somehow here always, just about to leave this moment, or just about to enter it, or living it.

Then his thoughts hitched and time moved again.

"Stop goading them, Gwenllian," Gansey said. "Do you think you're the only one with a right to bitterness here? Why don't you use your skills of seeing beneath to encourage instead of tear down?"

"I would like to see quite a bit of what's going on beneath all of the young men here," Gwenllian said. "You may volunteer first for my attention if you'd like."

Then Gansey rolled his eyes and blew out a breath in a very unkingly way. "Ignore her. Adam, give me an idea."

Adam was always called on, even when he didn't lift his hand. He thought of what Ronan had already failed to accomplish, and he thought of the moment on the mountaintop with Blue and Noah, and then, finally, he remembered what Persephone had said about the power of three. Then he said, "Ronan, did you bring your dream thing?"

Ronan gestured to the bag that hung below the dream light.

"The *what*?" Blue asked.

Adam waved his hand; this wasn't the time to explain. "Remember the Barns? You try to wake them like the cows, Ronan. I'll see if I can redirect the ley line to give you more energy to work with; Blue will amplify. Gansey can . . . move stones?"

Gansey nodded his approval. He didn't understand the plan, but he didn't need to: He trusted Adam's judgment.

Ronan unslung his bag, carefully unwrapping his dream thing from the now rather manky polar fleece. He hid it mostly from view as Adam crouched and pressed his fingers to the rock. He knew as soon as he touched it that they were not properly in Cabeswater anymore; they'd dug beneath it. The ley line was still there, though, and if he moved some of the stones, he might be able to point it at the skeletons.

"Blue, Gansey, help me," he said, directing them.

Gwenllian watched with curled lip.

"You could help, too," he told her.

"No," she replied. "I couldn't."

She didn't say that she couldn't help *him*, but it was understood. Gansey didn't even bother to chastise her this time. He merely worked with Blue to move the stones Adam indicated. Then they returned to the beast at the very front of the herd.

Ronan waited with the dream thing, eyes averted. Then, as they stood around it, he breathed over the top of the dream word, just as he had at the Barns.

His breath passed through it and on to the skeleton.

There was silence.

Adam could *feel* it, though. This vast underground valley was charged with energy, pulsing with life. It murmured against the walls. It darted from bone to bone in each skeleton, and then from one skeleton to the next. They wanted to spring; they remembered life. They remembered their bodies.

But there was still silence.

Adam felt the power of the ley line shaking and pulling at him, magnified by Blue. It was not destroying him, but it was diffusing. He was not the truest vessel for this energy, and he wouldn't be able to keep it focused for much longer.

Blue's lips were pressed together, and Adam knew she was feeling it, too.

Why wasn't it working?

Perhaps it was just as it had been at the Barns. They were

close, but not close enough. Perhaps Gwenllian was right; they were not worthy.

Gwenllian was backing up from them, her arms stretched by her sides, her eyes darting from beast to beast as if she expected one to break first and wanted to be watching.

Gansey's eyebrows drew together as he surveyed the herds and flocks, Gwenllian and the streaming light, his friends frozen in an invisible battle.

Adam could not stop seeing his fallible king, hanging in the pit of the ravens.

Gansey touched his lower lip very gently. He lowered his hand, and he said, "Wake up."

He said it like he had said *stop* earlier. He said it in a voice Adam had heard countless times, a voice he could never *not* listen to.

The beasts woke.

The stags and the horses, the lions and the hawks, the goats and the unicorns, and the creatures that Adam could not name.

One moment they were bones, and the next they were whole. Adam missed the moment of transformation. It was like Noah from smudged ghost to boy, from impossible to possible. Every creature was alive and shimmery and more beautiful than anything Adam could have ever imagined.

They reared and they called and they whinnied and they leapt.

Adam could see Gansey's chest heave with disbelief.

They had done this. Were still doing this.

"We have to go!" Blue shouted. "Look!"

The creatures were galloping away. Not as one, but as a hundred disparate minds with one goal, and that goal was a cave passage that had appeared on the other side of the valley. It was like a gaping mouth, though, slowly closing. If they didn't go through it, soon, it would disappear.

But no human could run that fast.

"This!" Blue shouted, and she flung herself onto the Irish elk. It tossed its massive antlers and twisted, but she clung on.

Adam couldn't believe it.

"Yes —" Ronan said, and snatched at a deer, and another, before he seized the ruff of a primordial creature and pulled himself on.

It was easier said than done, though. The beasts were fast and skittish, and Adam came away with handfuls of fur. A few yards away, he saw Gansey, frustrated, show him a palm coated with fur, too. Gwenllian laughed and ran after the creatures, clapping her hands and herding them.

"Run along, little creatures! Run! Run!"

Adam suddenly pitched forward, his shoulder stinging, as some sort of creature half-leapt over him. He rolled, covering his head. Another hoof knocked him — he thought of his old Latin teacher trampled to death in Cabeswater.

The difference was that Cabeswater wouldn't let Adam die.

It would let him get hurt, though. He scrambled farther out of the way and then back to his feet.

"Adam," Gansey said, pointing.

Adam's eyes found what he gestured to: Ronan's and Blue's beasts leaping through the diminished cave passage, right before it disappeared.

48

Blue found herself in a strange, low-ceilinged cavern of indeterminate space. Light from behind illuminated the ground as it sloped away from her and to a jagged-floored pit.

No. That was not the floor. That was the ceiling, reflected.

She was looking at a vast, still lake. The water mirrored the spiked ceiling perfectly, hiding the true depth of the dead lake. There was something dead and uncomforting about it. On the other side of the lake was another tunnel, barely visible in the dim light.

Blue shivered. Her shoulder ached where she had fallen on it, and so did her butt.

She turned away from the lake — uneasily, because who knew what a mirror might hold — and looked for signs of the others. She saw her great, white beast standing aloof and still, like a part of the cave. And she saw the cavern path that led back up the way she had hurtled.

"You're here," Blue said, relieved, because she was not alone: Here was Ronan. It was his ghost light, slung over his shoulder still, that lit the cavern.

He stood as aloof as the elk, eyes wary and dark and foreign as he strode out of the dimness. There was no sign of the creature he must have ridden to gain access, though.

Suddenly full of misgiving, she flicked out her switchblade. "Are you the real Ronan?"

He scoffed.

"I'm serious."

"Yes, maggot," Ronan said. He peered around as uneasily as she did, which made her feel a little better about him. It was the lake, or something on the underside of it, that was making her nervous.

"Why didn't you need to ride in on something?"

"I did. It got away."

"Got *away*? To where?"

He stalked closer to her, and then he leaned to scoop up a loose rock from the ground. He tossed it underhand into the lake. There was a sound like air blowing across their ears, and then the rock vanished. Blue saw the moment it hit the water and disappeared — not into the water, but into nothing.

There were no ripples.

"So, you know what?" Ronan asked Blue. "Fuck magic. Fuck this."

Blue walked slowly toward the lake's edge.

"Hey! Didn't you hear me? Don't do anything stupid. It ate my deer thing."

"I'm just looking," Blue said.

She got as close as she dared, and then she looked in, trying to see the bottom.

Once again she saw the golden reflection of the ceiling above, then the black of the water, and then her own face, her eyes hollowed out and strange.

Her face seemed to rise through the water toward her, closer and closer, skin paler and duller, until she saw that it was not her own face at all.

It was her mother's.

Her eyes were dead, mouth slack, cheeks hollow and water-logged. She floated just below the surface. Face closest, torso falling away, legs lost in the black.

Blue could feel herself begin to shake. It was everything she'd felt after Persephone's death. It was grief right in the moment, singeing her.

"No," she said out loud. *"No. No."*

But her mother's face kept floating, deader and deader, after all this, and Blue heard herself making a thin, awful sound.

Be sensible — Blue couldn't make herself so. *Drag her out.*

Suddenly, she felt arms around her, yanking her away from the lake's edge. The arms around her were trembling, too, but they were iron tight, scented with sweat and moss.

"It's not real," Ronan told her, voice low. "It's not real, Blue."

"I *saw* her," Blue said, and she heard the sob in her voice. "My mother."

He said, "I know. I saw my father."

"But she was *there* —"

"My father's dead in the ground. And Adam saw your mother farther on in this godforsaken cave. That lake is a *lie.*"

But it felt real to her heart, even if her head knew better.

For a moment they remained that way, Ronan holding her as tightly as he would hold his brother Matthew, his cheek on her shoulder. Every time she thought she could go on, she saw the face of her mother's corpse again.

Finally, she pulled back, and Ronan stood up. He looked away, but not before she saw the tear he flicked from his chin.

"Fuck this," he said again.

Blue took great pains to make her voice normal. "Why would it show us that? If it wasn't real, why would Cabeswater show us something so horrible?"

"This isn't Cabeswater anymore," Ronan replied. "This is underneath. The lake belongs to something else."

They both cast their eyes left and right, looking for some way to cross. But there was nothing in this barren, apocalyptic landscape except for them and the great beast, as still as a cave formation.

"I'm going to look again," Blue said finally. "I want to see if I can see how deep it really is."

Ronan did not tell her no, but he did not come with her, either. She walked to the edge, trying not to tremble at the thought of seeing her mother again, or something worse. Leaning, she scooped up another loose stone, and when she got to the edge, she dropped it in immediately, not waiting for a reflection to rise.

The stone vanished on the point of hitting the surface of the water.

Again, there wasn't so much as a ripple.

And now, undisturbed, the water began once more to form a vision for her, letting it float up from the depth.

As the horror rose, Blue suddenly remembered Gwenllian's lesson of the mirrors.

Mirror magic is nothing to mirrors.

If the dead lake had shown her Maura and shown Ronan his

father, then it was not creating anything — it was using thoughts of theirs and mirroring them back.

It was just a massive scrying bowl.

She began to build up the blocks inside her, just like when she'd cut off Noah and Adam. As the dead corpse face slowly rose toward her, she ignored it and continued.

She was a mirror.

Her gaze focused on the water once more. There was no corpse. There was no face. There was no reflection at all, just as there had been no reflection in Neeve's mirrors. There was just the still glass surface of the water, and then, if she squinted past the reflection of the roof, the silty, uneven surface of the bottom of the lake.

It was only a few inches deep. One or two. A faultless illusion.

She touched her lip — this reminded her of Gansey, and she stopped.

"I'm going to walk across it," she said.

Ronan laughed in an unfunny way. "Right, but seriously."

"Seriously," Blue told him. Then, hurriedly, "Not you, though. I don't think you can touch the water. You'd dissolve like that stone."

"And you won't?"

She looked at the water. It was unbelievable, really, that she was trusting a crazy person's wisdom. "I don't think so. Because of the way I am."

"Assuming that's even true," Ronan said, "you'd go on by yourself?"

"Don't leave this shore," Blue said. "Well, not forever. But — promise me you'll stay a reasonable amount of time. I'll just see what it looks like on the other side."

"Assuming you don't disappear, you mean."

He wasn't improving her already tested courage. "Ronan, *stop*."

He leveled a heavy gaze at her, the sort he normally used to bend Noah to his will.

"If she's over there . . ." Blue began.

"Yeah, I know," he snarled. "Fine. Wait."

Ducking his head, he pulled off his ghost light and hung it over her shoulder.

She didn't bother to say, *But you'll be waiting in darkness.* Nor did she say, *If I vanish immediately into the lake, you'll have to find your way out of here sightless.* Because he'd already known both these things when he'd given it to her.

Instead she said, "You know, you're not such a shithead."

"No," Ronan replied, "really I am."

Turning to the water, she allowed herself the brief gift of closing her eyes and shaking her head a little with the fear and awfulness of what she was about to do.

Then she stepped in.

49

The lake was wet, which shocked her.

Somehow she had believed that if the corpse was false, perhaps the water was, too. But it turned out that at least two inches of it was very real, and squishing coldly into her soles.

She had not disappeared.

She turned to find Ronan crouched down a few feet up onto dry land, arms wrapped around his knees, already waiting for the darkness to take him. When he met her eyes, he gave her an unsmiling salute before she turned back around.

Gingerly, she picked her way across the lake, her eyes on the true bottom of it and on the ceiling and on the walls — she did not trust anything in this place, especially as dread began to blossom in her, more and more.

She didn't like to think of leaving Ronan back there in the darkness.

But she kept going, alone, and when she thought that she could not take the blackness in her heart anymore, she came to the edge of the lake and to the tunnel that came after.

She stepped onto the rock, and for just a second, she stood there and tried to let her fear drip off her.

Why do I have to be alone for this?

She recognized the unfairness of this. Then she readjusted the ghost light and kept going.

Blue knew she was going the right way, because she began to feel the subtle tug of the third sleeper. It was like Adam had said — it was a voice in your head that sounded a lot like yours if you weren't paying attention.

But Blue *was* paying attention.

It was not far to the chamber he'd described. She crept through the dark hole, feeling a voice inside her say *come closer closer closer* when the real voice inside her was saying *I wish I could run away.*

And there it was, as he'd described. A small, scooped-out chamber, low enough that she had to crouch to enter. She didn't care for the crouching; it made her feel uncomfortably vulnerable.

It is a lot like kneeling.

But it wasn't the real voice in her head that thought this; it was the third sleeper's mimicked one.

She wished so much for the presence of the boys, or Calla, or her mother, or — she had so many people that she took for granted, all the time. She had never needed to be truly afraid before. There had always been another hand to catch her, or at least to hold hers as they fell together.

Blue crawled into the chamber. Ronan's ghost light illuminated the space. She flinched when she realized how close she was to a kneeling man. He was inches away, willow-limbed and somehow familiar, completely unmoving.

Not sleeping, like a dream creature, nor dead, like the valley of bones. But fixed, gazing, intent, upon a dull red door with an oily black handle.

Open

Blue pulled her eyes away from it.

I am a mirror, she thought. *Take a look at yourself while I look around in here.*

She moved around the motionless man, trying to steel her heart for what she was going to see. Trying to guard against that worst of things, that insidious hope, worse than the third sleeper's whispers in her head.

But it didn't help. Because on the other side of the man was Maura Sargent.

She was still, her hands stuffed in her armpits, but she was *alive.*

Alive, alive, alive, and Blue's mother, and she loved her, and she had found her.

Blue didn't care if Maura could feel it or not — she scrambled over and threw her arms ferociously around her mother's neck. It felt so very comfortingly like her mother, because it *was* her mother.

To her very great surprise, Maura moved slightly beneath her, and then whispered, "Don't let me move!"

"What?"

"I won't be able to prevent myself from opening it, now that there's three of us!"

Blue glanced over at the man. His brow had furrowed deeper.

"We should just go," Blue said. "How did you get across the lake?"

"Went around," Maura whispered. "From above."

"There was another way?" Now that Blue knew Maura was alive, she had room in her heart for other emotions, like being pissed. She peered around the cave and saw a small opening at the top of one of the low walls just as she saw that the man was beginning to creep toward the door.

Blue didn't think. Bent over double, she darted over and flicked the switchblade out. "Oh, no. Come with me, dude."

He seemed to genuinely consider impaling himself on a blade preferable to moving away from the door. Finally he shuffled back a few inches. Then a few inches more. Blue looked for something to tie his hands, but she only had the ghost light. She pulled it over her head and said, "Don't take this personally, whoever you are, but I don't trust you when you have your enchanty face on."

She put the handle of her switchblade between her teeth, feeling slightly heroic, and used the soft handle of the light to tie his hands behind his back. He didn't protest, and his eyebrows softened in something like gratitude. Now that he couldn't open the door, he sank onto his knees, shoulders slumped, and let out a shaky sigh.

How long had Maura and this man been down here, resisting the call of whatever slept behind that door? This entire time?

"Are you Artemus?" Blue asked him.

He peered up at her in haggard acknowledgment.

So that was why he was familiar. She didn't have the long face or deep crow's feet, but his mouth and eyes were the ones she'd seen looking back in the mirror her entire life.

Huh. Hi, Dad. Then she thought, *Really, with these genetics, I should be taller.*

She looked back to the other opening, the one at the top of the wall. It was not the most welcoming sort of hole, but her mother had no climbing experience that Blue knew of, so it could not be any worse than the way she had already come.

She didn't have time for further pondering. Still bent, she shuffled toward the tunnel opening she'd entered by. She called into the darkness: "Ronan?"

Her voice spread and softened in the space, eaten by the black.

A pause. Somewhere, water dripped. Then: "Sargent?"

"I found her! There's another way out! Can you manage to get out the way we came?"

Another pause. "Yeah."

"Then go!"

"Really?"

"Yeah, there's no point if you can't cross!" It was more dangerous for him to be there in the dark and unknown, and she wouldn't be able to take her mother and Artemus back that way.

My parents, she thought. *I can't take* my parents *back that way.*

This made her frown.

She returned to Maura. "Come on. You can move without opening the door. We're going to leave."

But Maura didn't seem to be listening anymore. She was gazing at the door once more, frowning.

Artemus's voice sounded in the dim, surprising her. "How are you able to bear it?"

His voice was — accented. She wasn't sure why she was surprised. It was something like British, but clipped, as if English was not his native language.

Blue considered other options for tying her mother's hands;

she wondered if she could force her to leave. It would be horrific if she had to fight her. "I'm a mirror, I guess. I've just turned it back on itself."

"But that's not possible," Artemus said.

"Okay," she replied. "Well, then, that's probably not what I'm doing and you know better. Now if you don't mind, I'm trying to figure out how to get my mother out of this cavern."

"But she can't be your mother."

Blue was taking less of a shine to her father than she'd hoped all these years. "You, sir, have a lot of suppositions that you're considering fact, and I think, in a better time, you should take a long think about everything you're sure is true. But for now, tell me if I can drag her out of this place and up that hole. That is the way out, right?"

He twisted his hands so the light showed on her a bit better. "You do, in fact, look a little like her."

"Good *God*, man," Blue said. "Are you still on that? Do you know who else I look a little like? Your face. Have a think on that and I'll just figure this out myself."

Artemus fell silent, sitting with his arms tied behind him, expression thoughtful. Blue wasn't sure if he was indeed having a think on what her face looked like or if he was falling back into the thrall of the third sleeper.

Blue took her mother's arm and gave an experimental tug. "Let's go."

Her mother's arm went rigid, resisting not Blue, but the concept of moving at all. Then, when Blue released her, Maura immediately stretched out a hand to the door.

Blue slapped it. She turned to the door. "Let her *go!*"

The voice tried to creep in around her defenses. *Open the door and you'll all go free, and with a favor. Surely you want to save that boy's life.*

The third sleeper was good at what it did.

Even though Blue knew there was no chance that she would open the door or accept its help, she felt the offer chisel its way into her heart.

She wondered what it whispered to her mother.

Blue slid off her sweater. She took Maura's hands — Maura resisted — and then tied them as well as she could by twisting the sweater arms around them. She tried not to care about how the sweater was surely ruined and stretched out now, but Persephone had made it for her, and that felt as dire as everything else. Every concern and every joy had become equal, priority erased by terror.

Blue took Artemus's arm by the elbow and Maura's arm by the elbow, and she dragged them up. At least as far up as they could go in this little room. Shoving them against each other and pausing a lot to lift them back off their knees, she began to inch them away from the door and toward the hole of the cave. She didn't care if they were all bruised and bleeding by the time they got out of here — just as long as they got out of here.

But then a mass of bodies suddenly tumbled in through their exit.

50

The cavern had never been large to begin with, but as Blue keeled back onto her butt, it seemed ever smaller. The population of the room had suddenly increased by three people. The person in front had glorious blond hair and a gun, and the man behind her had pinched nostrils and a gun, and the person behind him was —

"Mr. Gray," Blue cried gladly. She was so grateful to see him that she couldn't believe he was real.

"Blue?" the Gray Man asked. "Oh no."

Oh no?

A second later she saw that his hands were tied behind his back.

"What?" asked the blond woman with the gun. She directed a flashlight at Blue's face, momentarily blinding her. "Are you a real person?"

"Yes, I'm a real person!" Blue replied indignantly.

The woman pointed the gun at her.

"Piper, *no!*" the Gray Man said, and jostled himself so hard against the woman that her flashlight dropped from her hand. It hit the rock and went out immediately. The only light came from the ghost light that tied Artemus's hands.

"Classy, Mr. Gray," Piper said, blinking, eyes glancing in the direction of the ghost light and then returning to him. "I wasn't going to shoot her. But it might be time to shoot *you* now. What do you think, Morris? I defer to your professional judgment."

"Please don't," said Blue. "Please, really, don't."

"We could shoot this one, too," Morris replied. "No one will ever make it down this far to find them."

Behind her, a few pebbles skittered down from the ceiling, or somewhere near it. Blue wondered with dim anxiety if they had unsettled the caverns by letting a herd of animals gallop through them.

Piper pointed at Maura and Artemus, finally giving them her attention. "Are these people real, too? Why do they look like that?"

"Maura," the Gray Man said, only now taking his gaze from Piper and Blue. There was a breathless note to his ordinarily brisk voice. "Blue — how did it come to —" He frowned, a familiar sort of frown, and Blue knew that he was hearing the third sleeper whispering doubts and promises in his head.

Another pebble dropped down onto the cavern floor.

"All right, never mind," Piper said. Her eyes, clear and intent and certain, were on the door. There was not a doubt in Blue's mind that she had come to wake the sleeper. "Let me think. It's so damn claustrophobic in here. You know what, you can just go, strange girl. That's fine. Just pretend like you never saw us."

"I'm not leaving Mr. Gray here," Blue said. She supposed after she said it that it was a brave thing to say, but at the time, she'd just said it because it was the truth, even if it was scary.

"It's a touching thought, but no," Piper replied. "He can't go. Please don't make me ask not nicely."

The Gray Man was all hunched to fit in the cavern, his hands behind his back. Stones and dust shivered down the walls behind him in an ominous way. To Blue, he said, "Listen to me. Take them and go. I've earned this. This is how I've lived and this is what it's come to. You haven't done anything to deserve this, nor has your mother. Now is the time to be a hero."

"Listen to the man," Piper said. "When he says 'earned this,' he means that he held a gun to my head in my own kitchen, and he's right."

Think, Blue, think — her head felt buzzy and clouded. Probably it was the third sleeper poking round the corner of her consciousness. Maybe it was the dread of that lake creeping up the tunnel. Perhaps it was just the growing supposition that something terrible was about to happen here. A bigger rock rolled free from the tunnel the others had emerged from. This little cavern was so small already; it didn't seem at all like a difficult thing for it to collapse entirely.

"Sorry, can you speed it up?" Piper asked. "I know no one wants to say 'Oh, look, this particular shitty cave is collapsing,' but I'm going to point it out to lend some urgency to the proceedings."

"You're beginning to sound like Colin," the Gray Man said.

"Say that again and I'll shoot you in the nuts." Piper gestured to Blue. "Are you going, or what?"

Blue bit her lip. "Can I — can I hug him good-bye? Please?"

She shrank her shoulders down, arms clinging round herself, looking miserable. The last part wasn't hard.

"You want to hug *him*? What a zoo," Piper said. "Fine."

Boredly, she pointed a gun in their general direction as Blue ducked over to the Gray Man.

"Ah, Blue," he said.

She threw her arms and hugged him tightly in a hug he couldn't return. Leaning her cheek against his stubble, she whispered, "I wish I could remember how you said that hero bit in Old English."

The Gray Man said it.

"Sounds like cat puke," Piper observed. "What's it mean?"

"'A coward's heart is no prize, but the man of valor deserves his shining helmet.'"

"I'm working on it," Blue replied as she used the switchblade she had hidden in her hand to silently slice the zip ties that bound his wrists. She stepped back. He remained bowed over, with his hands behind his back, but he raised one colorless eyebrow at her.

"Okay, get out of here. Scram. Farewell," Piper said as more of the wall moved uneasily, the uppermost surface shifting dustily to the floor. "Go be short somewhere else."

Blue hoped fervently the Gray Man could do something now.

The problem was that Maura and Artemus were no more mobile than before, even if Blue had been willing to utterly abandon the Gray Man in the cavern. The only thing she could do was return to struggling them toward the cavern exit. It was like a fever dream, though, except instead of her own legs being turned to lead, Maura and Artemus were the hideously slow ones.

Piper permitted this for about thirty seconds before she said, "This is ridiculous" and clicked off her gun's safety.

"Blue, down!" the Gray Man shouted. He was already moving.

He must have hit Piper, or Morris, because bodies shoved wildly against Artemus and then Blue. Did it count as falling down if you were already on your knees?

A gun blasted nearby, and for half a second, it was silent. Every sound had been smashed up against the walls of this tiny room, and when it came back, it was only ringing. Dust moved through the space from wherever the bullet had ended up or glanced off. More rocks slid precipitously. They glanced off Blue's shoulders — it was the *ceiling*.

Blue couldn't tell whose arms were whose, and if she should be ducking or punching or stabbing. All she was certain of was that someone could die in a moment here. The threat of it was thick in the murky air.

Morris was strangling the Gray Man. Blue wanted to attend to that — could she? But she saw Piper scrabbling around between shuffling legs for her gun, which she must have dropped. Blue, scouring the floor herself, spotted *someone's* gun. She snatched for it and missed just as the Gray Man and Morris staggered by together. One of them kicked the gun, and it chattered crazily across the rocks and into the black of the tunnel.

The other gun went off in someone else's hand. The sound made it impossible to think. Had someone been shot? Who was shooting? Was it going to happen again?

In that moment of stillness, Blue saw that Morris was still choking the Gray Man. She stabbed his arm, right in the meaty part. She felt considerably less bad than she had when she'd stabbed Adam.

Morris immediately released Mr. Gray, who picked him up and began bashing him against the ceiling.

"Okay, stop," Piper said. "Or I kill her."

Everyone turned to look. Piper had a gun pointed to Maura's head. She tossed her head to get her blond hair out of her eyes, and then blew out her lips to remove a few strands from her mouth.

"What do you want, Piper?" the Gray Man asked. He put Morris down. Morris stayed down.

"I *want* what I asked for before," Piper said. "Remember when I was letting the women and children go so I could feel good about myself? *That* was what I wanted. I guess none of us are getting *that* now."

Behind her, Artemus blinked, which was notable because he hadn't really been blinking before. His shoulder was bleeding in a way that seemed like he might have been shot. Every time he dripped on the cave floor, the blood ran together and trickled through the fallen rock toward the red door.

Uphill.

They all stopped to watch it.

Piper's gaze followed it all the way to the door, and to the handle, and her bubble-gum pink lips parted.

Then Artemus used his tied hands to swing the ghost light at her hands.

It careened into the gun, colliding with an unremarkable *snick* sound. The ghost light went dark, and they all stood in the perfect blackness of the cave.

No one moved, or if they did, they were soundless. No one except Piper knew if she was still holding the gun to Maura's head.

There was silence except for the chitinous rattle of stones from the ceiling. The worst sound was one that came from above or around the cavern: a sort of creaking roar as rocks moved in a cavern above them. From closer by there was a groan, which Blue thought was Morris.

She felt oddly breathless, like the cave was running out of air. She knew what the feeling really was: panic.

Then everyone began to move.

It started with a shuffling sound from the direction of either Piper or Artemus or Maura, and then maybe the Gray Man, and it became so jumbled it was impossible to tell who was who. Blue snapped away her switchblade, because the odds were good that she'd stab someone she didn't want to stab, and began feeling around the floor for the dropped flashlight. Maybe the top just needed to be screwed on again for it to work once more.

Maura's voice suddenly said, "Don't open that door! Don't open it!"

Blue couldn't even tell where the door was now. There was shuffling in every direction.

But she could also hear the third sleeper now. It was as if its collective whispers in everyone *else's* head had become so loud that they spilled into the cavern itself. It didn't tug on Blue, but it billowed through the darkness and condensed on her arms. Dripping down her fingers.

Blue thought she knew how the mirror lake had come to be now.

"Stop her!"

It was impossible to tell whose voice it was. Somewhere close by, she heard someone's breathing getting faster.

Her fingers closed over the flashlight. *Come on, come on —*

Suddenly, there was a thud and a half shout.

The flashlight came on in time to illuminate Piper curled in front of the red door, clutching the back of her head.

"Come on," Mr. Gray said. He dropped a very bloody rock to the ground. "At once."

Rocks were showering down now, bigger than before.

"We're getting out of here. Right now," the Gray Man said, brisk and efficient. He turned his head to Artemus. "You. You're bleeding. Let me see? Oh, you're fine. Blue? You're all right?"

Blue nodded.

"And Maura?" the Gray Man turned to her. She had an ugly scratch on her jaw and she looked studiously at the ground, arms tied behind her. He gently lifted her dirty bangs from her forehead to examine her face.

"We need to get her away from the door," Blue said. "What about . . . the others?"

She meant Piper and Morris. Both of them were on the ground. Blue didn't want to think too hard about it.

There was no kindness on Mr. Gray's face. "Unless you have hidden reserves of strength you didn't display on the way down, we cannot carry her and Maura, and I know which one I prefer. We need to go."

As if to confirm, the tunnel Blue had entered by collapsed in a hail of stones and dirt.

They seized hands. With Blue and the flashlight leading the way, they climbed back into the small hole at the top of the cavern. Blue crawled up it a few yards and then waited, counting bodies as they climbed up.

One (Artemus), two (Maura), and three (the Gray Man), four —

Four

Piper, nearly unrecognizable behind all of the dirt, appeared in the tunnel opening. She had not climbed in, but she was framed in the opening. In one shaking hand was the gun.

"*You —*" she said, and stopped, as if she couldn't imagine what to say next.

"Just go!" shouted the Gray Man. "Go, Blue, fast, take the light away!"

Blue scurried up the tunnel.

Behind her, a shot exploded again. But none of the tunnel was disturbed.

"Keep going!" the Gray Man's voice called. "It's okay!"

Then there was half a high-pitched shout, too throaty for a scream, and an explosion of sound as the cavern collapsed behind them.

Blue wanted to stop hearing that cry. She didn't care that it was someone who had just been trying to kill her mother. She couldn't make herself feel like that made it better.

But she couldn't, so she just kept climbing and leading them out of the cave.

It was dark outside when they emerged, but nothing could ever be as dark as that cavern by the red door. Nothing could ever smell as wonderful as the grass and the trees and even the asphalt of a nearby highway.

The entrance here was just a jagged hole in the side of a hill; it was impossible to tell where they were except *out*. Artemus woozily leaned against the hillside, touching his wound gingerly.

Blue untied her mother; Maura threw her arms around Blue's neck and crushed her to her.

"I'm so sorry," she said after a few minutes. "I'm so so so sorry. I'm going to buy you a car and make your bedroom bigger and all we'll ever eat is yogurt and . . ."

She trailed off, and finally they released each other.

The Gray Man stood by her elbow, and when she turned, she made a face, and then she touched his stubbled cheek.

"Mr. Gray," she said.

He just nodded. He traced one of her eyebrows with his finger in an efficient, competent, in-love kind of way, and then he looked to Blue.

She said, "Let's go find the others."

51

Adam Parrish was awake.

The opposite of *awake* was supposed to be *asleep*, but Adam had spent much of the last two years of his life being both at once, or neither. In retrospect, he wasn't sure he had known what *awake* really felt like until now.

He sat in the backseat of the Camaro with Ronan and Blue, watching the D.C. streetlights go by, feeling the pulse of the ley line ebb the farther away he got from Henrietta. A week had passed since they emerged from the valley of bones, and things were returning to normal.

No, not normal.

There was no normal.

Maura was back at 300 Fox Way, but Persephone was not. The boys were back at school, but Greenmantle wasn't. Jesse Dittley's death dominated the newspapers. One of the articles had noted that the valley was beginning to look like a dangerous place to live: Niall Lynch, Joseph Kavinsky, Jesse Dittley, Persephone Poldma.

Everyone had been surprised to discover Persephone had a last name.

"Was it everything you expected?" Gansey asked Malory.

Malory and the Dog looked up from their boarding passes. "More. Much more. Too much. No offense meant to you and your company, Gansey, but I shall be very relieved to go back to my drowsy ley line for a while."

Adam worked a scab off his hand; the smallest of the scratches he'd gotten from sliding down into the pit of ravens and then climbing back out. The most lasting wound was invisible but persistent: The knowledge of Persephone's death hummed constantly through Adam like the pulse of the ley line.

She had told him that there were three sleepers. One to wake, one to not wake. One in between. The others thought that Gwenllian was the one in between, but that didn't really make sense, because she'd never been asleep.

So he didn't know if it was true or not, but he sort of liked to believe that the third sleeper had been him.

"You must come visit me," Malory said. "You can see the tapestry. We will mince along the old tracks for nostalgia's sake. The Dog would like it if Jane came as well."

"I'd like that," Gansey said politely. Like he would, but it wouldn't happen. Malory probably couldn't hear it, but Adam could. He would stay here, searching for Glendower and his favor.

The night before, Adam had restlessly started one of his old tricks to get to sleep: rehearsing the various wordings of the favor, trying to hit upon the right one, the one that wouldn't squander the opportunity, the one that would fix everything that was wrong. Only he discovered that he couldn't quite invest himself in the game. He didn't so much care about asking for success; he was going to survive Aglionby, he thought, and he figured it was quite probable that he'd get a scholarship to at least one place he wanted to go. And he used to think he needed to use it to ask to be free of Cabeswater, but now it seemed like a strange thing to ask for. Like asking to be freed from Gansey or Ronan.

Then he realized the only thing he needed the favor for was to save Gansey's life.

"Here we are," Malory said, eyes on the airport terminal. The Dog wagged his tail for the first time. "Tell your mother good luck with her election. American politics! More dangerous than a ley line."

"I'll let her know," Gansey said.

"Don't you go into politics," Malory said sternly as they pulled up on the curb.

"Unlikely."

He still sounded anxious to Adam, even though there was nothing inherently anxious about the conversation. It was time to find Glendower. They all knew it.

Gansey stepped on the parking brake and said, "Once I send the professor off, one of you guys can get into the front. Adam? Unless he's sleeping."

"No," Adam said. "I'm awake."

EPILOGUE

It wasn't that Piper had been unconscious for hours. In action movies of the sort Colin had always hated and she had always loved, heroes were always knocking out henchmen instead of shooting them. It's how you could tell they were the hero. Villains shot minions; heroes knocked them out with a punch to the head. Then, a few hours later, they came to and went about their lives. Piper had read a blog post pointing out that this wasn't really possible, however, because if you were unconscious for longer than a minute or two, it was because you had brain damage. And the post was written by a doctor, or someone who said they used to be a doctor, or someone married to a medical professional, so Piper thought it was probably true. Truer than those action movies, anyway.

As she lay there in the cave, she thought about all the brain-damaged thugs in Hollywood, spared by dashing heroes who thought it would be kinder than killing them.

She was not really unconscious for hours, but she did stay down on the ground for hours, or days. She swam in and out of sleep. Every so often she heard another moan from in the cave. Morris, maybe, or just her own voice. Sometimes she cracked her eyes and thought that it was time to get up, probably, but then it seemed like too much work, so she stayed down.

Finally, though, she stopped hitting the cavern's snooze button and got herself together. This was ridiculous. She sat up, head throbbing, and let her eyes adjust. She wasn't sure exactly where the light was coming from. There was rubble and water all around her. She remembered suddenly that Colin had buggered off, leaving her to die in this cave that had been his idea in the first place. Typical. He was always off doing things for himself and pretending it was for both of them.

Suddenly, she realized where the light was coming from: a lantern, an old-fashioned kind, like a miner's lamp. And there were hands folded together on the other side of it. Plump, pretty hands. Attached to arms. Attached to a body. It was a woman. She was looking at Piper with an unwaving and unblinking gaze.

"Are you real?" Piper asked.

The woman gave a serene nod. Piper didn't take the nod as a guarantee of realness, though. This didn't seem like the sort of place random women would appear.

"Are you paralyzed?" the woman asked kindly.

"No," Piper said. Then she paused. "Yes. No."

One of her legs was not obeying her, but that didn't count as paralysis. She thought it was probably broken. She was starting to feel not great about the situation.

"We can fix that," the woman said. "If we wake it up."

They both looked at the tomb door.

"If we wake him, he will give us a favor," the woman added. "There are three of us, but just barely. Not for long."

She gestured vaguely in the direction of Morris's moaning.

Piper, who was interested in her own well-being above all others, was instantly suspicious. "Why didn't you just wake him yourself, then?"

"It would be lonely to be a queen alone," the woman said. "It would've been better with three, but two will have to do. Two is less stable than three, but better than one."

Piper was supremely disinterested in magic math. Now that she was beginning to think about it, her leg really hurt. It also was leaking. She was getting angry about everything here. "Okay, fine. Fine."

The woman lifted the lamp and helped Piper struggle to her feet. Piper said a word that usually made her feel better, but didn't in this case. At least she now believed the other woman was real; she was squashing Piper's rib cage in her effort to help her stand. "Who are you, anyway?"

"My name is Neeve."

As they hobbled to the door, Piper observed, "That's a kind of stupid name."

"So," replied Neeve mildly, "is Piper."

In the end, there was not really any ceremony. They just both put their hands on the door and pushed. It didn't feel magical; it just felt like a chunk of wood.

The tomb was already light inside. It was a similar amount of light as the lantern Neeve had at her feet. It was, in fact, the exact same amount of light, mirrored back at them.

The two of them staggered in. There was a raised coffin, the lid already ajar.

The sleeper wasn't human. Piper wasn't sure why she'd

expected it would be. Instead, it was small, and black, and shiny, with more legs than she'd expected. It was powerful.

Neeve said, "We have to do it at the same time to get the fa —"

Piper reached out and touched it before Neeve could move. "Wake up."

Maggie Stiefvater is the #1 *New York Times* bestselling author of the novels *Shiver, Linger, Forever,* and *Sinner.* Her novel *The Scorpio Races* was named a Michael L. Printz Honor Book by the American Library Association. The first book in The Raven Cycle, *The Raven Boys,* was a *Publishers Weekly* Best Book of the Year and the second book, *The Dream Thieves,* was an ALA Best Book for Young Adults. She is also an artist and musician. She lives in Virginia with her husband and their two children. You can visit her online at www.maggiestiefvater.com.